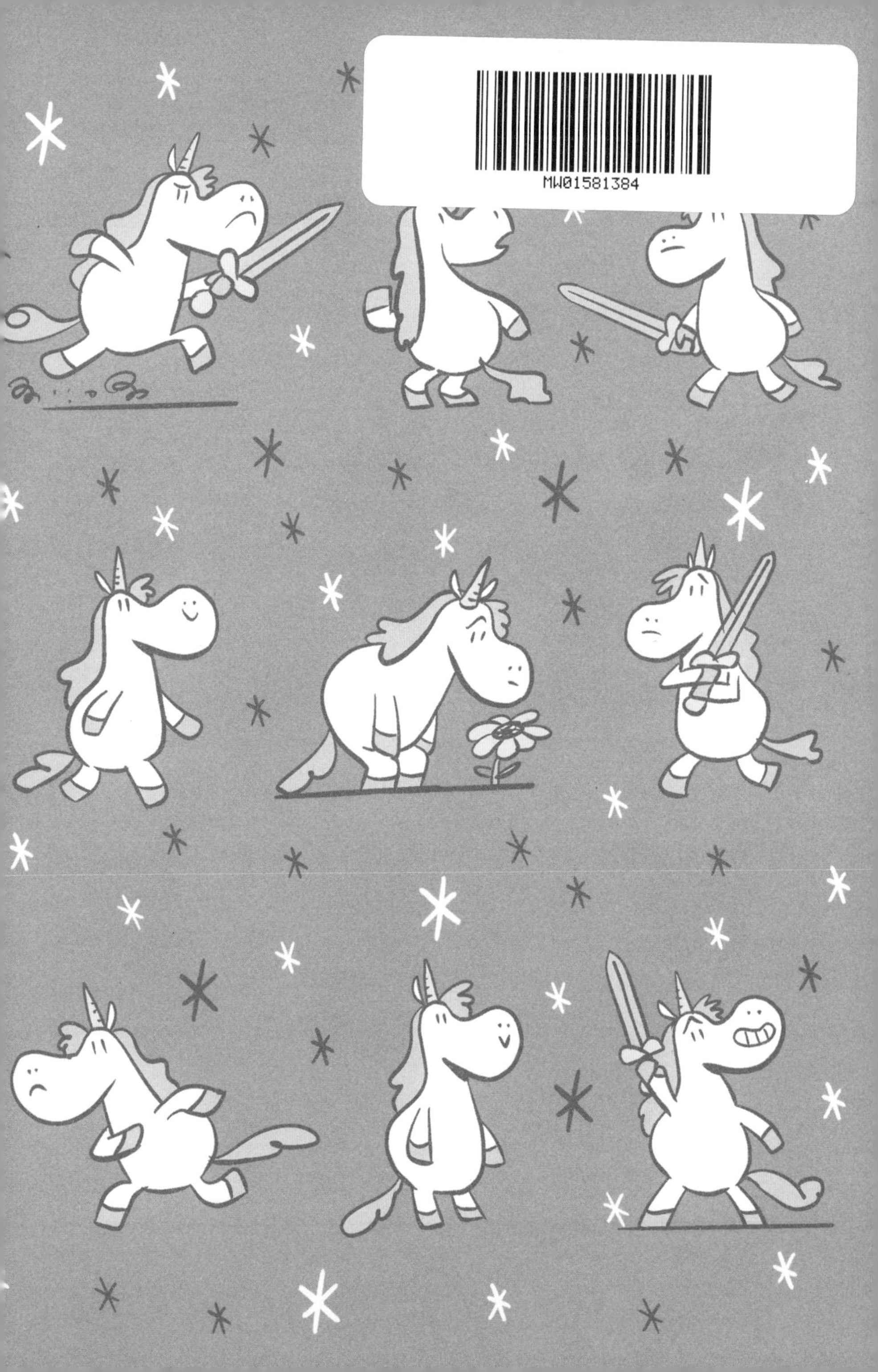

Punycorn
and the PRINCESS of THIEVES

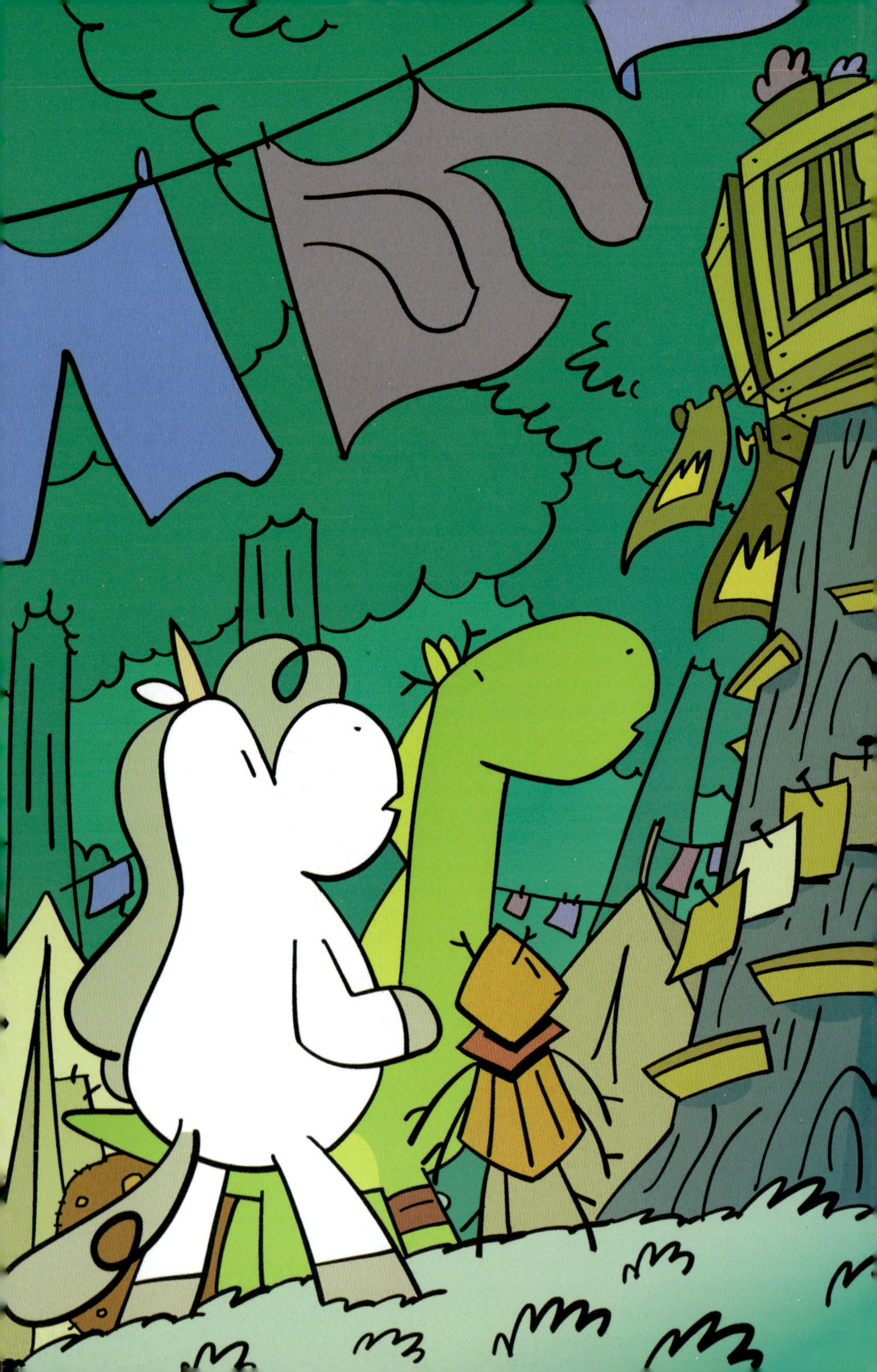

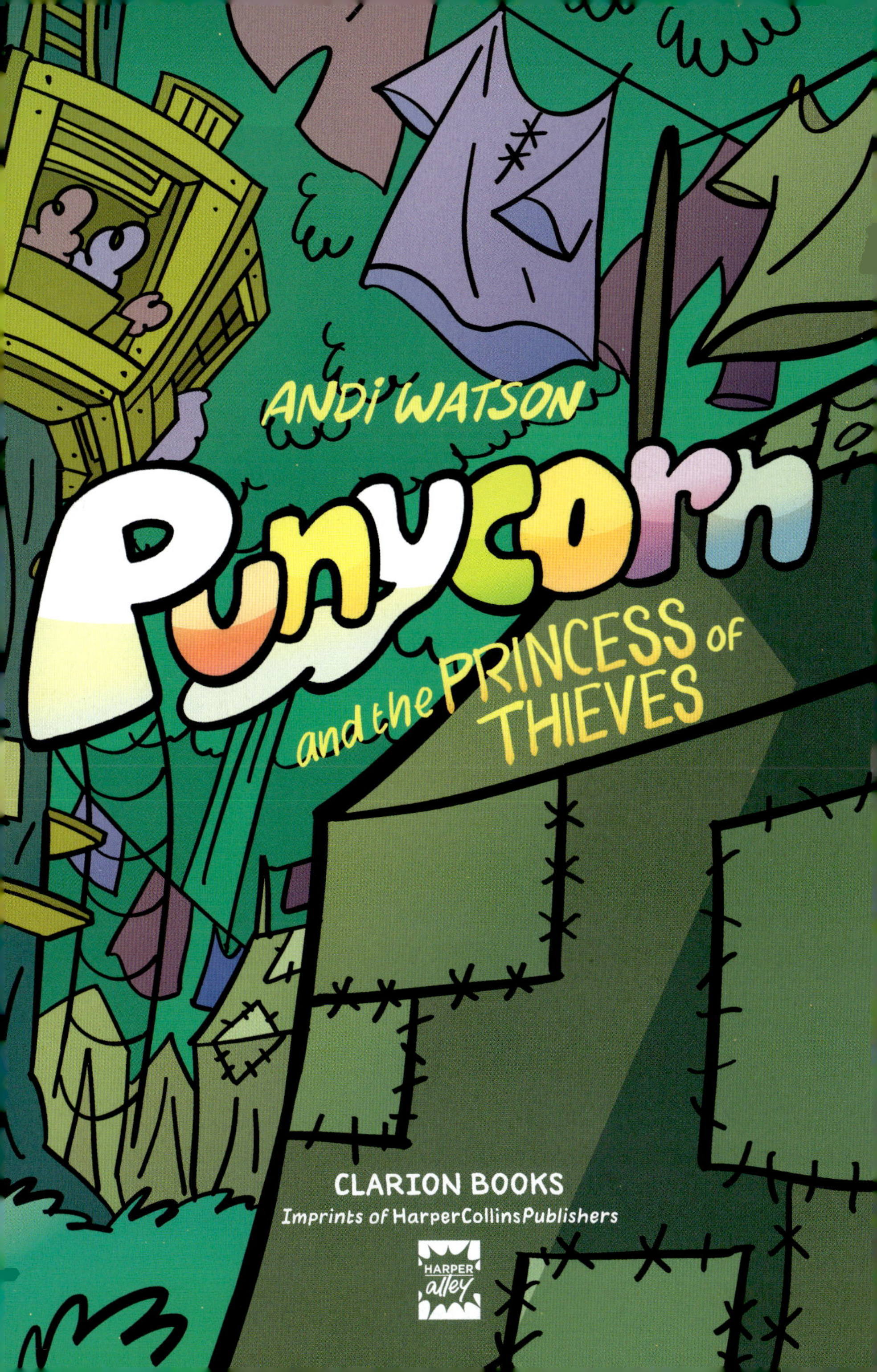

ANDI WATSON

Punycorn and the PRINCESS of THIEVES

CLARION BOOKS
Imprints of HarperCollinsPublishers
HARPER alley

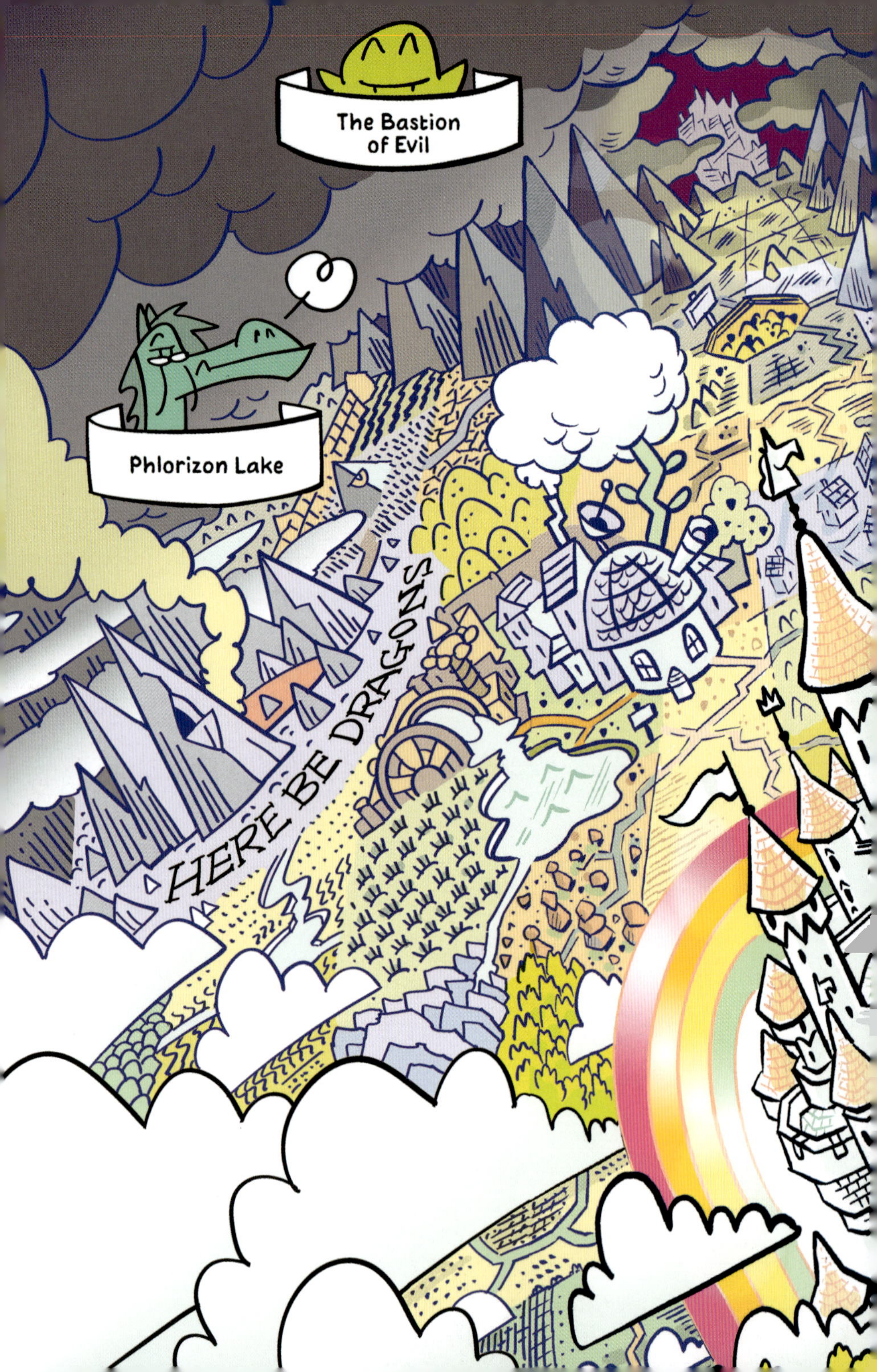
The Bastion of Evil
Phlorizon Lake
HERE BE DRAGONS

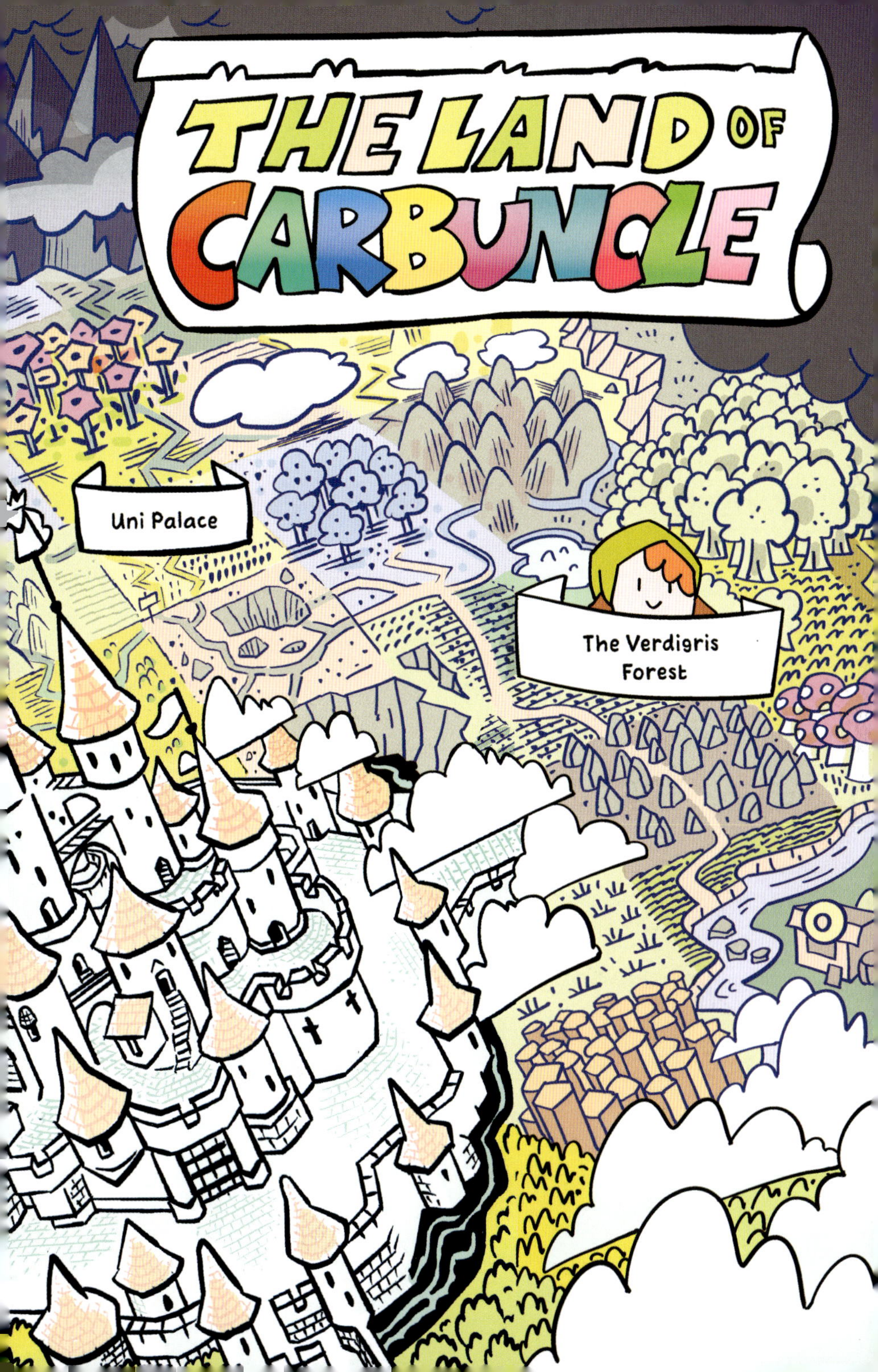
THE LAND OF CARBUNCLE
Uni Palace
The Verdigris Forest

CHAPTER ONE

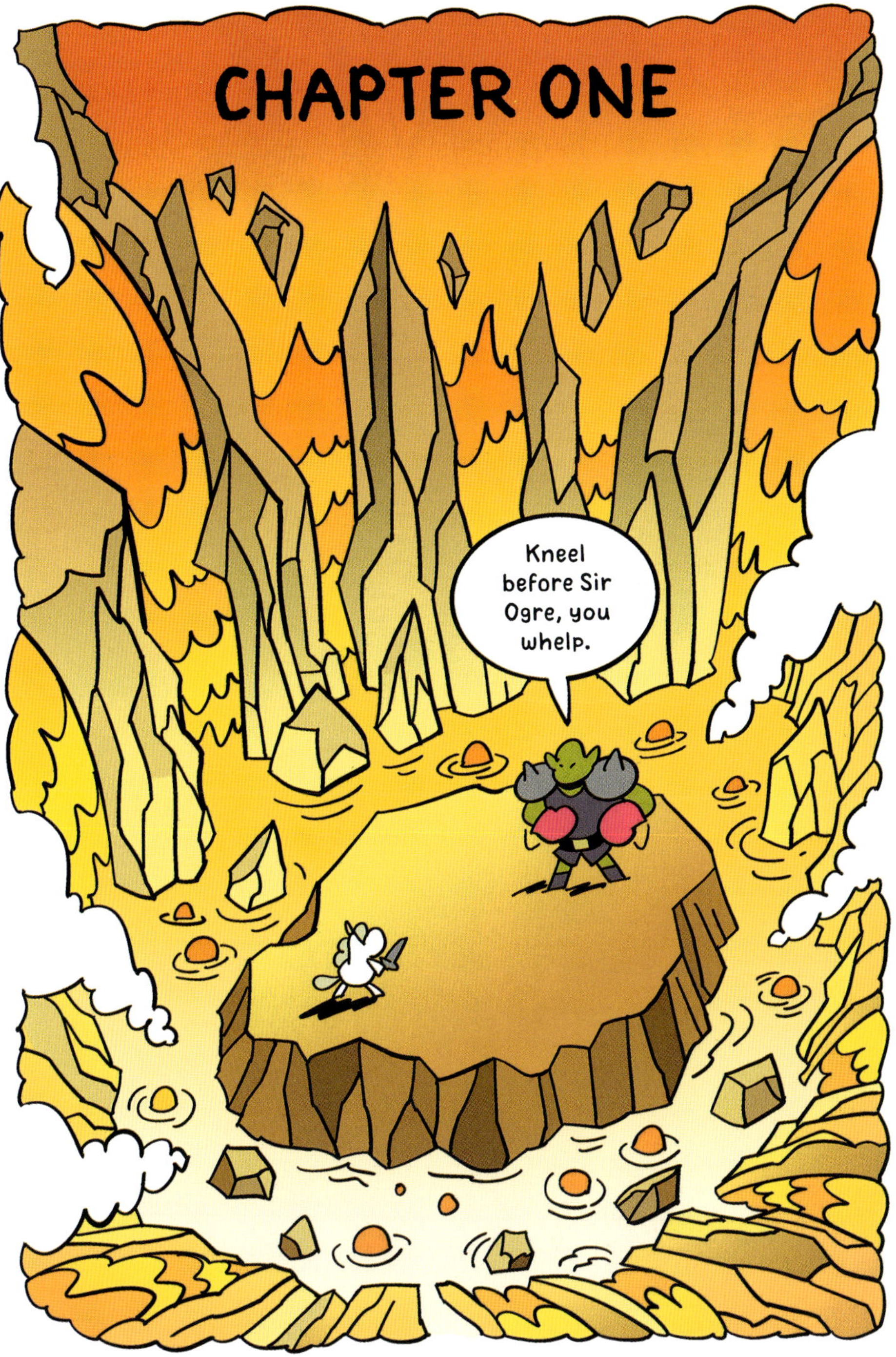
Kneel before Sir Ogre, you whelp.

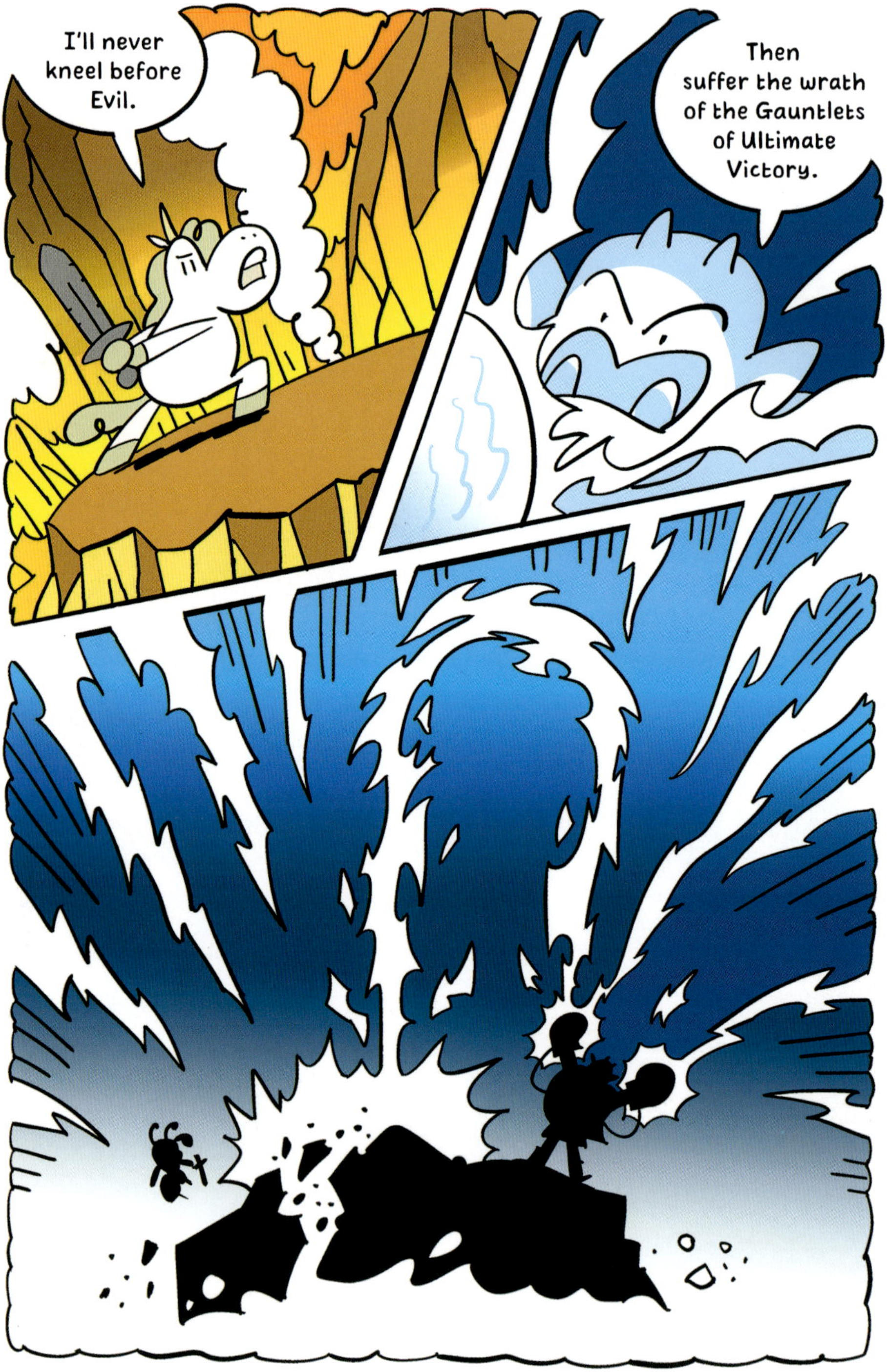
I'll never kneel before Evil.
Then suffer the wrath of the Gauntlets of Ultimate Victory.

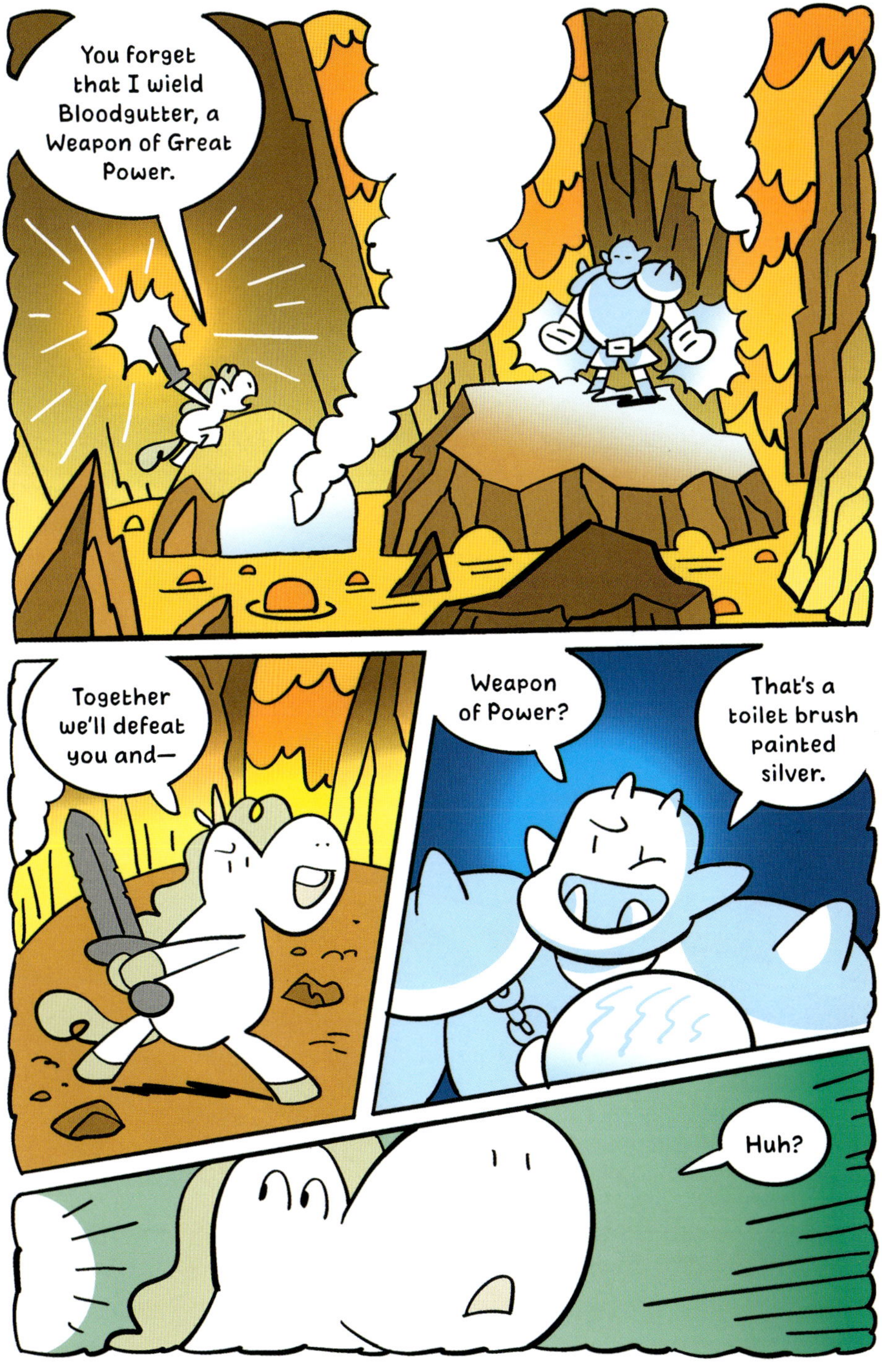
You forget that I wield Bloodgutter, a Weapon of Great Power.
Together we'll defeat you and—
Weapon of Power?
That's a toilet brush painted silver.
Huh?

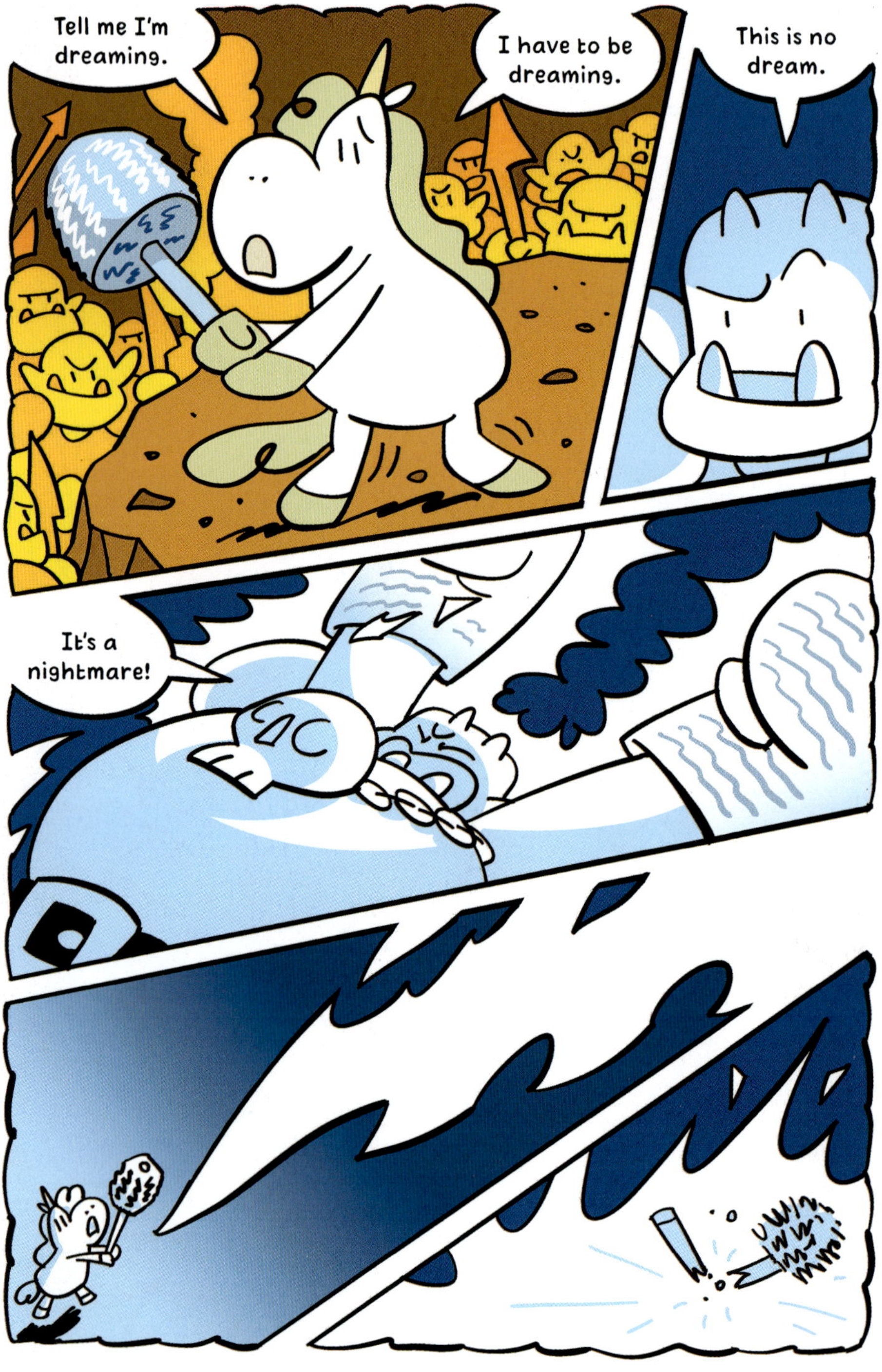
Tell me I'm dreaming.
I have to be dreaming.
This is no dream.
It's a nightmare!

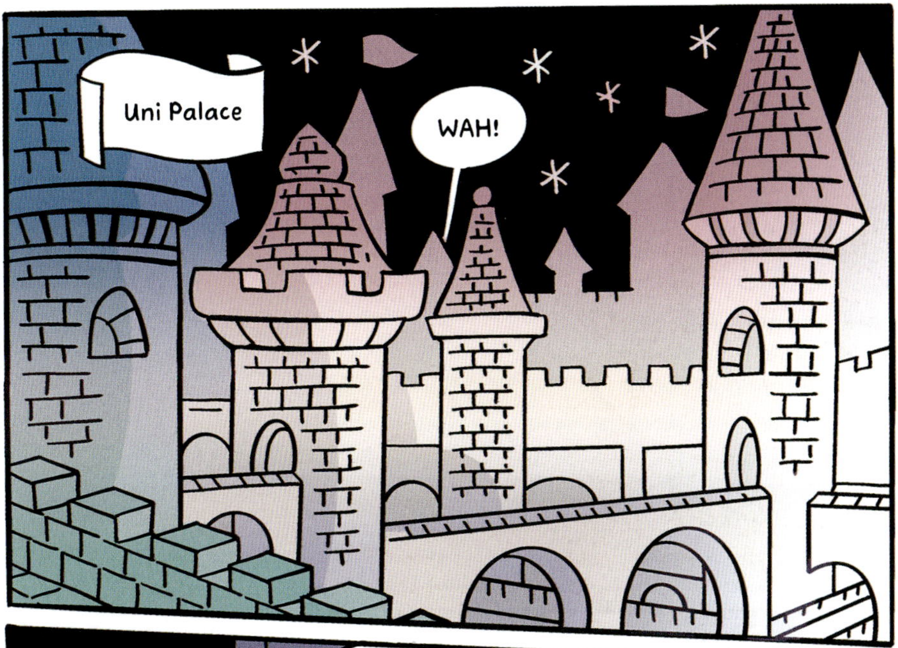
Uni Palace
WAH!

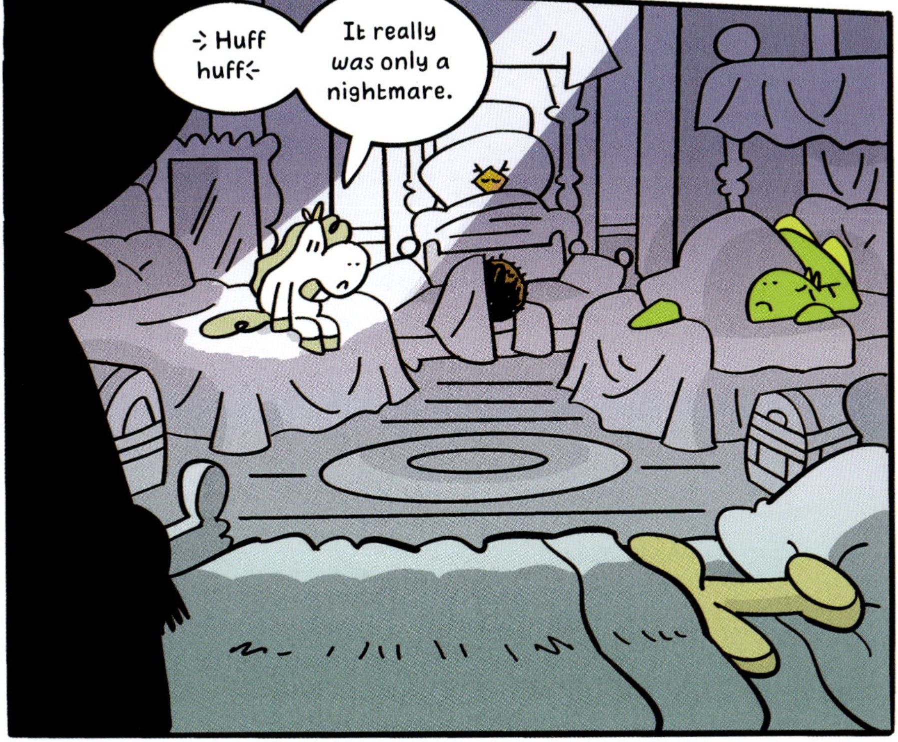
Huff huff
It really was only a nightmare.

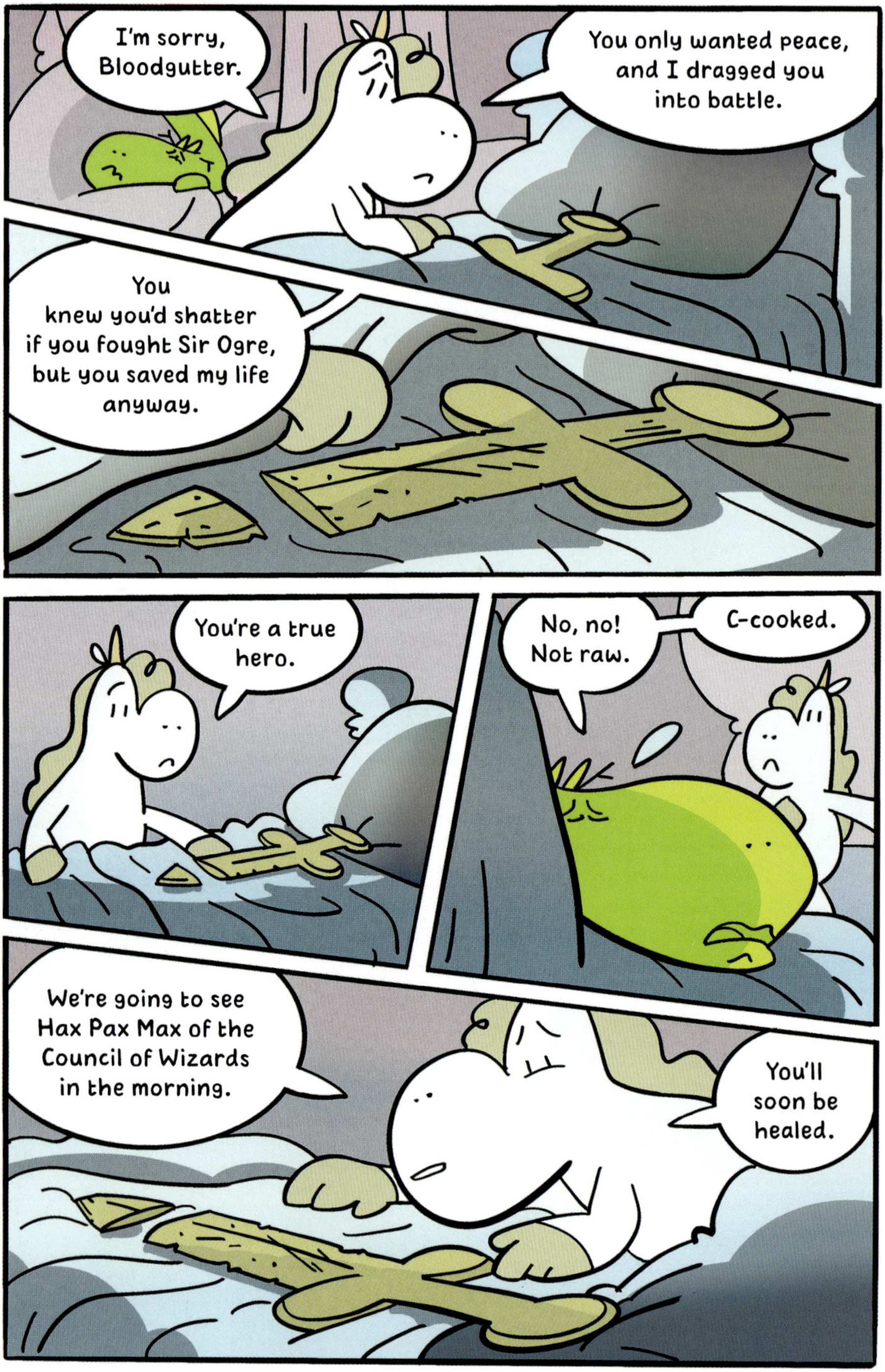

I'm sorry, Bloodgutter.
You only wanted peace, and I dragged you into battle.
You knew you'd shatter if you fought Sir Ogre, but you saved my life anyway.
You're a true hero.
No, no! Not raw.
C-cooked.
We're going to see Hax Pax Max of the Council of Wizards in the morning.
You'll soon be healed.

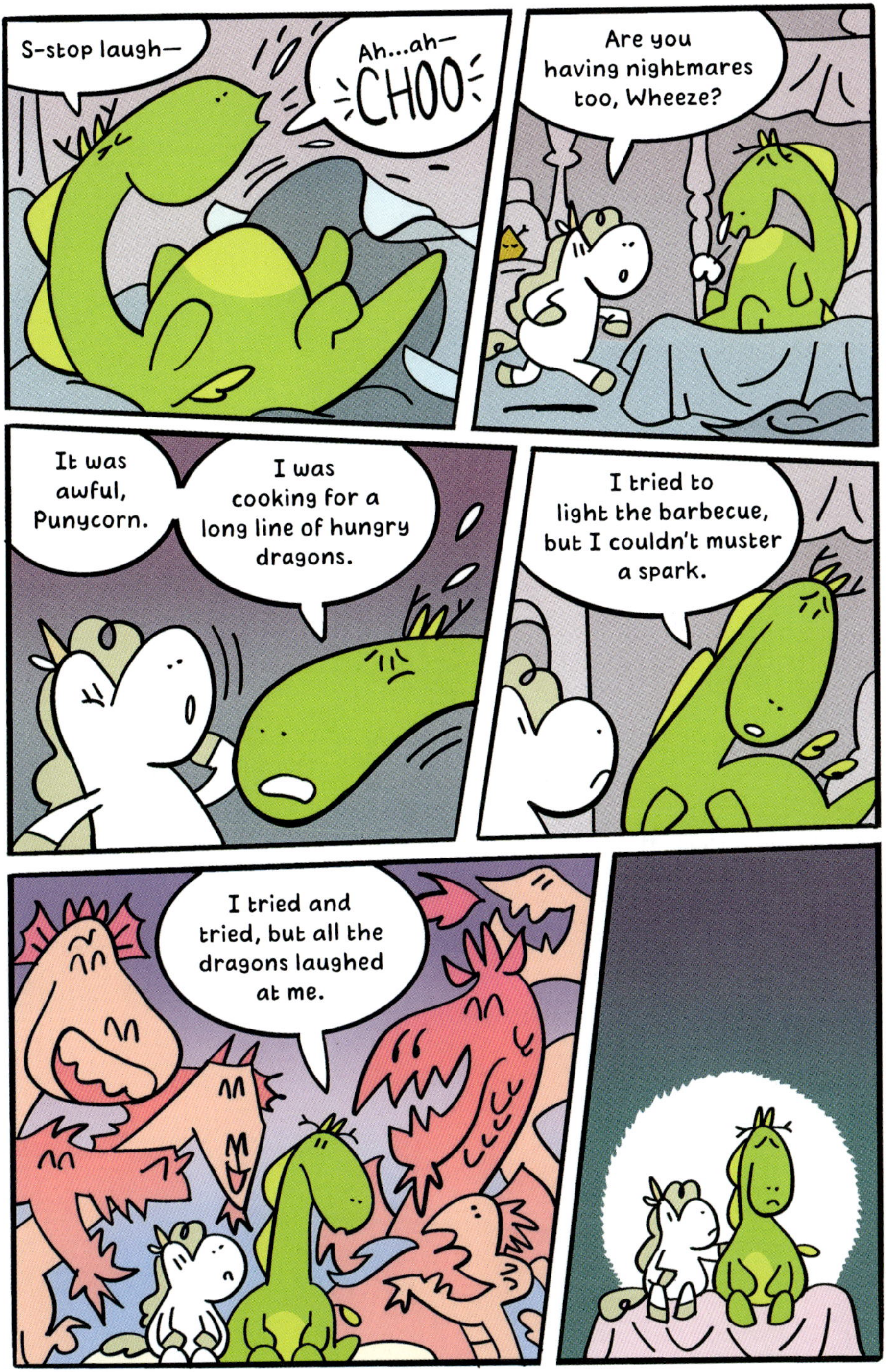
S-stop laugh—
Ah...ah—
CHOO
Are you having nightmares too, Wheeze?
It was awful, Punycorn.
I was cooking for a long line of hungry dragons.
I tried to light the barbecue, but I couldn't muster a spark.
I tried and tried, but all the dragons laughed at me.

CHAPTER TWO

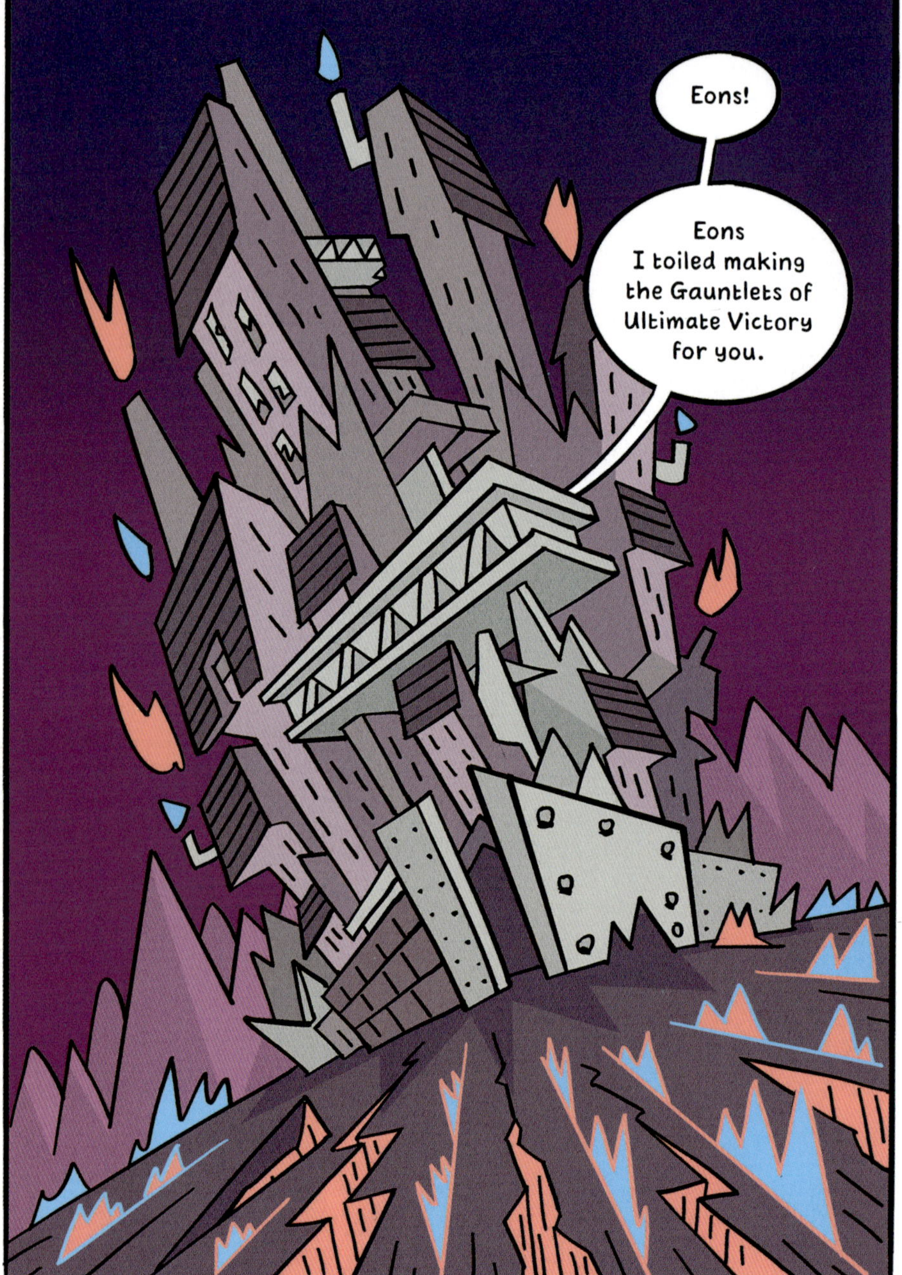
Eons!
Eons I toiled making the Gauntlets of Ultimate Victory for you.

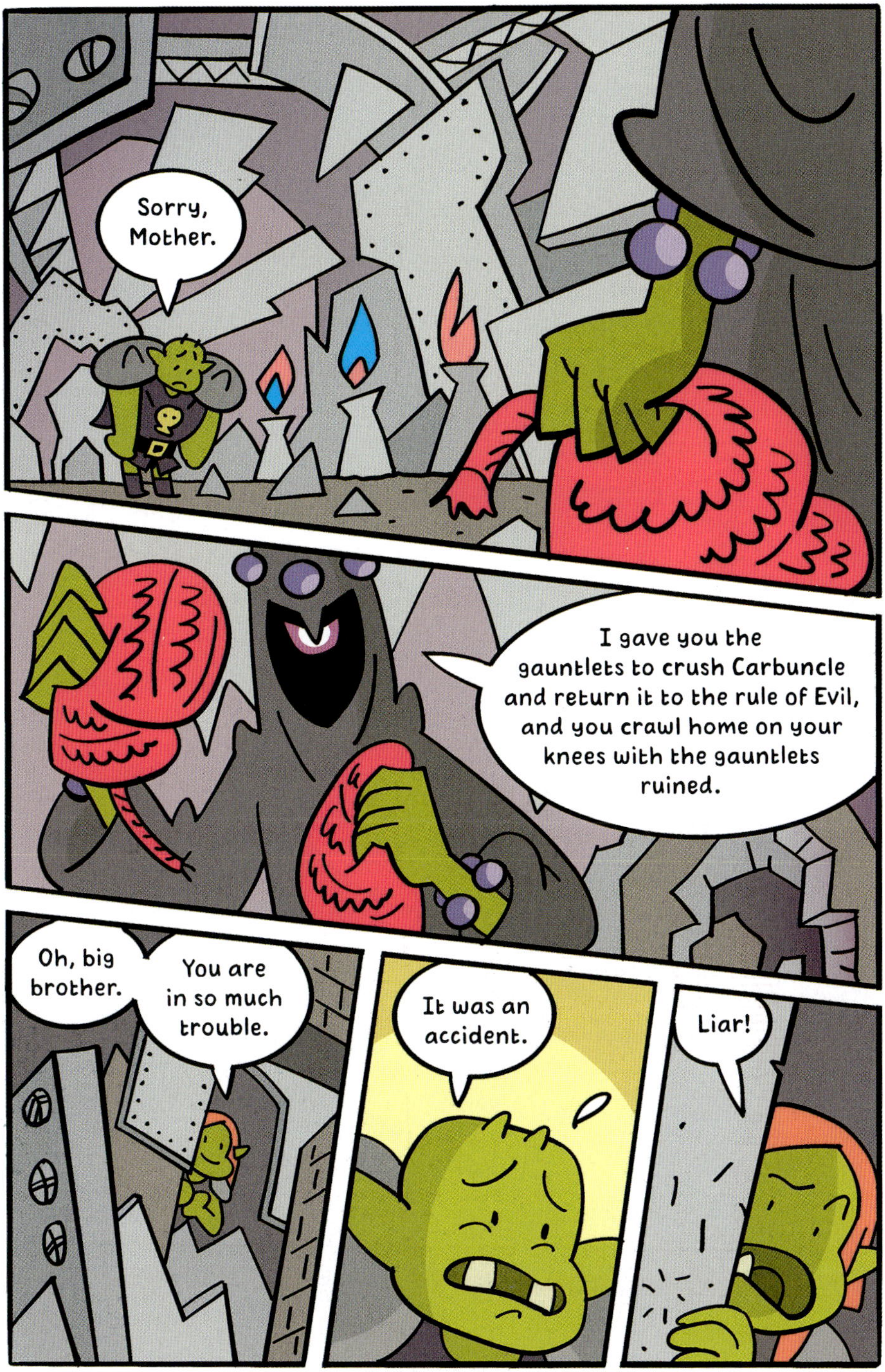
Sorry, Mother.
I gave you the gauntlets to crush Carbuncle and return it to the rule of Evil, and you crawl home on your knees with the gauntlets ruined.
Oh, big brother.
You are in so much trouble.
It was an accident.
Liar!

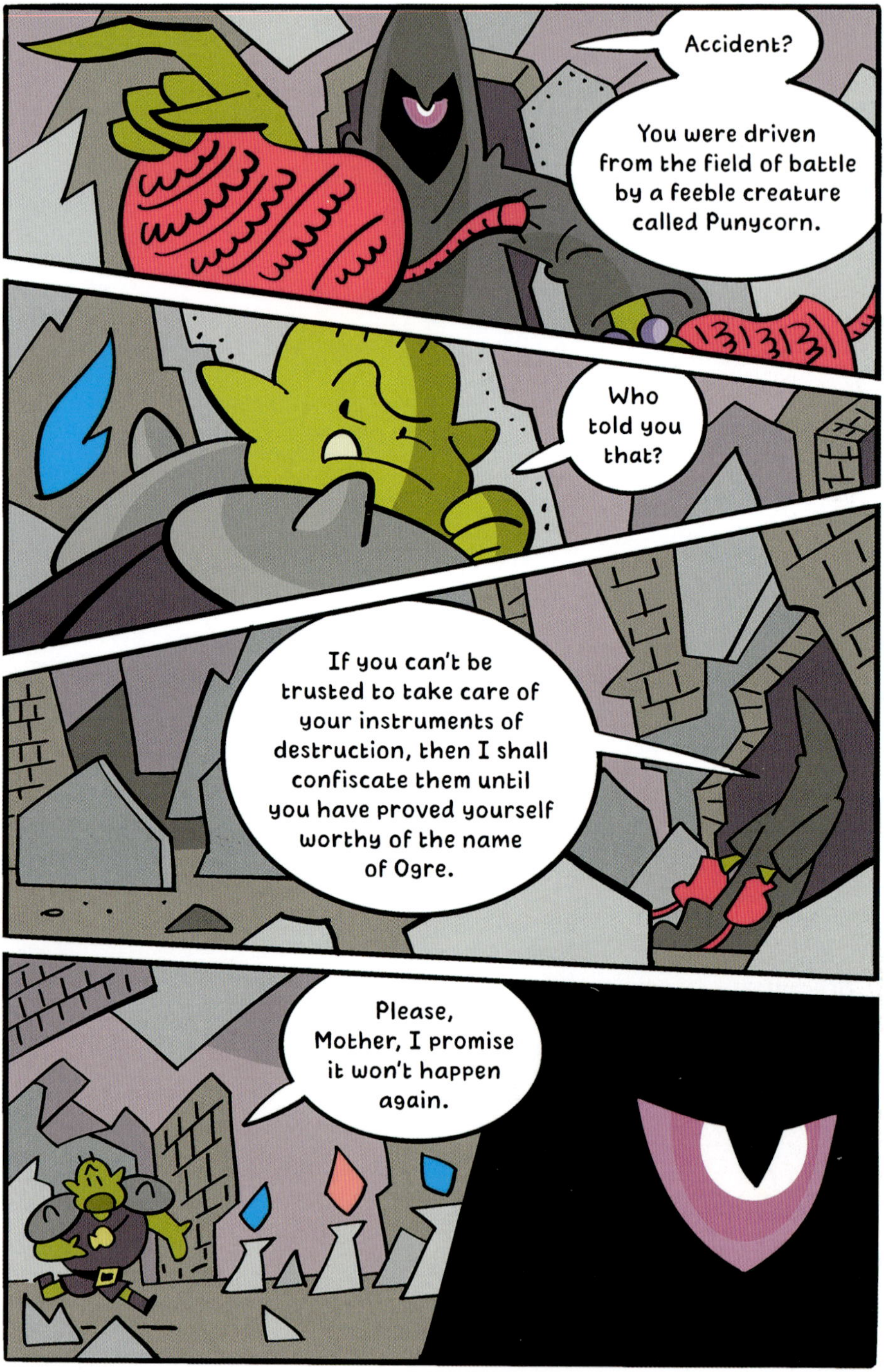
Accident?
You were driven from the field of battle by a feeble creature called Punycorn.
Who told you that?
If you can't be trusted to take care of your instruments of destruction, then I shall confiscate them until you have proved yourself worthy of the name of Ogre.
Please, Mother, I promise it won't happen again.

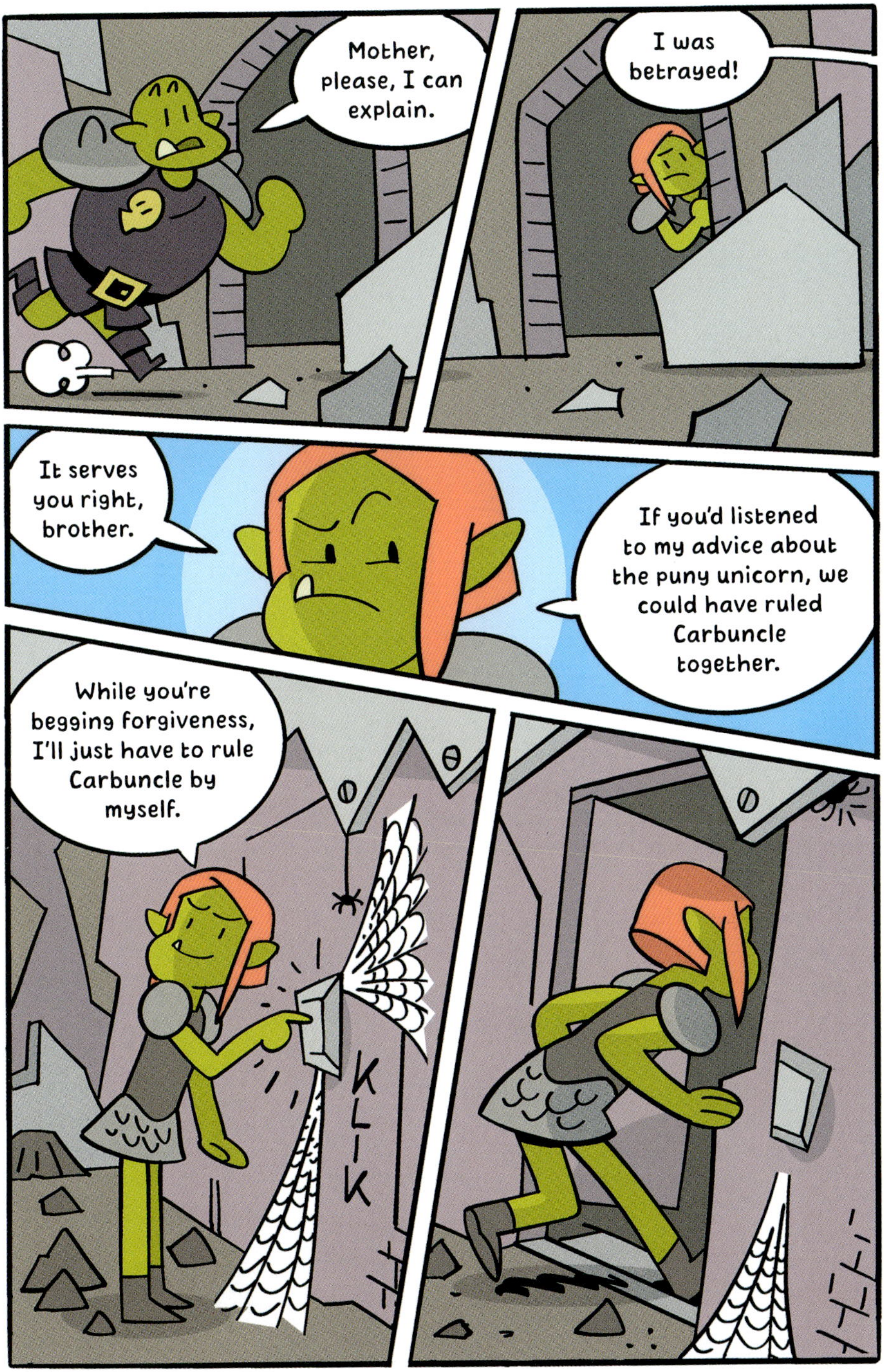
Mother, please, I can explain.
I was betrayed!
It serves you right, brother.
If you'd listened to my advice about the puny unicorn, we could have ruled Carbuncle together.
While you're begging forgiveness, I'll just have to rule Carbuncle by myself.
KLIK

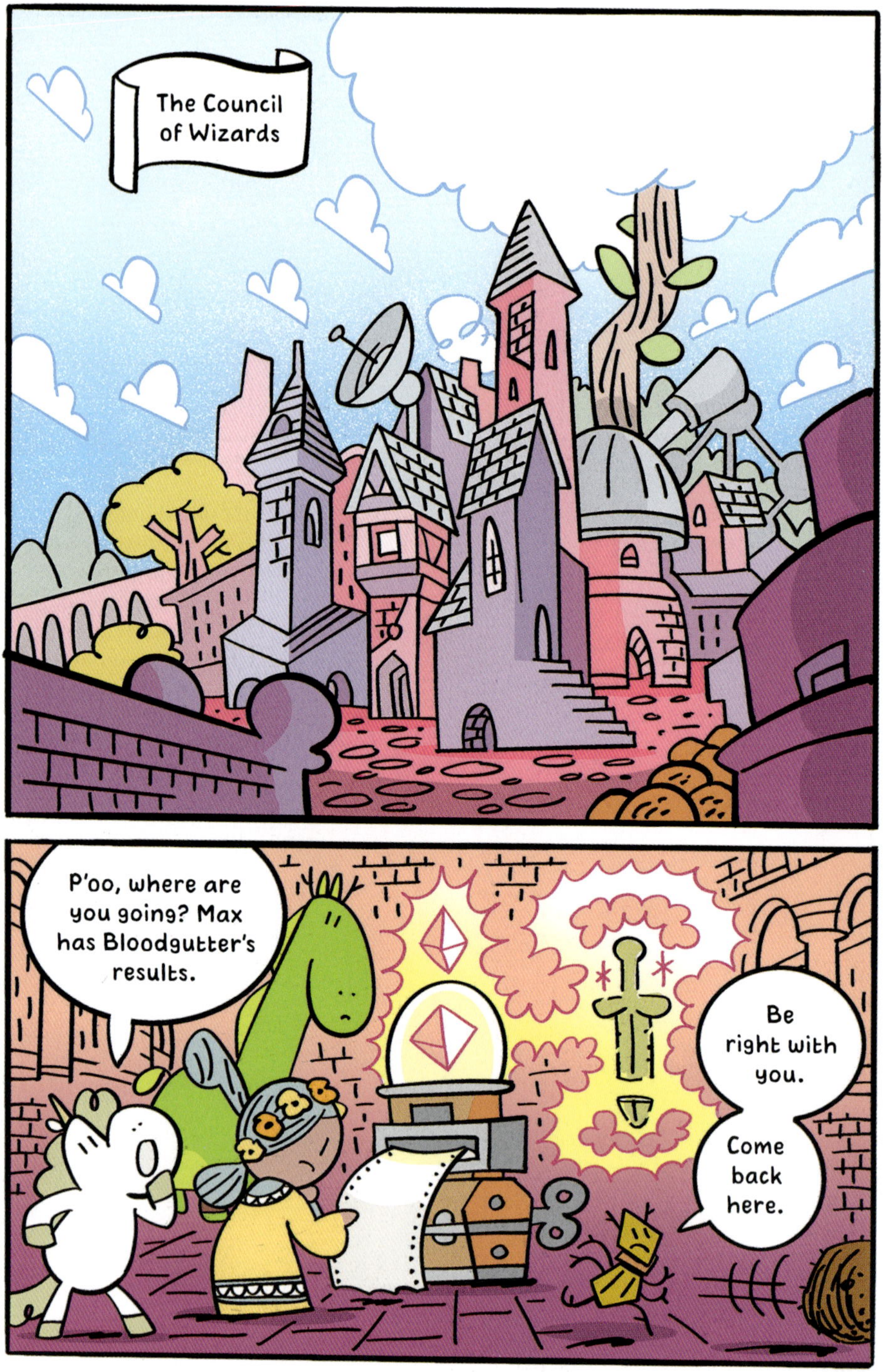
The Council of Wizards
P'oo, where are you going? Max has Bloodgutter's results.
Be right with you.
Come back here.

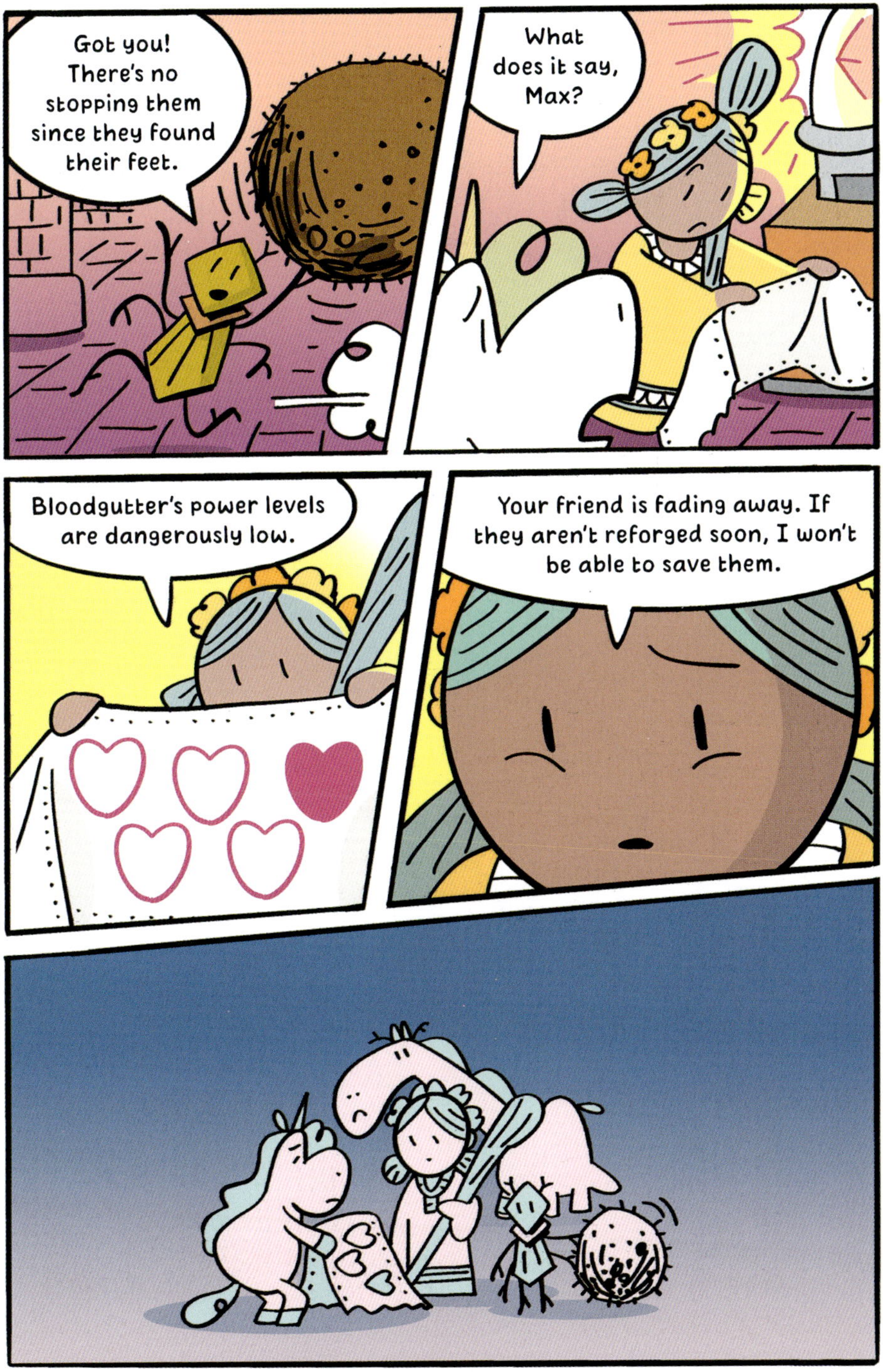
Got you! There's no stopping them since they found their feet.
What does it say, Max?
Bloodgutter's power levels are dangerously low.
Your friend is fading away. If they aren't reforged soon, I won't be able to save them.

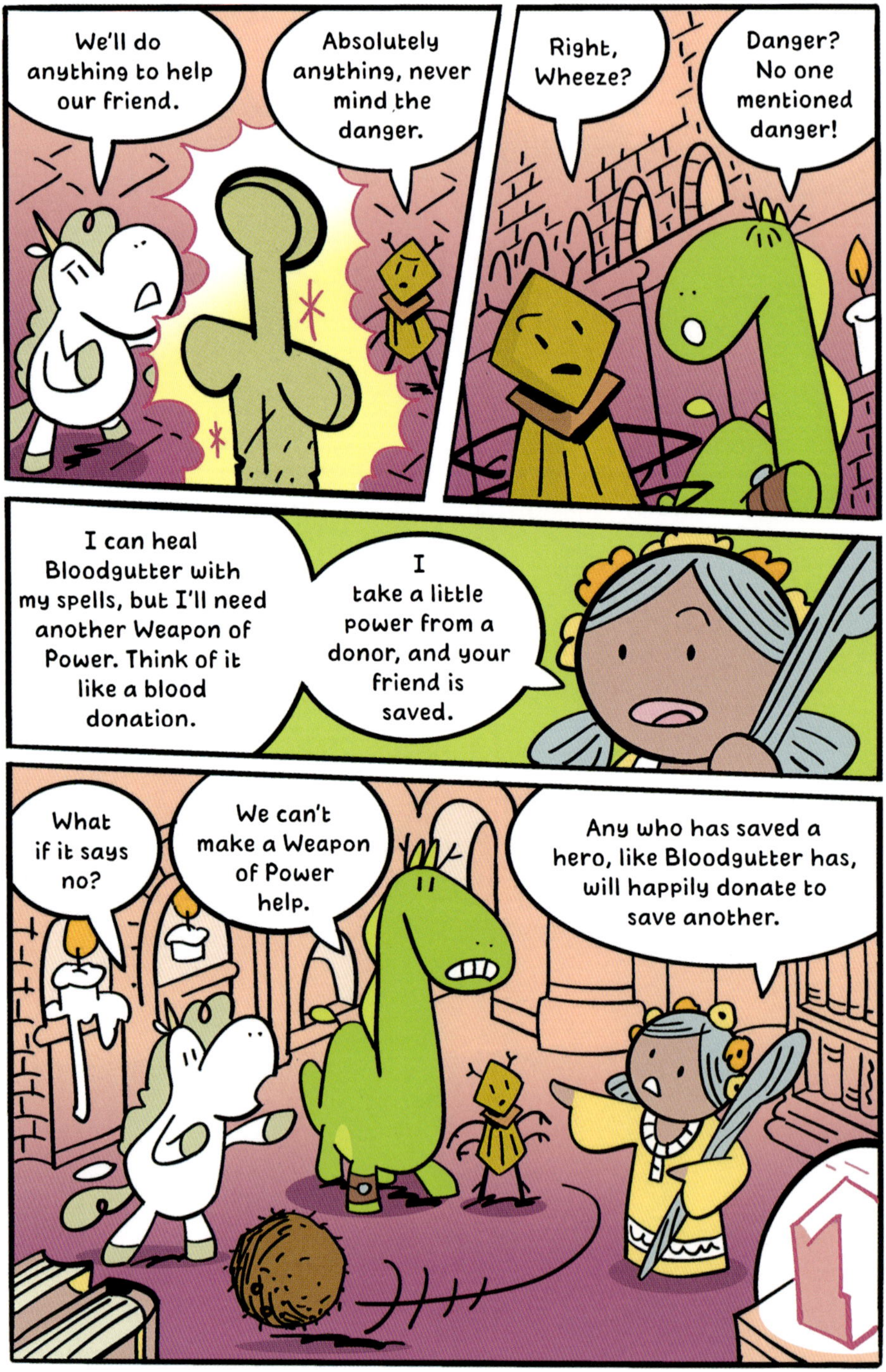
We'll do anything to help our friend.
Absolutely anything, never mind the danger.
Right, Wheeze?
Danger? No one mentioned danger!
I can heal Bloodgutter with my spells, but I'll need another Weapon of Power. Think of it like a blood donation.
I take a little power from a donor, and your friend is saved.
What if it says no?
We can't make a Weapon of Power help.
Any who has saved a hero, like Bloodgutter has, will happily donate to save another.

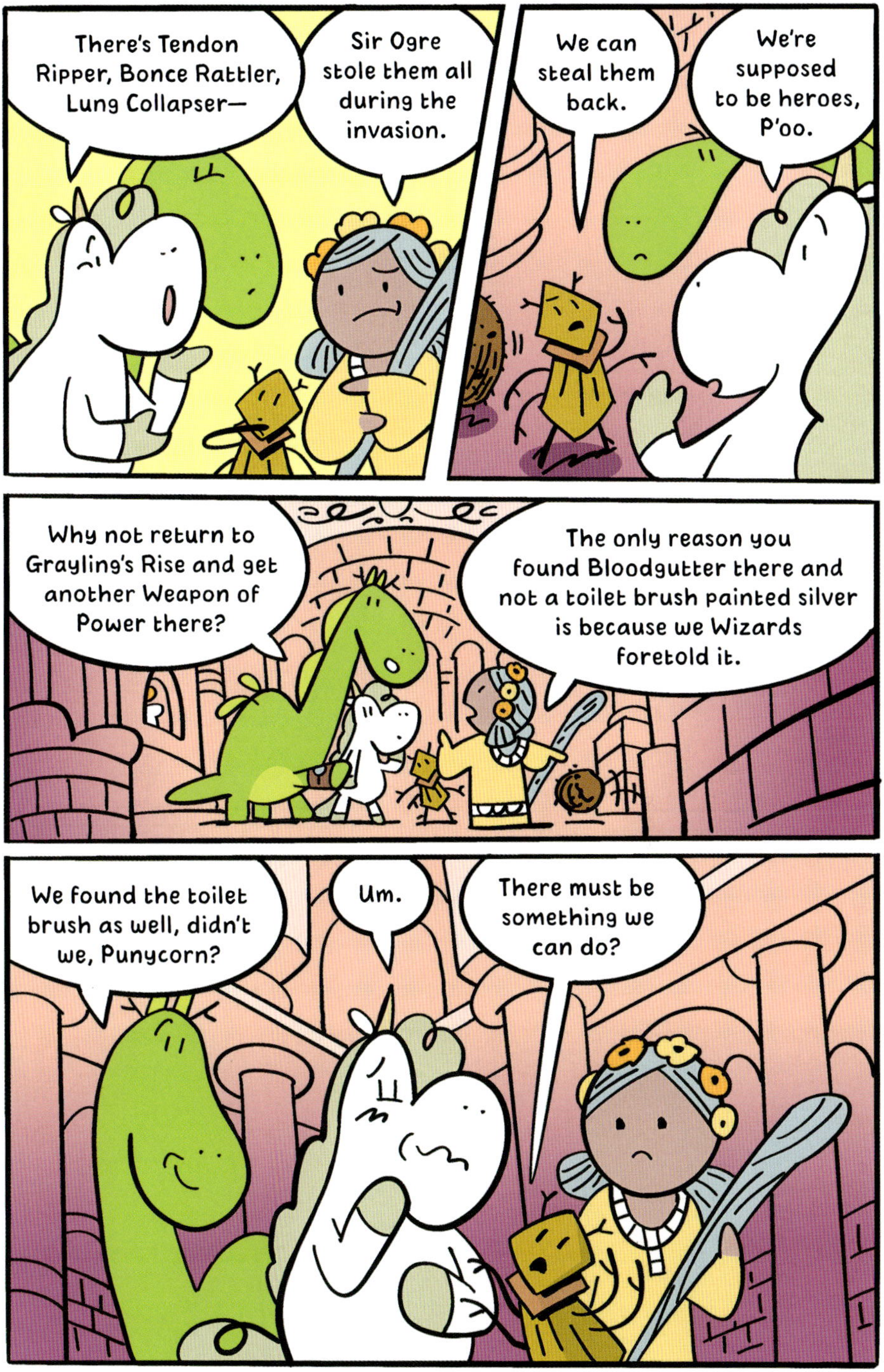
There's Tendon Ripper, Bonce Rattler, Lung Collapser—
Sir Ogre stole them all during the invasion.
We can steal them back.
We're supposed to be heroes, P'oo.
Why not return to Grayling's Rise and get another Weapon of Power there?
The only reason you found Bloodgutter there and not a toilet brush painted silver is because we Wizards foretold it.
We found the toilet brush as well, didn't we, Punycorn?
Um.
There must be something we can do?

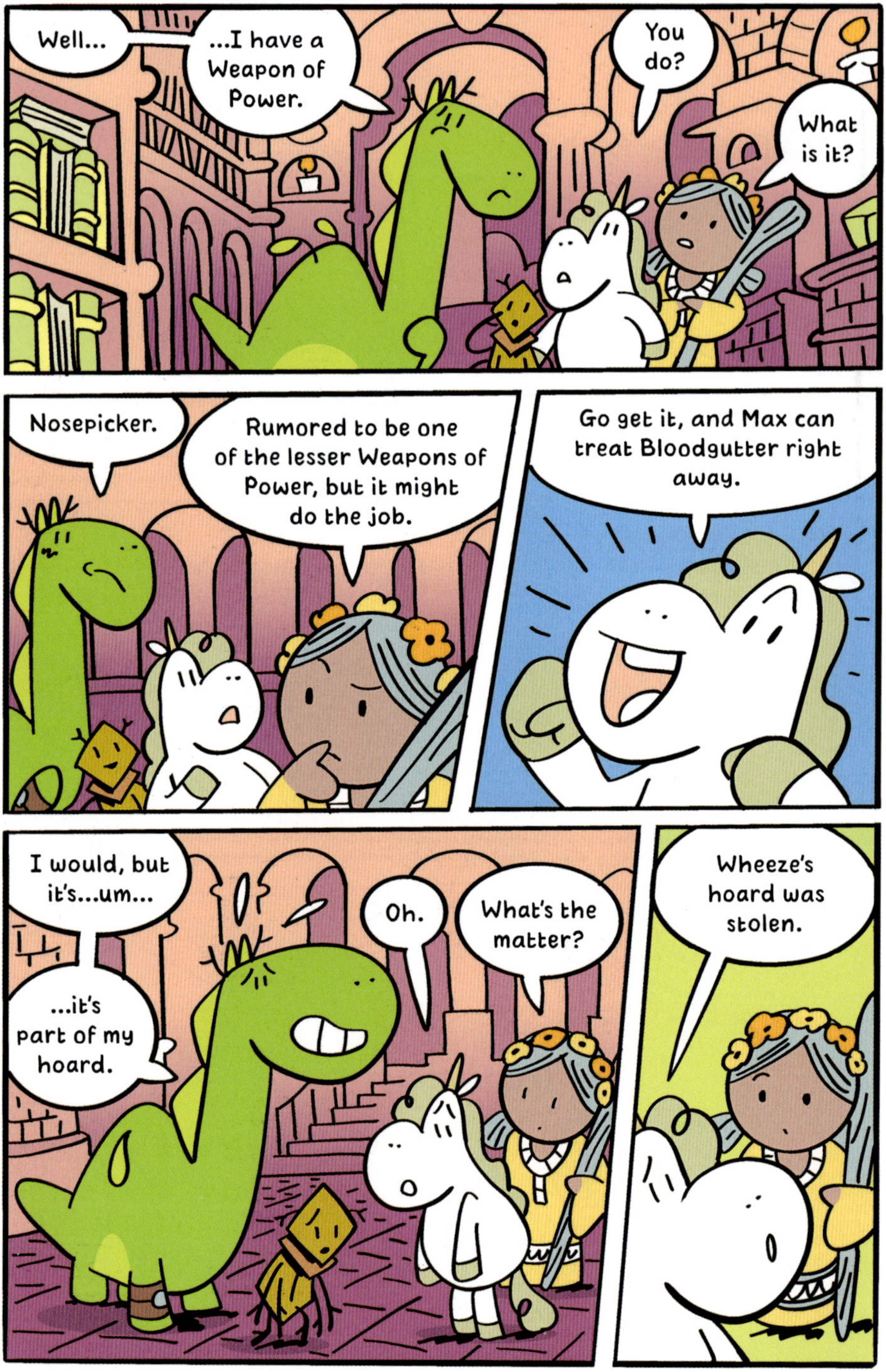
Well...
...I have a Weapon of Power.
You do?
What is it?
Nosepicker.
Rumored to be one of the lesser Weapons of Power, but it might do the job.
Go get it, and Max can treat Bloodgutter right away.
I would, but it's...um...
...it's part of my hoard.
Oh.
What's the matter?
Wheeze's hoard was stolen.

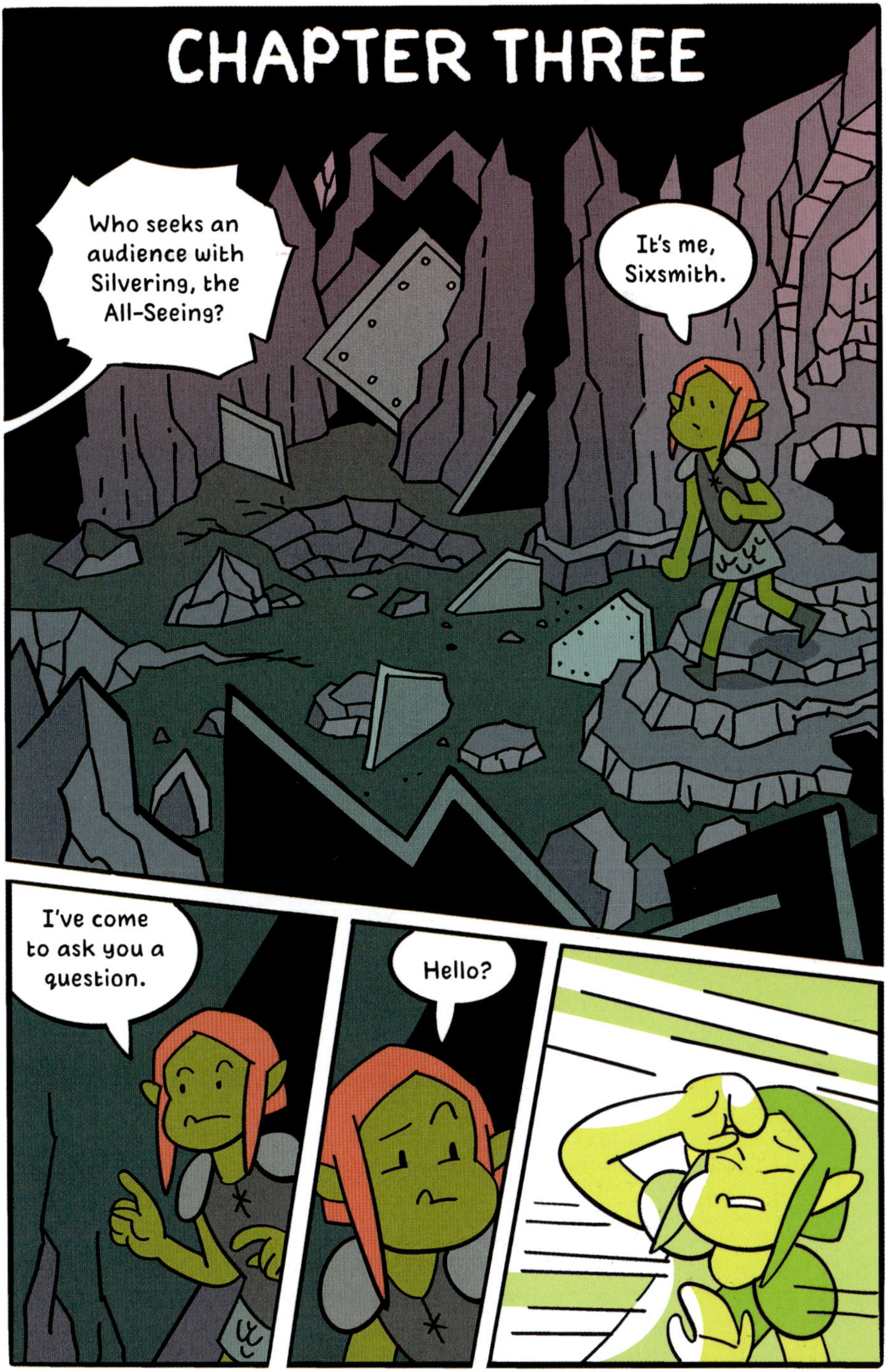
CHAPTER THREE
Who seeks an audience with Silvering, the All-Seeing?
It's me, Sixsmith.
I've come to ask you a question.
Hello?

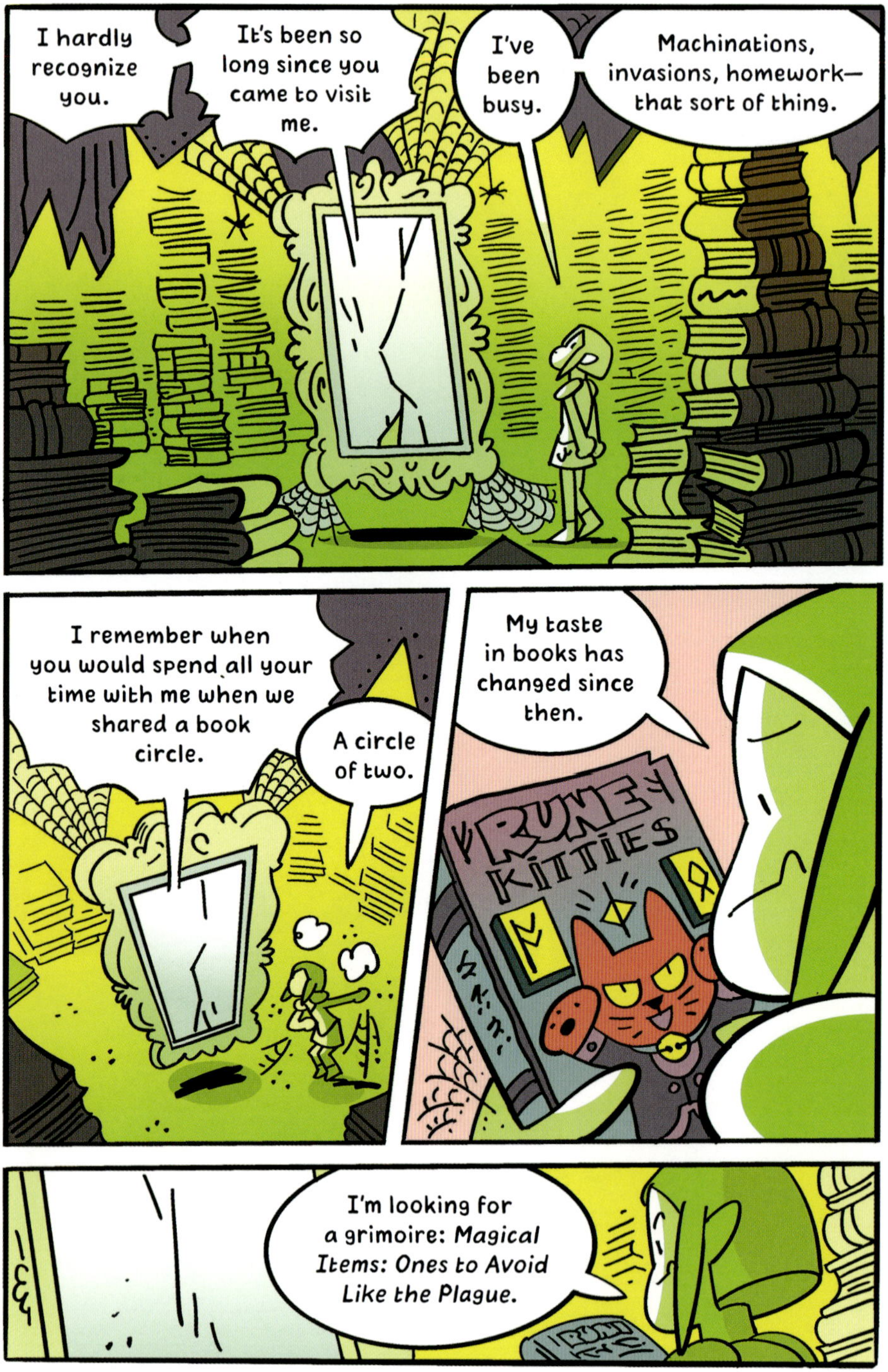
I hardly recognize you.
It's been so long since you came to visit me.
I've been busy.
Machinations, invasions, homework—that sort of thing.
I remember when you would spend all your time with me when we shared a book circle.
A circle of two.
My taste in books has changed since then.
RUNE KITTIES
I'm looking for a grimoire: *Magical Items: Ones to Avoid Like the Plague.*

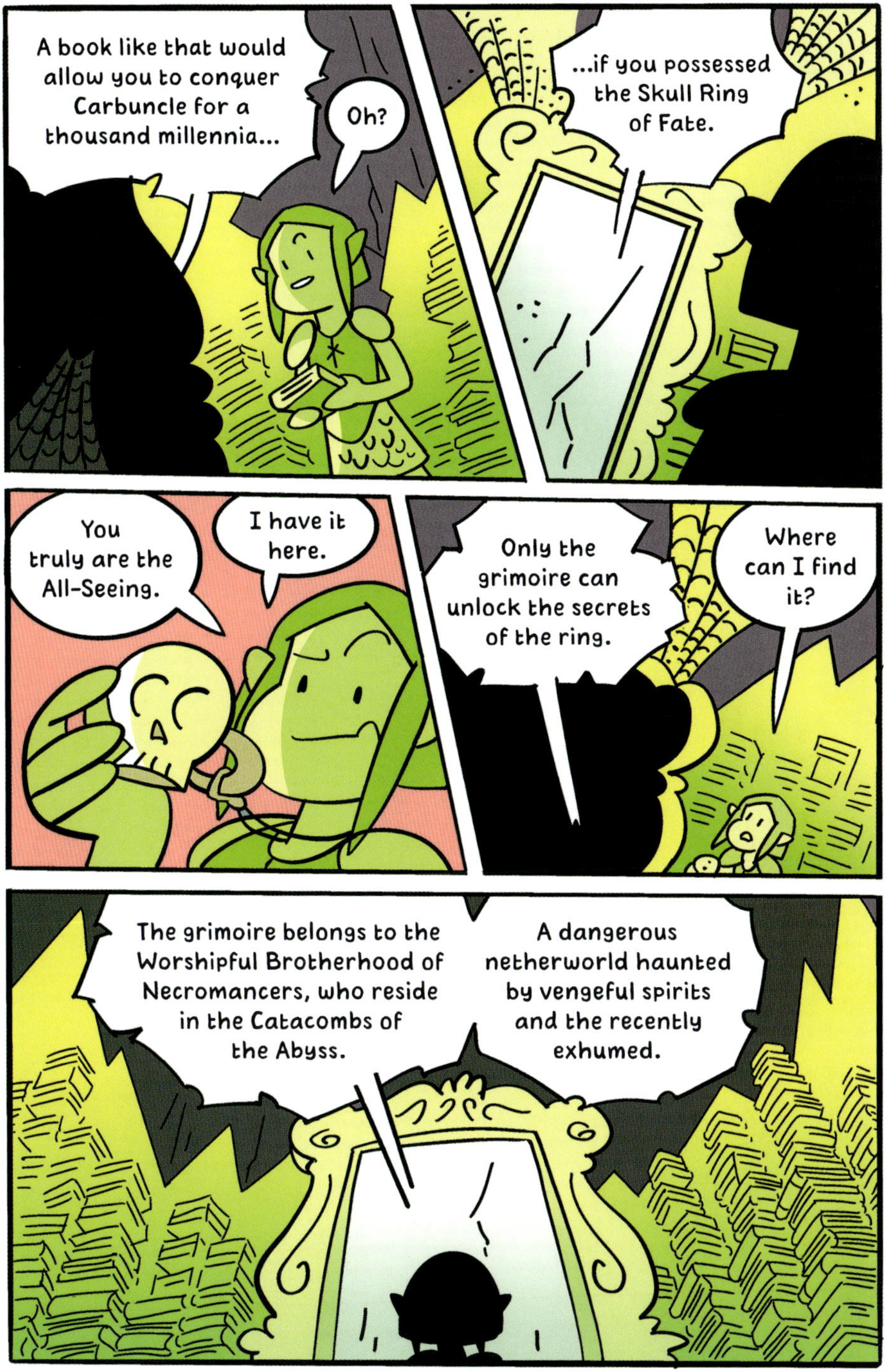
A book like that would allow you to conquer Carbuncle for a thousand millennia...
Oh?
...if you possessed the Skull Ring of Fate.
You truly are the All-Seeing.
I have it here.
Only the grimoire can unlock the secrets of the ring.
Where can I find it?
The grimoire belongs to the Worshipful Brotherhood of Necromancers, who reside in the Catacombs of the Abyss.
A dangerous netherworld haunted by vengeful spirits and the recently exhumed.

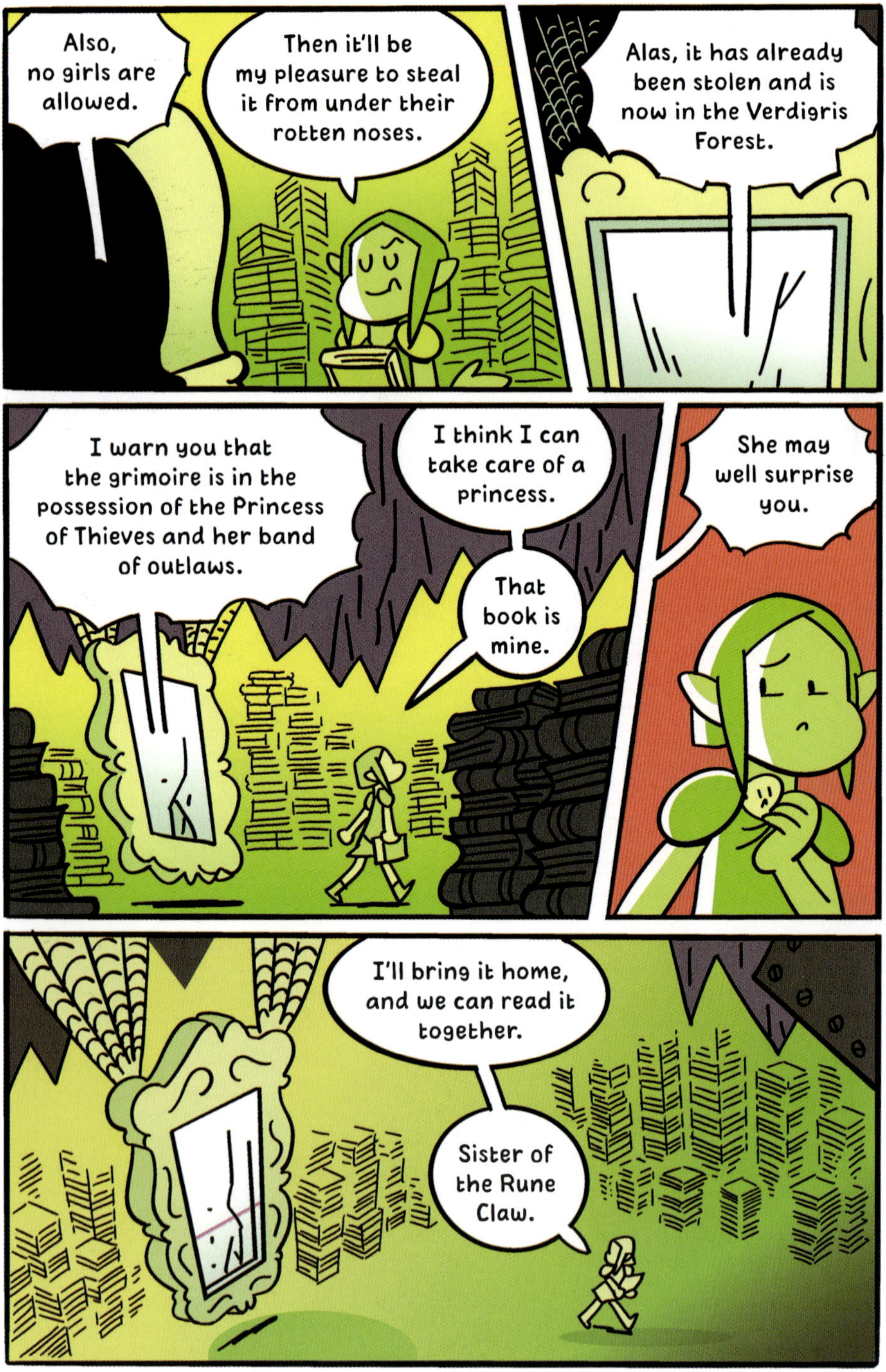
Also, no girls are allowed.
Then it'll be my pleasure to steal it from under their rotten noses.
Alas, it has already been stolen and is now in the Verdigris Forest.
I warn you that the grimoire is in the possession of the Princess of Thieves and her band of outlaws.
I think I can take care of a princess.
That book is mine.
She may well surprise you.
I'll bring it home, and we can read it together.
Sister of the Rune Claw.

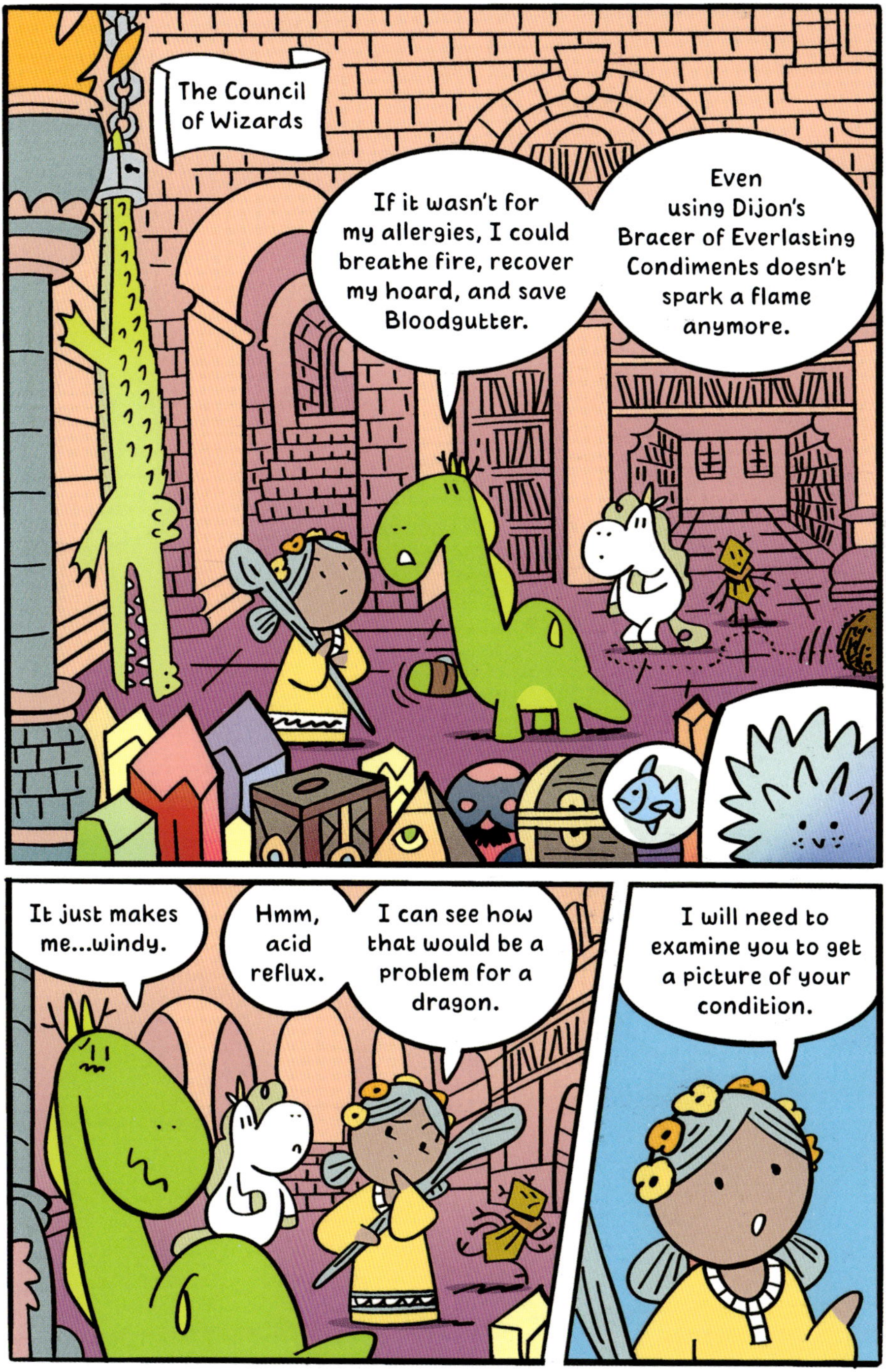
The Council of Wizards
If it wasn't for my allergies, I could breathe fire, recover my hoard, and save Bloodgutter.
Even using Dijon's Bracer of Everlasting Condiments doesn't spark a flame anymore.
It just makes me...windy.
Hmm, acid reflux.
I can see how that would be a problem for a dragon.
I will need to examine you to get a picture of your condition.

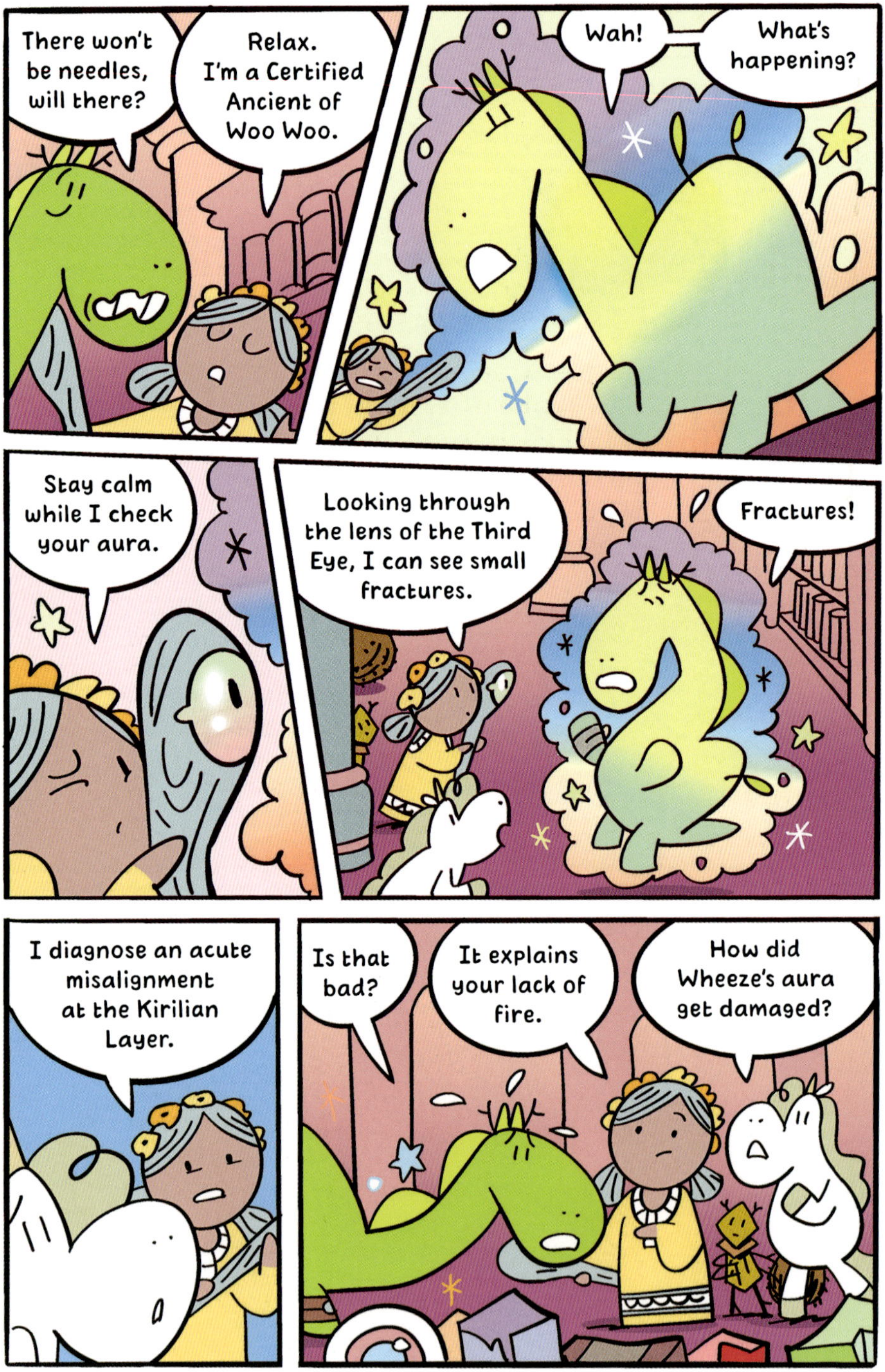
There won't be needles, will there?
Relax. I'm a Certified Ancient of Woo Woo.
Wah!
What's happening?
Stay calm while I check your aura.
Looking through the lens of the Third Eye, I can see small fractures.
Fractures!
I diagnose an acute misalignment at the Kirilian Layer.
Is that bad?
It explains your lack of fire.
How did Wheeze's aura get damaged?

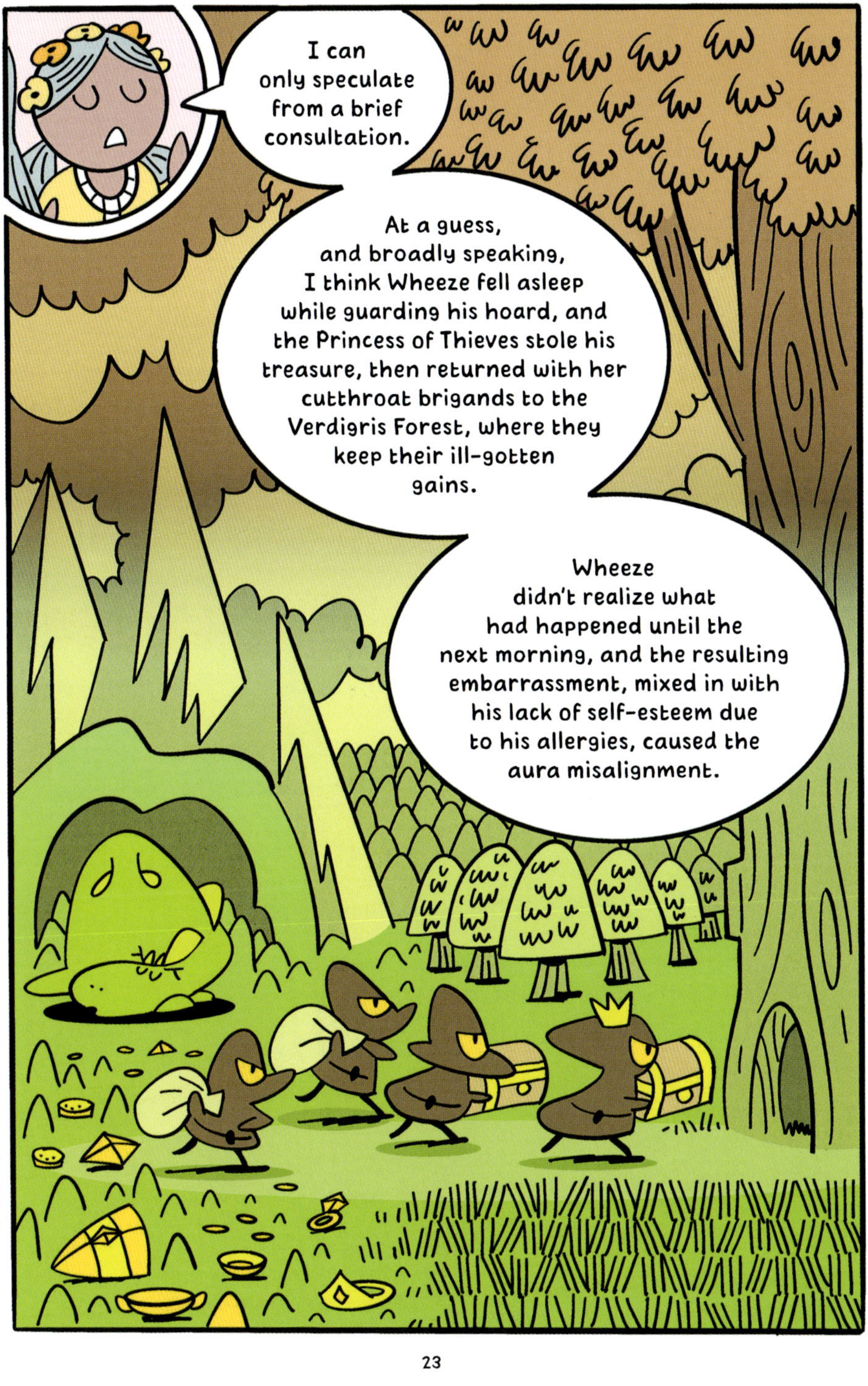
I can only speculate from a brief consultation.
At a guess, and broadly speaking, I think Wheeze fell asleep while guarding his hoard, and the Princess of Thieves stole his treasure, then returned with her cutthroat brigands to the Verdigris Forest, where they keep their ill-gotten gains.
Wheeze didn't realize what had happened until the next morning, and the resulting embarrassment, mixed in with his lack of self-esteem due to his allergies, caused the aura misalignment.

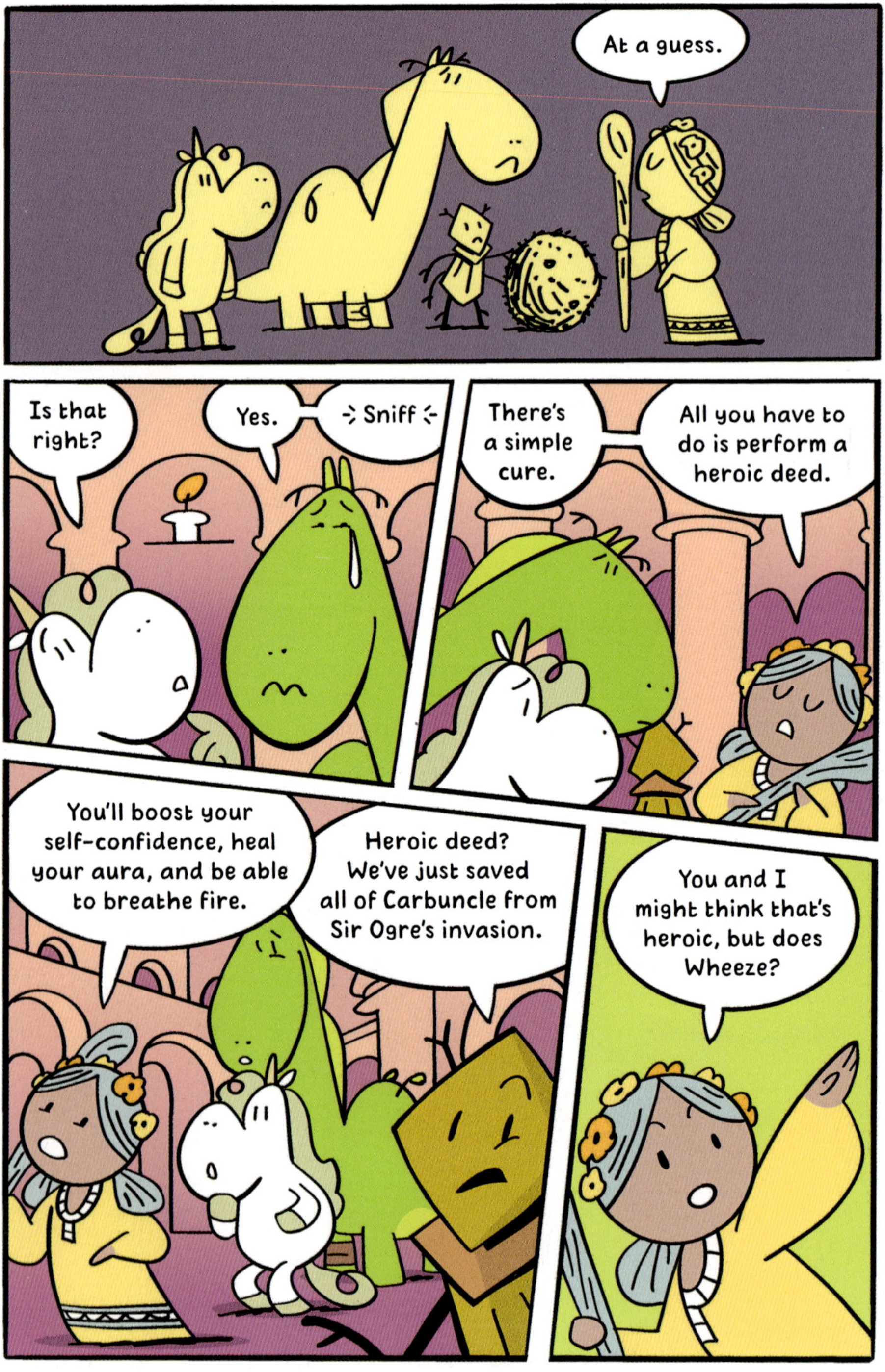
At a guess.
Is that right?
Yes.
Sniff
There's a simple cure.
All you have to do is perform a heroic deed.
You'll boost your self-confidence, heal your aura, and be able to breathe fire.
Heroic deed? We've just saved all of Carbuncle from Sir Ogre's invasion.
You and I might think that's heroic, but does Wheeze?

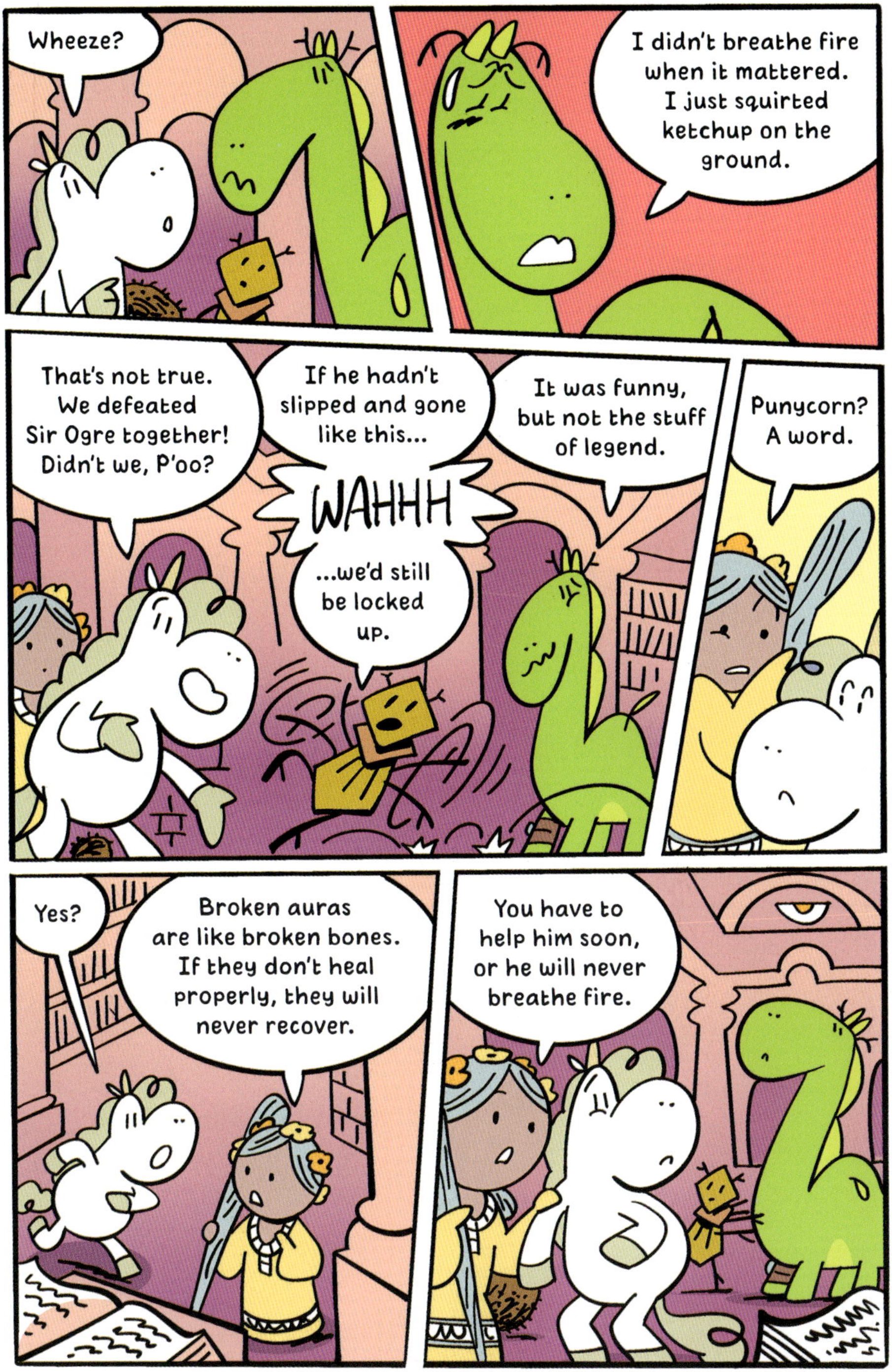
Wheeze?
I didn't breathe fire when it mattered. I just squirted ketchup on the ground.
That's not true. We defeated Sir Ogre together! Didn't we, P'oo?
If he hadn't slipped and gone like this...
WAHHH
...we'd still be locked up.
It was funny, but not the stuff of legend.
Punycorn? A word.
Yes?
Broken auras are like broken bones. If they don't heal properly, they will never recover.
You have to help him soon, or he will never breathe fire.

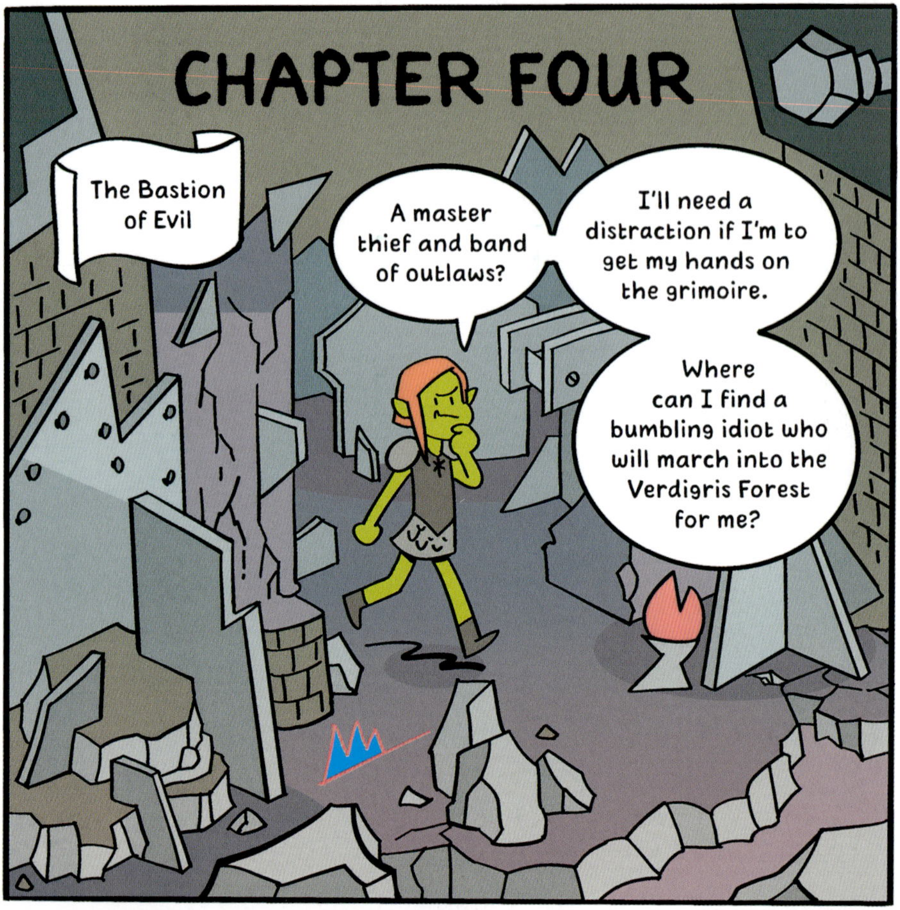
CHAPTER FOUR
The Bastion of Evil
A master thief and band of outlaws?
I'll need a distraction if I'm to get my hands on the grimoire.
Where can I find a bumbling idiot who will march into the Verdigris Forest for me?

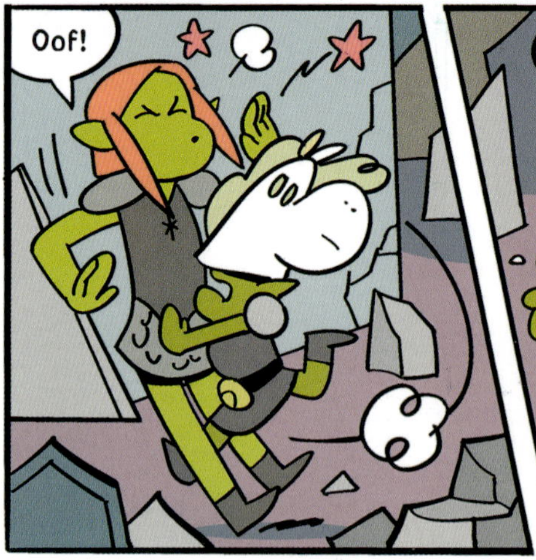
Oof!

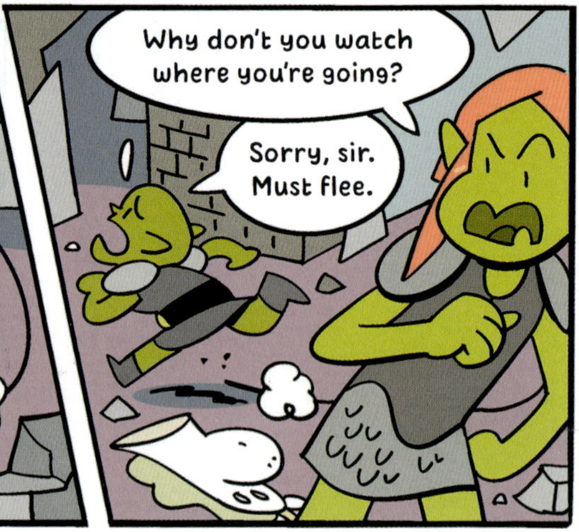
Why don't you watch where you're going?
Sorry, sir. Must flee.

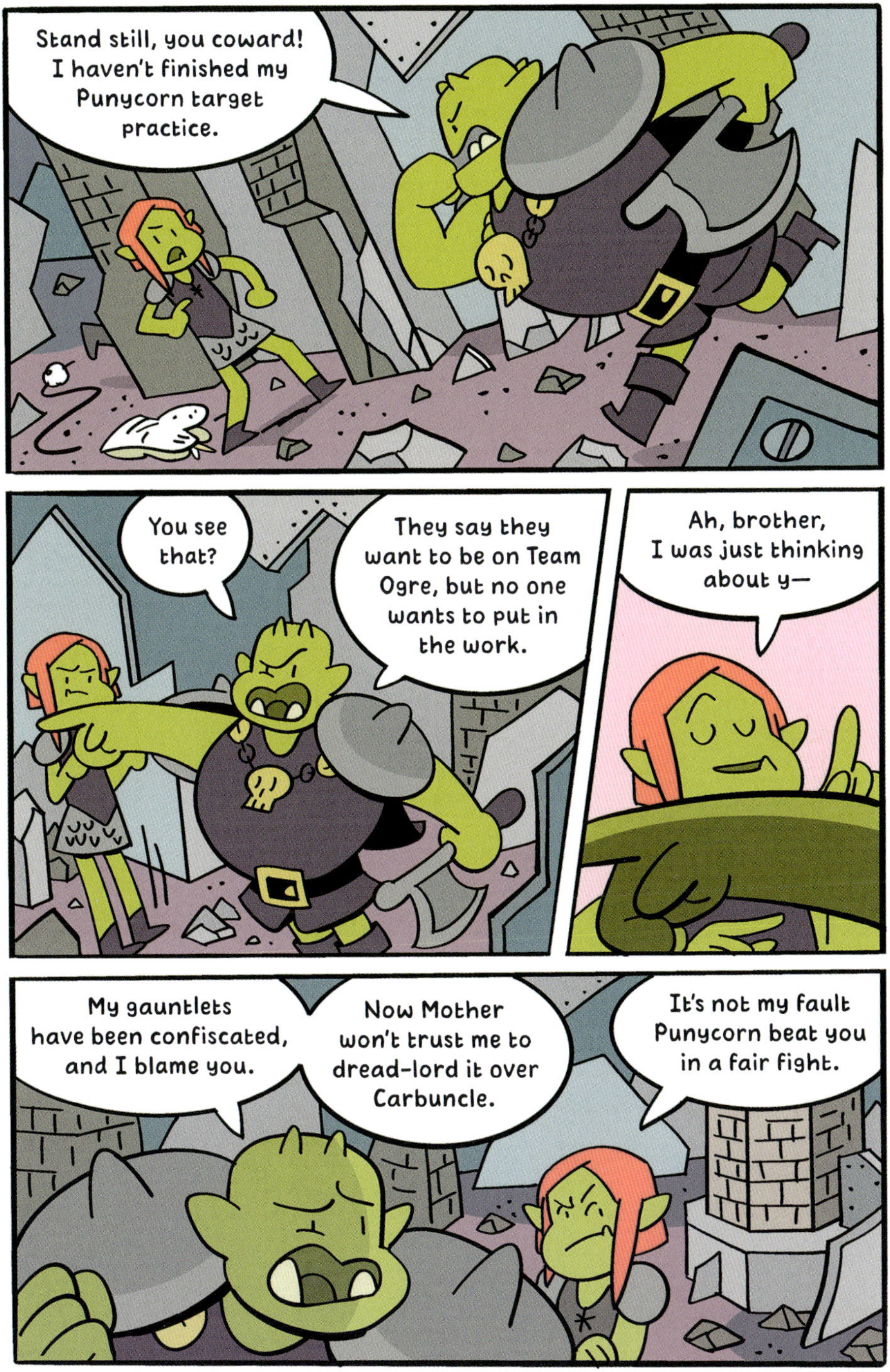

Stand still, you coward! I haven't finished my Punycorn target practice.
You see that?
They say they want to be on Team Ogre, but no one wants to put in the work.
Ah, brother, I was just thinking about y—
My gauntlets have been confiscated, and I blame you.
Now Mother won't trust me to dread-lord it over Carbuncle.
It's not my fault Punycorn beat you in a fair fight.

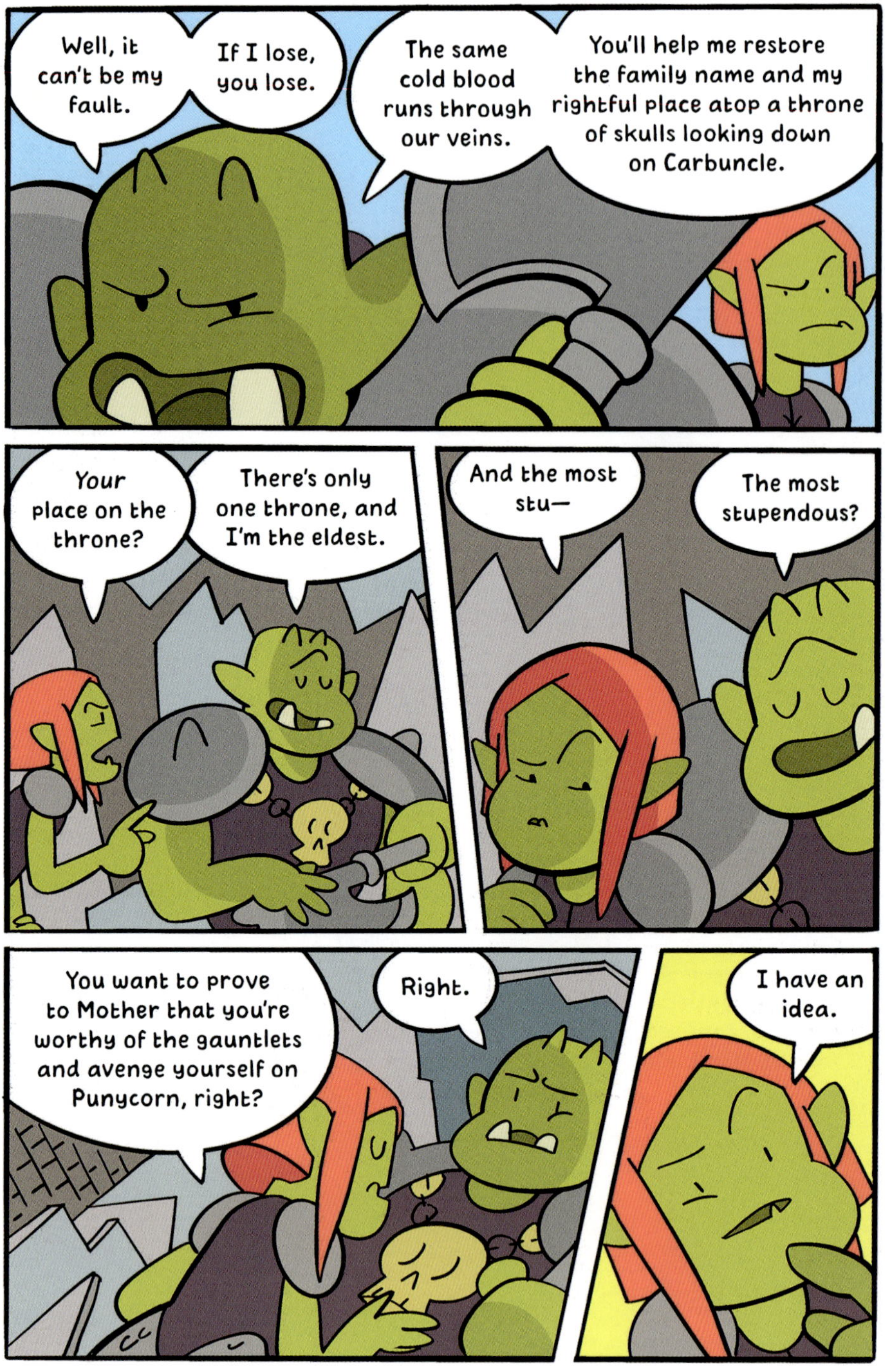
Well, it can't be my fault.
If I lose, you lose.
The same cold blood runs through our veins.
You'll help me restore the family name and my rightful place atop a throne of skulls looking down on Carbuncle.
Your place on the throne?
There's only one throne, and I'm the eldest.
And the most stu—
The most stupendous?
You want to prove to Mother that you're worthy of the gauntlets and avenge yourself on Punycorn, right?
Right.
I have an idea.

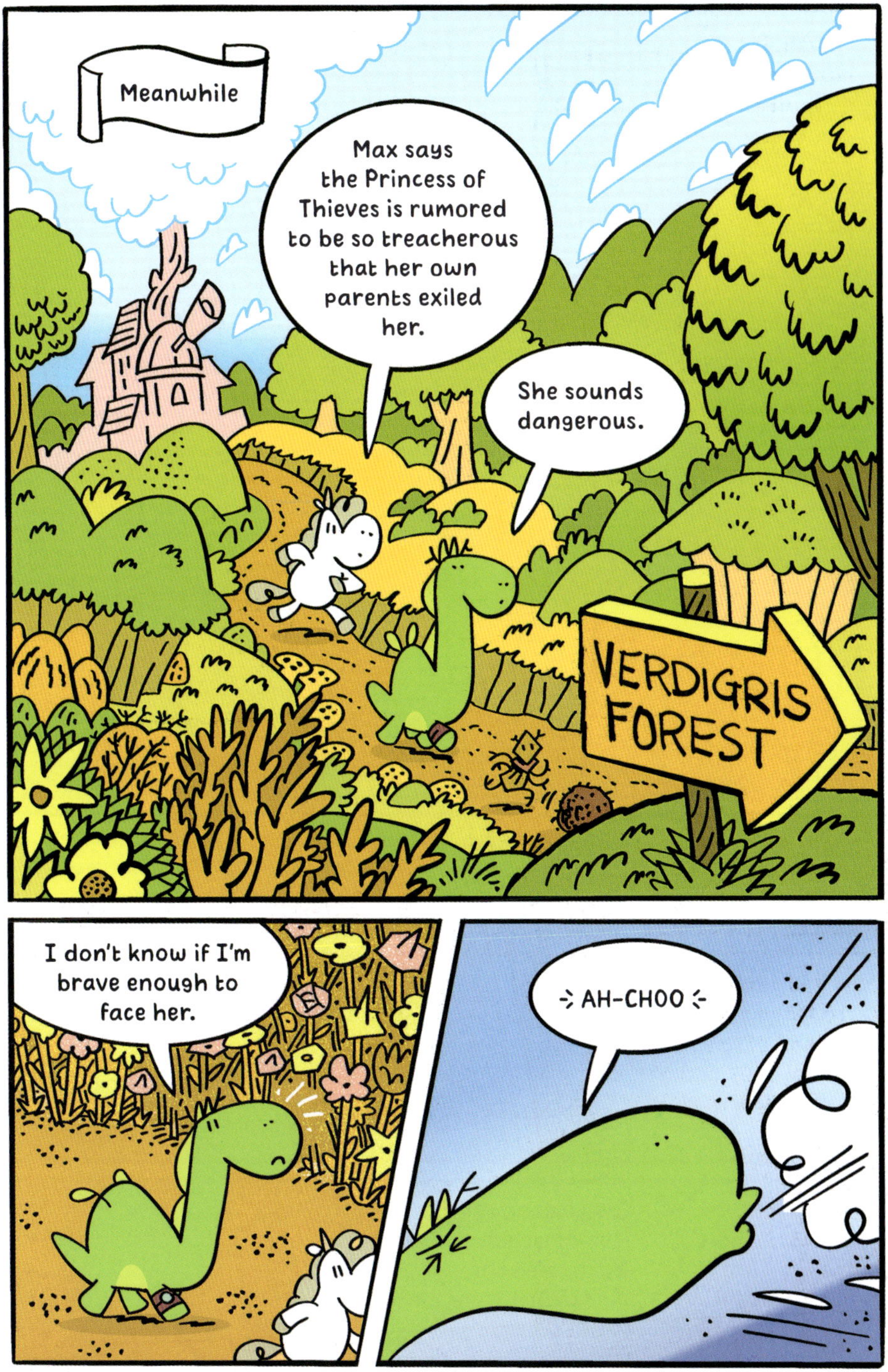
Meanwhile
Max says the Princess of Thieves is rumored to be so treacherous that her own parents exiled her.
She sounds dangerous.
VERDIGRIS FOREST
I don't know if I'm brave enough to face her.
AH-CHOO

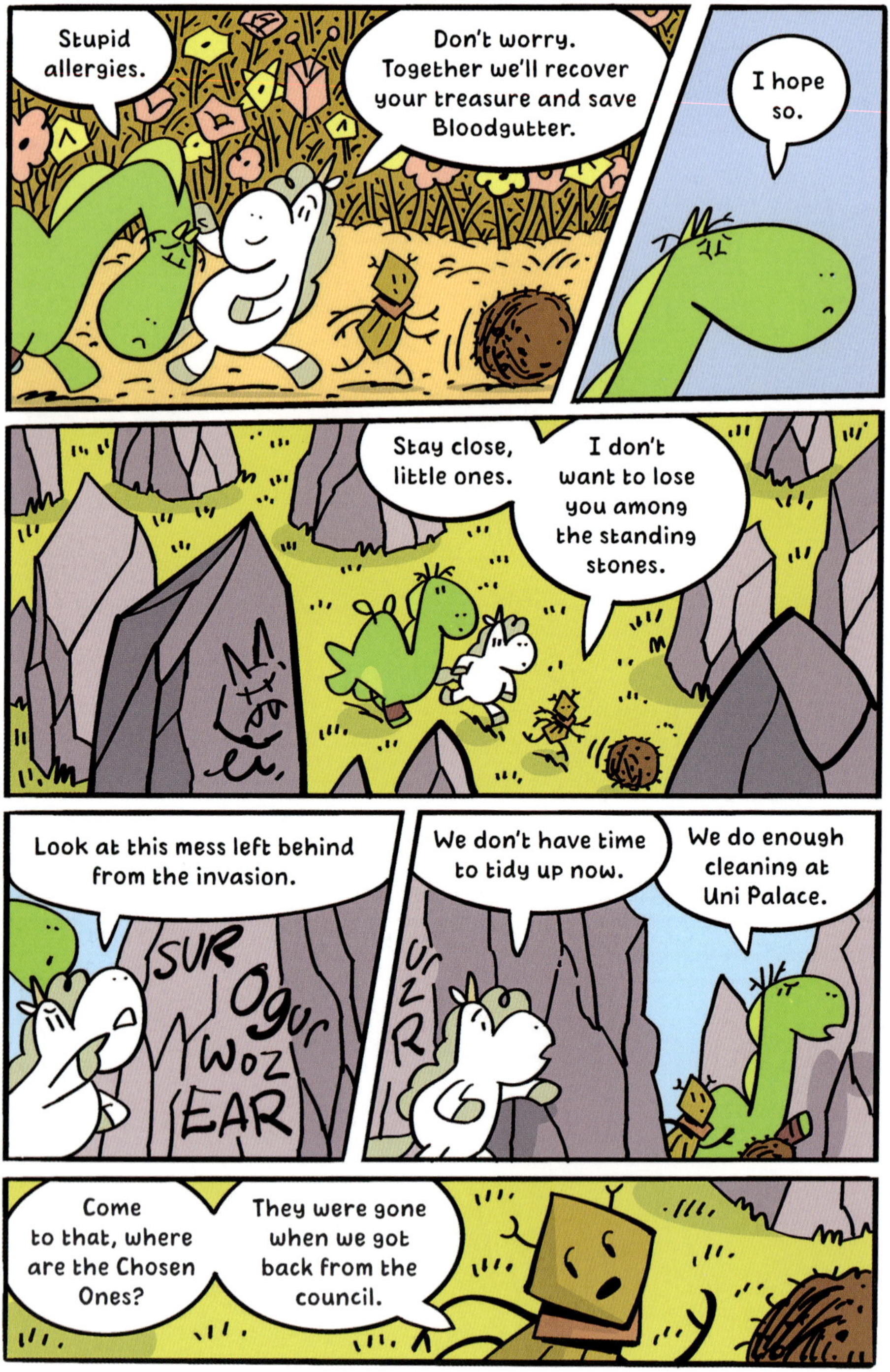
Stupid allergies.
Don't worry. Together we'll recover your treasure and save Bloodgutter.
I hope so.
Stay close, little ones.
I don't want to lose you among the standing stones.
Look at this mess left behind from the invasion.
SUR Ogur WOZ EAR
We don't have time to tidy up now.
We do enough cleaning at Uni Palace.
Come to that, where are the Chosen Ones?
They were gone when we got back from the council.

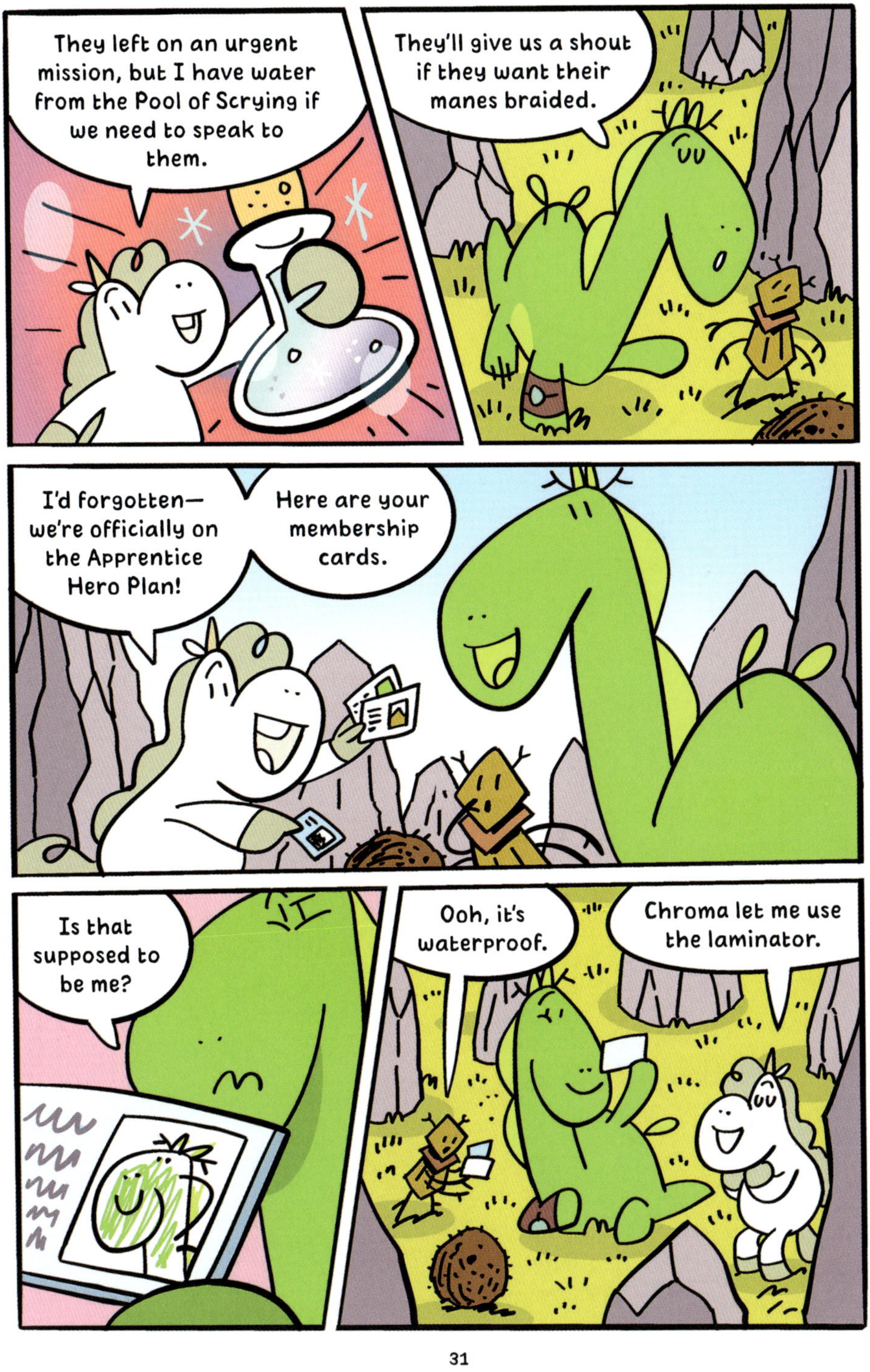
They left on an urgent mission, but I have water from the Pool of Scrying if we need to speak to them.
They'll give us a shout if they want their manes braided.
I'd forgotten—we're officially on the Apprentice Hero Plan!
Here are your membership cards.
Is that supposed to be me?
Ooh, it's waterproof.
Chroma let me use the laminator.

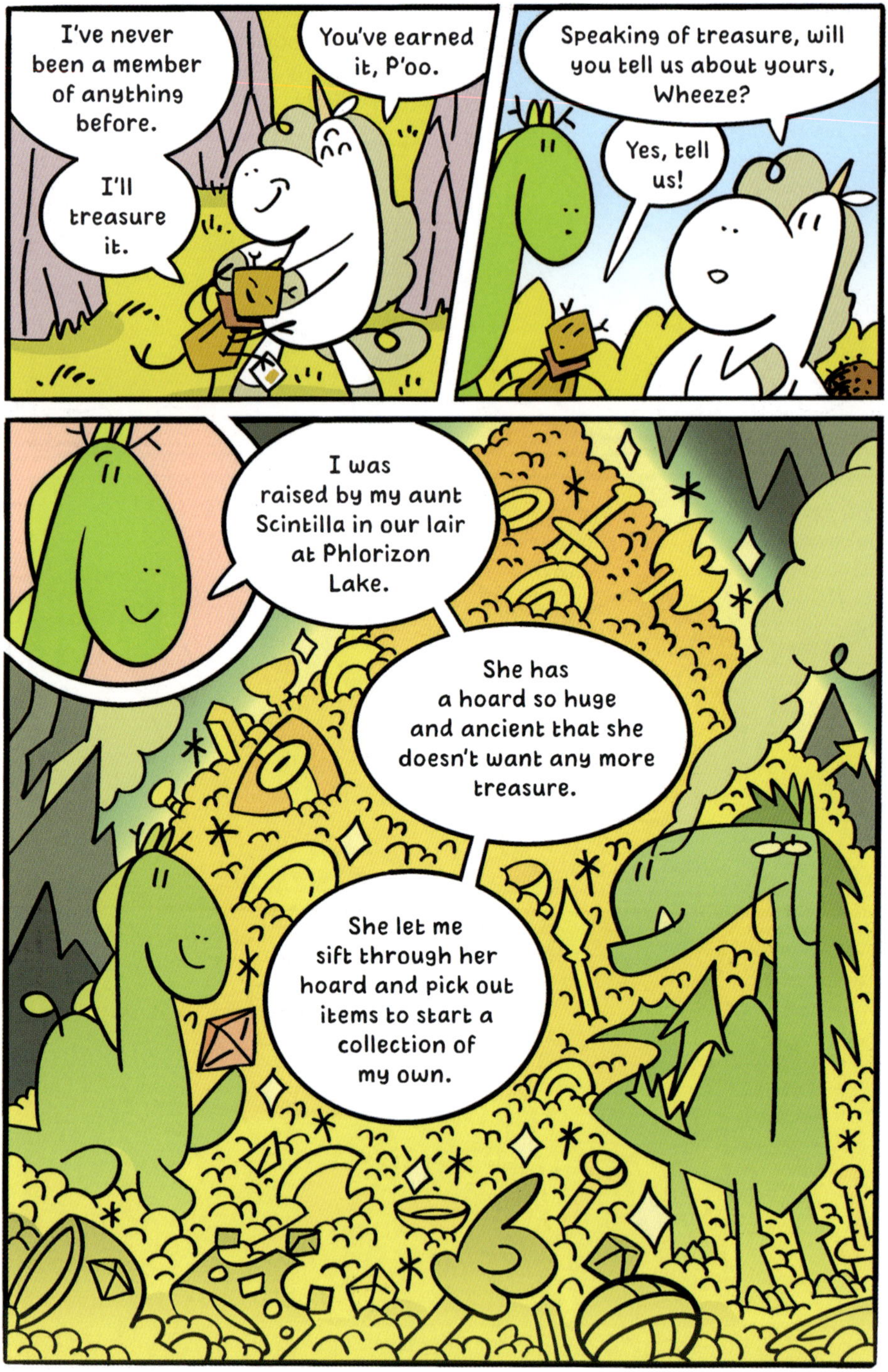
I've never been a member of anything before.
I'll treasure it.
You've earned it, P'oo.
Speaking of treasure, will you tell us about yours, Wheeze?
Yes, tell us!
I was raised by my aunt Scintilla in our lair at Phlorizon Lake.
She has a hoard so huge and ancient that she doesn't want any more treasure.
She let me sift through her hoard and pick out items to start a collection of my own.

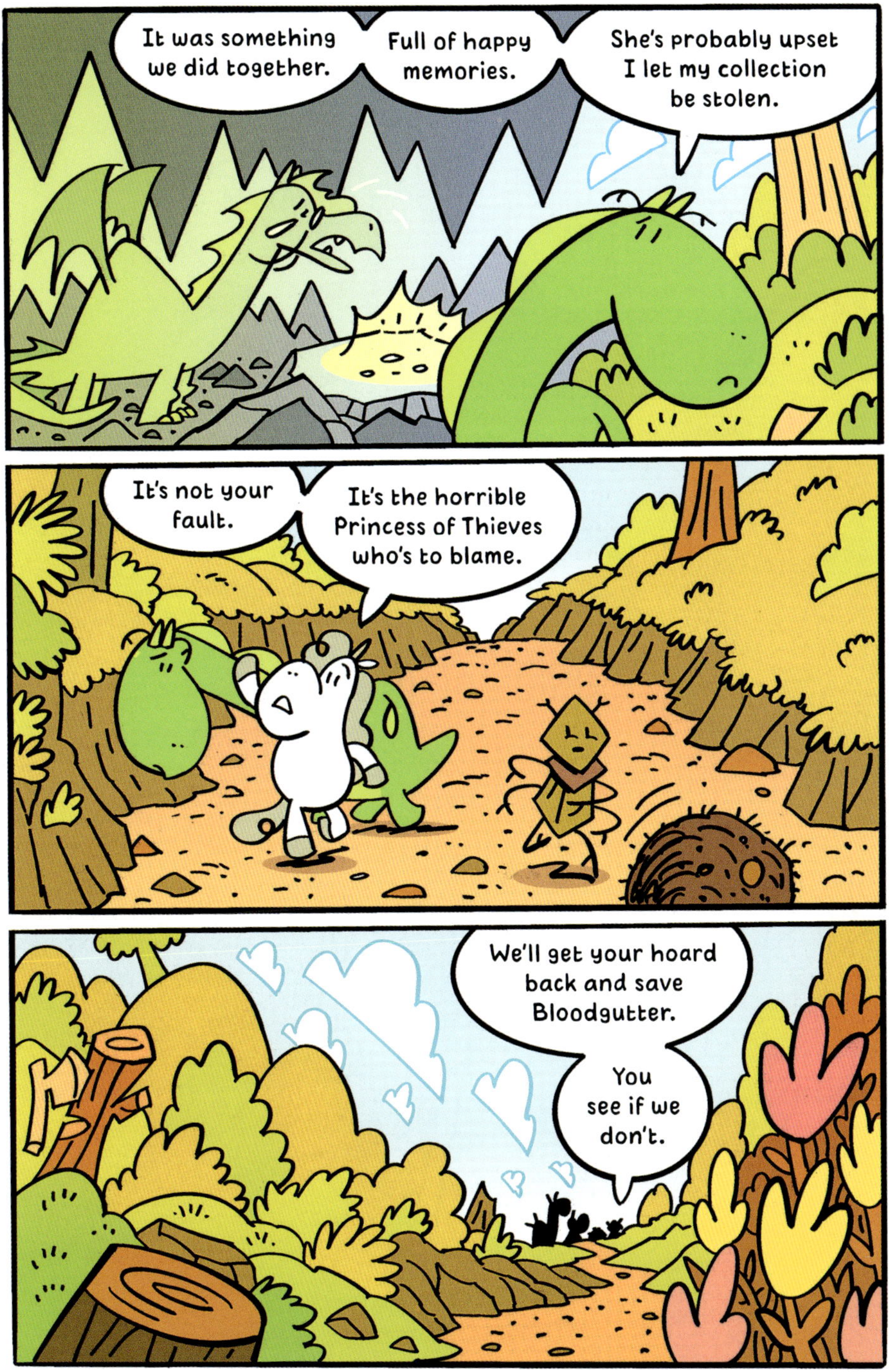
It was something we did together.
Full of happy memories.
She's probably upset I let my collection be stolen.
It's not your fault.
It's the horrible Princess of Thieves who's to blame.
We'll get your hoard back and save Bloodgutter.
You see if we don't.

CHAPTER FIVE

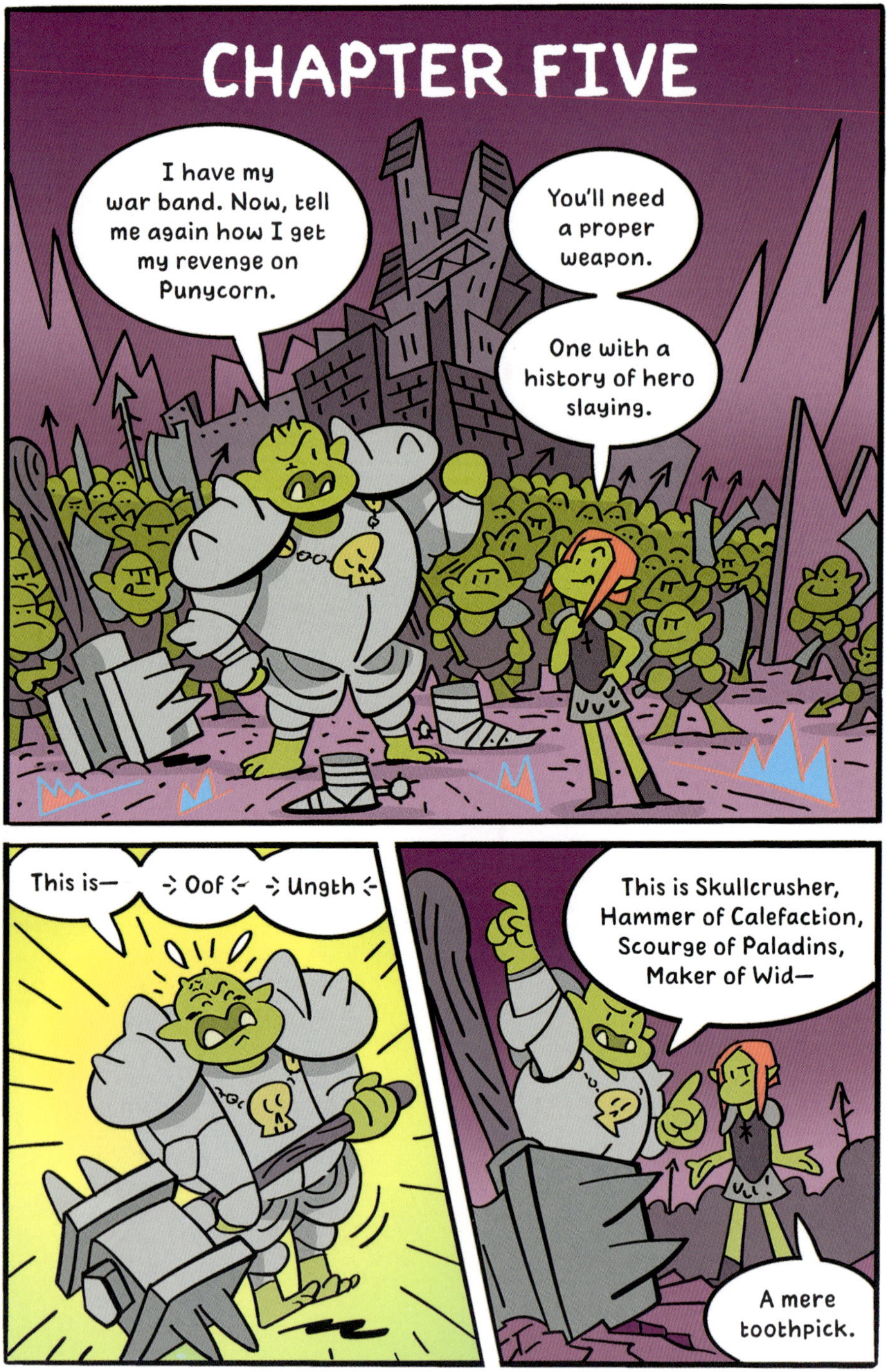
I have my war band. Now, tell me again how I get my revenge on Punycorn.
You'll need a proper weapon.
One with a history of hero slaying.
This is—
Oof
Ungth
This is Skullcrusher, Hammer of Calefaction, Scourge of Paladins, Maker of Wid—
A mere toothpick.

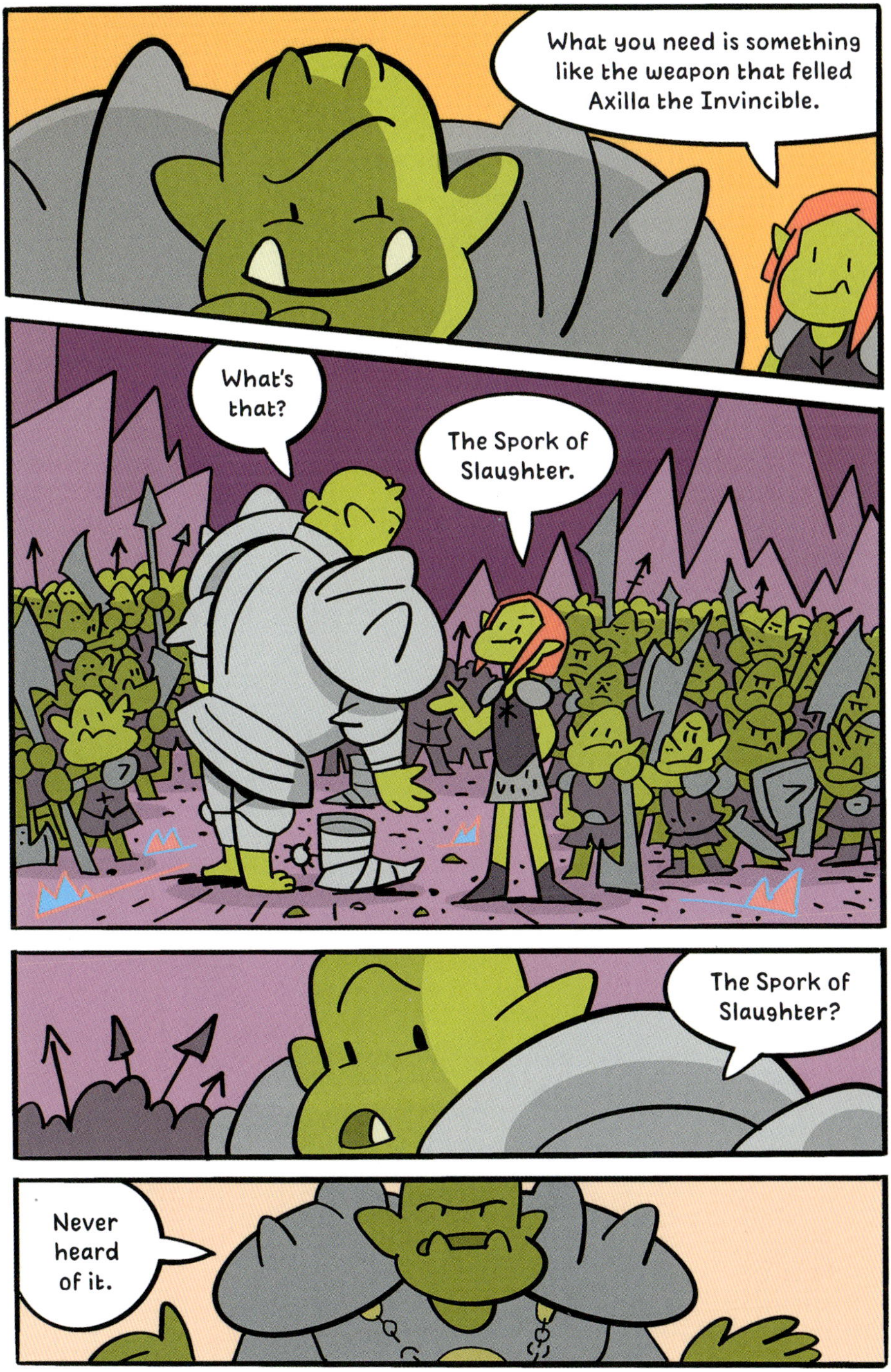
What you need is something like the weapon that felled Axilla the Invincible.
What's that?
The Spork of Slaughter.
The Spork of Slaughter?
Never heard of it.

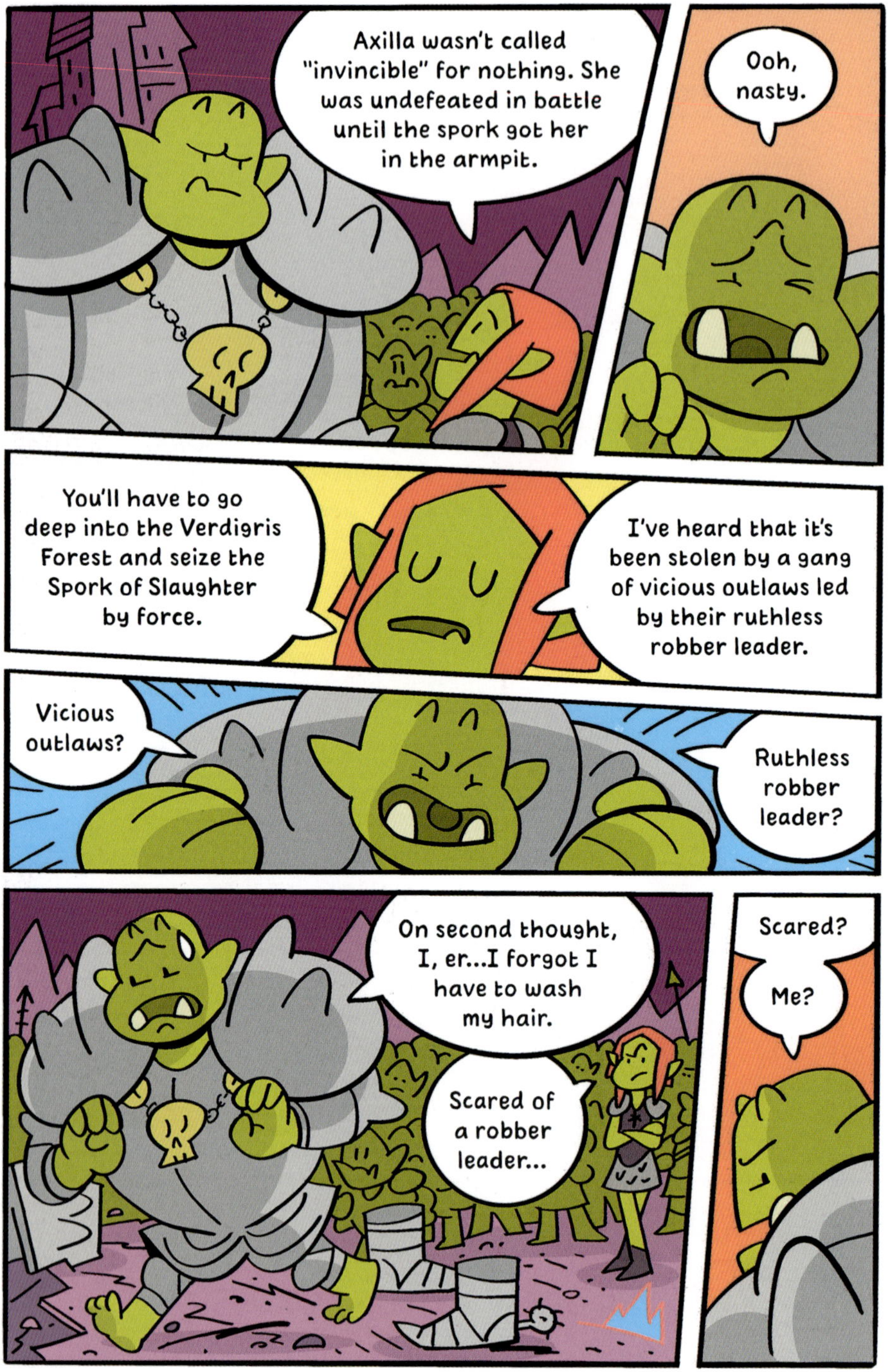
Axilla wasn't called "invincible" for nothing. She was undefeated in battle until the spork got her in the armpit.
Ooh, nasty.
You'll have to go deep into the Verdigris Forest and seize the Spork of Slaughter by force.
I've heard that it's been stolen by a gang of vicious outlaws led by their ruthless robber leader.
Vicious outlaws?
Ruthless robber leader?
On second thought, I, er...I forgot I have to wash my hair.
Scared of a robber leader...
Scared?
Me?

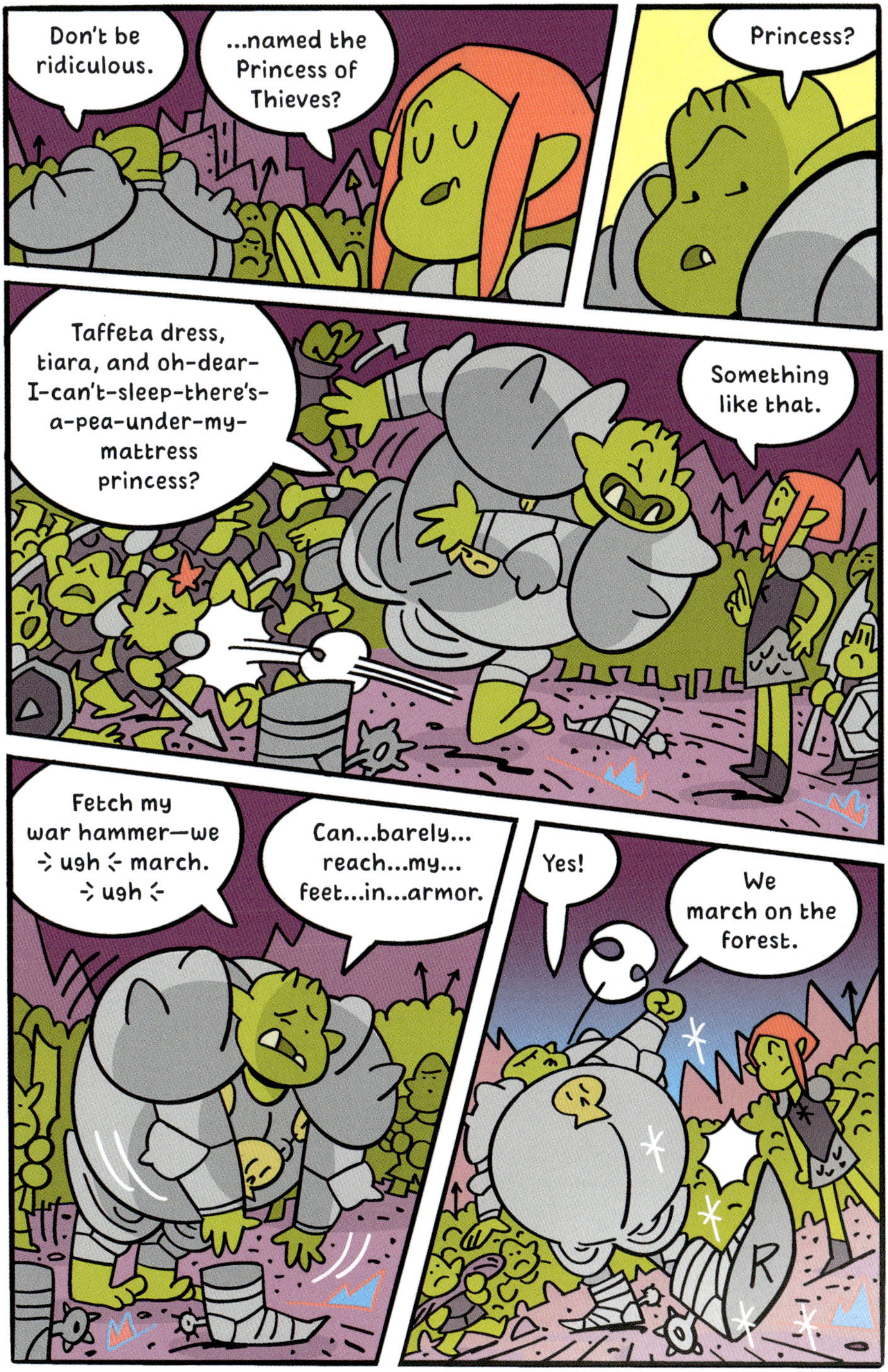
Don't be ridiculous.
...named the Princess of Thieves?
Princess?
Taffeta dress, tiara, and oh-dear-I-can't-sleep-there's-a-pea-under-my-mattress princess?
Something like that.
Fetch my war hammer—we ⁓ ugh ⁓ march. ⁓ ugh ⁓
Can...barely... reach...my... feet...in...armor.
Yes!
We march on the forest.

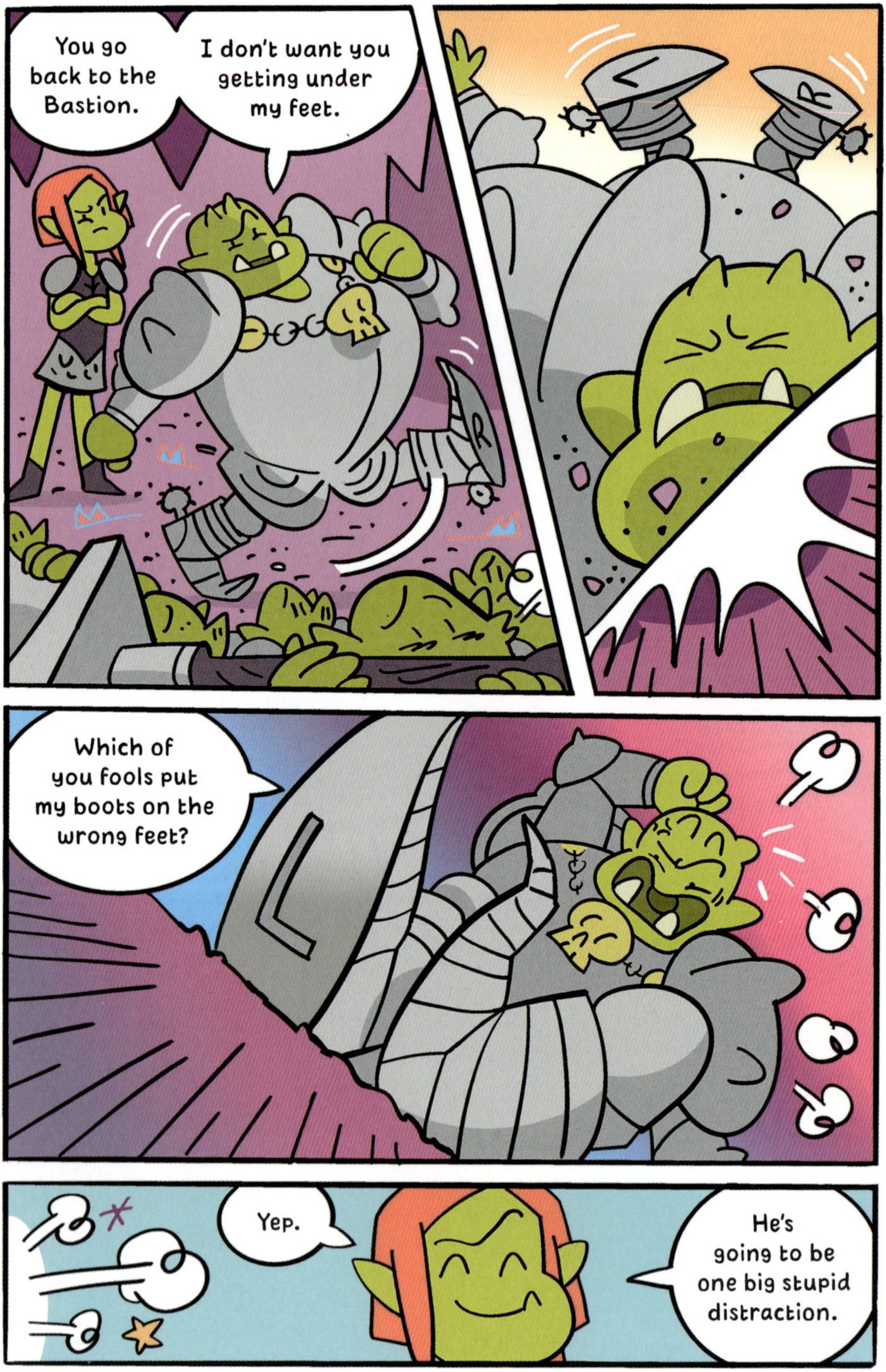
You go back to the Bastion.
I don't want you getting under my feet.
Which of you fools put my boots on the wrong feet?
Yep.
He's going to be one big stupid distraction.

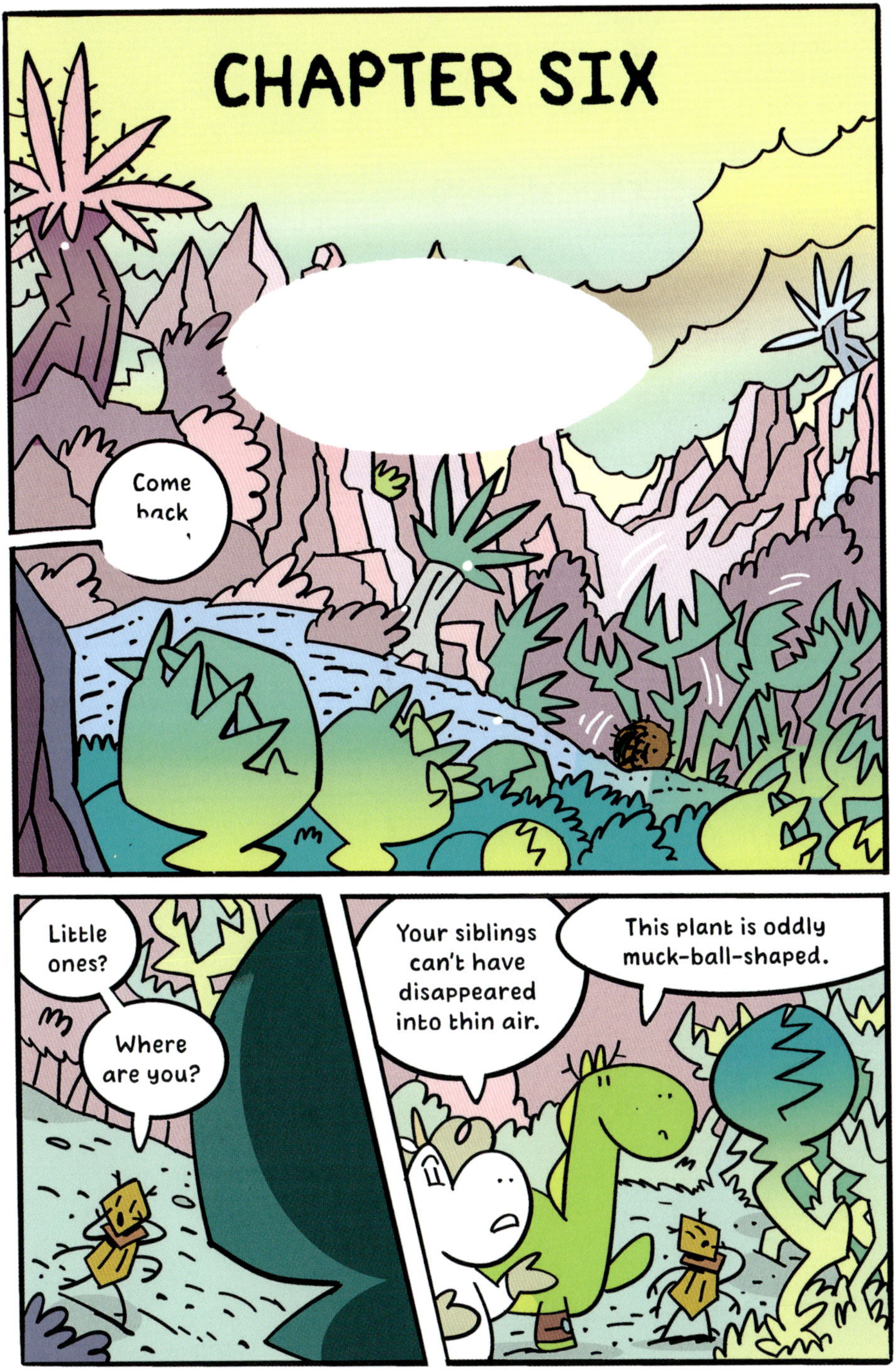
CHAPTER SIX
Come back
Little ones?
Where are you?
Your siblings can't have disappeared into thin air.
This plant is oddly muck-ball-shaped.

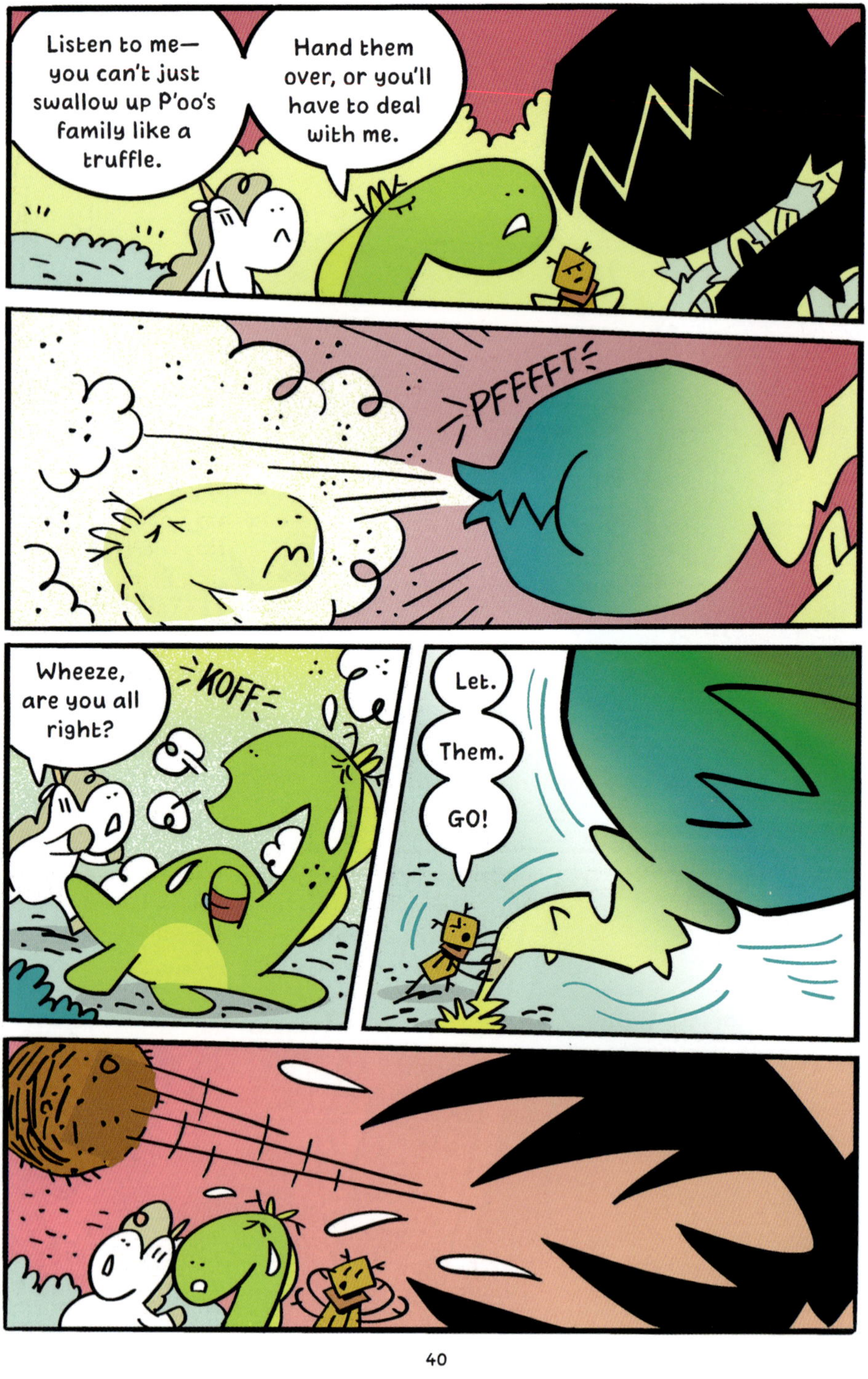

Listen to me—you can't just swallow up P'oo's family like a truffle.
Hand them over, or you'll have to deal with me.
PFFFFT
Wheeze, are you all right?
KOFF
Let.
Them.
GO!

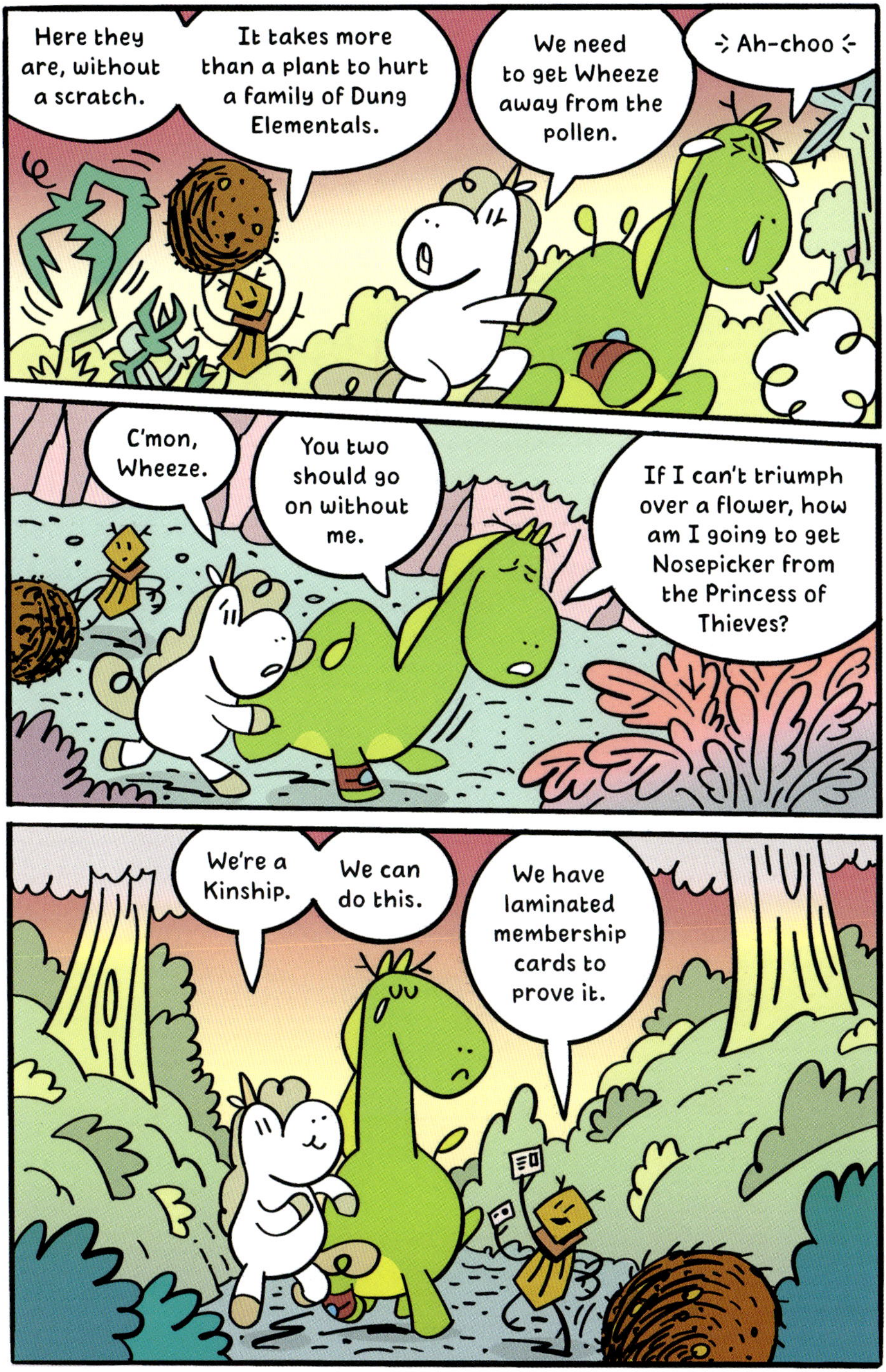
Here they are, without a scratch.
It takes more than a plant to hurt a family of Dung Elementals.
We need to get Wheeze away from the pollen.
Ah-choo
C'mon, Wheeze.
You two should go on without me.
If I can't triumph over a flower, how am I going to get Nosepicker from the Princess of Thieves?
We're a Kinship.
We can do this.
We have laminated membership cards to prove it.

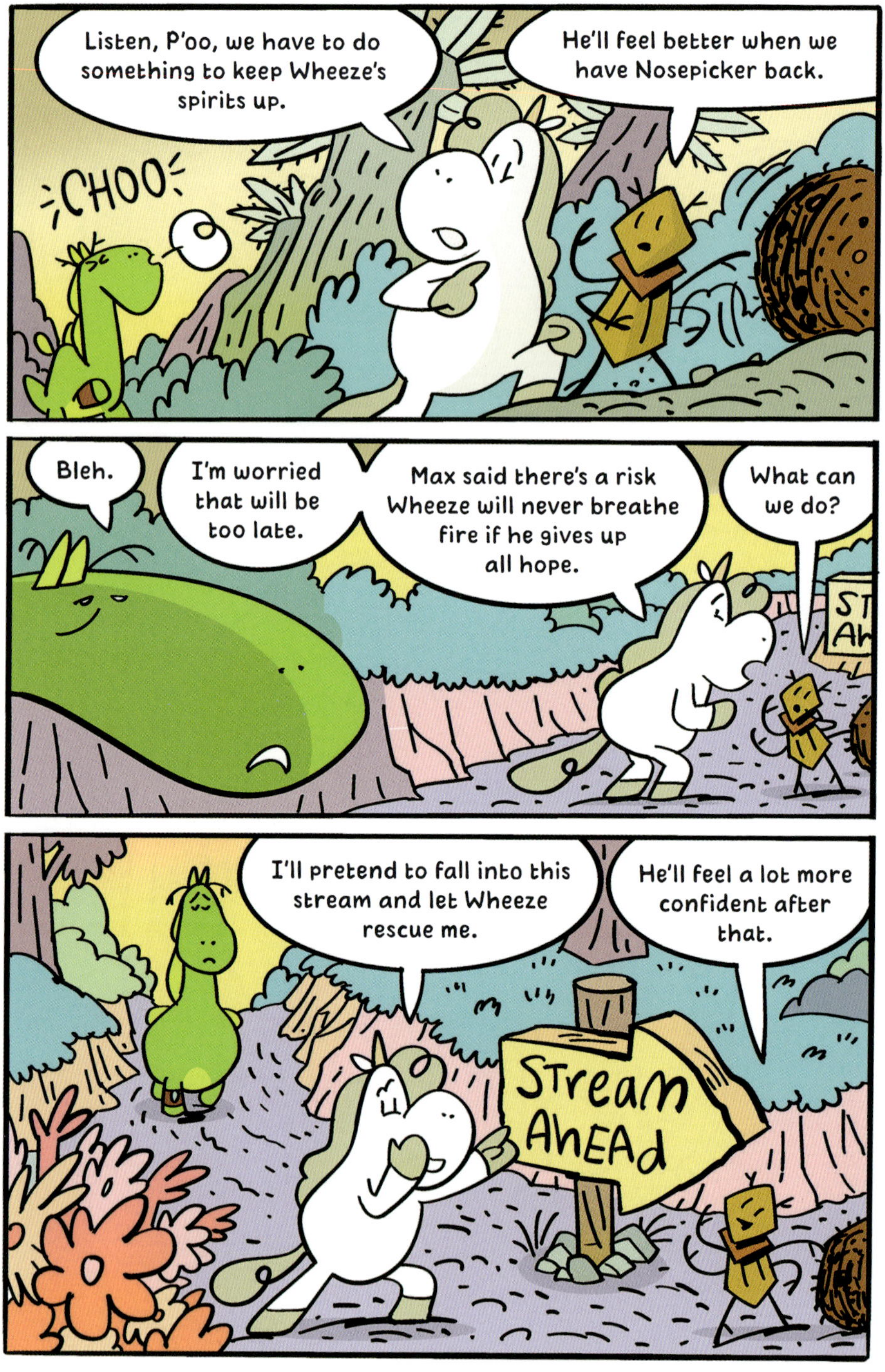
Listen, P'oo, we have to do something to keep Wheeze's spirits up.
He'll feel better when we have Nosepicker back.
CHOO
Bleh.
I'm worried that will be too late.
Max said there's a risk Wheeze will never breathe fire if he gives up all hope.
What can we do?
I'll pretend to fall into this stream and let Wheeze rescue me.
He'll feel a lot more confident after that.
Stream Ahead

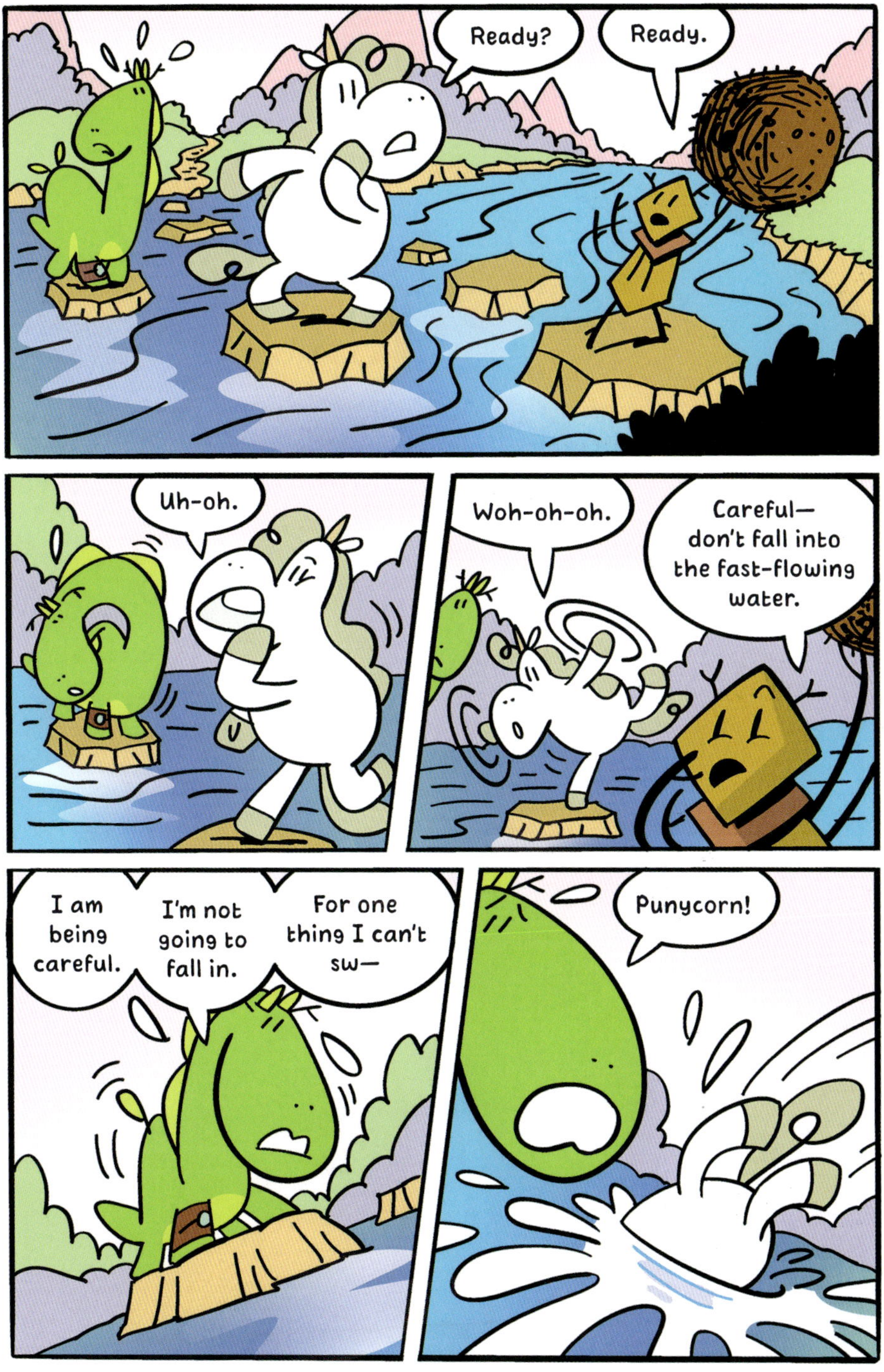
Ready?
Ready.
Uh-oh.
Woh-oh-oh.
Careful— don't fall into the fast-flowing water.
I am being careful.
I'm not going to fall in.
For one thing I can't sw—
Punycorn!

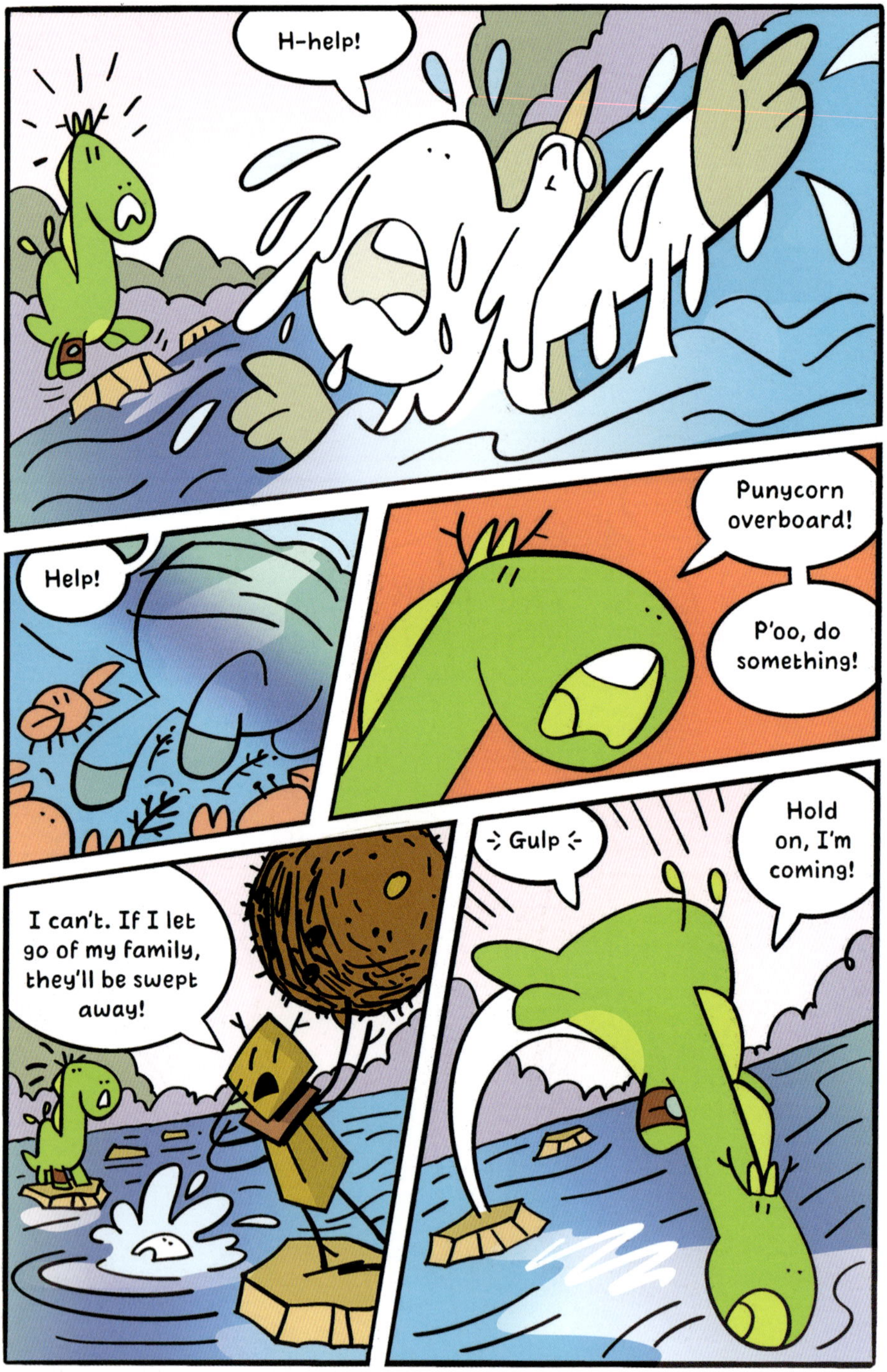
H-help!
Help!
Punycorn overboard!
P'oo, do something!
I can't. If I let go of my family, they'll be swept away!
Gulp
Hold on, I'm coming!

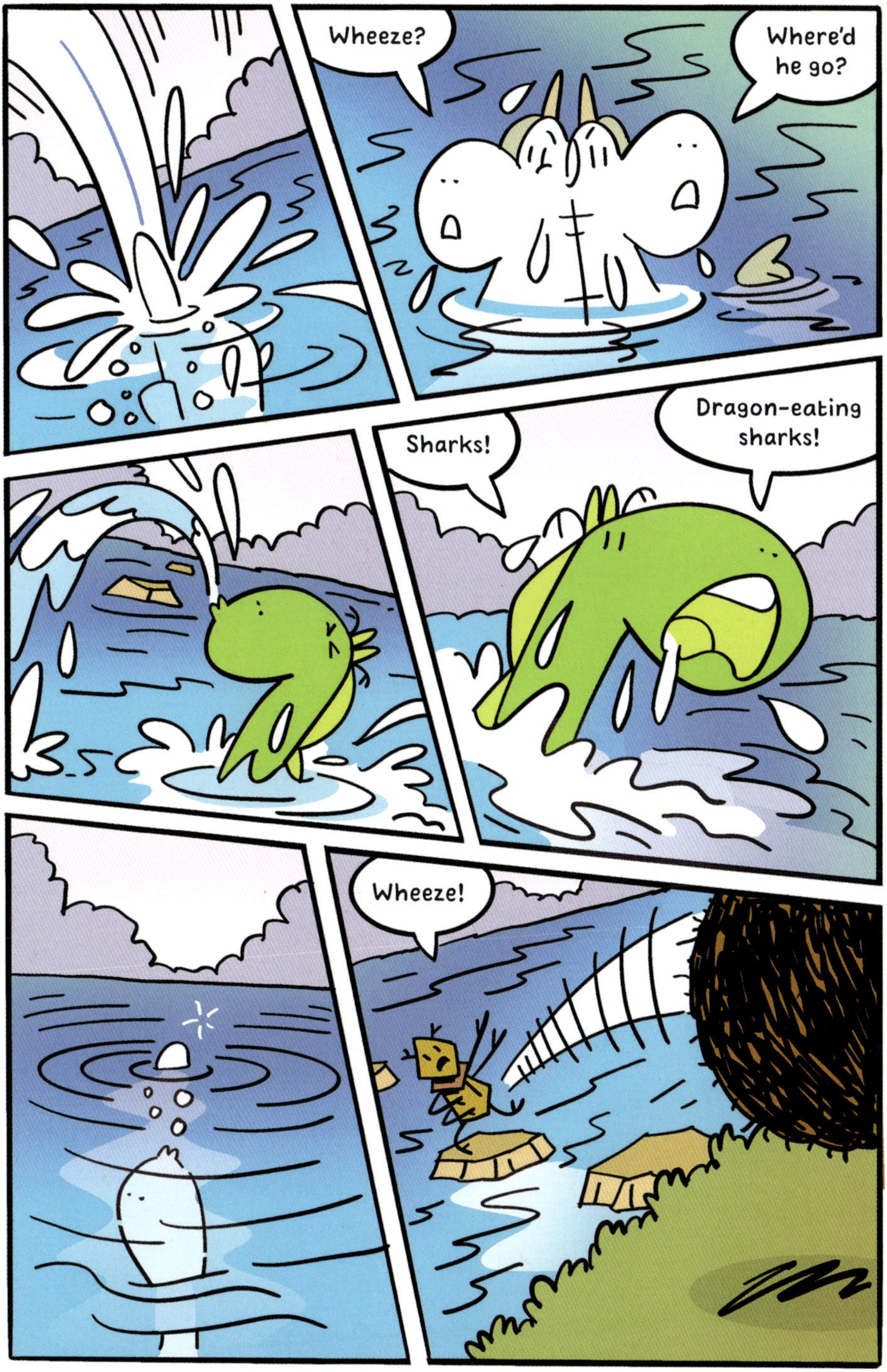
Wheeze?
Where'd he go?
Sharks!
Dragon-eating sharks!
Wheeze!

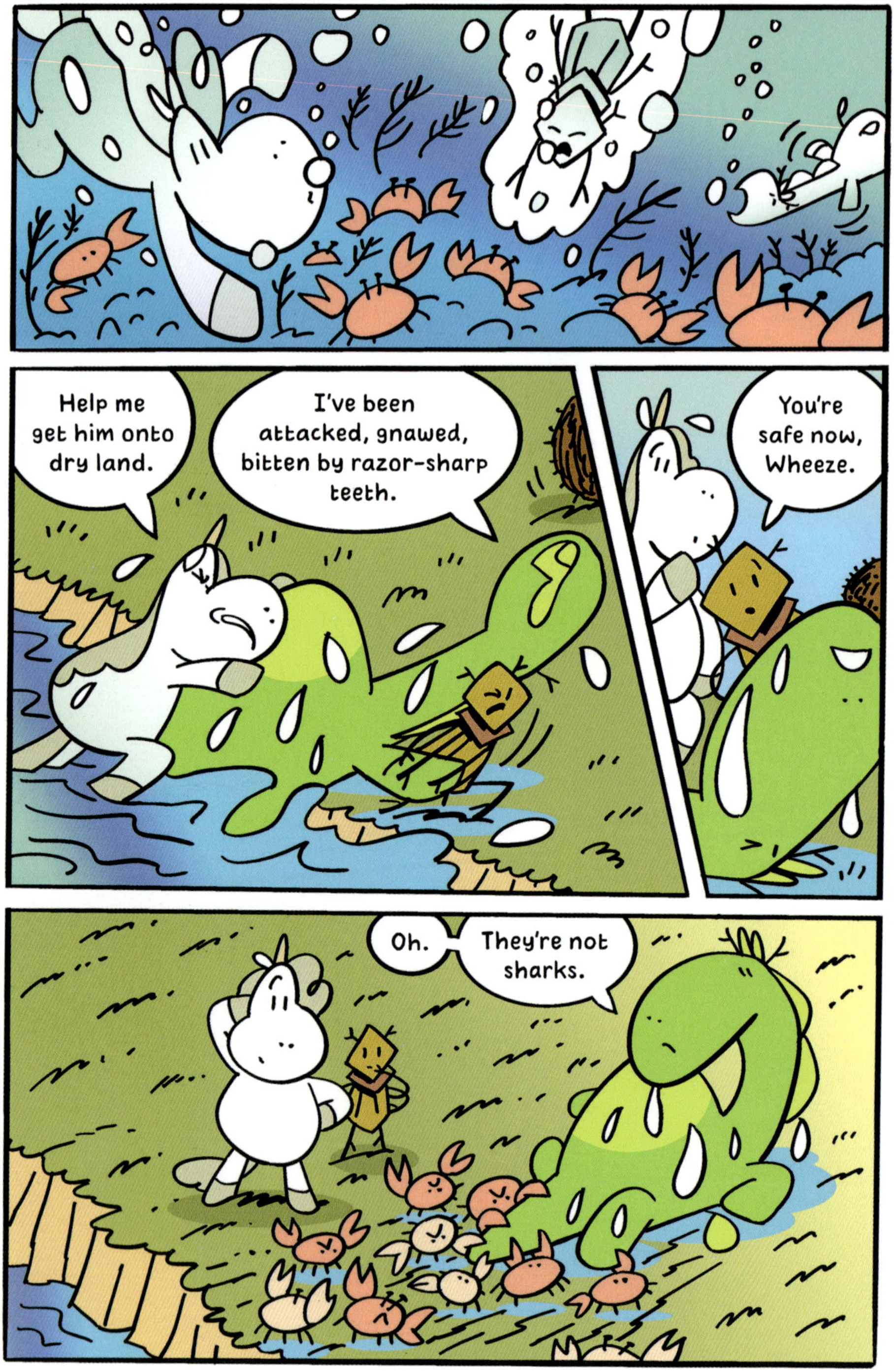
Help me get him onto dry land.
I've been attacked, gnawed, bitten by razor-sharp teeth.
You're safe now, Wheeze.
Oh.
They're not sharks.

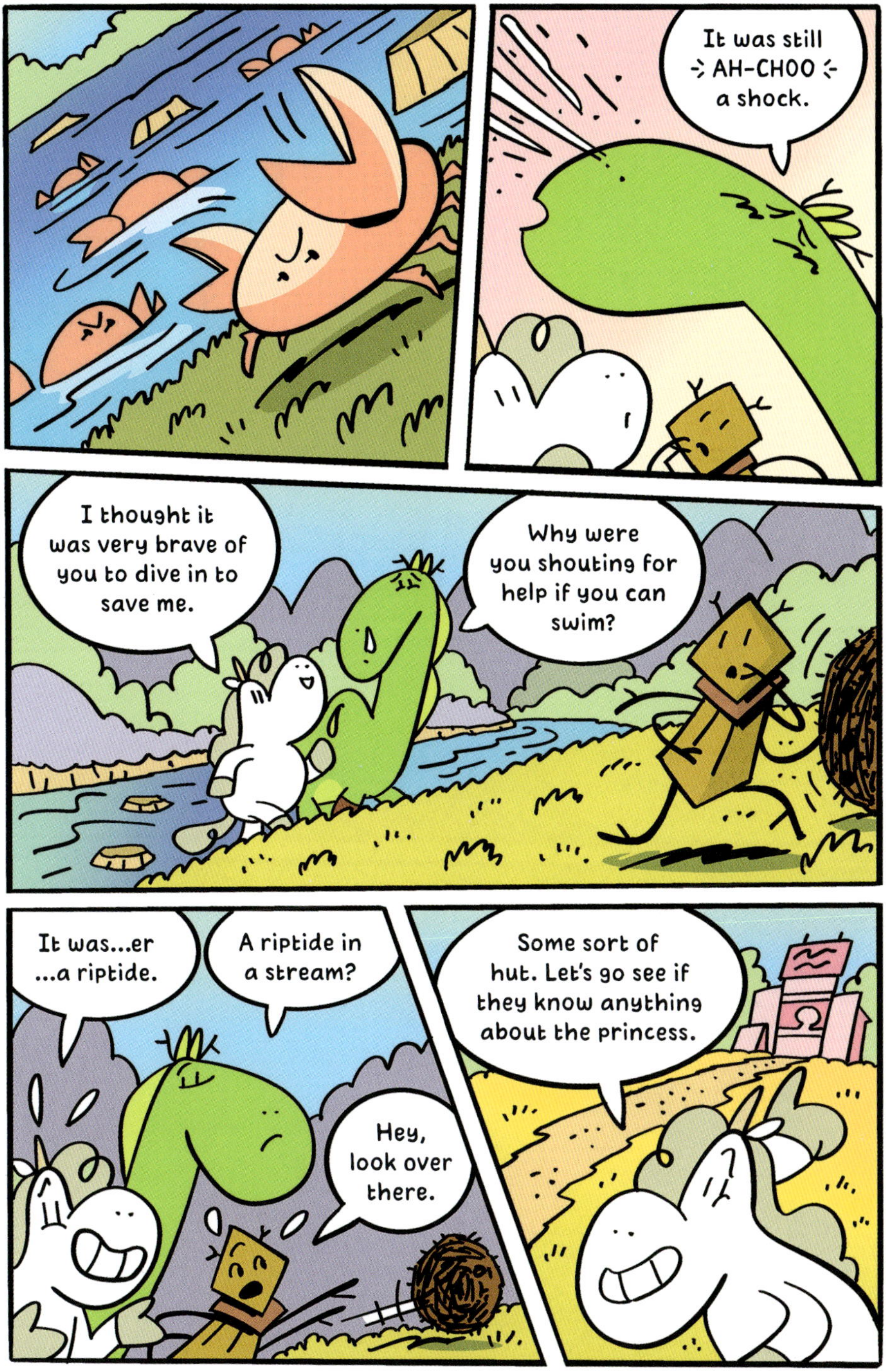
It was still AH-CHOO a shock.
I thought it was very brave of you to dive in to save me.
Why were you shouting for help if you can swim?
It was...er ...a riptide.
A riptide in a stream?
Hey, look over there.
Some sort of hut. Let's go see if they know anything about the princess.

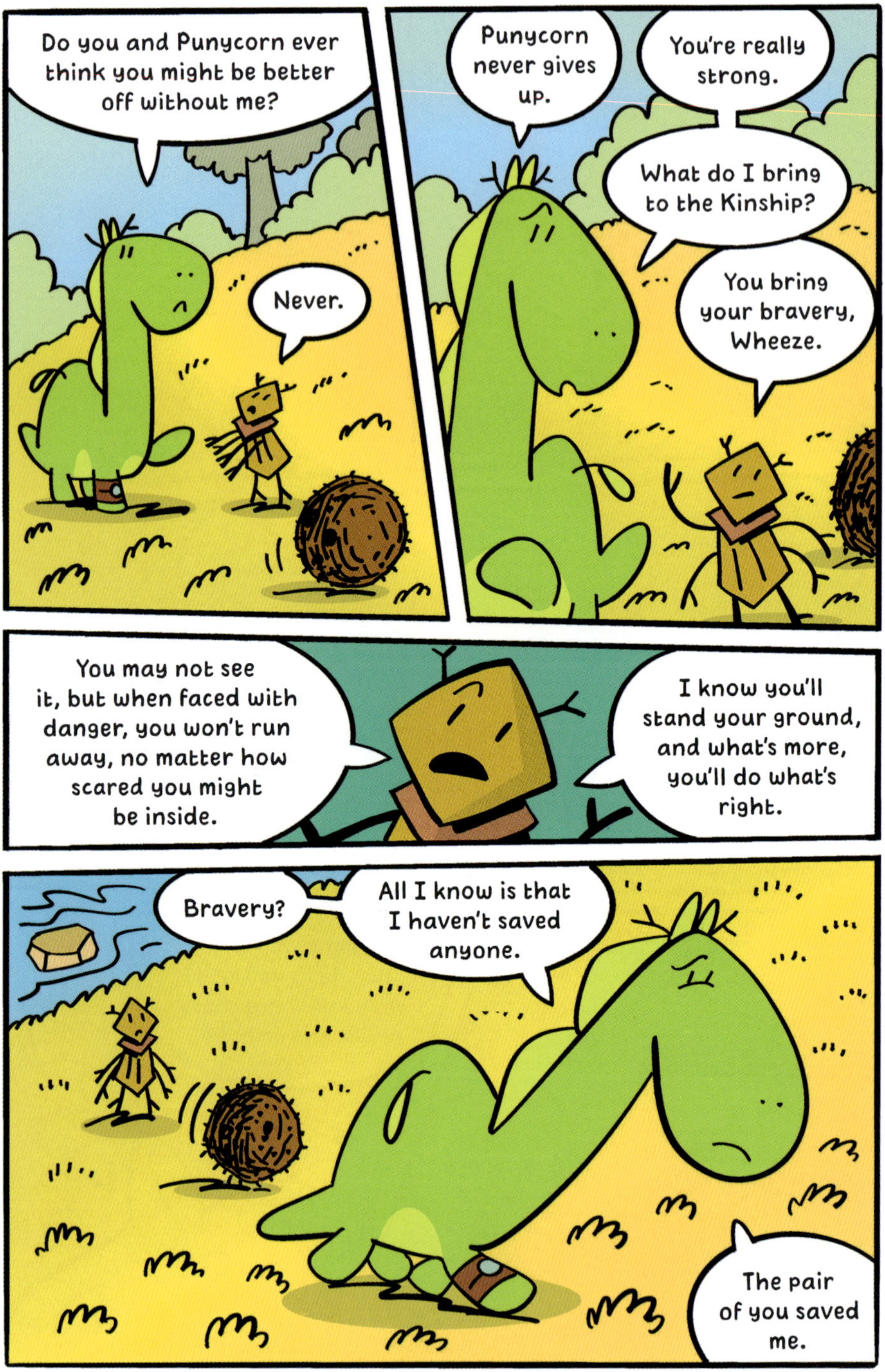
Do you and Punycorn ever think you might be better off without me?
Never.
Punycorn never gives up.
You're really strong.
What do I bring to the Kinship?
You bring your bravery, Wheeze.
You may not see it, but when faced with danger, you won't run away, no matter how scared you might be inside.
I know you'll stand your ground, and what's more, you'll do what's right.
Bravery?
All I know is that I haven't saved anyone.
The pair of you saved me.

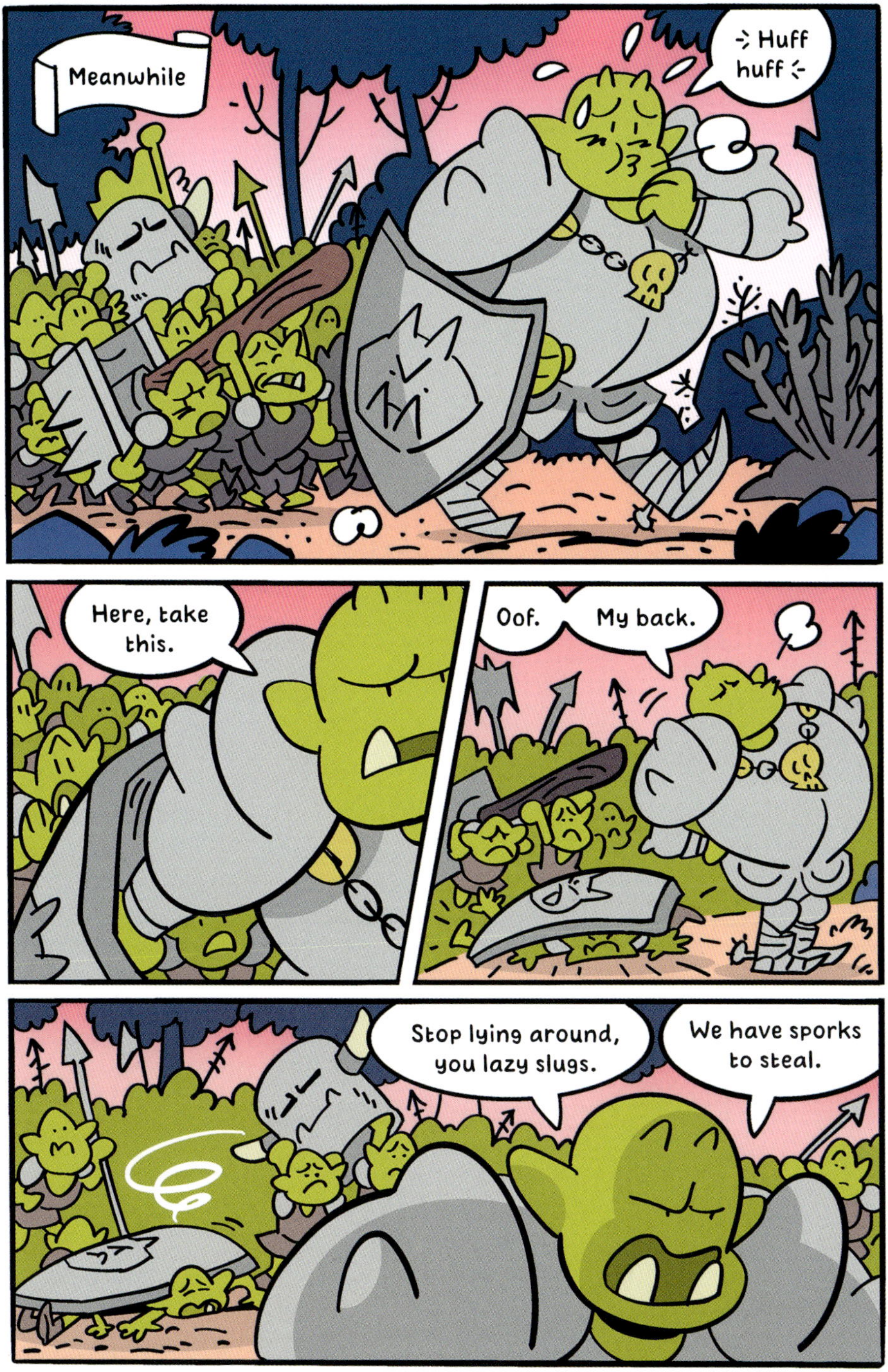
Meanwhile
Huff huff
Here, take this.
Oof.
My back.
Stop lying around, you lazy slugs.
We have sporks to steal.

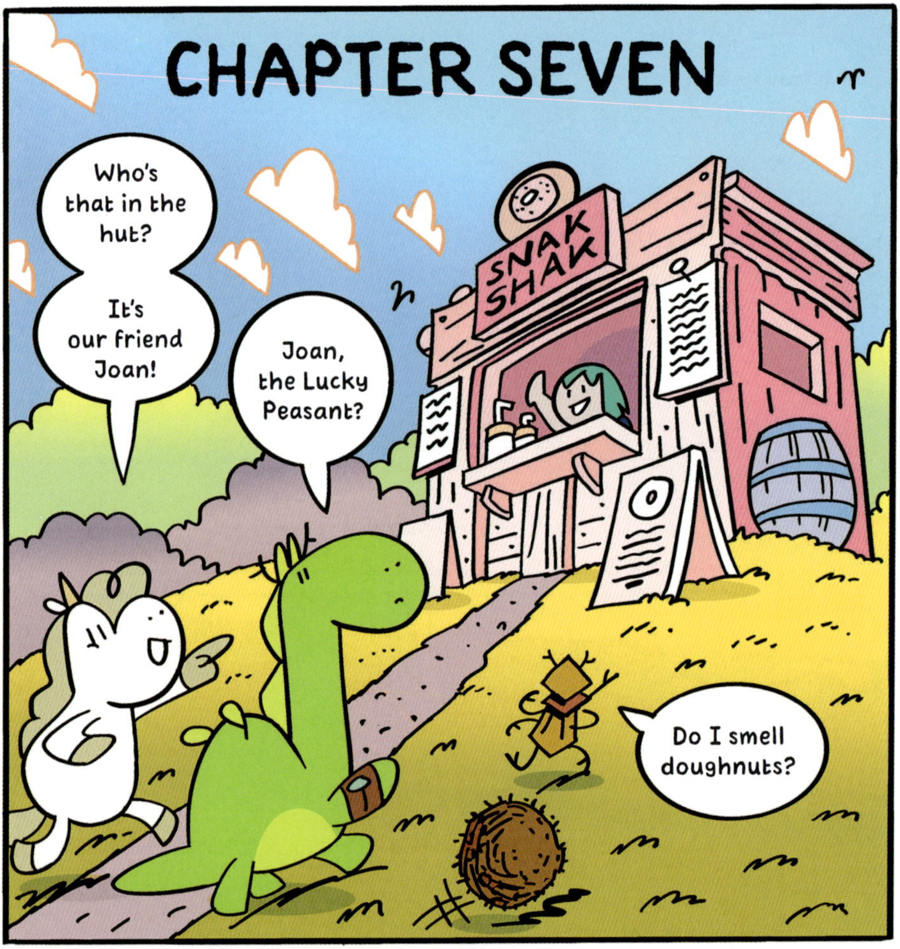
CHAPTER SEVEN
Who's that in the hut?
It's our friend Joan!
Joan, the Lucky Peasant?
SNAK SHAK
Do I smell doughnuts?

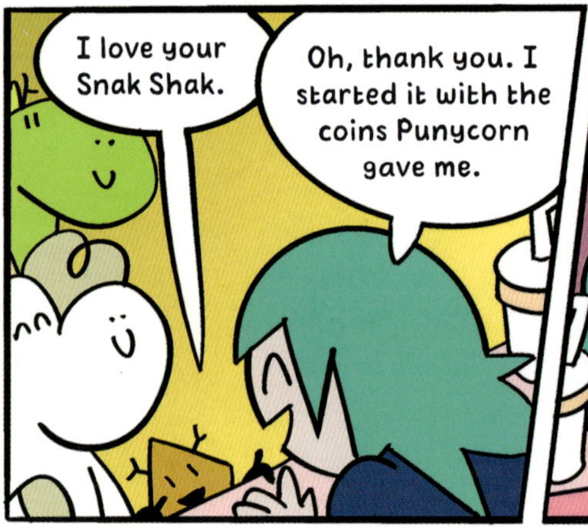
I love your Snak Shak.
Oh, thank you. I started it with the coins Punycorn gave me.

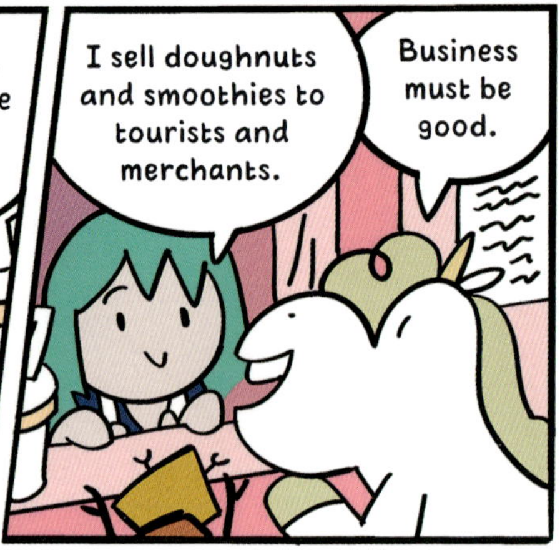
I sell doughnuts and smoothies to tourists and merchants.
Business must be good.

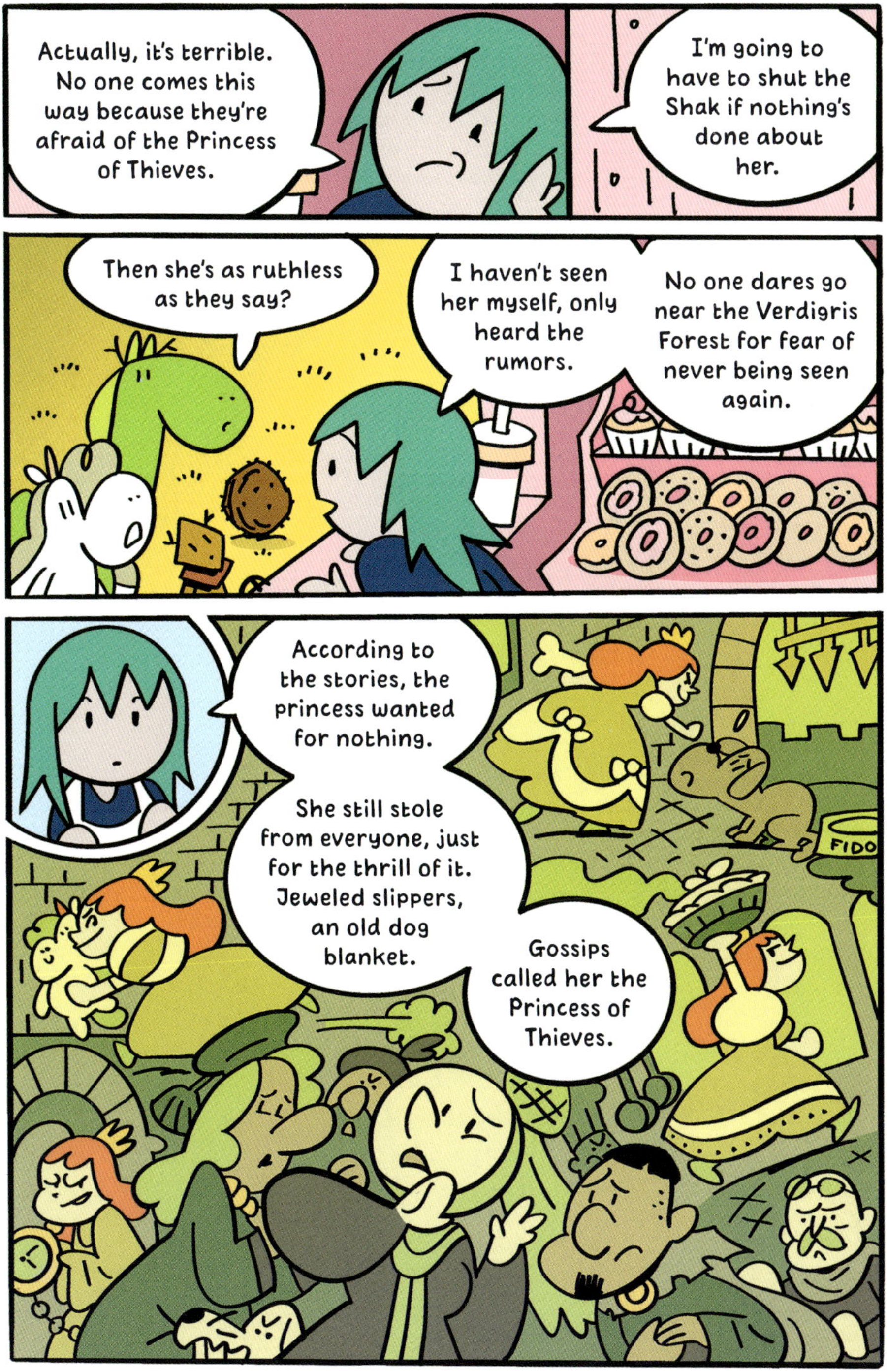
Actually, it's terrible. No one comes this way because they're afraid of the Princess of Thieves.
I'm going to have to shut the Shak if nothing's done about her.
Then she's as ruthless as they say?
I haven't seen her myself, only heard the rumors.
No one dares go near the Verdigris Forest for fear of never being seen again.
According to the stories, the princess wanted for nothing.
She still stole from everyone, just for the thrill of it. Jeweled slippers, an old dog blanket.
Gossips called her the Princess of Thieves.
FIDO

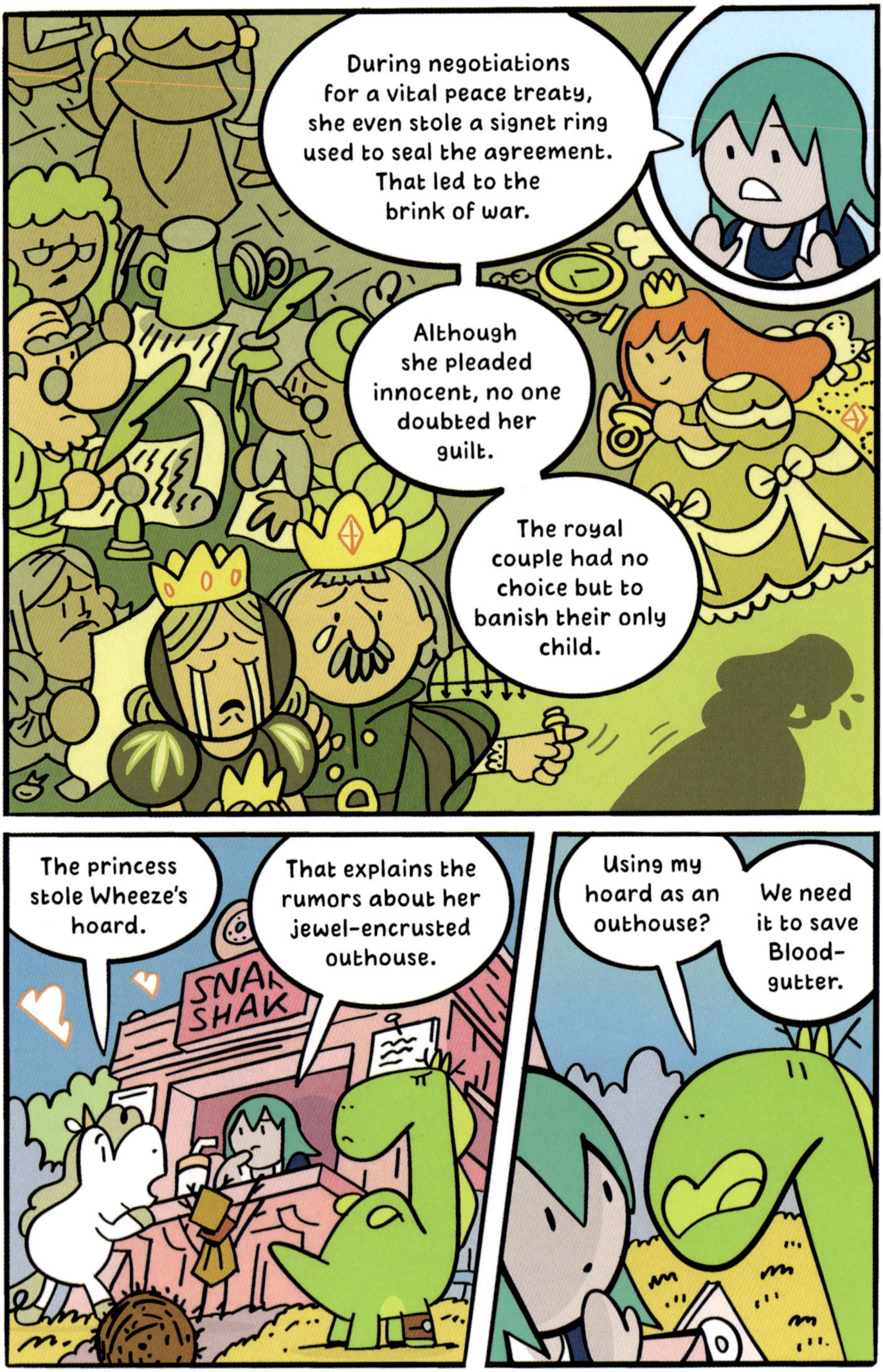
During negotiations for a vital peace treaty, she even stole a signet ring used to seal the agreement. That led to the brink of war.
Although she pleaded innocent, no one doubted her guilt.
The royal couple had no choice but to banish their only child.
The princess stole Wheeze's hoard.
That explains the rumors about her jewel-encrusted outhouse.
SNA SHAK
Using my hoard as an outhouse?
We need it to save Blood-gutter.

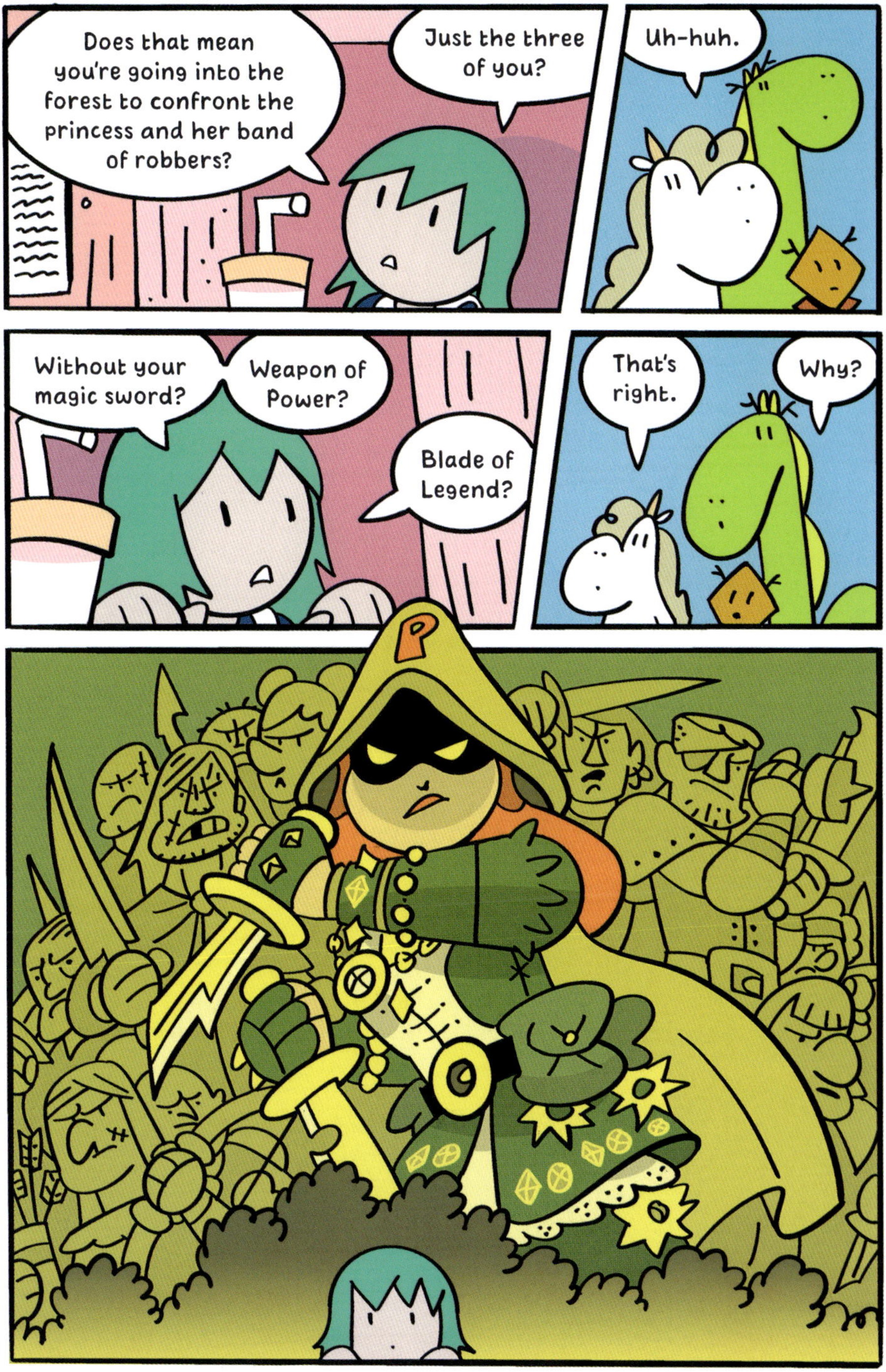
Does that mean you're going into the forest to confront the princess and her band of robbers?
Just the three of you?
Uh-huh.
Without your magic sword?
Weapon of Power?
Blade of Legend?
That's right.
Why?

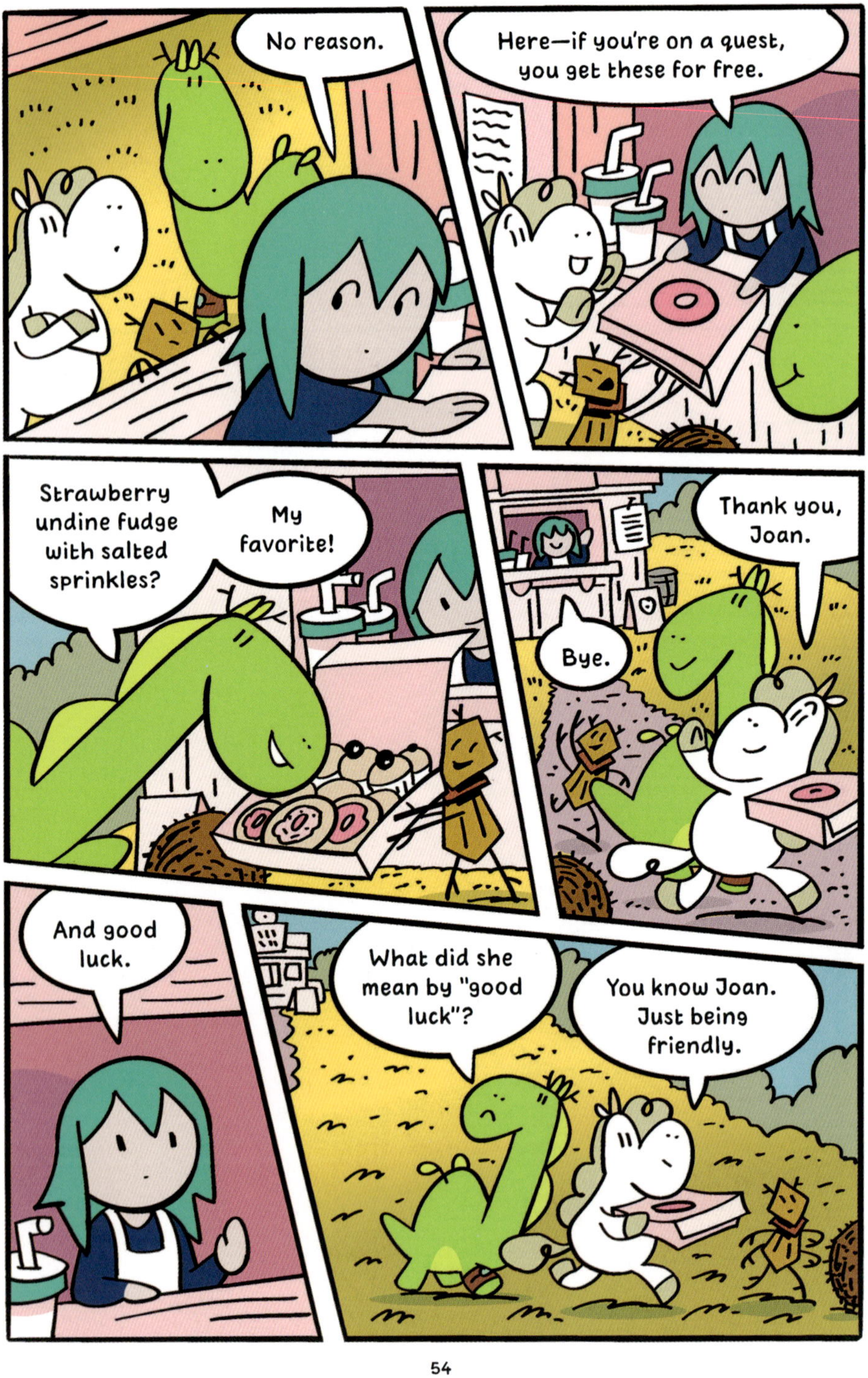
No reason.
Here—if you're on a quest, you get these for free.
Strawberry undine fudge with salted sprinkles?
My favorite!
Thank you, Joan.
Bye.
And good luck.
What did she mean by "good luck"?
You know Joan. Just being friendly.

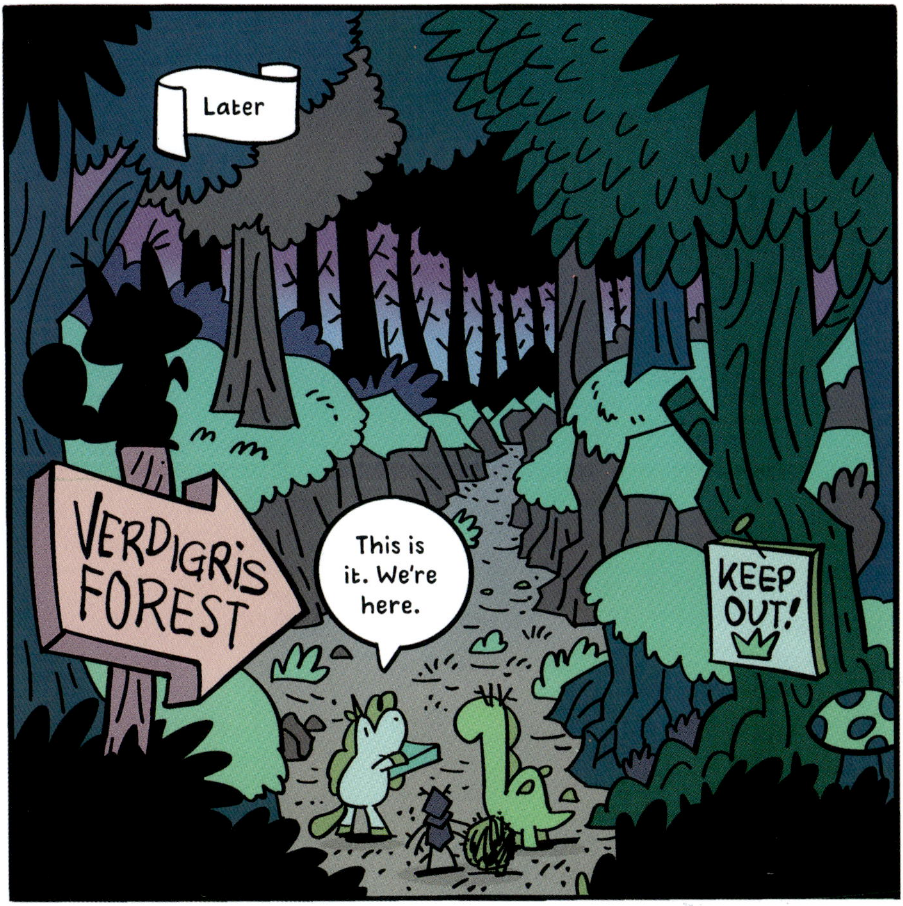
Later
VERDIGRIS FOREST
This is it. We're here.
KEEP OUT!

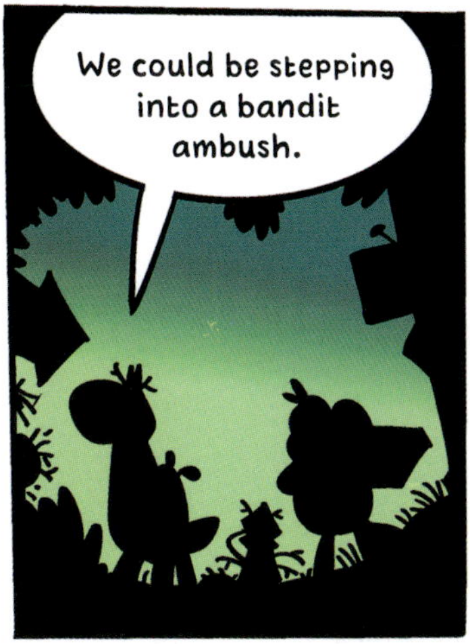
We could be stepping into a bandit ambush.

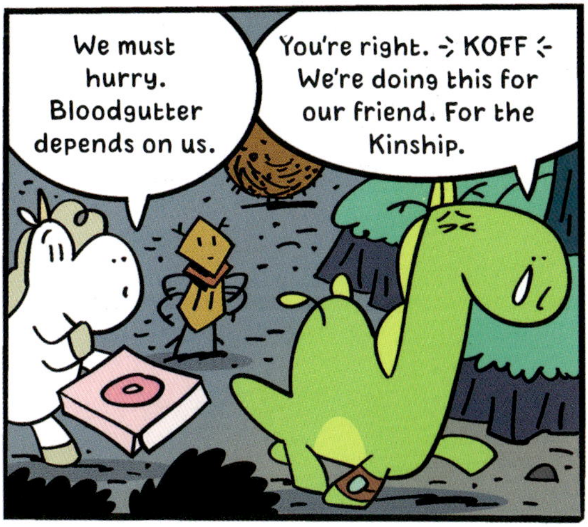
We must hurry. Bloodgutter depends on us.
You're right. KOFF We're doing this for our friend. For the Kinship.

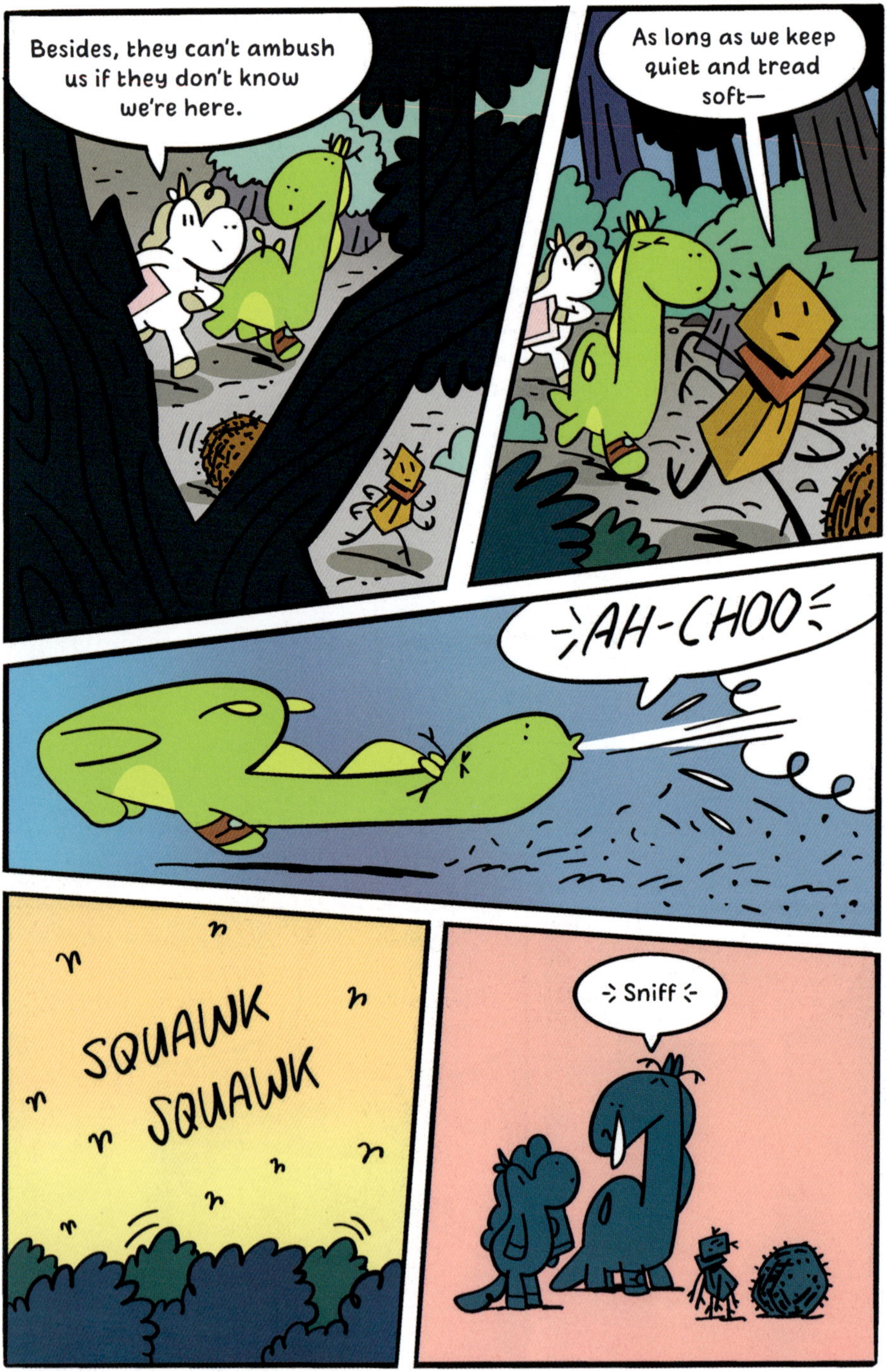
Besides, they can't ambush us if they don't know we're here.
As long as we keep quiet and tread soft—
AH-CHOO
SQUAWK SQUAWK
Sniff

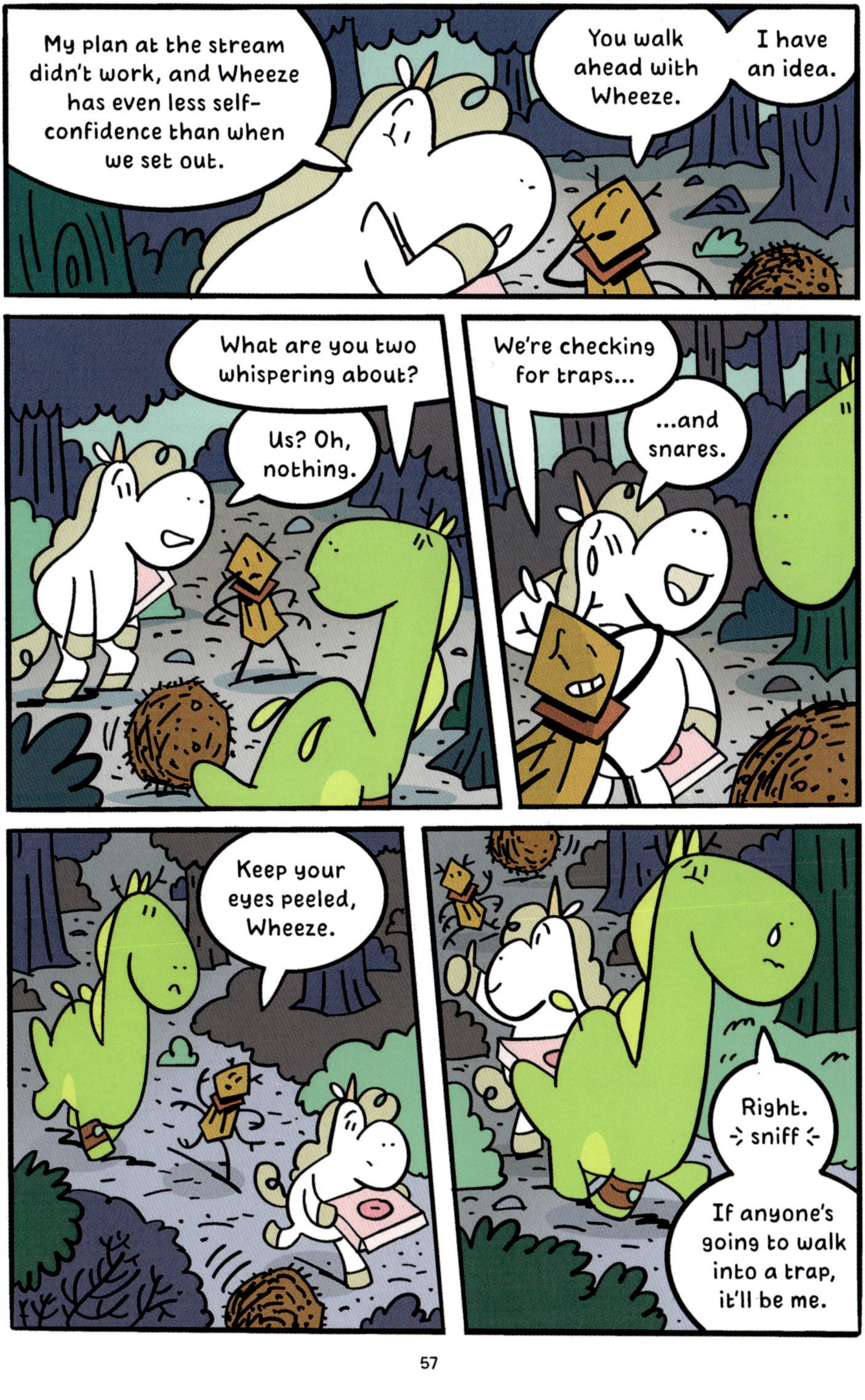
My plan at the stream didn't work, and Wheeze has even less self-confidence than when we set out.
You walk ahead with Wheeze.
I have an idea.
What are you two whispering about?
Us? Oh, nothing.
We're checking for traps...
...and snares.
Keep your eyes peeled, Wheeze.
Right. sniff
If anyone's going to walk into a trap, it'll be me.

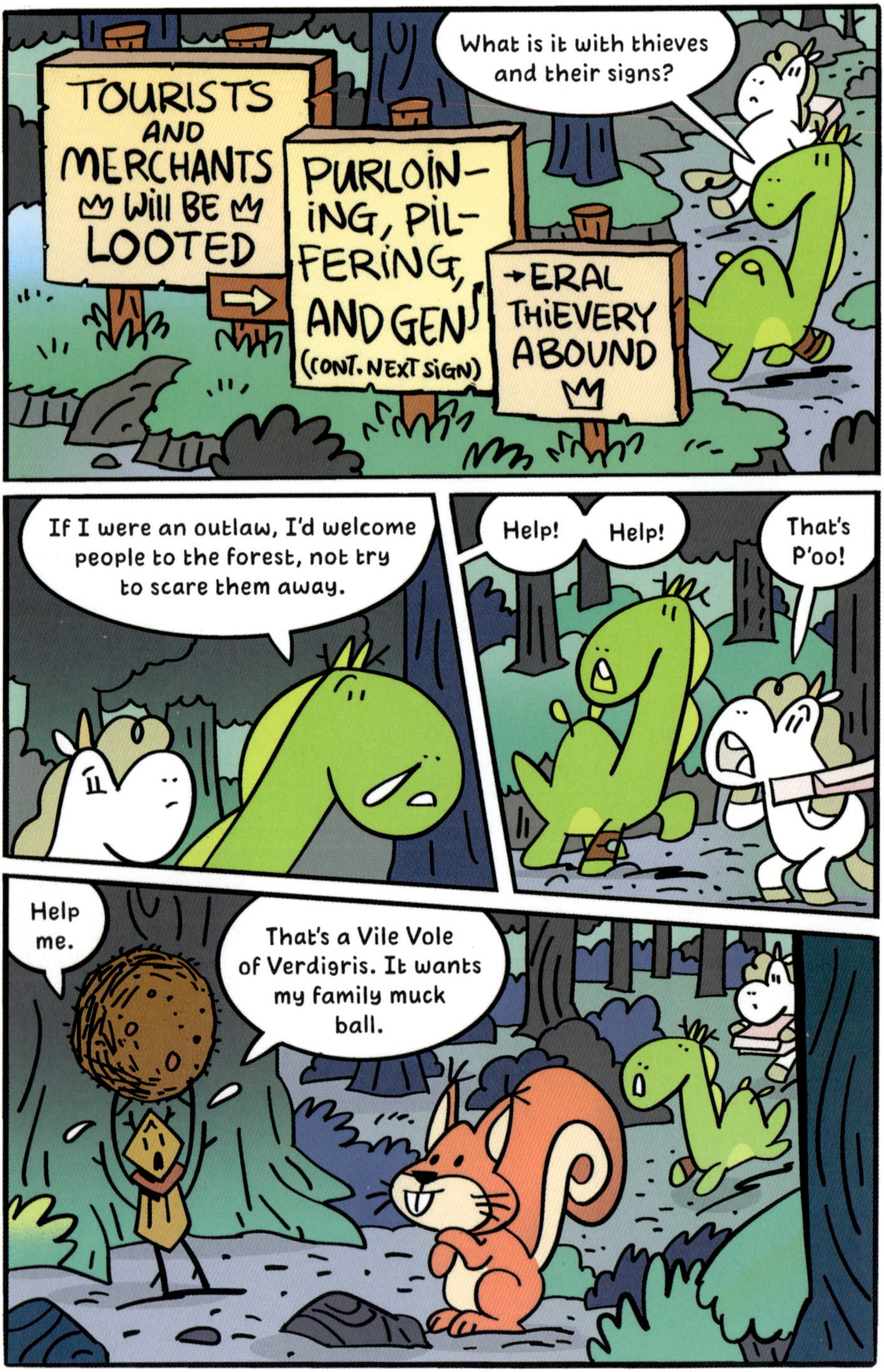

TOURISTS AND MERCHANTS WILL BE LOOTED
PURLOINING, PILFERING, AND GEN (CONT. NEXT SIGN)
→ERAL THIEVERY ABOUND
What is it with thieves and their signs?
If I were an outlaw, I'd welcome people to the forest, not try to scare them away.
Help!
Help!
That's P'oo!
Help me.
That's a Vile Vole of Verdigris. It wants my family muck ball.

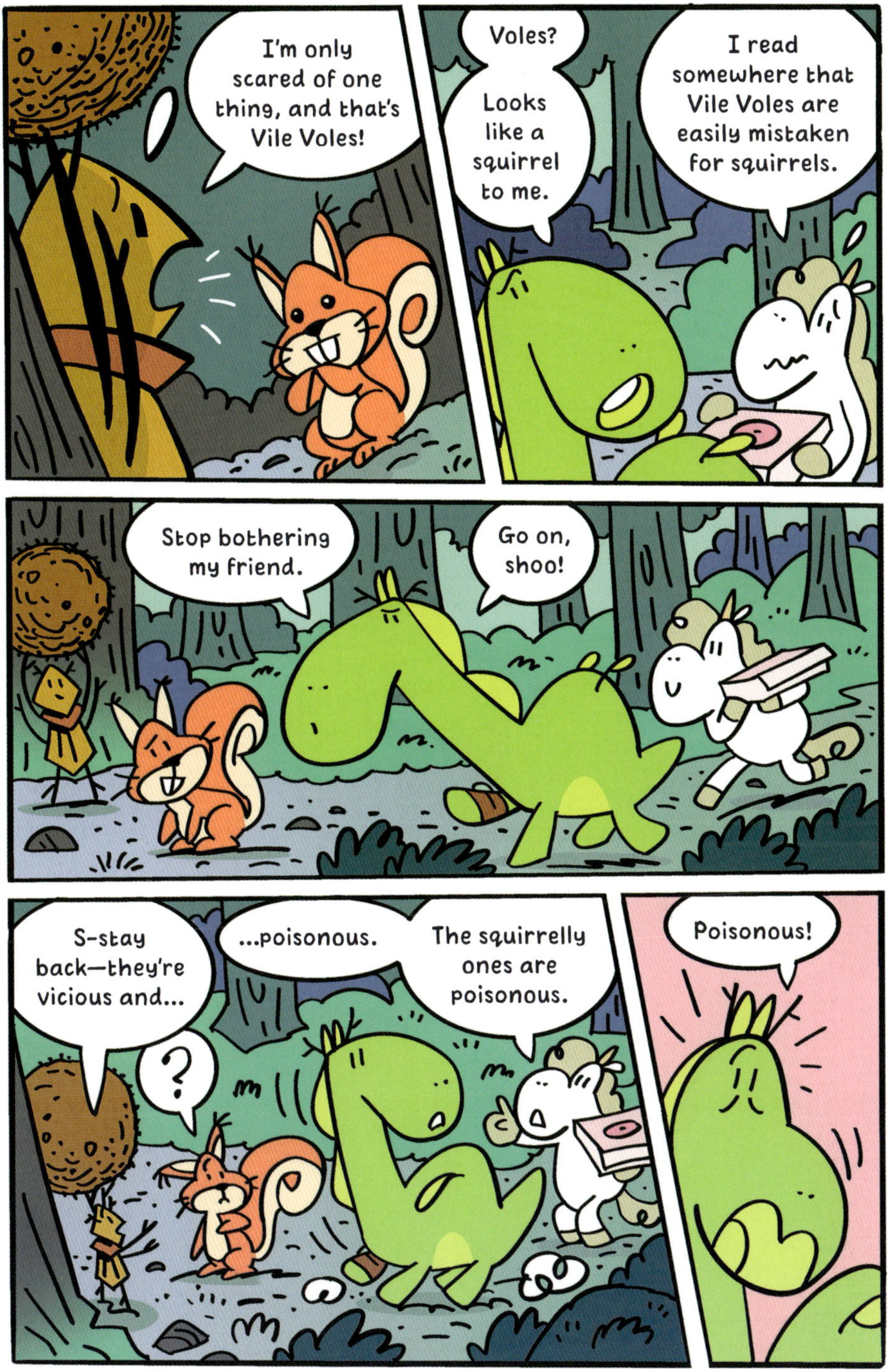
I'm only scared of one thing, and that's Vile Voles!
Voles?
Looks like a squirrel to me.
I read somewhere that Vile Voles are easily mistaken for squirrels.
Stop bothering my friend.
Go on, shoo!
S-stay back—they're vicious and...
...poisonous.
?
The squirrelly ones are poisonous.
Poisonous!

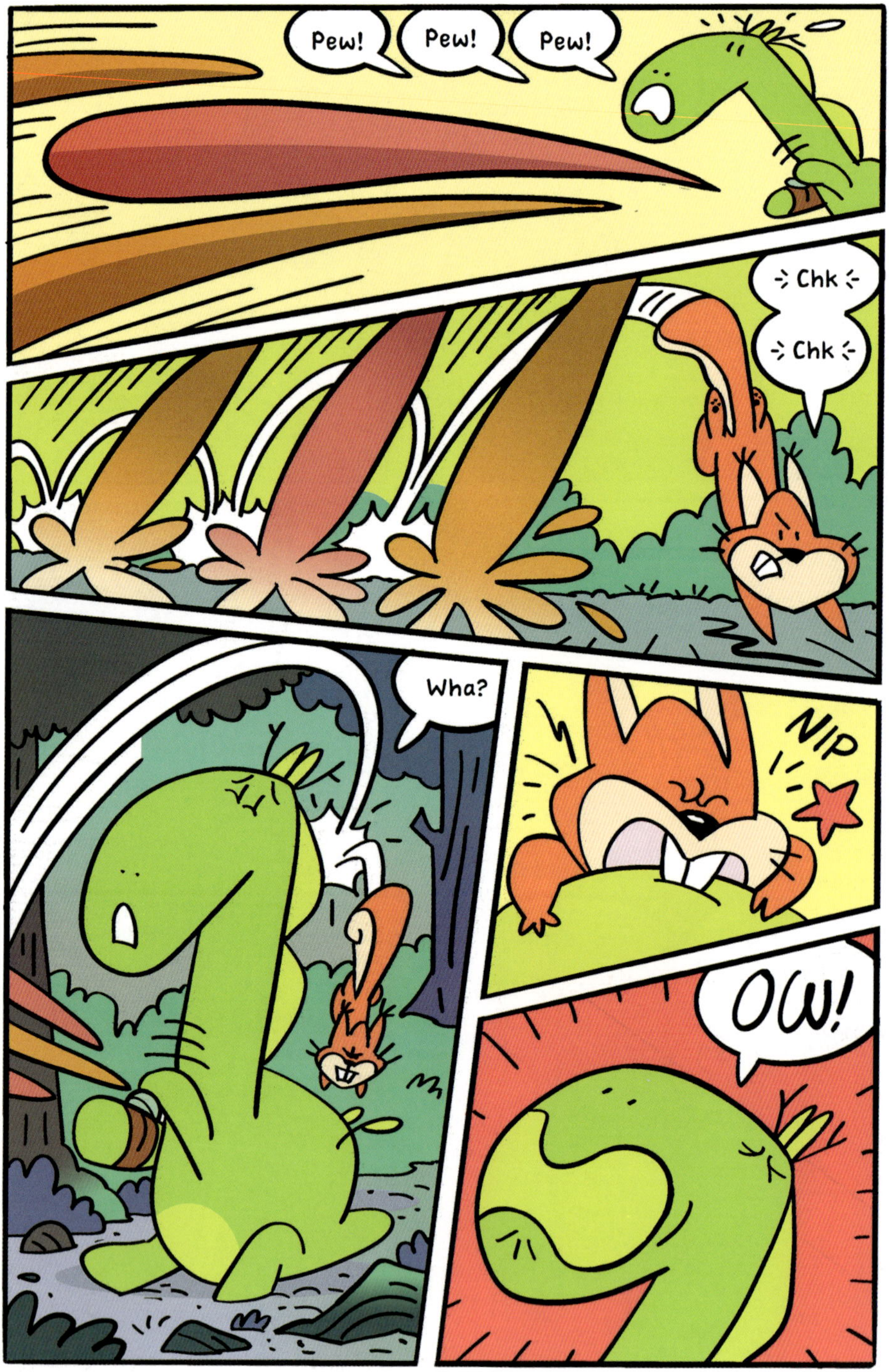
Pew!
Pew!
Pew!
Chk
Chk
Wha?
NIP
OW!

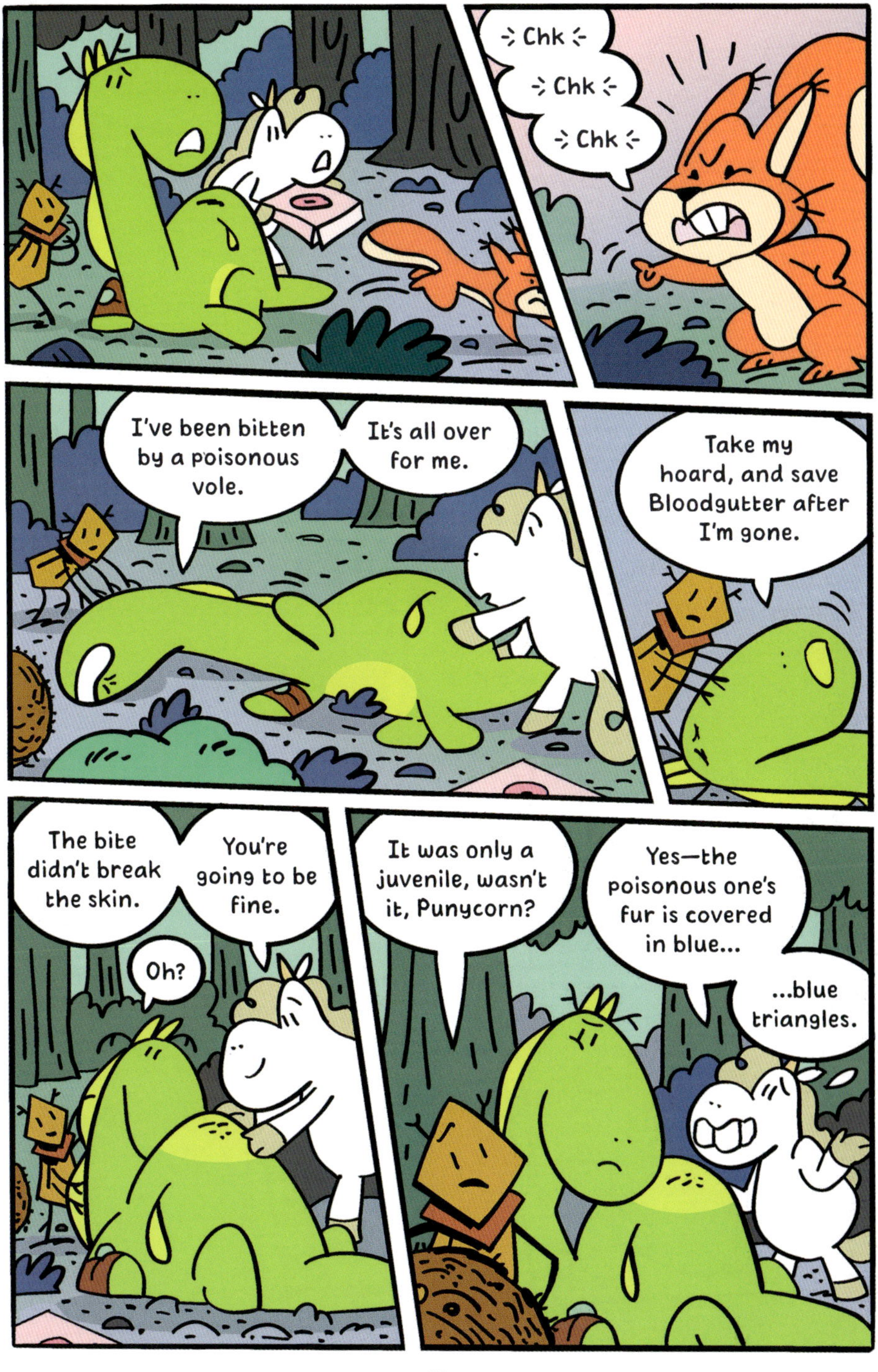
Chk
Chk
Chk
I've been bitten by a poisonous vole.
It's all over for me.
Take my hoard, and save Bloodgutter after I'm gone.
The bite didn't break the skin.
You're going to be fine.
Oh?
It was only a juvenile, wasn't it, Punycorn?
Yes—the poisonous one's fur is covered in blue...
...blue triangles.

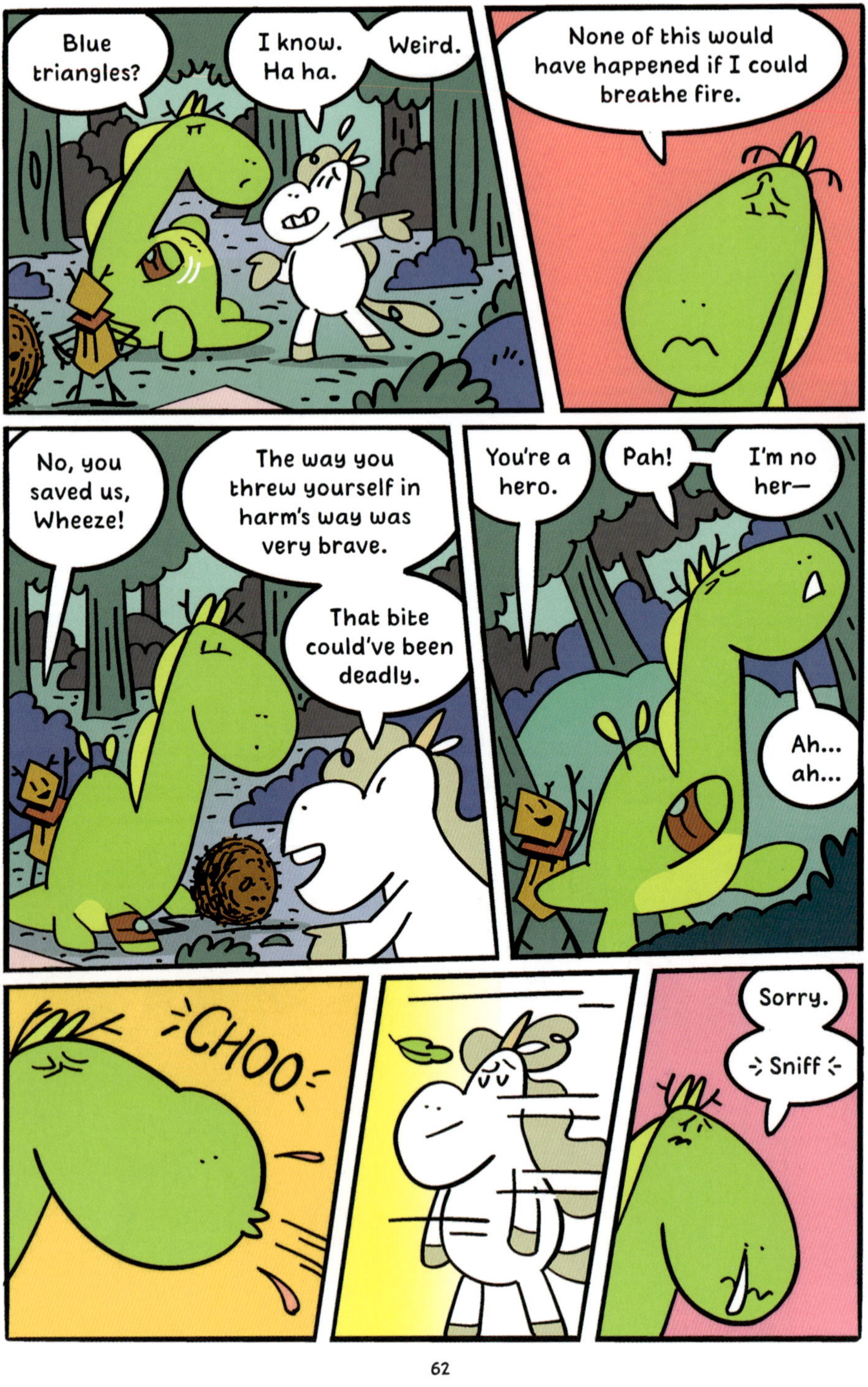

Blue triangles?
I know. Ha ha.
Weird.
None of this would have happened if I could breathe fire.
No, you saved us, Wheeze!
The way you threw yourself in harm's way was very brave.
That bite could've been deadly.
You're a hero.
Pah!
I'm no her—
Ah... ah...
CHOO
Sorry.
Sniff

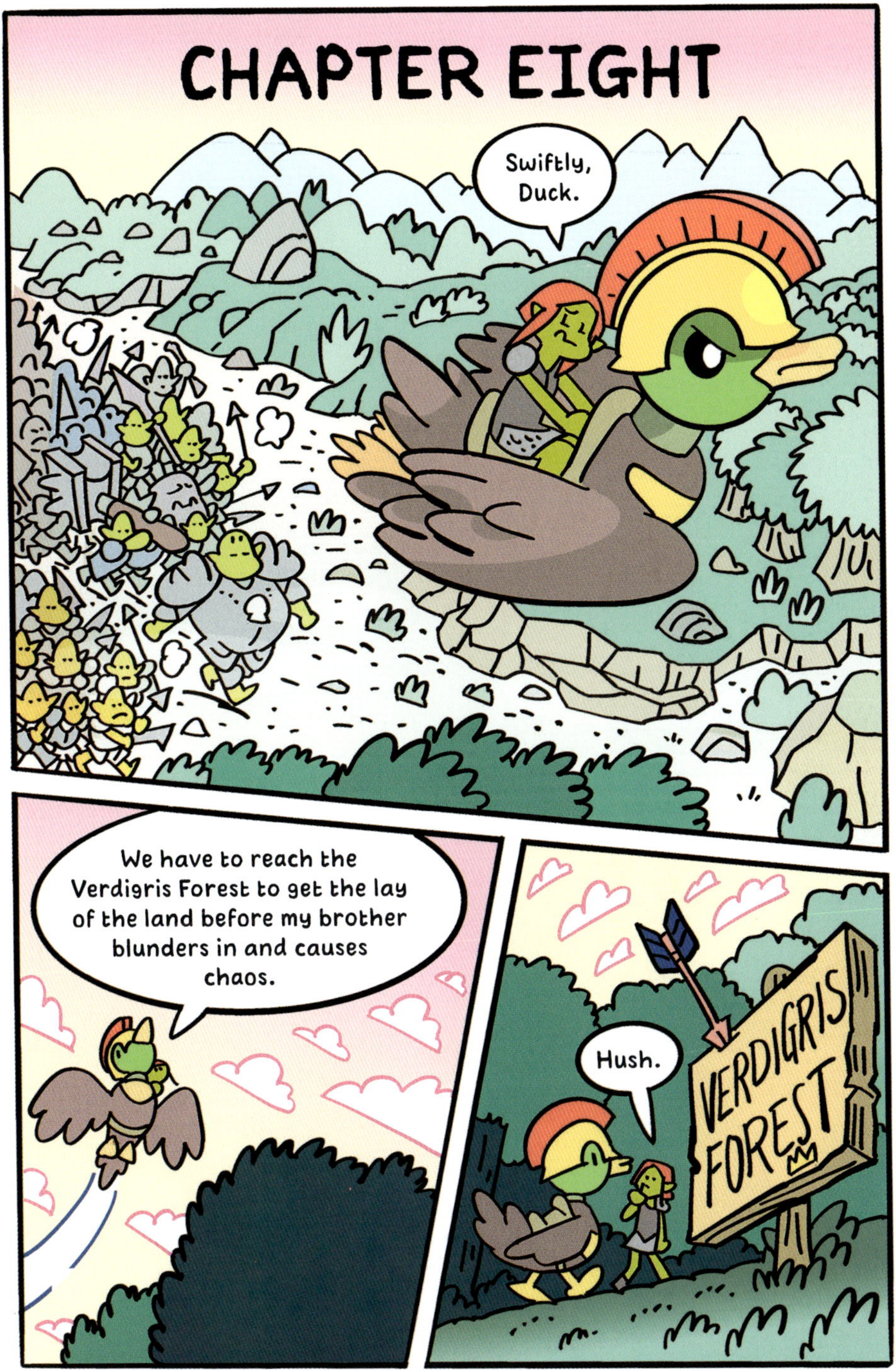
CHAPTER EIGHT
Swiftly, Duck.
We have to reach the Verdigris Forest to get the lay of the land before my brother blunders in and causes chaos.
Hush.
VERDIGRIS FOREST

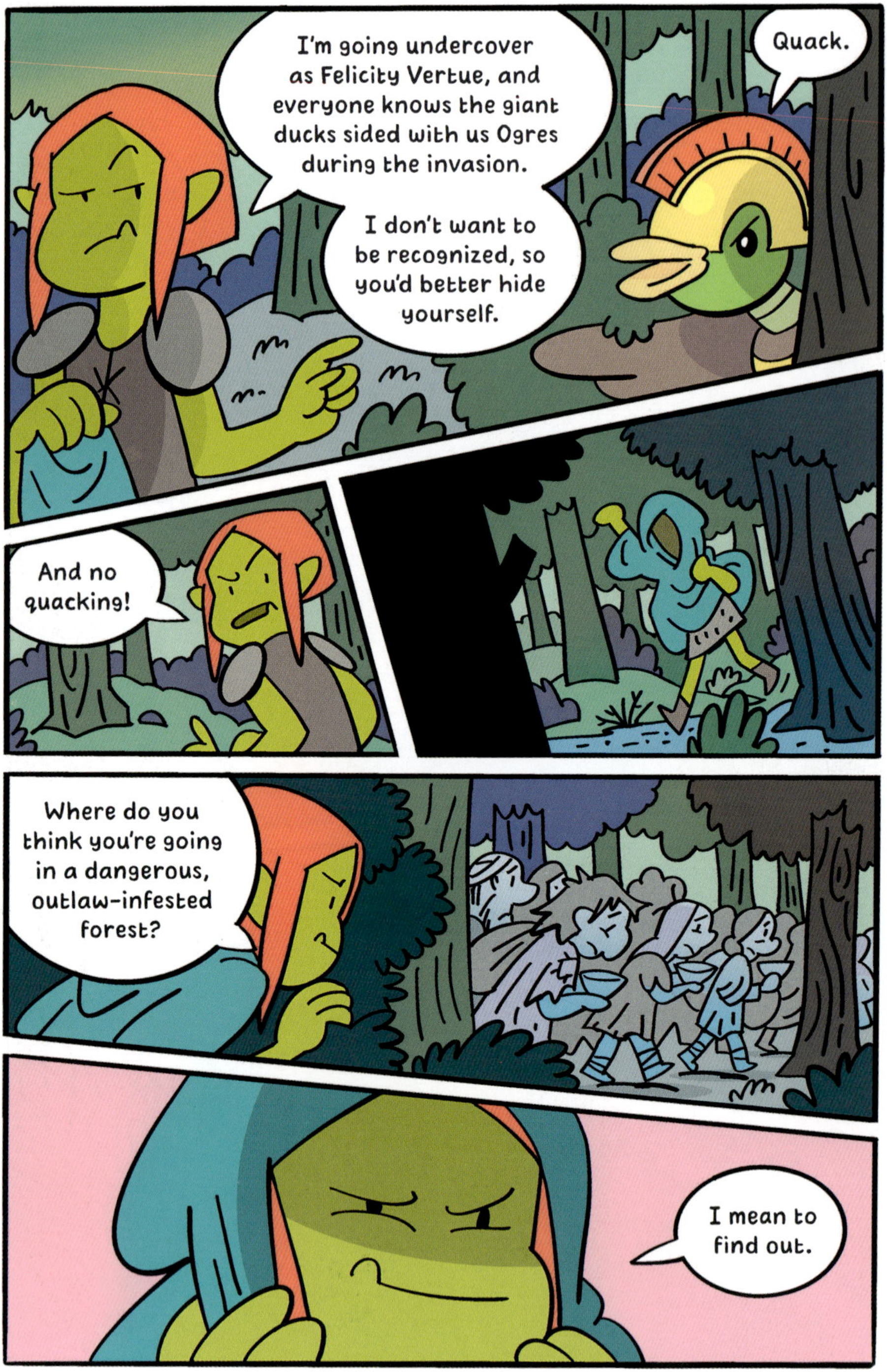
I'm going undercover as Felicity Vertue, and everyone knows the giant ducks sided with us Ogres during the invasion.
I don't want to be recognized, so you'd better hide yourself.
Quack.
And no quacking!
Where do you think you're going in a dangerous, outlaw-infested forest?
I mean to find out.

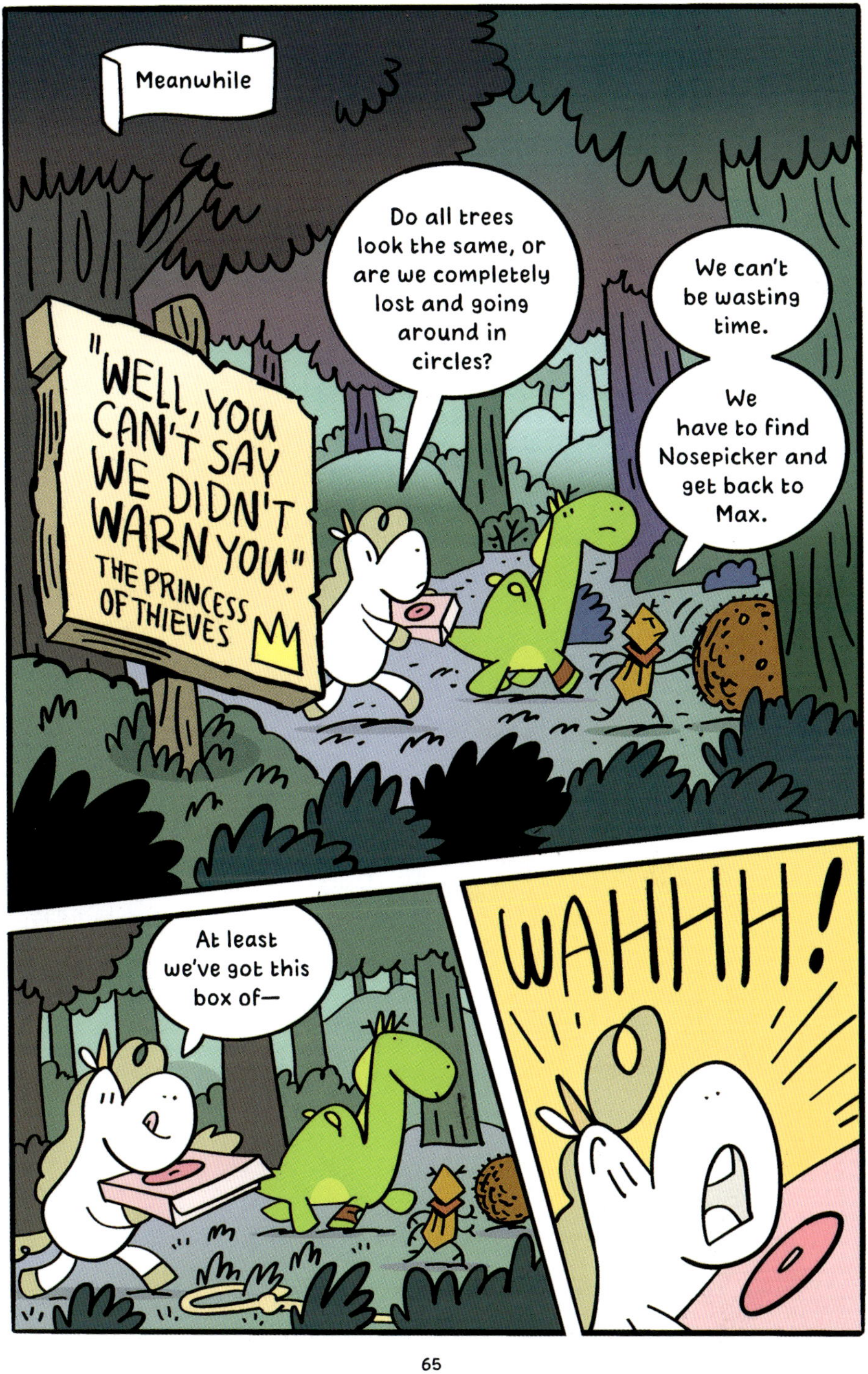
Meanwhile
"WELL, YOU CAN'T SAY WE DIDN'T WARN YOU." THE PRINCESS OF THIEVES
Do all trees look the same, or are we completely lost and going around in circles?
We can't be wasting time.
We have to find Nosepicker and get back to Max.
At least we've got this box of—
WAHHH!

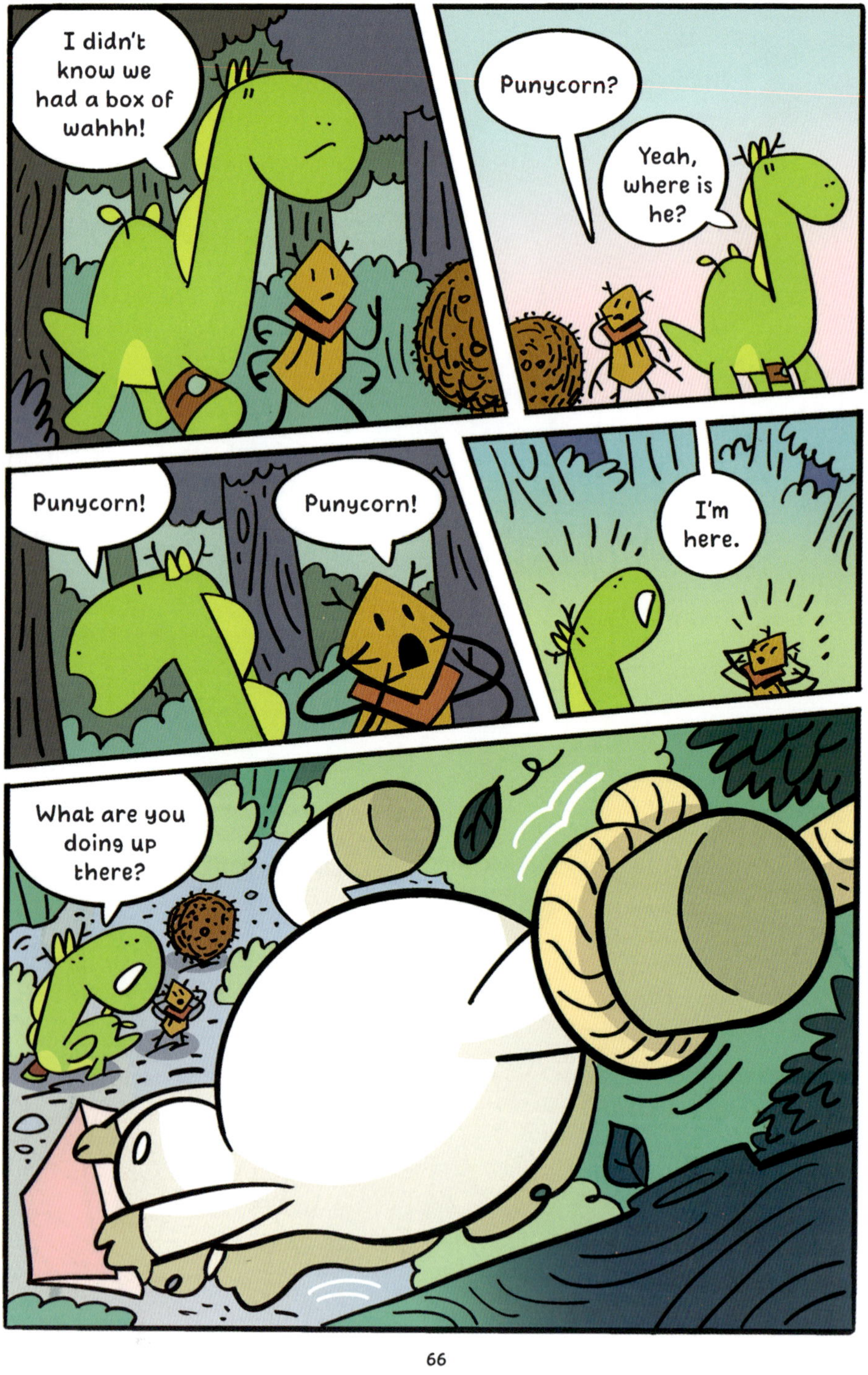
I didn't know we had a box of wahhh!
Punycorn?
Yeah, where is he?
Punycorn!
Punycorn!
I'm here.
What are you doing up there?

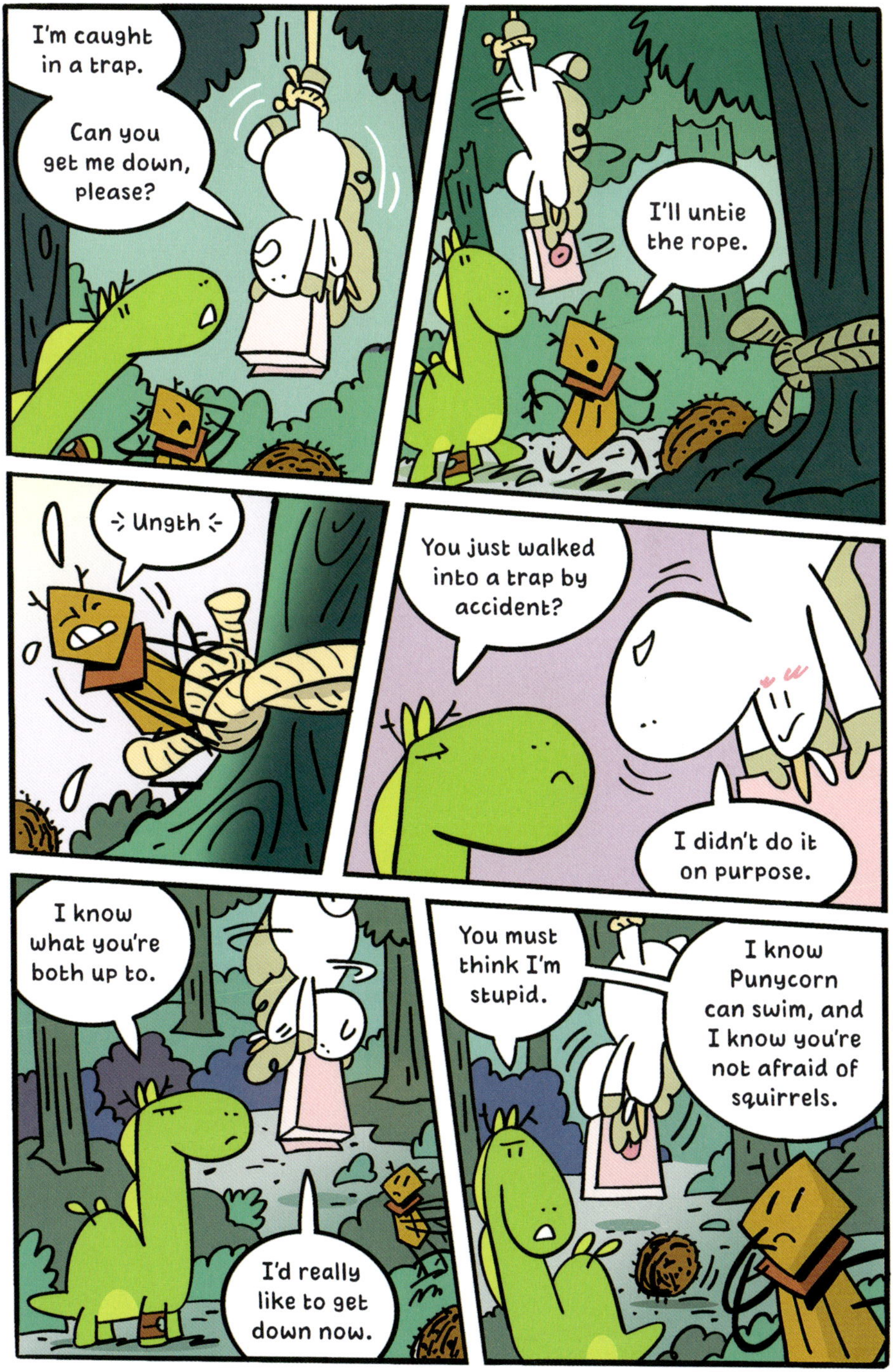

I'm caught in a trap.
Can you get me down, please?
I'll untie the rope.
Ungth
You just walked into a trap by accident?
I didn't do it on purpose.
I know what you're both up to.
I'd really like to get down now.
You must think I'm stupid.
I know Punycorn can swim, and I know you're not afraid of squirrels.

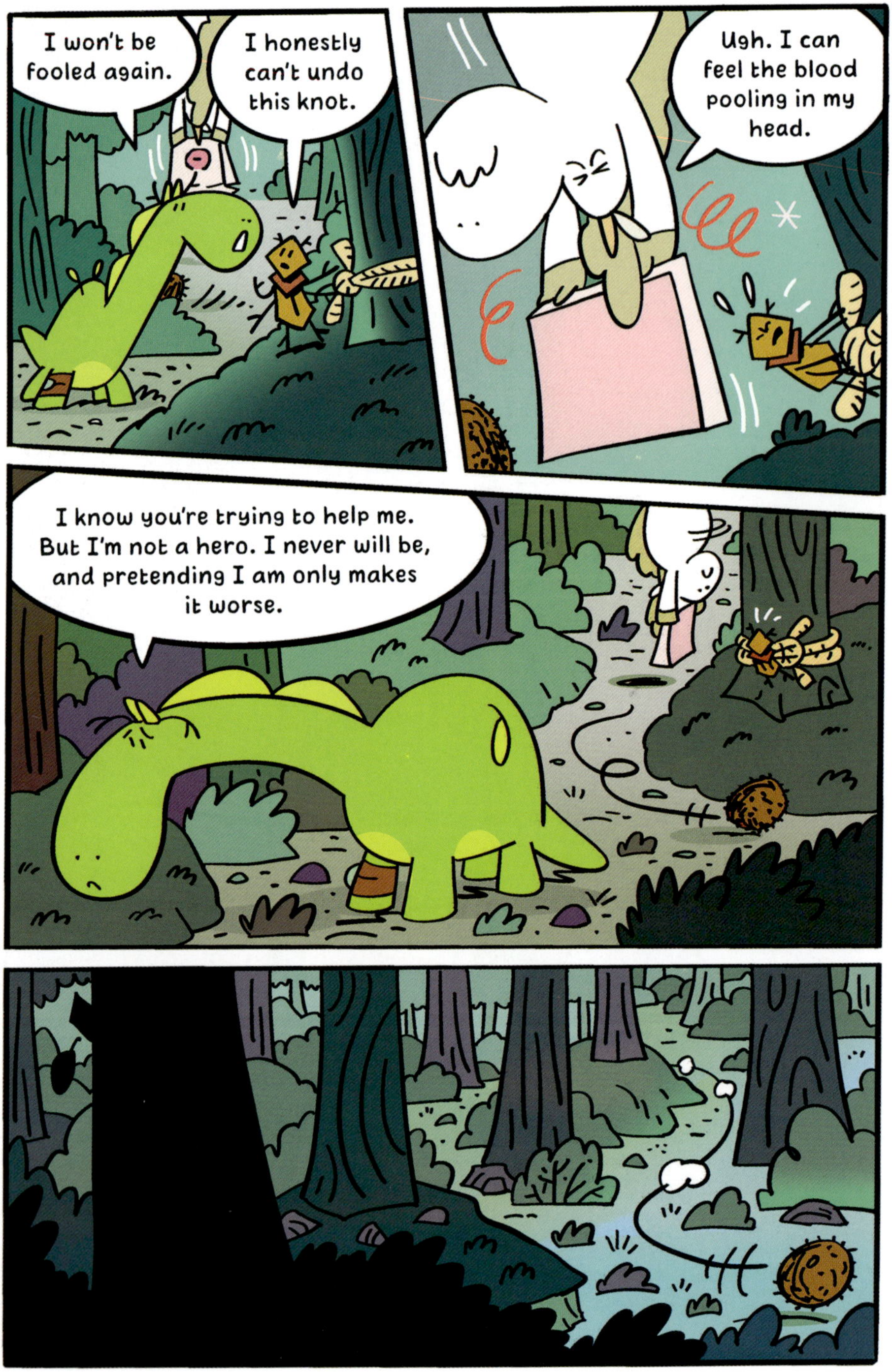
I won't be fooled again.
I honestly can't undo this knot.
Ugh. I can feel the blood pooling in my head.
I know you're trying to help me. But I'm not a hero. I never will be, and pretending I am only makes it worse.

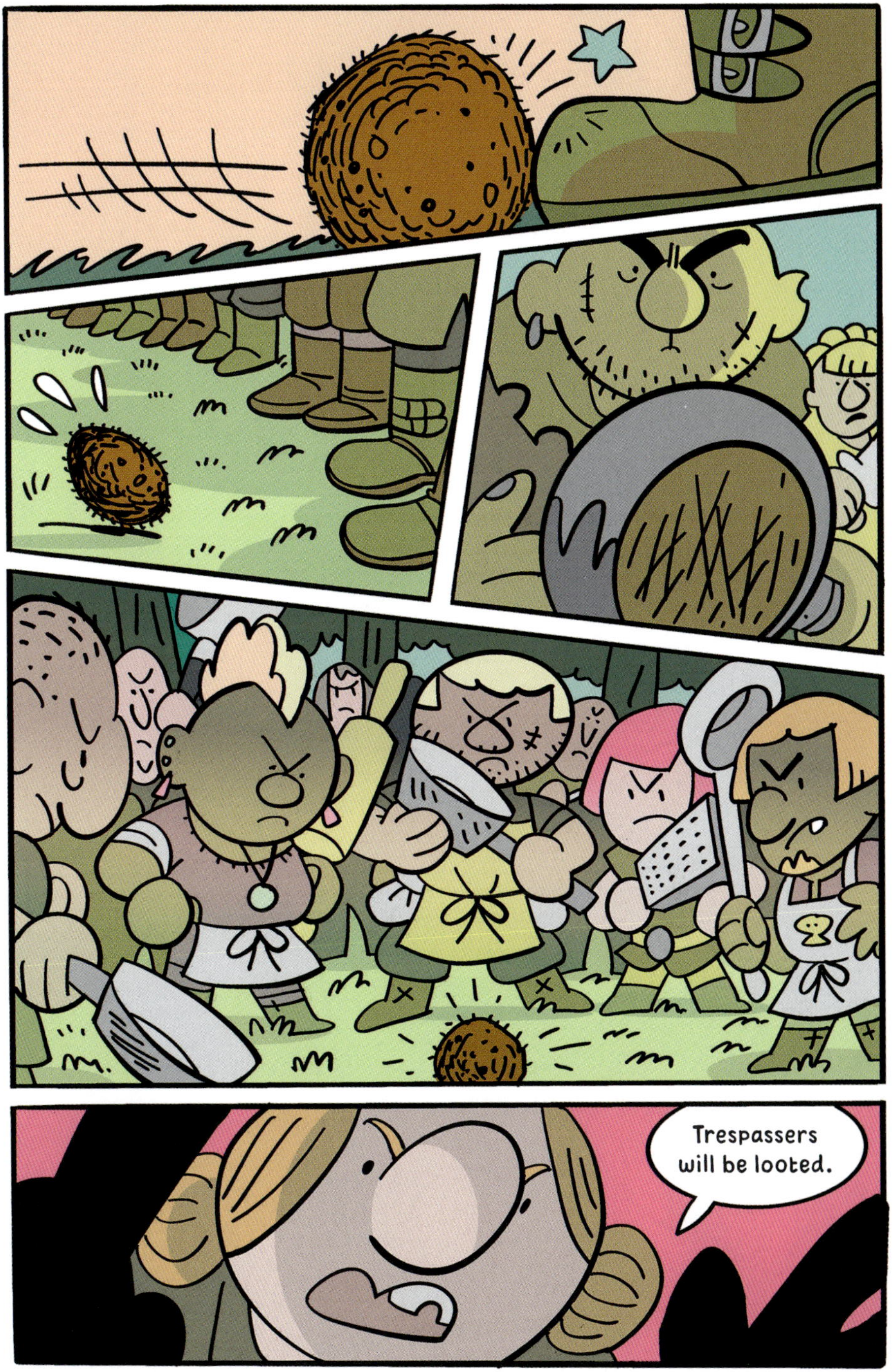
Trespassers will be looted.

CHAPTER NINE

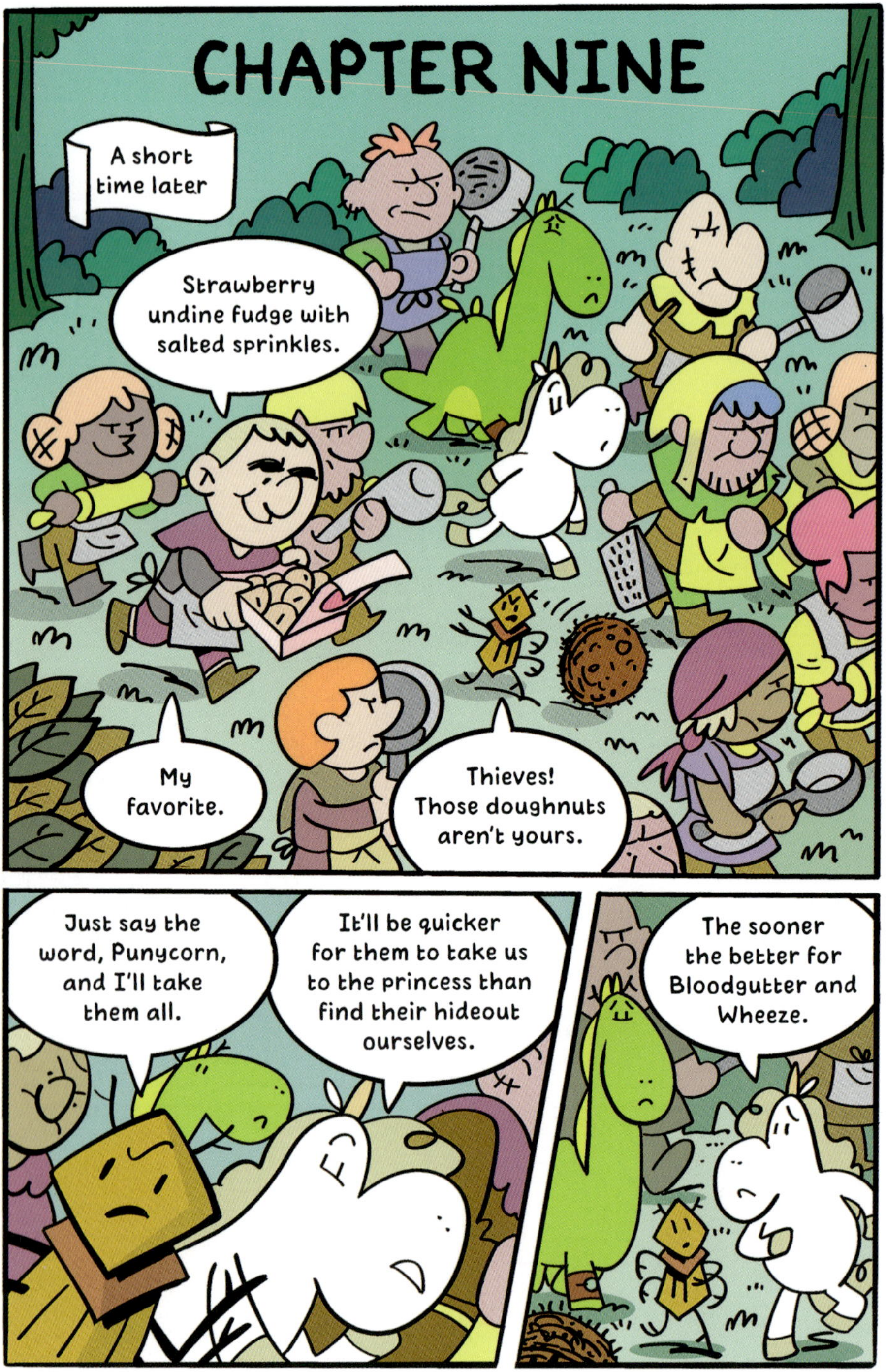
A short time later
Strawberry undine fudge with salted sprinkles.
My favorite.
Thieves! Those doughnuts aren't yours.
Just say the word, Punycorn, and I'll take them all.
It'll be quicker for them to take us to the princess than find their hideout ourselves.
The sooner the better for Bloodgutter and Wheeze.

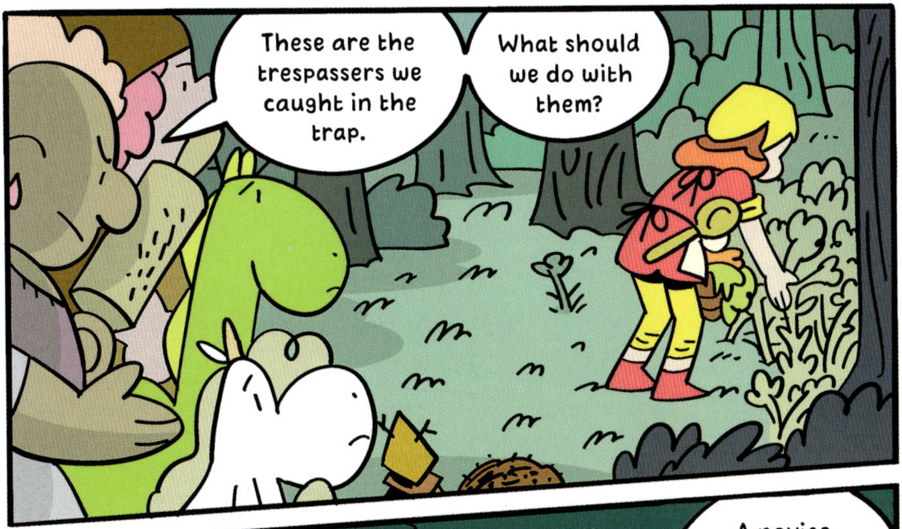
These are the trespassers we caught in the trap.
What should we do with them?

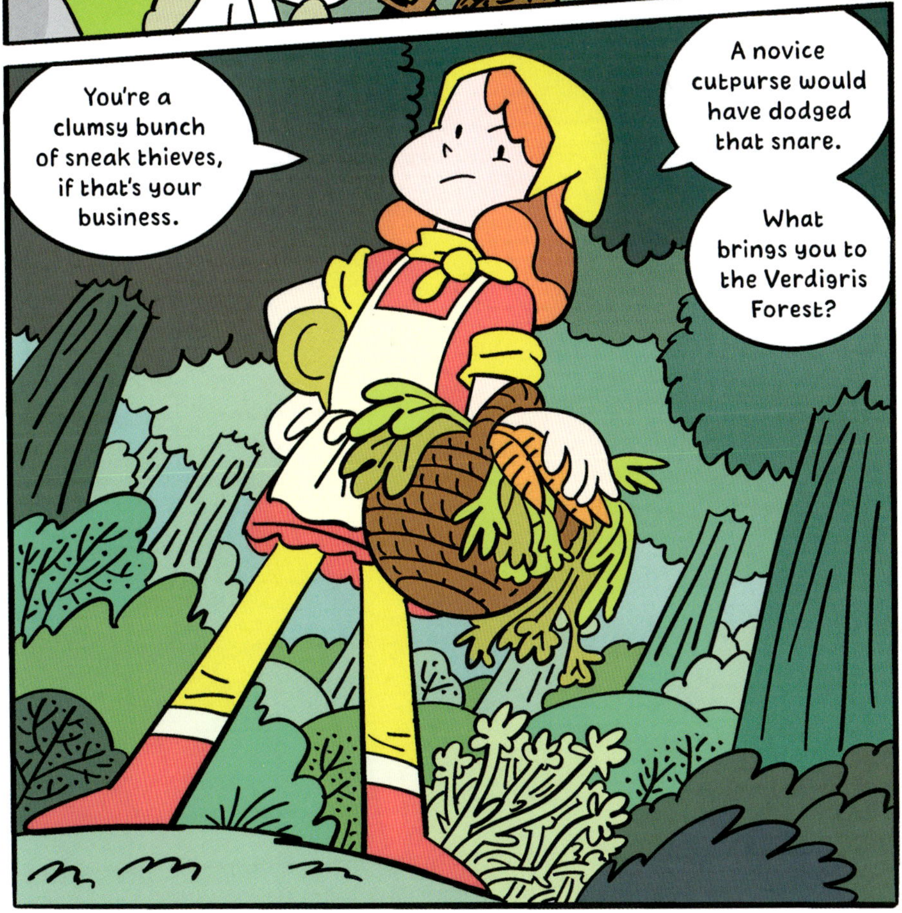
You're a clumsy bunch of sneak thieves, if that's your business.
A novice cutpurse would have dodged that snare.
What brings you to the Verdigris Forest?

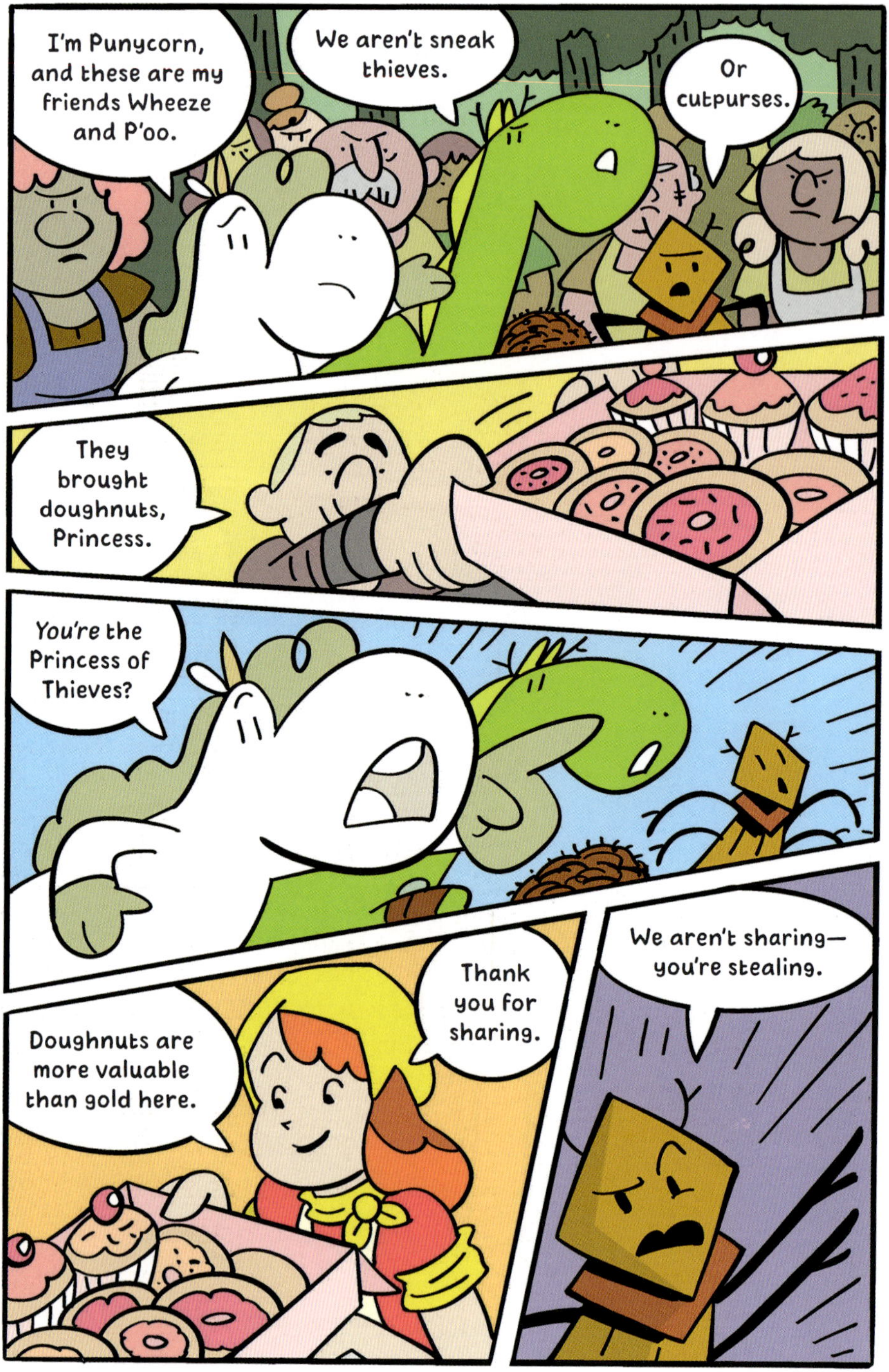
I'm Punycorn, and these are my friends Wheeze and P'oo.
We aren't sneak thieves.
Or cutpurses.
They brought doughnuts, Princess.
You're the Princess of Thieves?
Doughnuts are more valuable than gold here.
Thank you for sharing.
We aren't sharing—you're stealing.

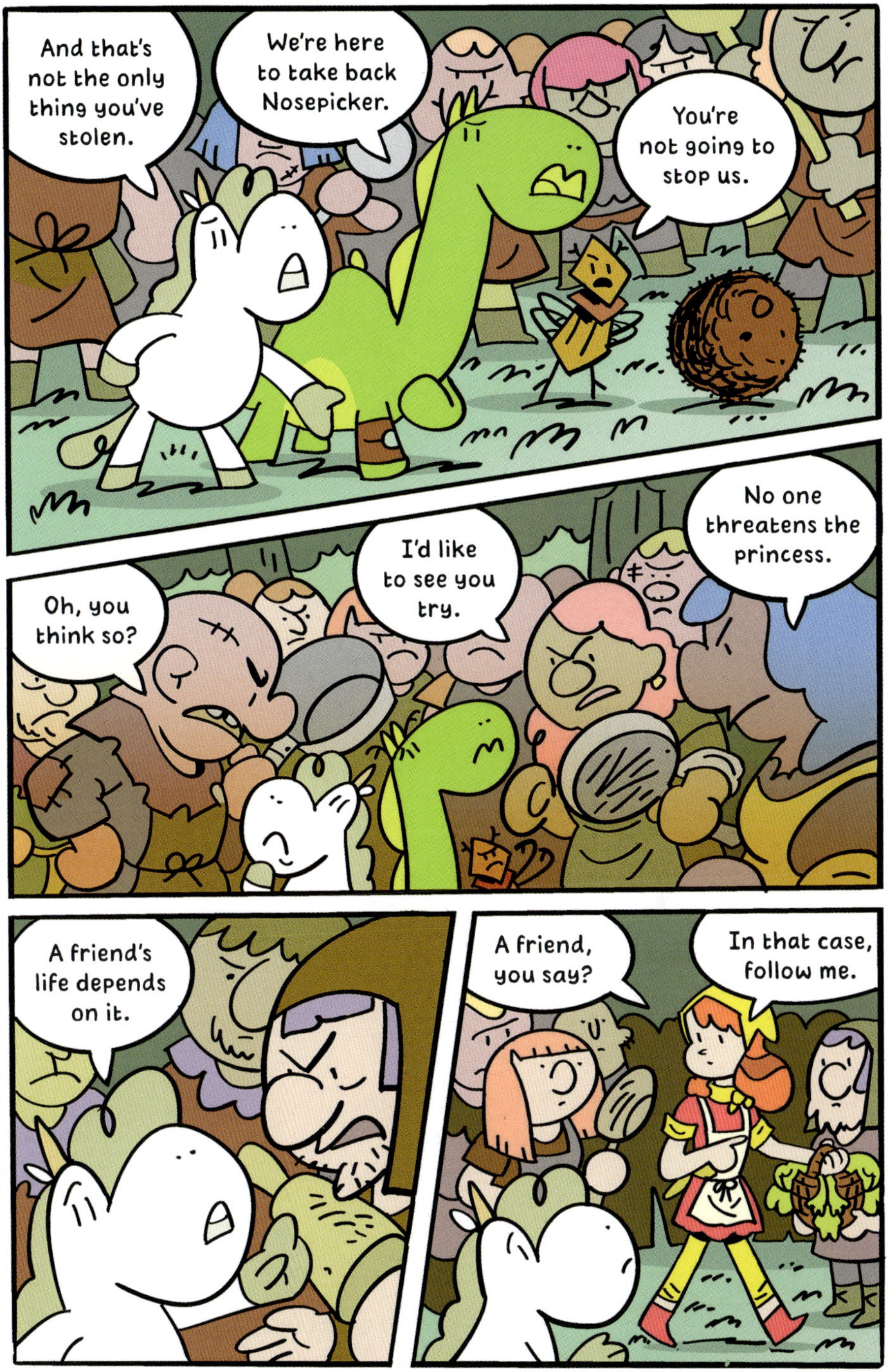
And that's not the only thing you've stolen.
We're here to take back Nosepicker.
You're not going to stop us.
Oh, you think so?
I'd like to see you try.
No one threatens the princess.
A friend's life depends on it.
A friend, you say?
In that case, follow me.

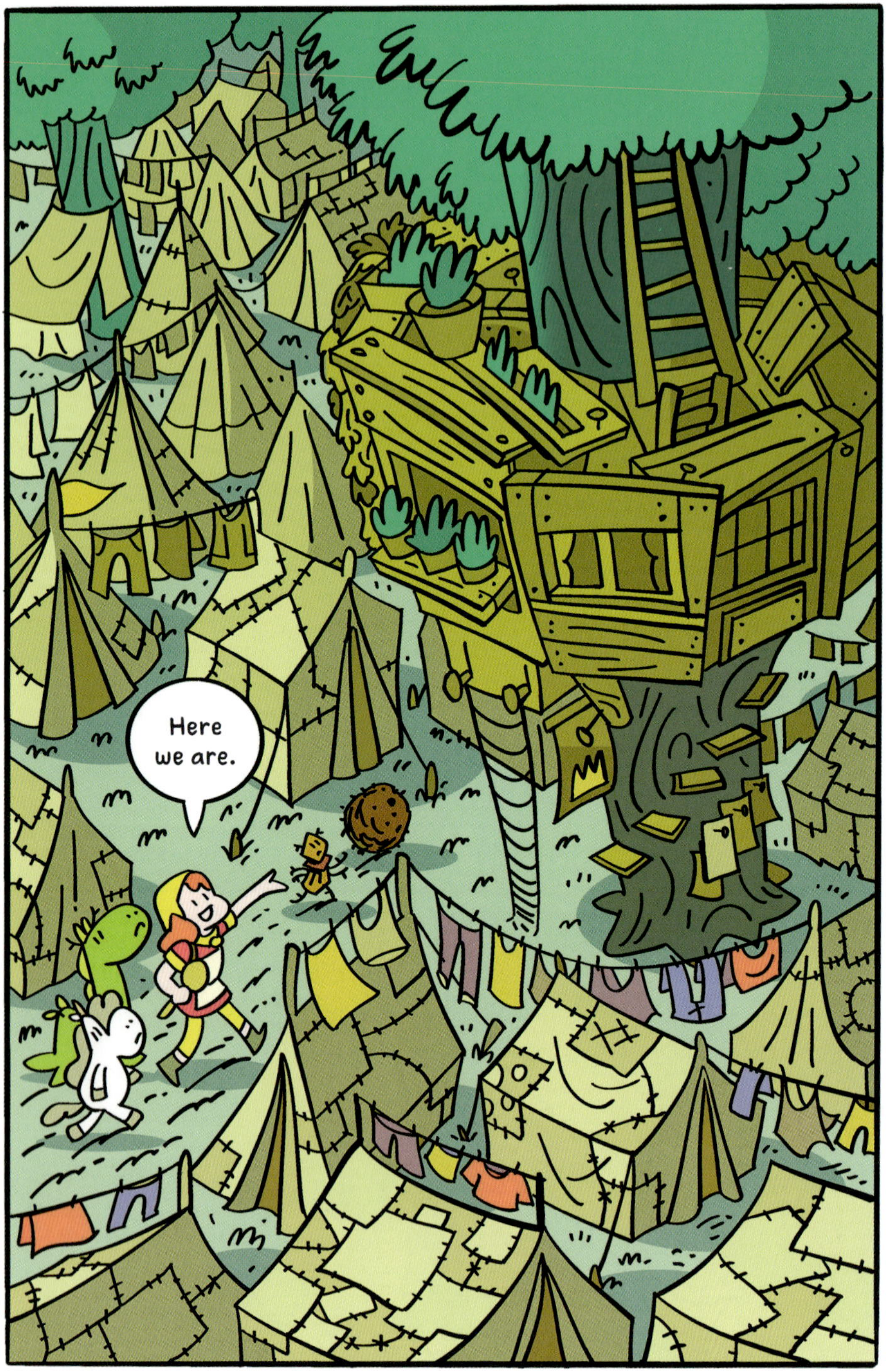
Here we are.

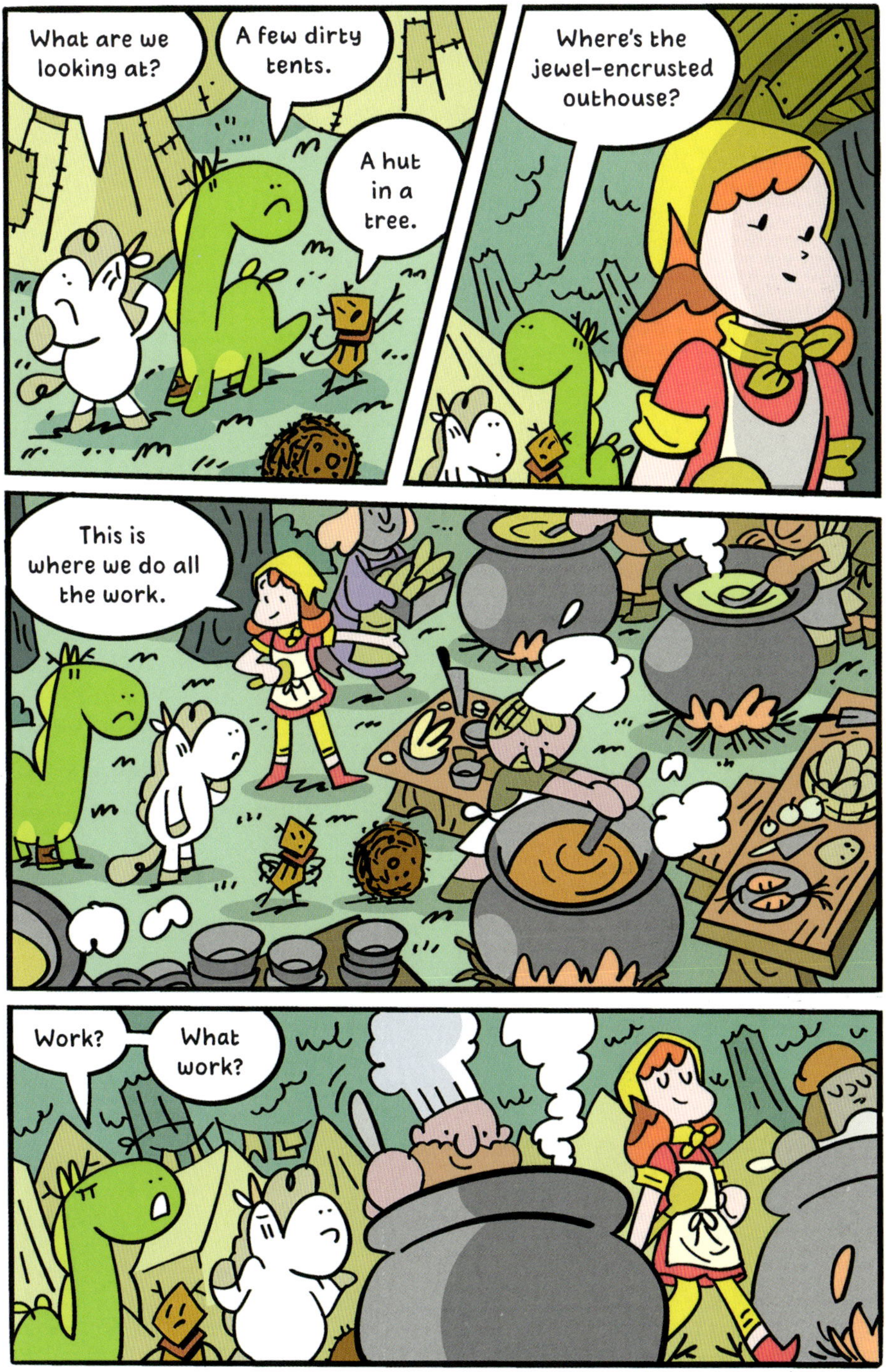
What are we looking at?
A few dirty tents.
A hut in a tree.
Where's the jewel-encrusted outhouse?
This is where we do all the work.
Work?
What work?

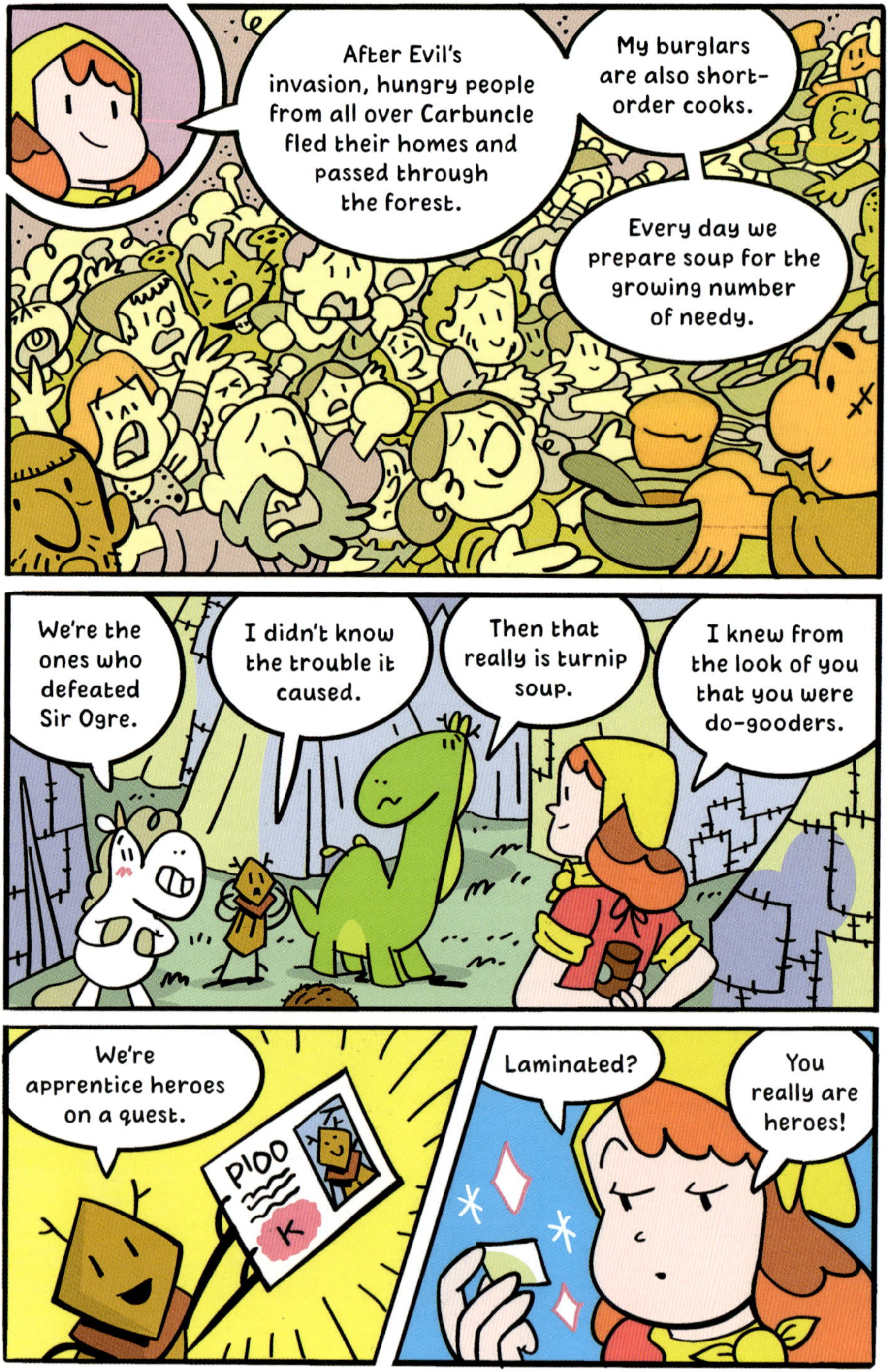
After Evil's invasion, hungry people from all over Carbuncle fled their homes and passed through the forest.
My burglars are also short-order cooks.
Every day we prepare soup for the growing number of needy.
We're the ones who defeated Sir Ogre.
I didn't know the trouble it caused.
Then that really is turnip soup.
I knew from the look of you that you were do-gooders.
We're apprentice heroes on a quest.
PIDD
K
Laminated?
You really are heroes!

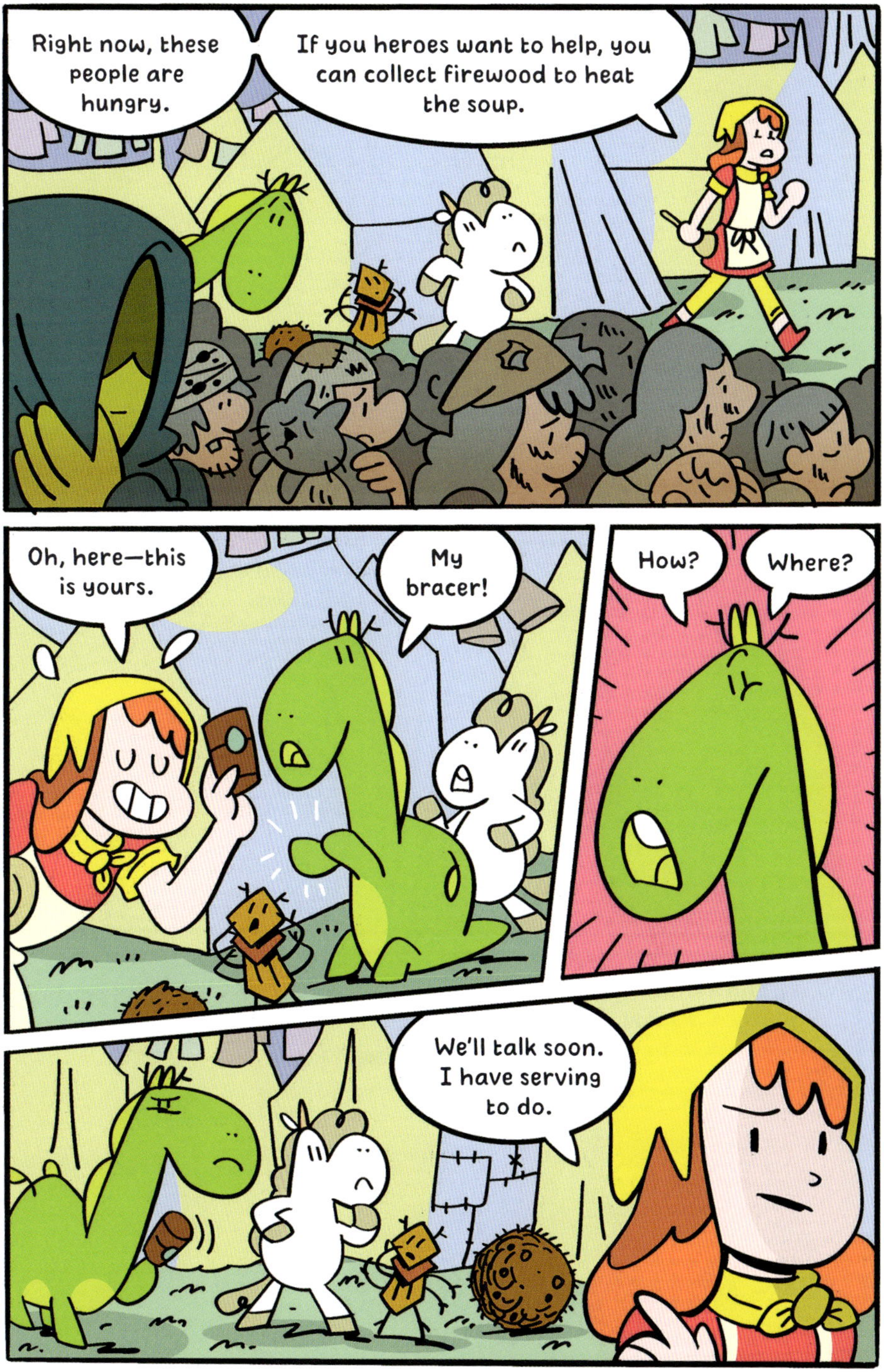

Right now, these people are hungry.
If you heroes want to help, you can collect firewood to heat the soup.
Oh, here—this is yours.
My bracer!
How?
Where?
We'll talk soon. I have serving to do.

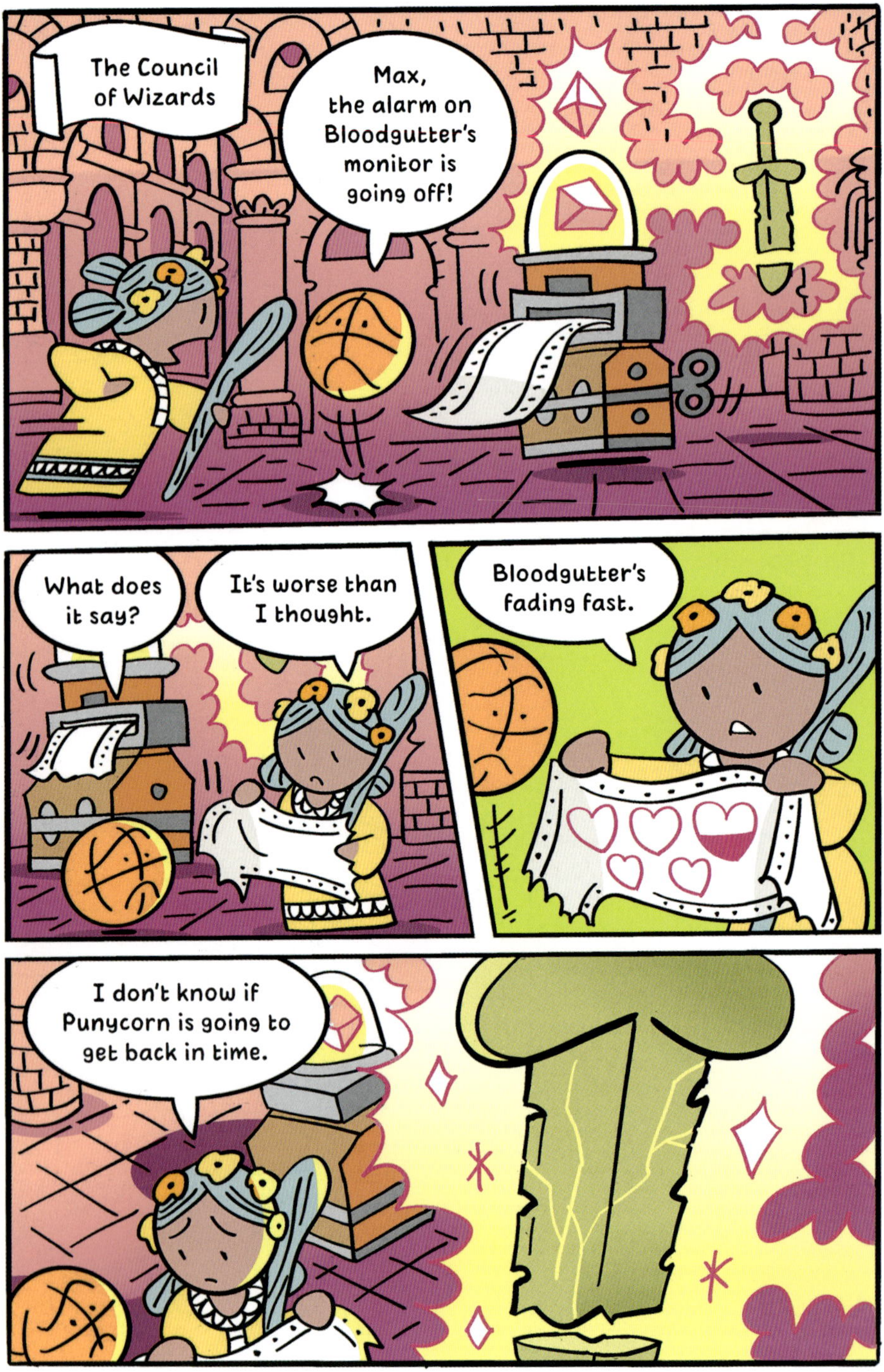
The Council of Wizards
Max, the alarm on Bloodgutter's monitor is going off!
What does it say?
It's worse than I thought.
Bloodgutter's fading fast.
I don't know if Punycorn is going to get back in time.

CHAPTER TEN

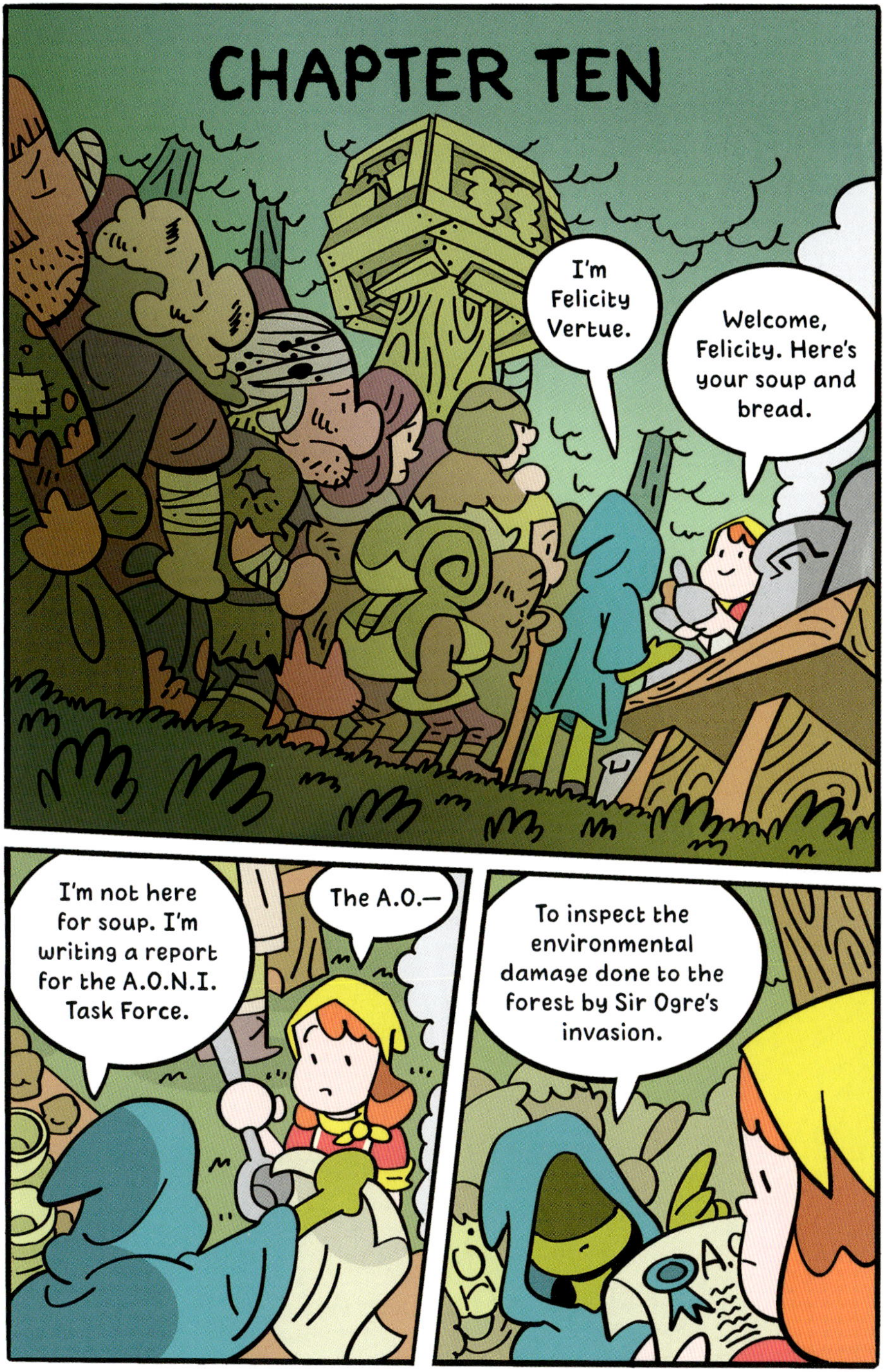

I'm Felicity Vertue.
Welcome, Felicity. Here's your soup and bread.
I'm not here for soup. I'm writing a report for the A.O.N.I. Task Force.
The A.O.—
To inspect the environmental damage done to the forest by Sir Ogre's invasion.

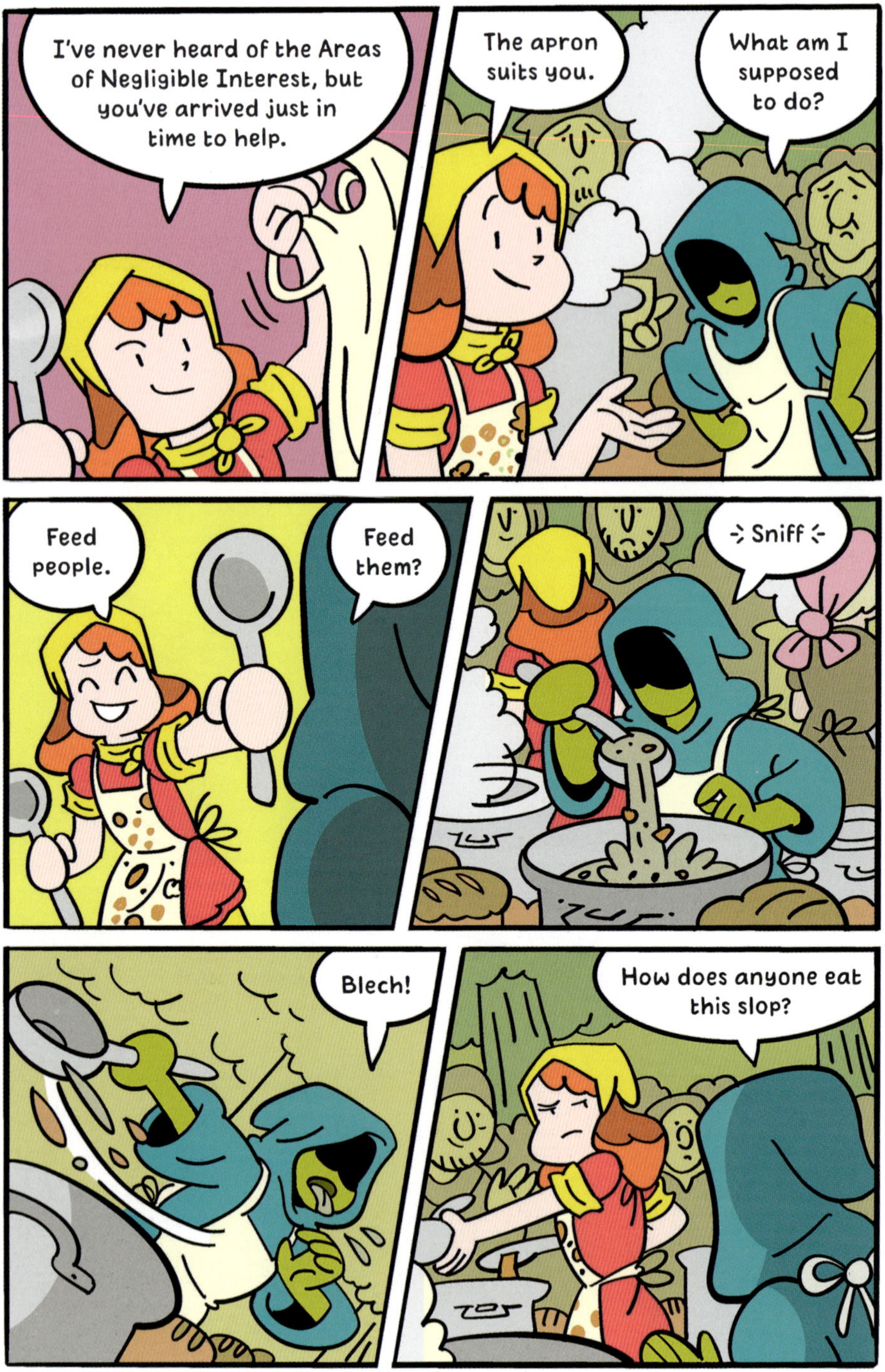
I've never heard of the Areas of Negligible Interest, but you've arrived just in time to help.
The apron suits you.
What am I supposed to do?
Feed people.
Feed them?
Sniff
Blech!
How does anyone eat this slop?

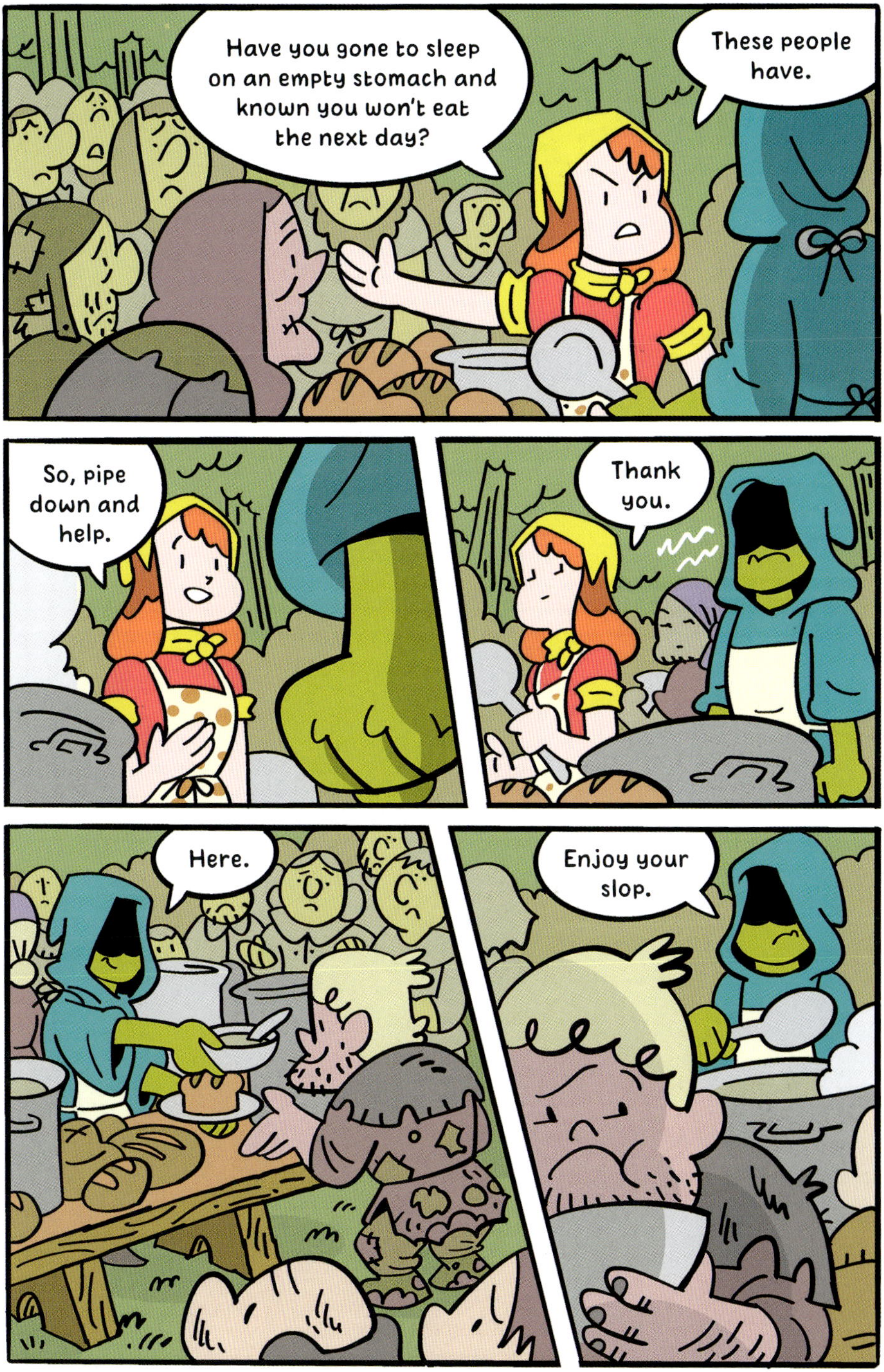
Have you gone to sleep on an empty stomach and known you won't eat the next day?
These people have.
So, pipe down and help.
Thank you.
Here.
Enjoy your slop.

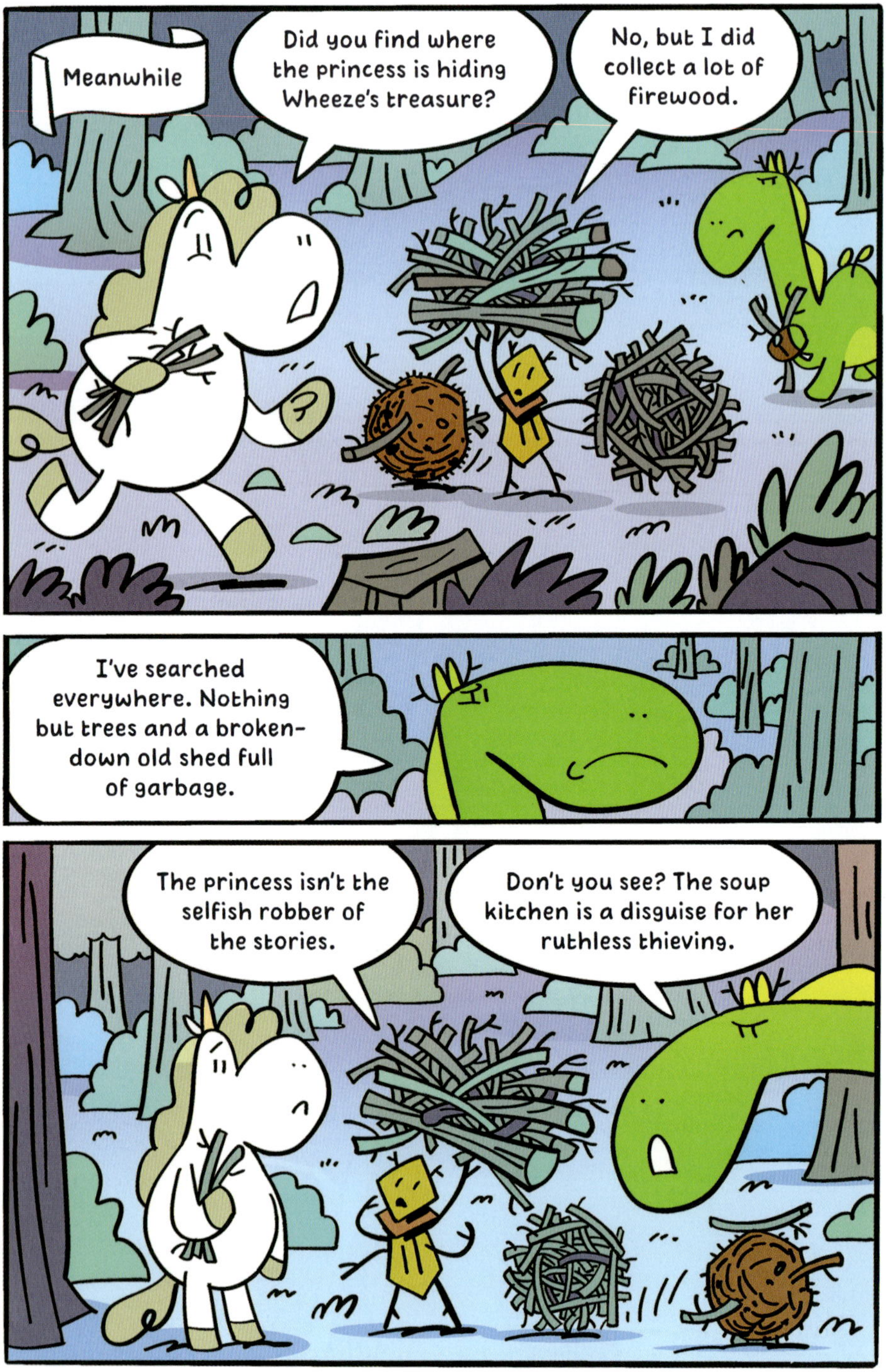
Meanwhile
Did you find where the princess is hiding Wheeze's treasure?
No, but I did collect a lot of firewood.
I've searched everywhere. Nothing but trees and a broken-down old shed full of garbage.
The princess isn't the selfish robber of the stories.
Don't you see? The soup kitchen is a disguise for her ruthless thieving.

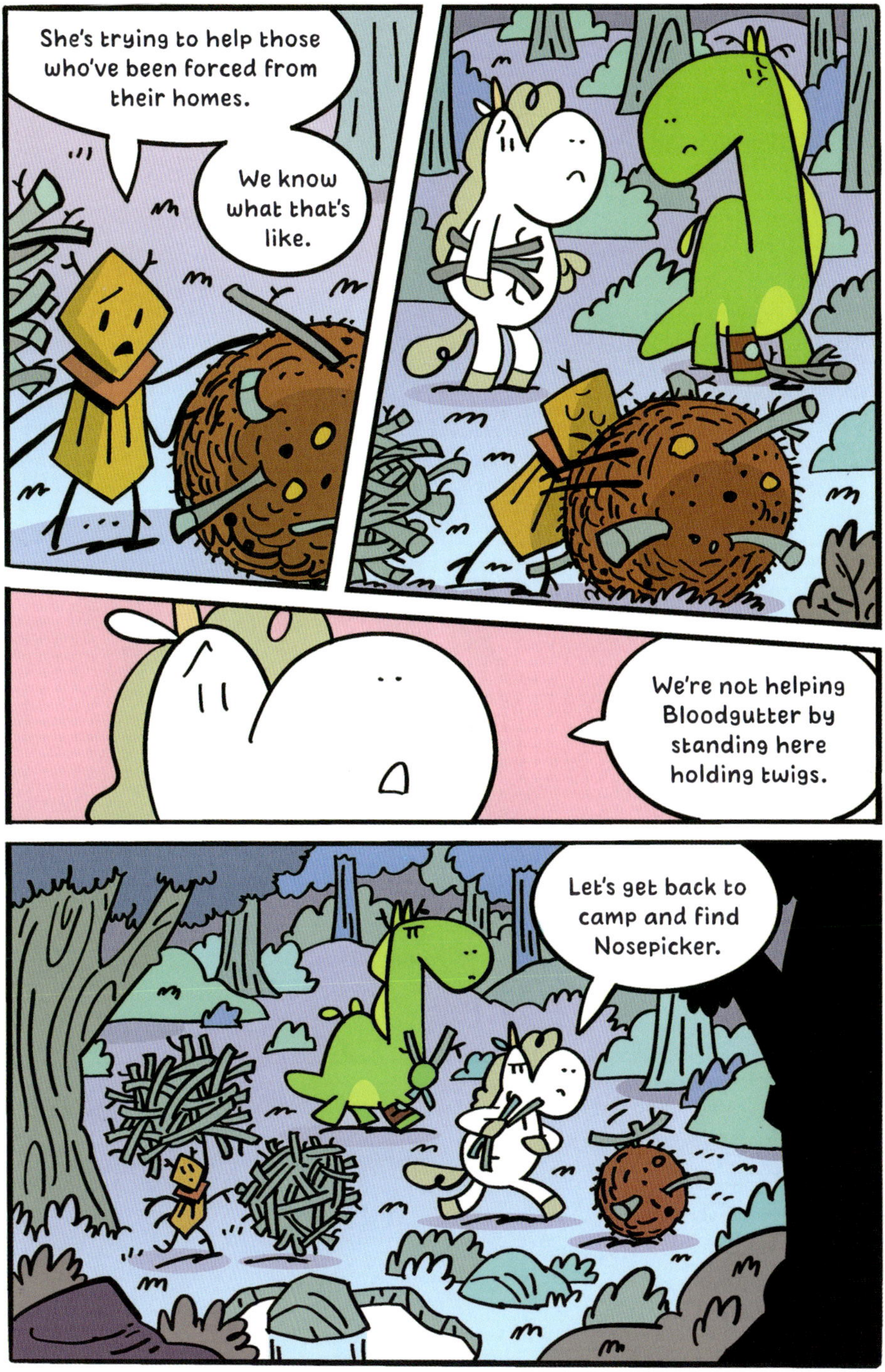
She's trying to help those who've been forced from their homes.
We know what that's like.
We're not helping Bloodgutter by standing here holding twigs.
Let's get back to camp and find Nosepicker.

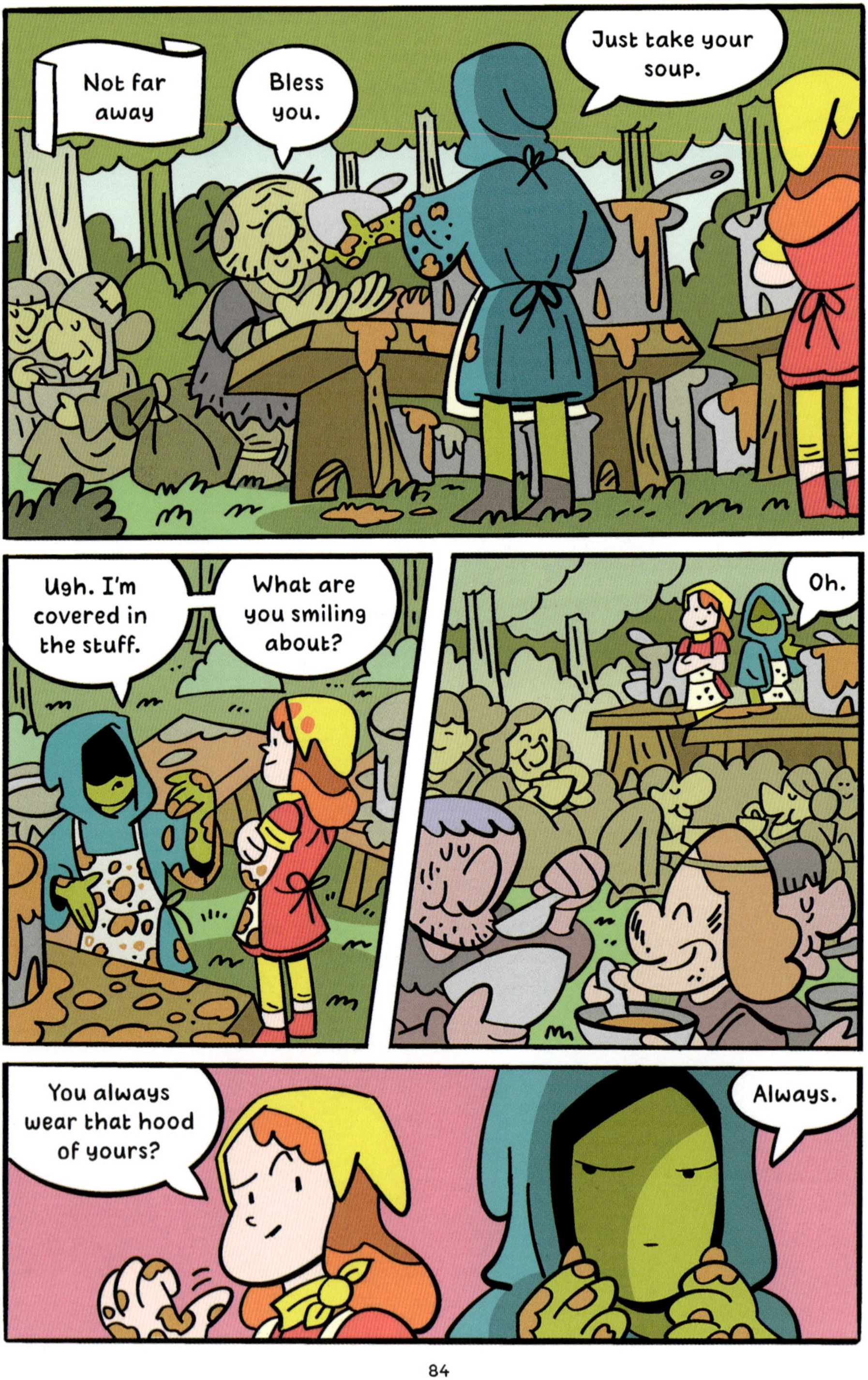
Not far away
Bless you.
Just take your soup.
Ugh. I'm covered in the stuff.
What are you smiling about?
Oh.
You always wear that hood of yours?
Always.

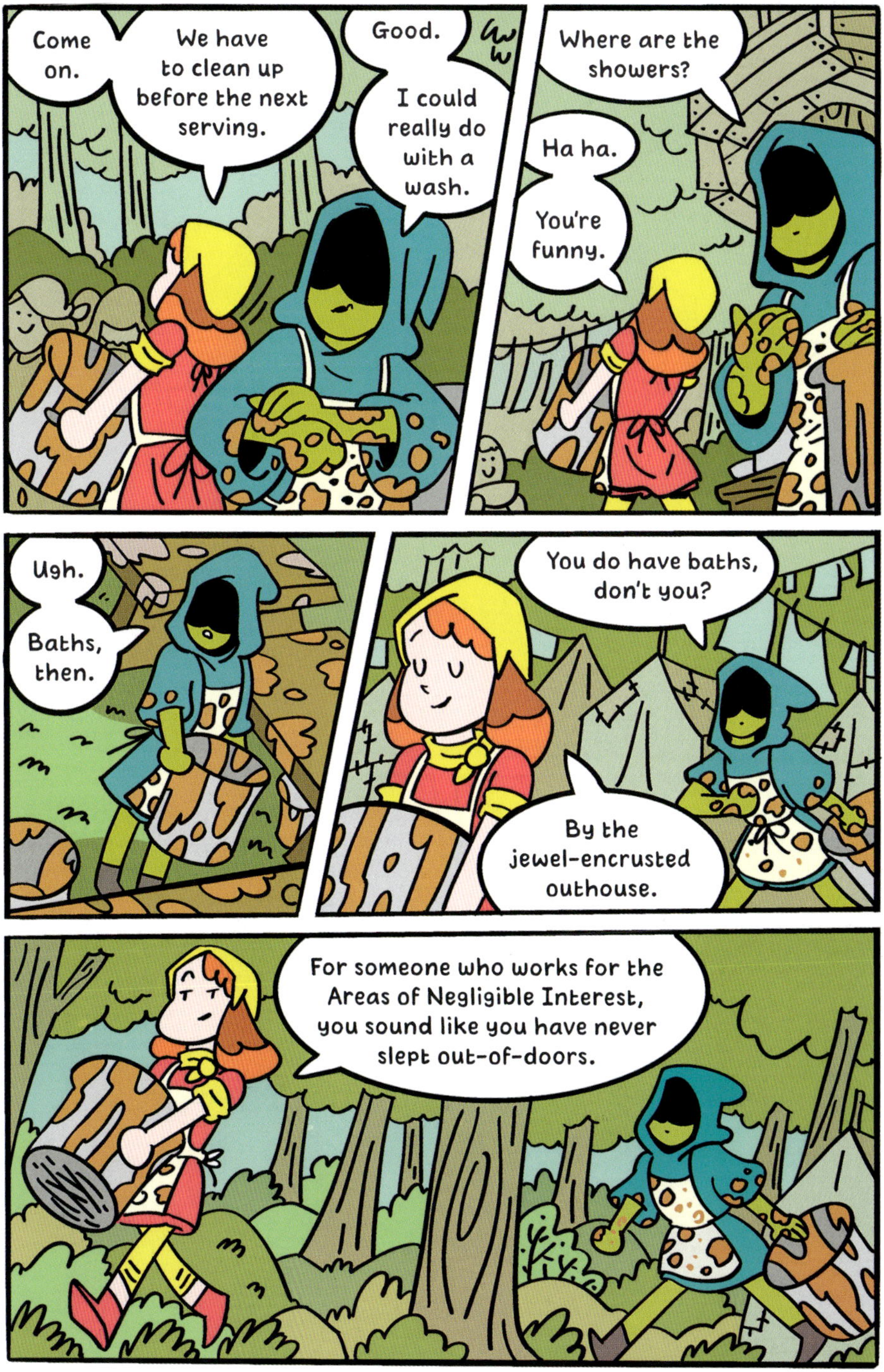
Come on.
We have to clean up before the next serving.
Good.
I could really do with a wash.
Where are the showers?
Ha ha.
You're funny.
Ugh.
Baths, then.
You do have baths, don't you?
By the jewel-encrusted outhouse.
For someone who works for the Areas of Negligible Interest, you sound like you have never slept out-of-doors.

CHAPTER ELEVEN

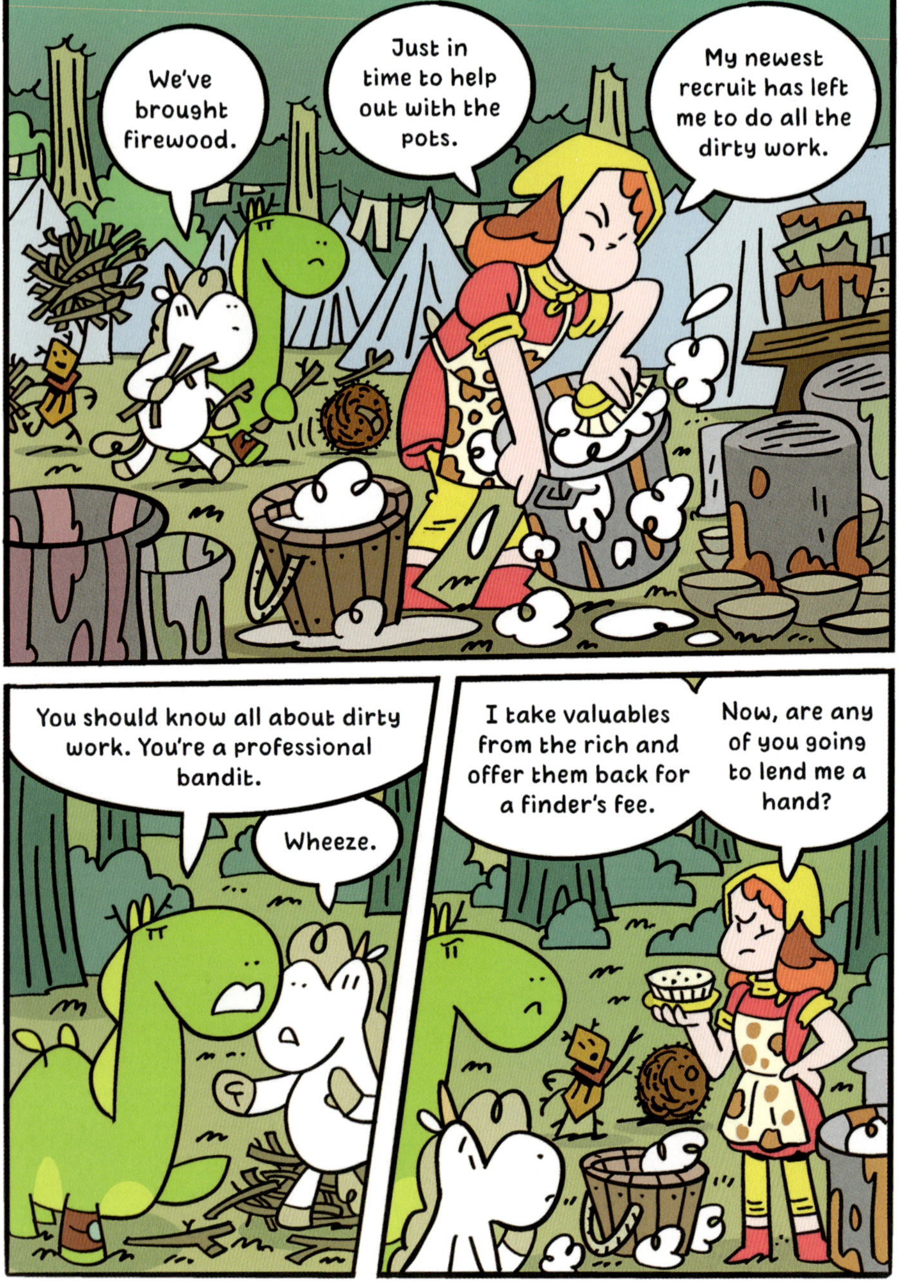
We've brought firewood.
Just in time to help out with the pots.
My newest recruit has left me to do all the dirty work.
You should know all about dirty work. You're a professional bandit.
Wheeze.
I take valuables from the rich and offer them back for a finder's fee.
Now, are any of you going to lend me a hand?

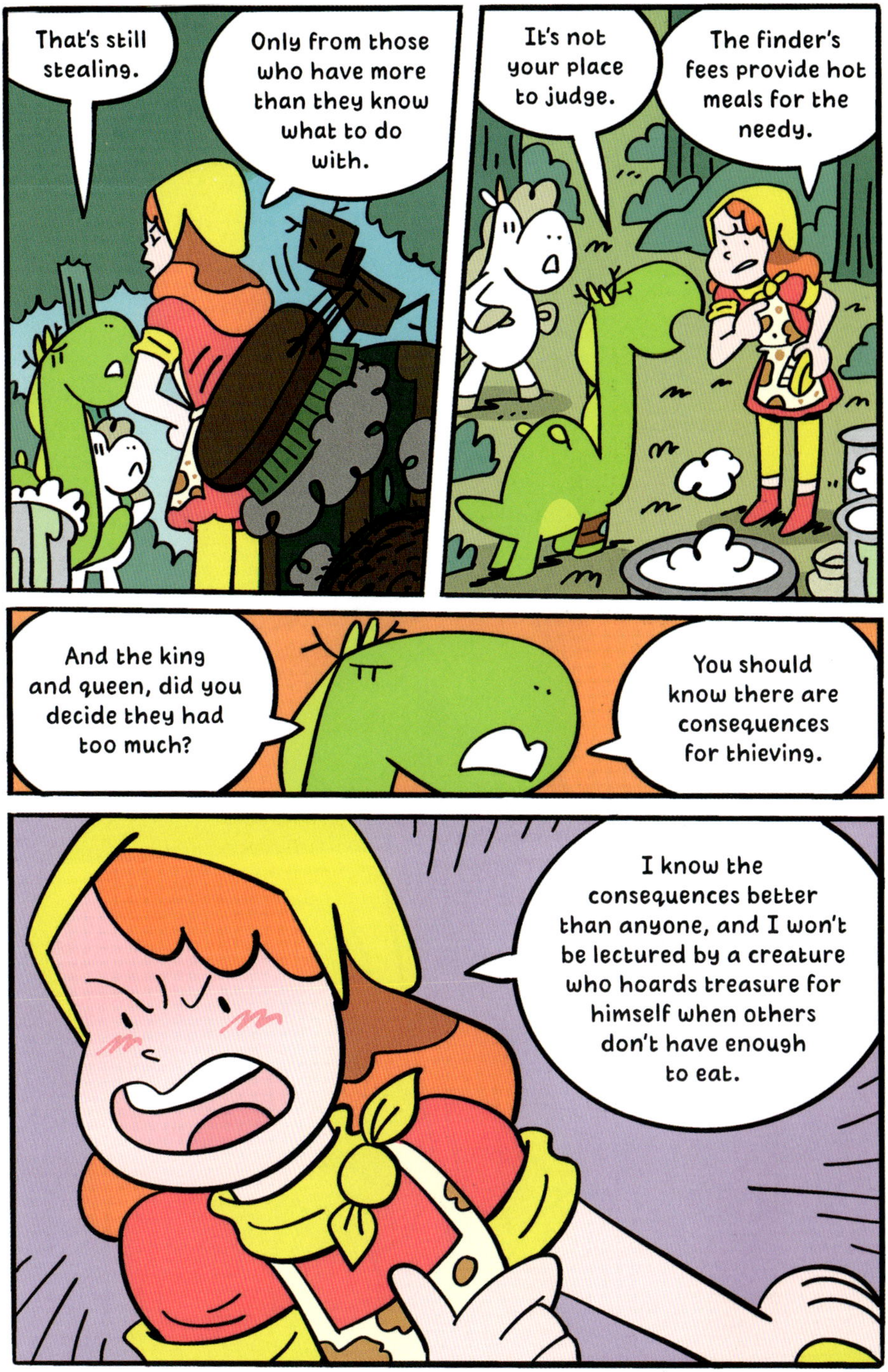
That's still stealing.
Only from those who have more than they know what to do with.
It's not your place to judge.
The finder's fees provide hot meals for the needy.
And the king and queen, did you decide they had too much?
You should know there are consequences for thieving.
I know the consequences better than anyone, and I won't be lectured by a creature who hoards treasure for himself when others don't have enough to eat.

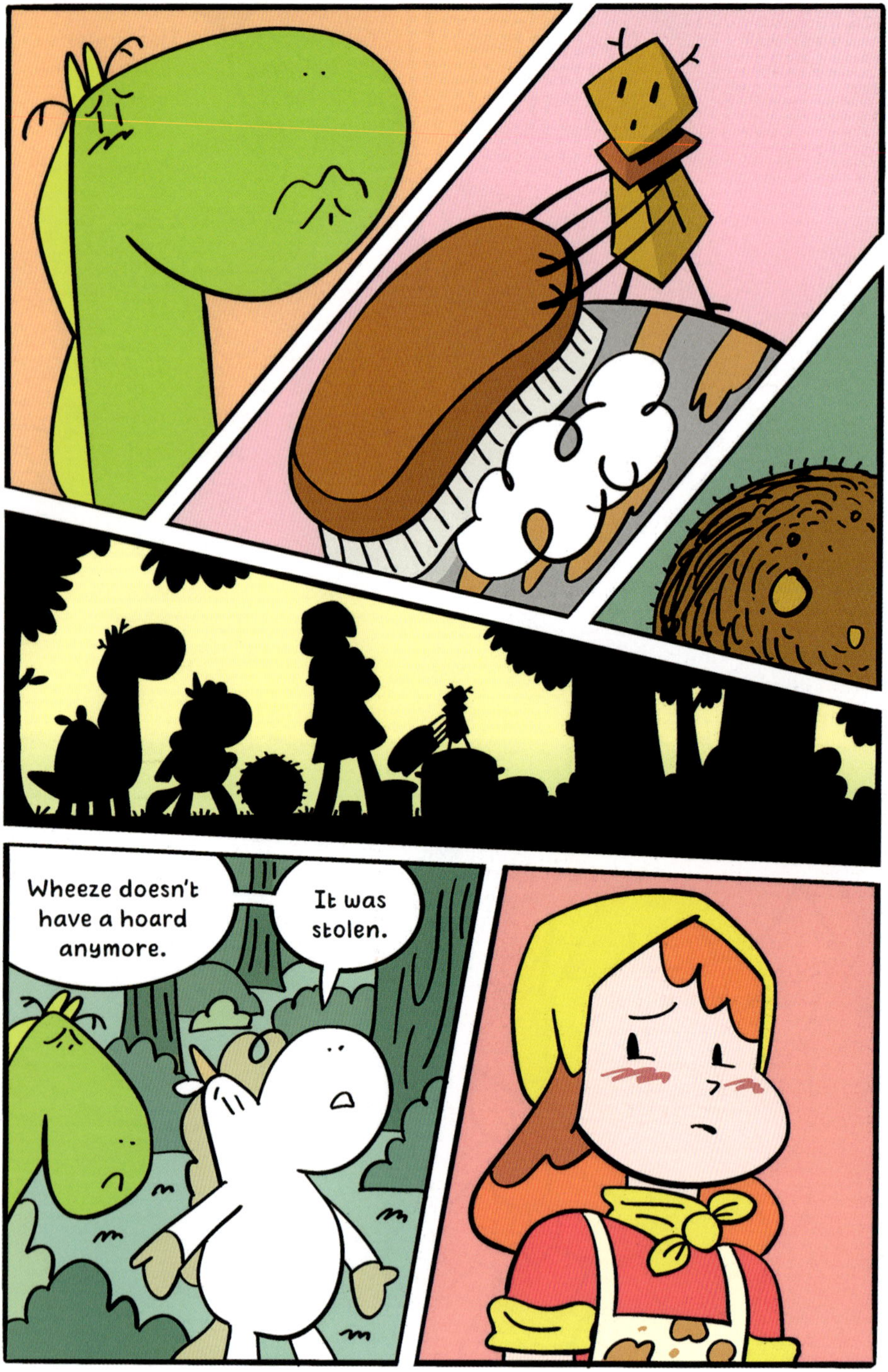
Wheeze doesn't have a hoard anymore.
It was stolen.

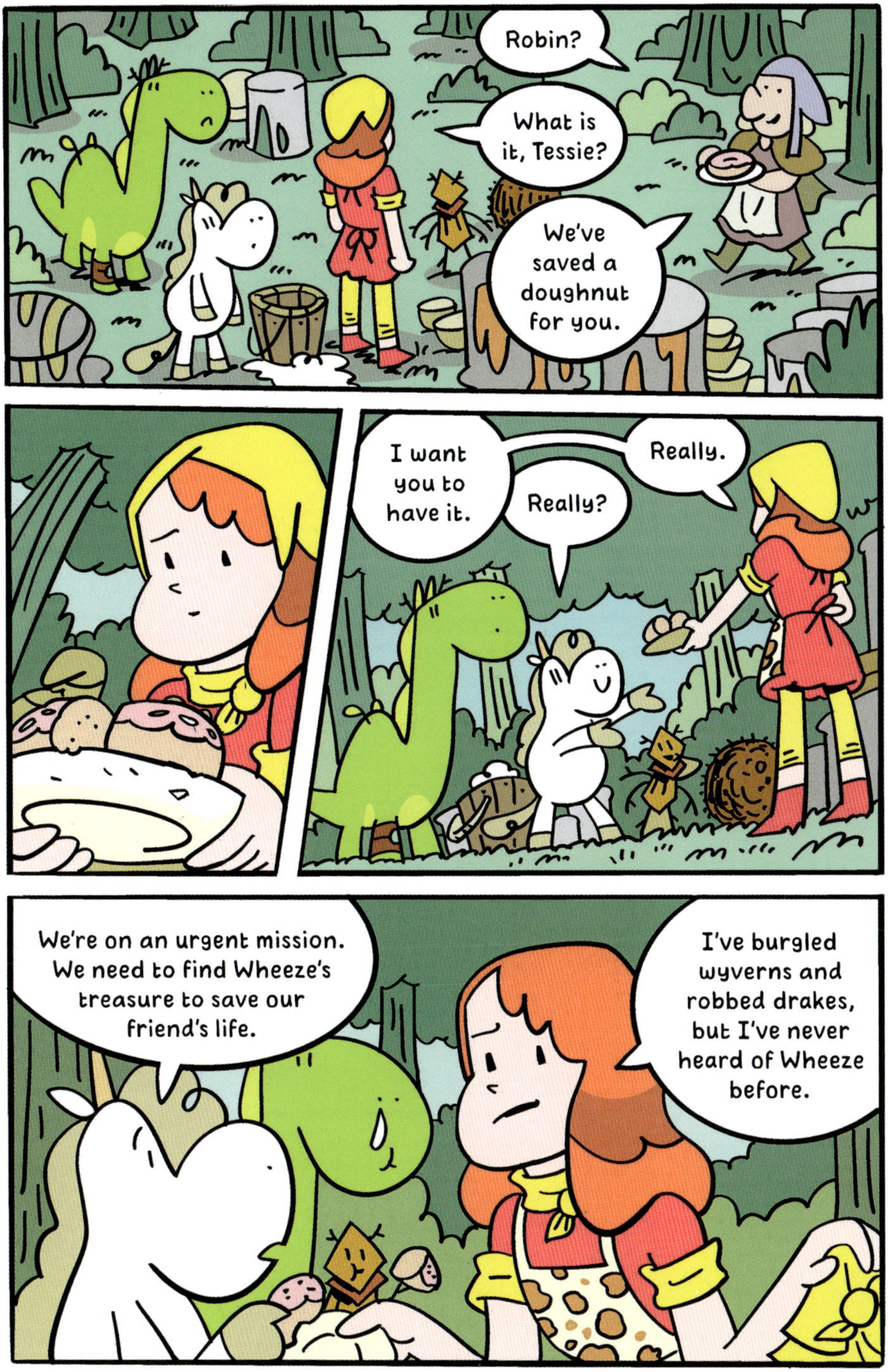
Robin?
What is it, Tessie?
We've saved a doughnut for you.
I want you to have it.
Really?
Really.
We're on an urgent mission. We need to find Wheeze's treasure to save our friend's life.
I've burgled wyverns and robbed drakes, but I've never heard of Wheeze before.

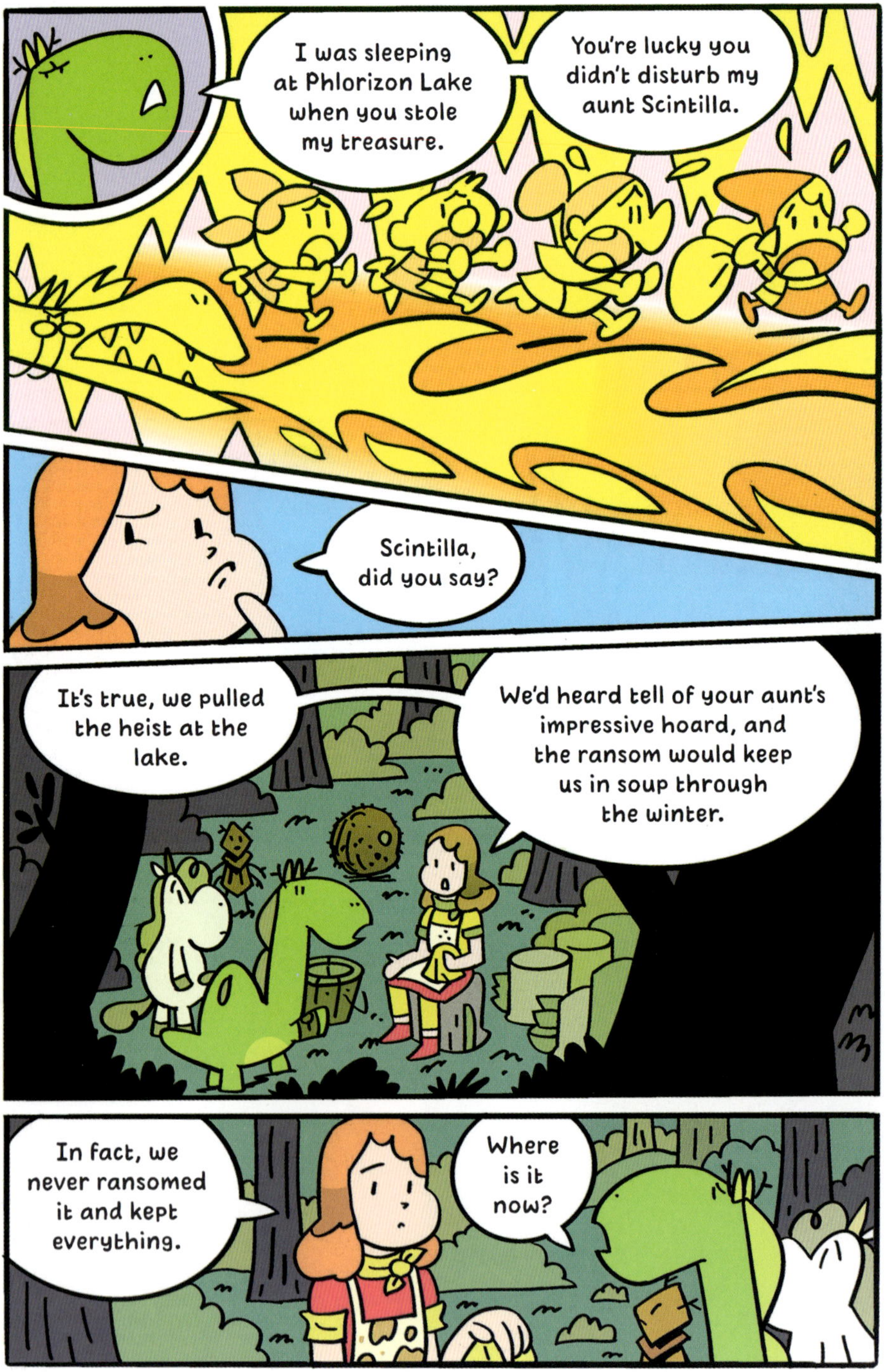
I was sleeping at Phlorizon Lake when you stole my treasure.
You're lucky you didn't disturb my aunt Scintilla.
Scintilla, did you say?
It's true, we pulled the heist at the lake.
We'd heard tell of your aunt's impressive hoard, and the ransom would keep us in soup through the winter.
In fact, we never ransomed it and kept everything.
Where is it now?

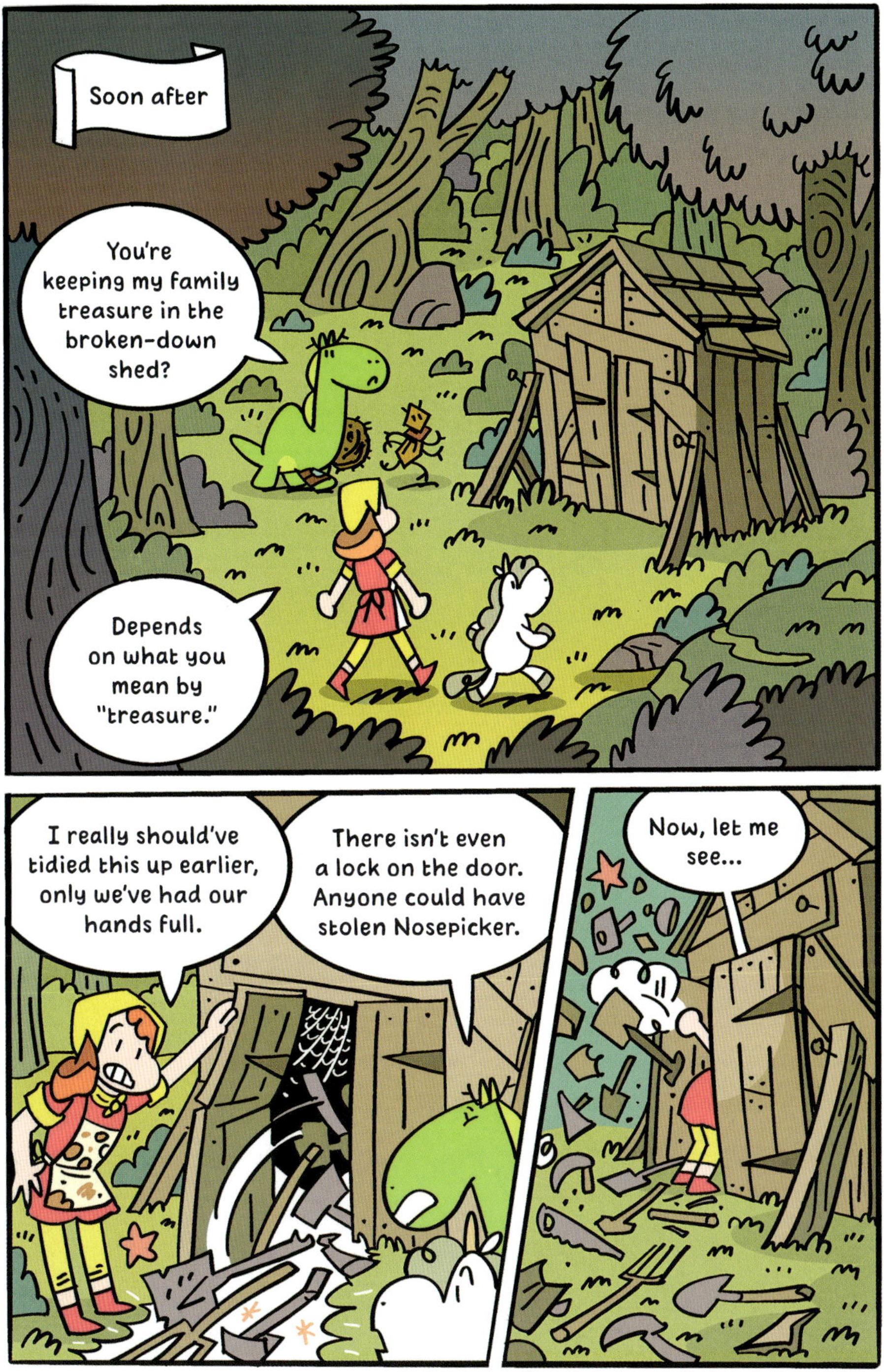
Soon after
You're keeping my family treasure in the broken-down shed?
Depends on what you mean by "treasure."
I really should've tidied this up earlier, only we've had our hands full.
There isn't even a lock on the door. Anyone could have stolen Nosepicker.
Now, let me see...

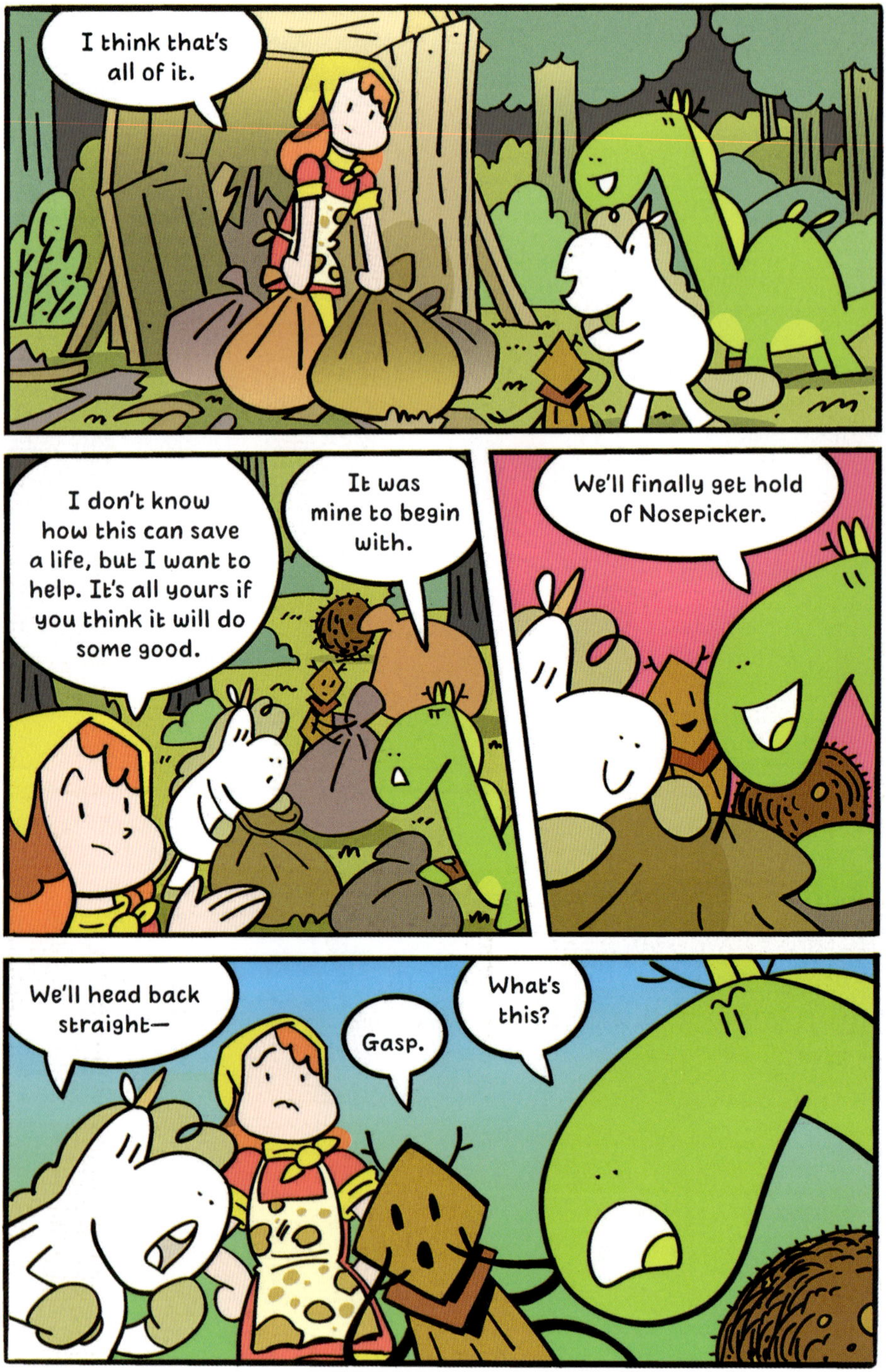
I think that's all of it.
I don't know how this can save a life, but I want to help. It's all yours if you think it will do some good.
It was mine to begin with.
We'll finally get hold of Nosepicker.
We'll head back straight—
Gasp.
What's this?

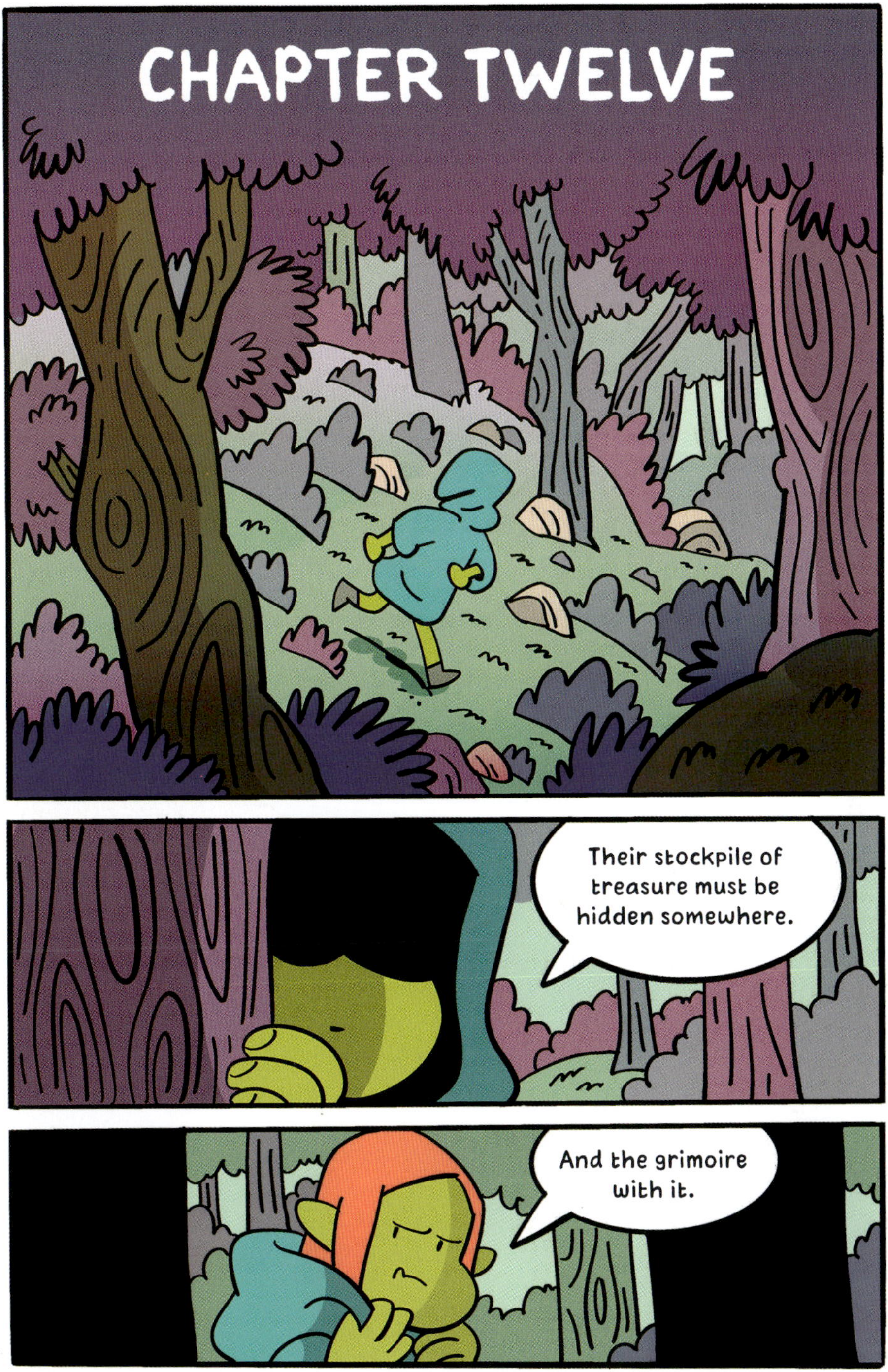
CHAPTER TWELVE
Their stockpile of treasure must be hidden somewhere.
And the grimoire with it.

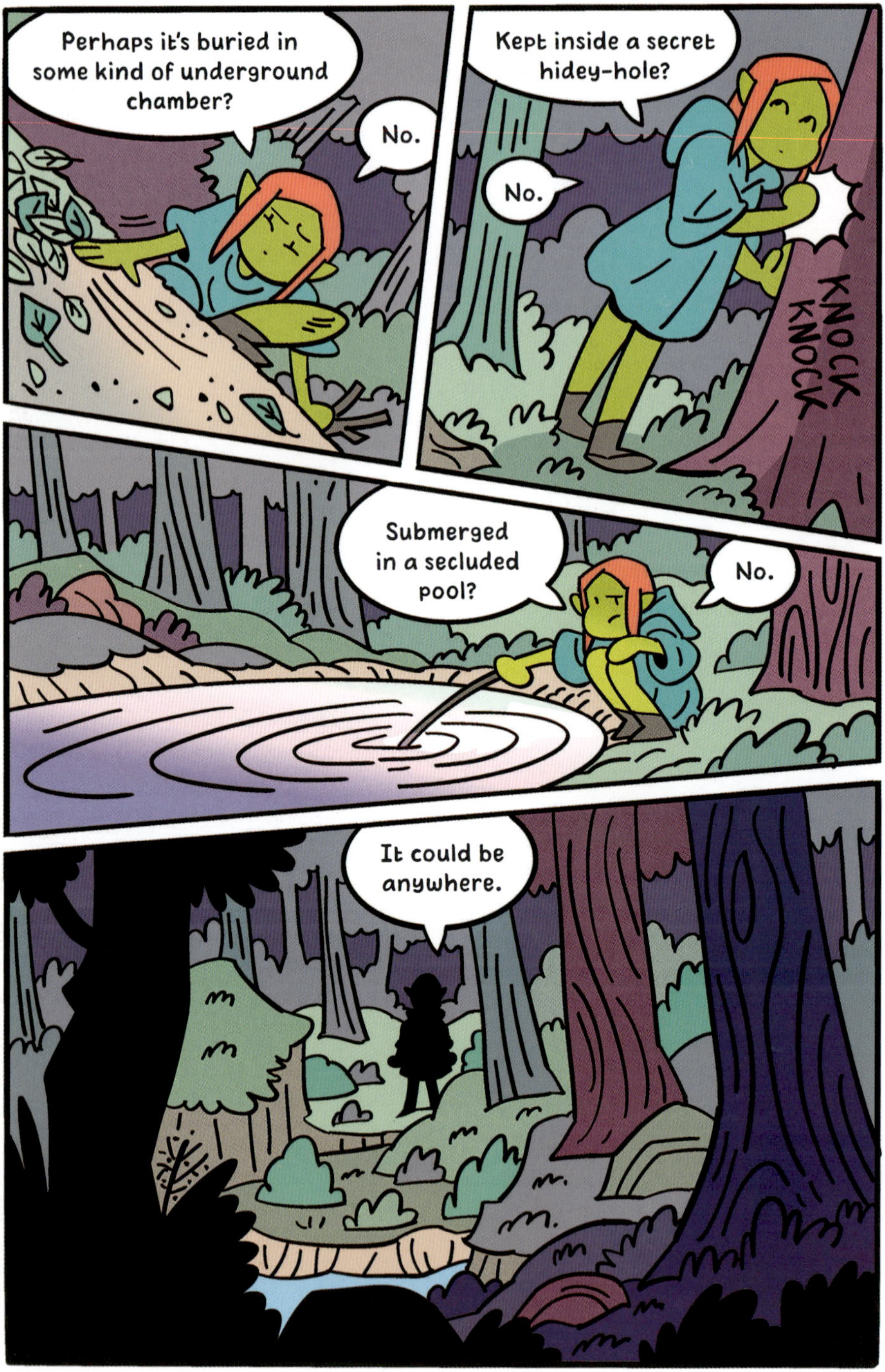
Perhaps it's buried in some kind of underground chamber?
No.
Kept inside a secret hidey-hole?
No.
KNOCK KNOCK
Submerged in a secluded pool?
No.
It could be anywhere.

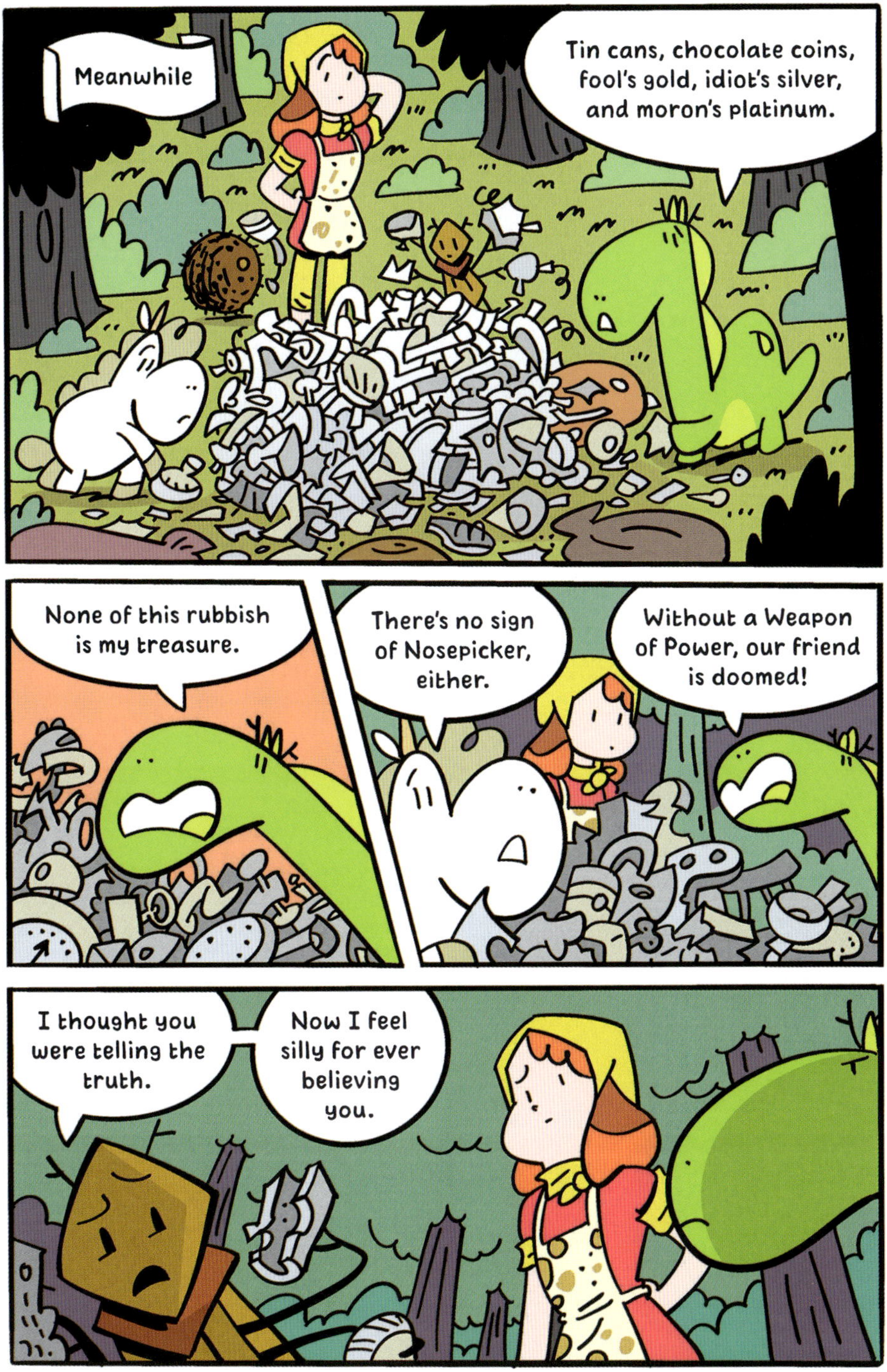
Meanwhile
Tin cans, chocolate coins, fool's gold, idiot's silver, and moron's platinum.
None of this rubbish is my treasure.
There's no sign of Nosepicker, either.
Without a Weapon of Power, our friend is doomed!
I thought you were telling the truth.
Now I feel silly for ever believing you.

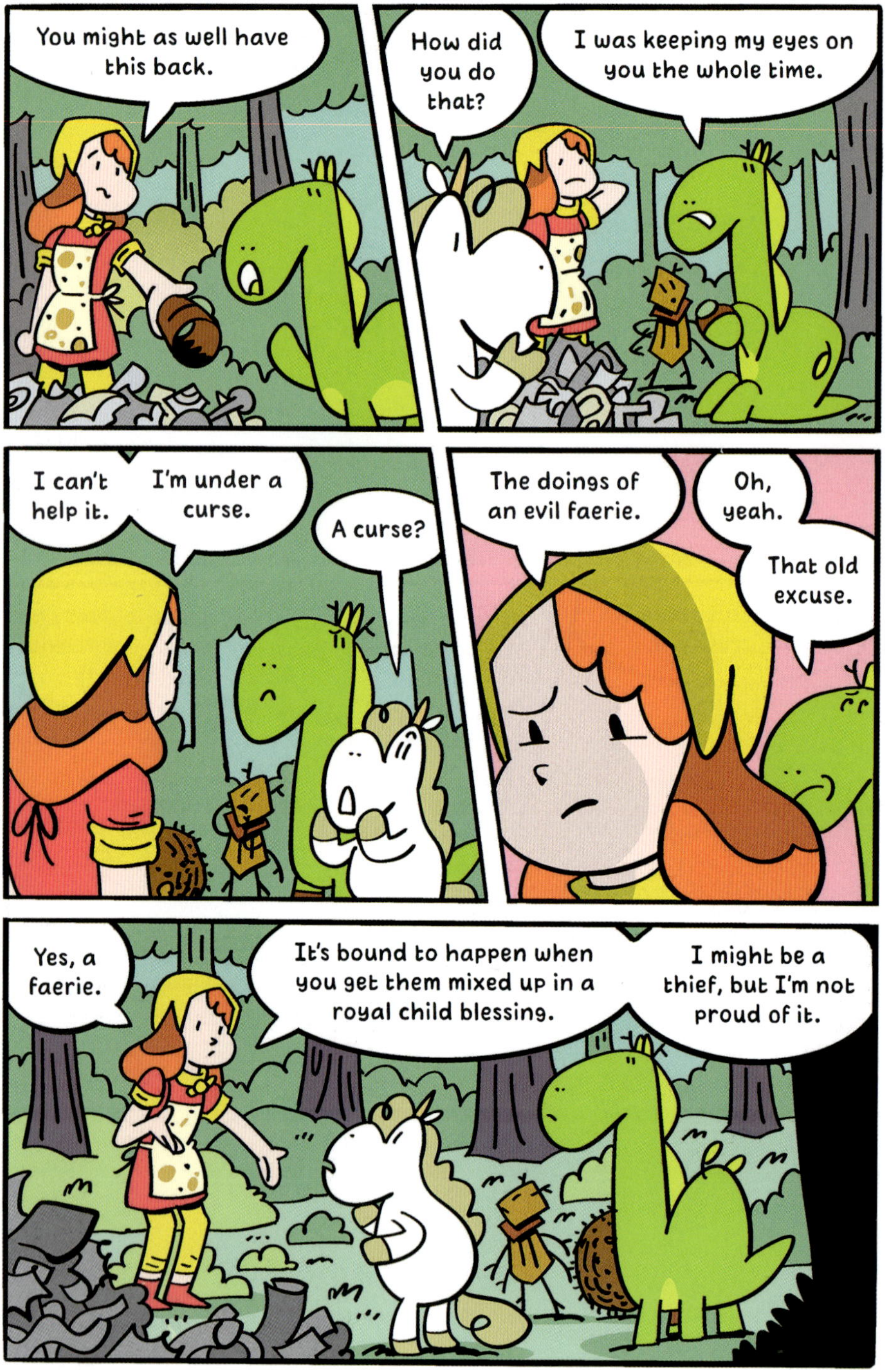
You might as well have this back.
How did you do that?
I was keeping my eyes on you the whole time.
I can't help it.
I'm under a curse.
A curse?
The doings of an evil faerie.
Oh, yeah.
That old excuse.
Yes, a faerie.
It's bound to happen when you get them mixed up in a royal child blessing.
I might be a thief, but I'm not proud of it.

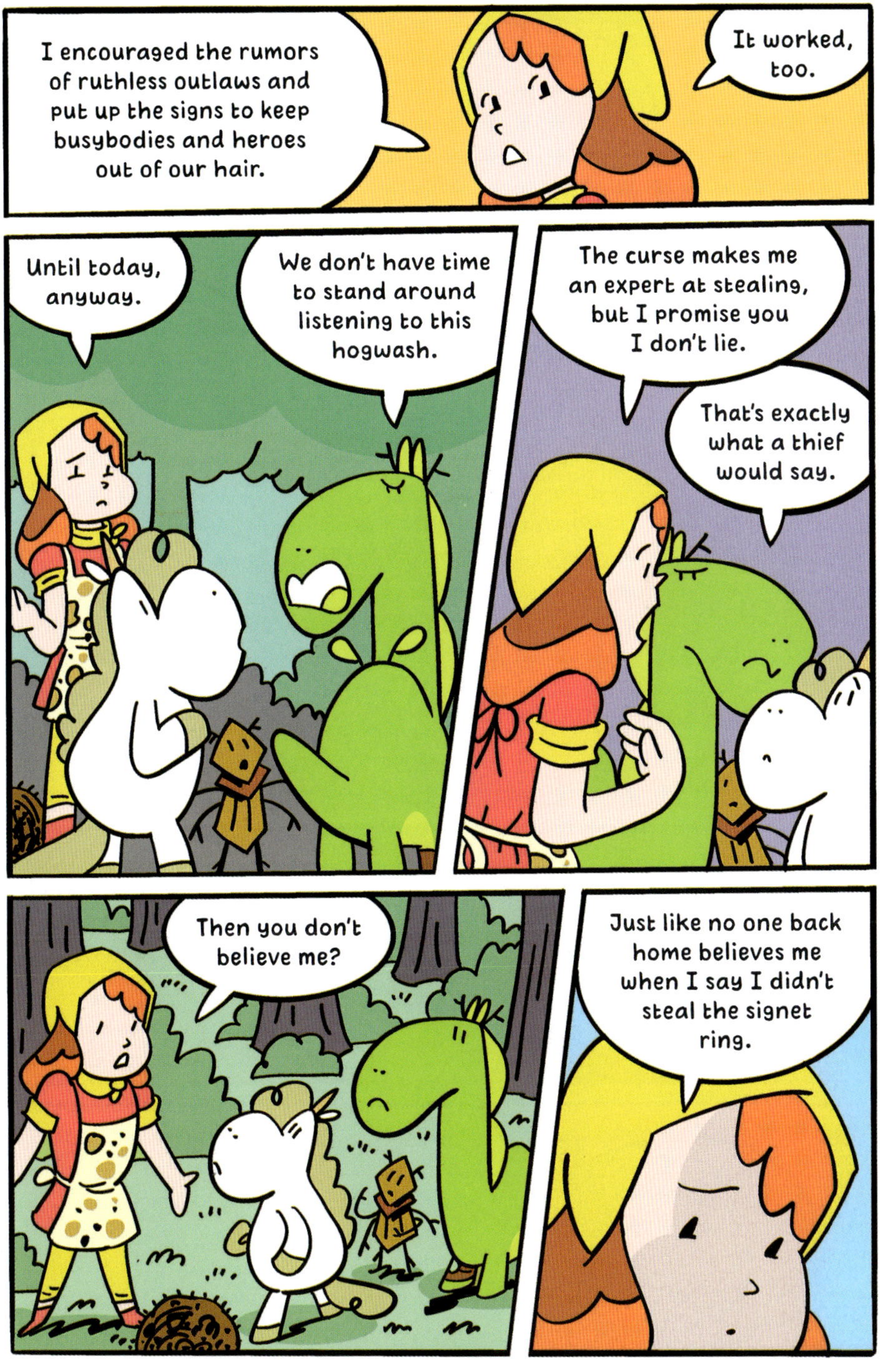
I encouraged the rumors of ruthless outlaws and put up the signs to keep busybodies and heroes out of our hair.
It worked, too.
Until today, anyway.
We don't have time to stand around listening to this hogwash.
The curse makes me an expert at stealing, but I promise you I don't lie.
That's exactly what a thief would say.
Then you don't believe me?
Just like no one back home believes me when I say I didn't steal the signet ring.

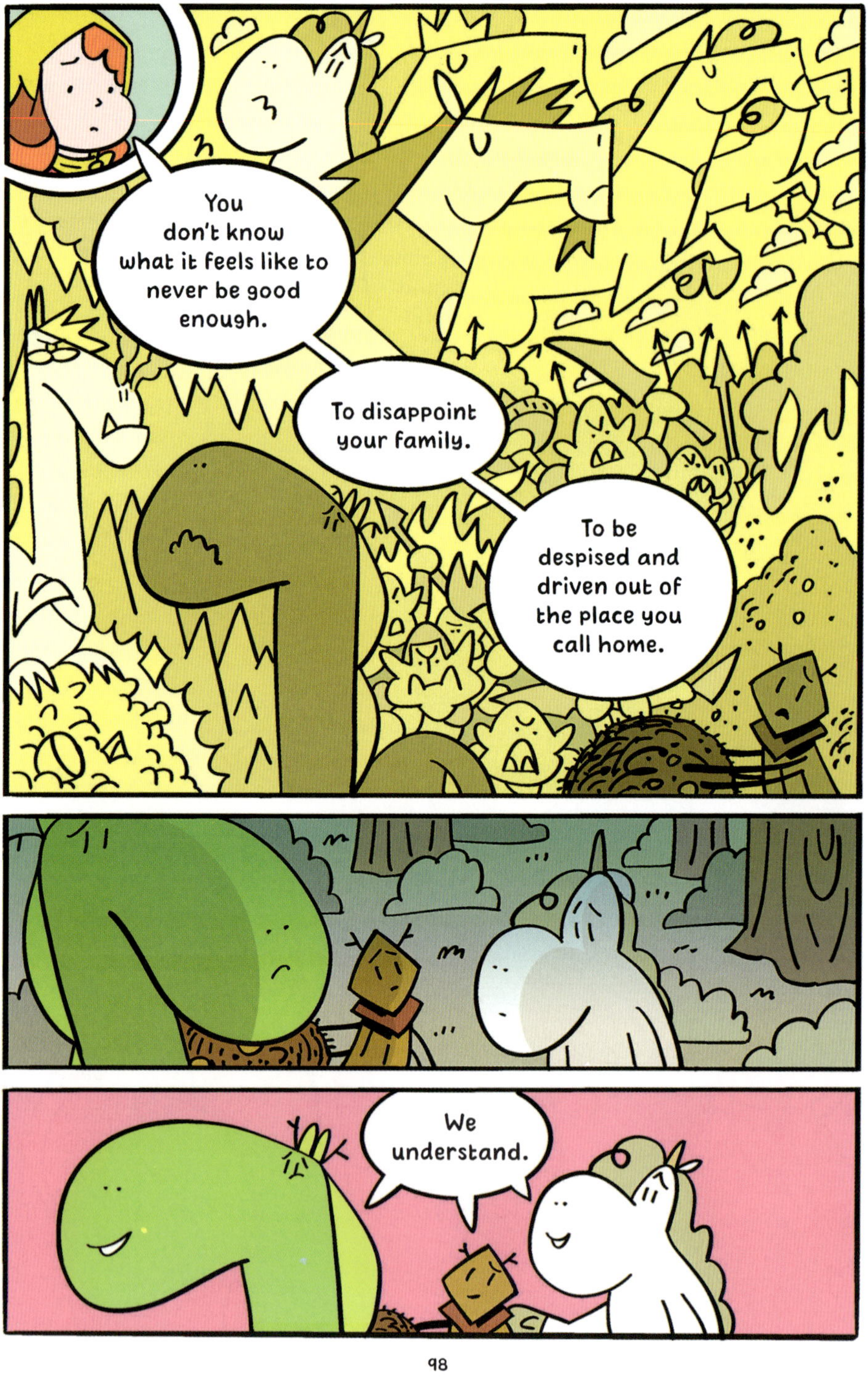
You don't know what it feels like to never be good enough.
To disappoint your family.
To be despised and driven out of the place you call home.
We understand.

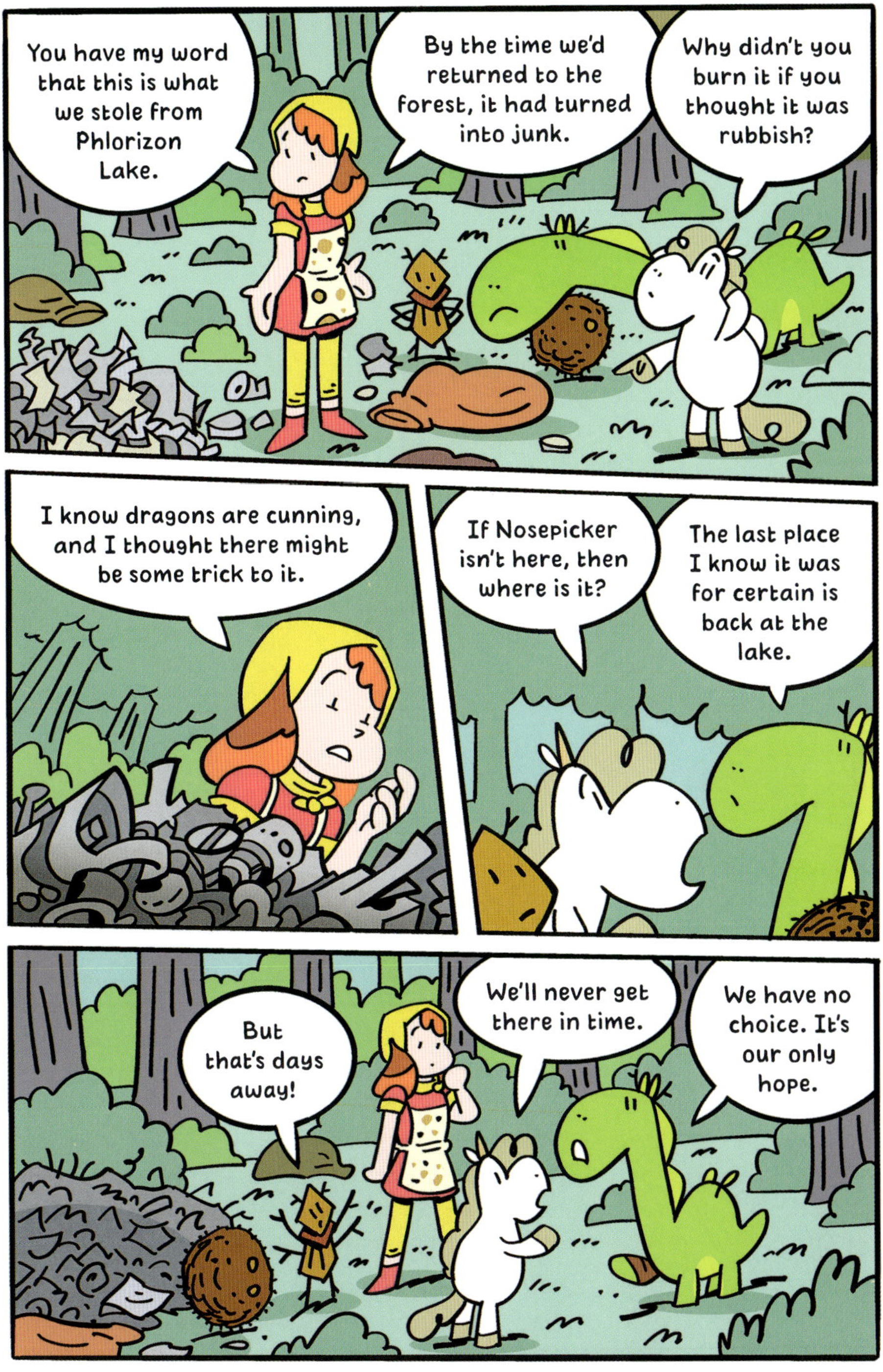
You have my word that this is what we stole from Phlorizon Lake.
By the time we'd returned to the forest, it had turned into junk.
Why didn't you burn it if you thought it was rubbish?
I know dragons are cunning, and I thought there might be some trick to it.
If Nosepicker isn't here, then where is it?
The last place I know it was for certain is back at the lake.
But that's days away!
We'll never get there in time.
We have no choice. It's our only hope.

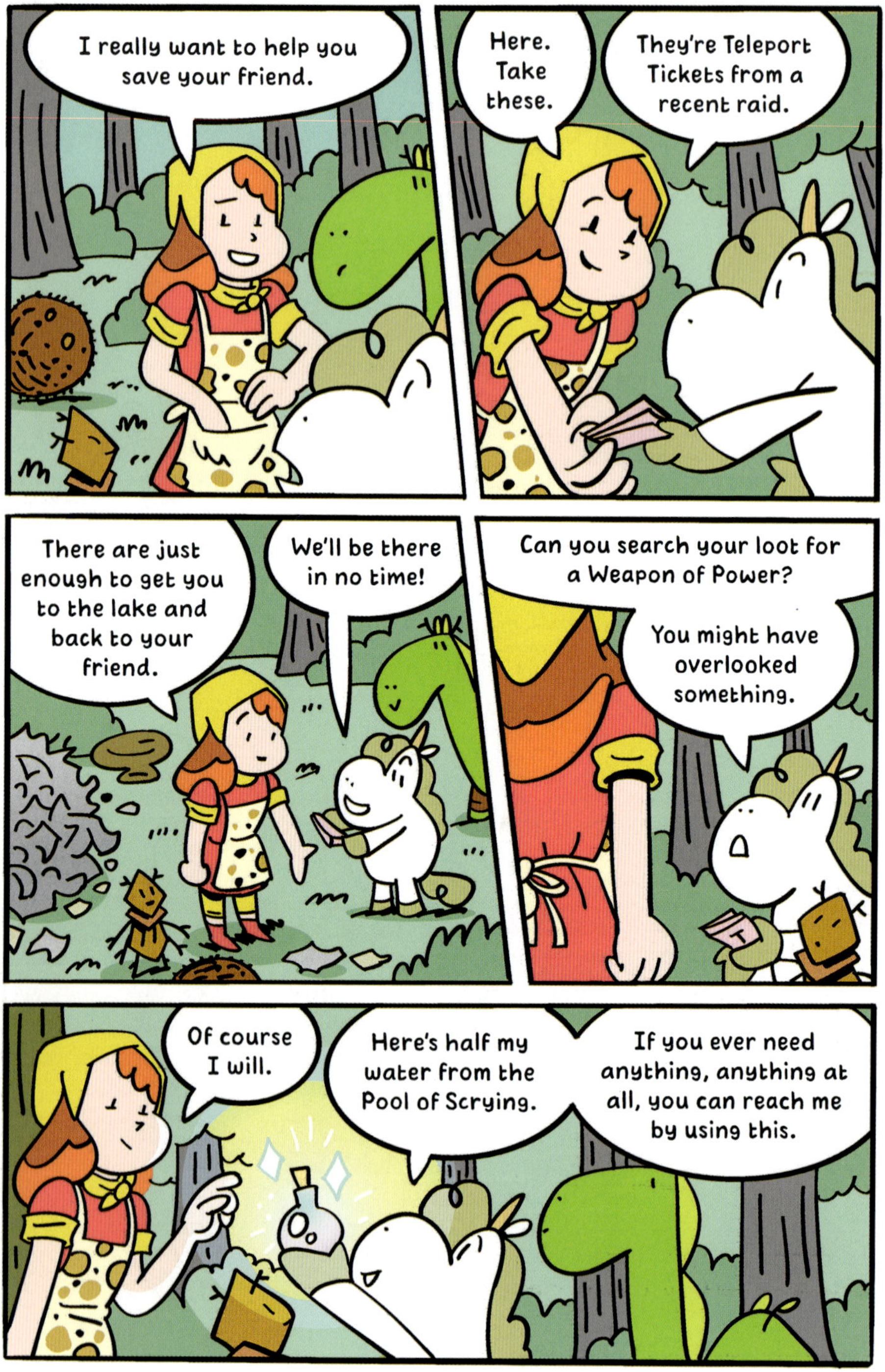
I really want to help you save your friend.
Here. Take these.
They're Teleport Tickets from a recent raid.
There are just enough to get you to the lake and back to your friend.
We'll be there in no time!
Can you search your loot for a Weapon of Power?
You might have overlooked something.
Of course I will.
Here's half my water from the Pool of Scrying.
If you ever need anything, anything at all, you can reach me by using this.

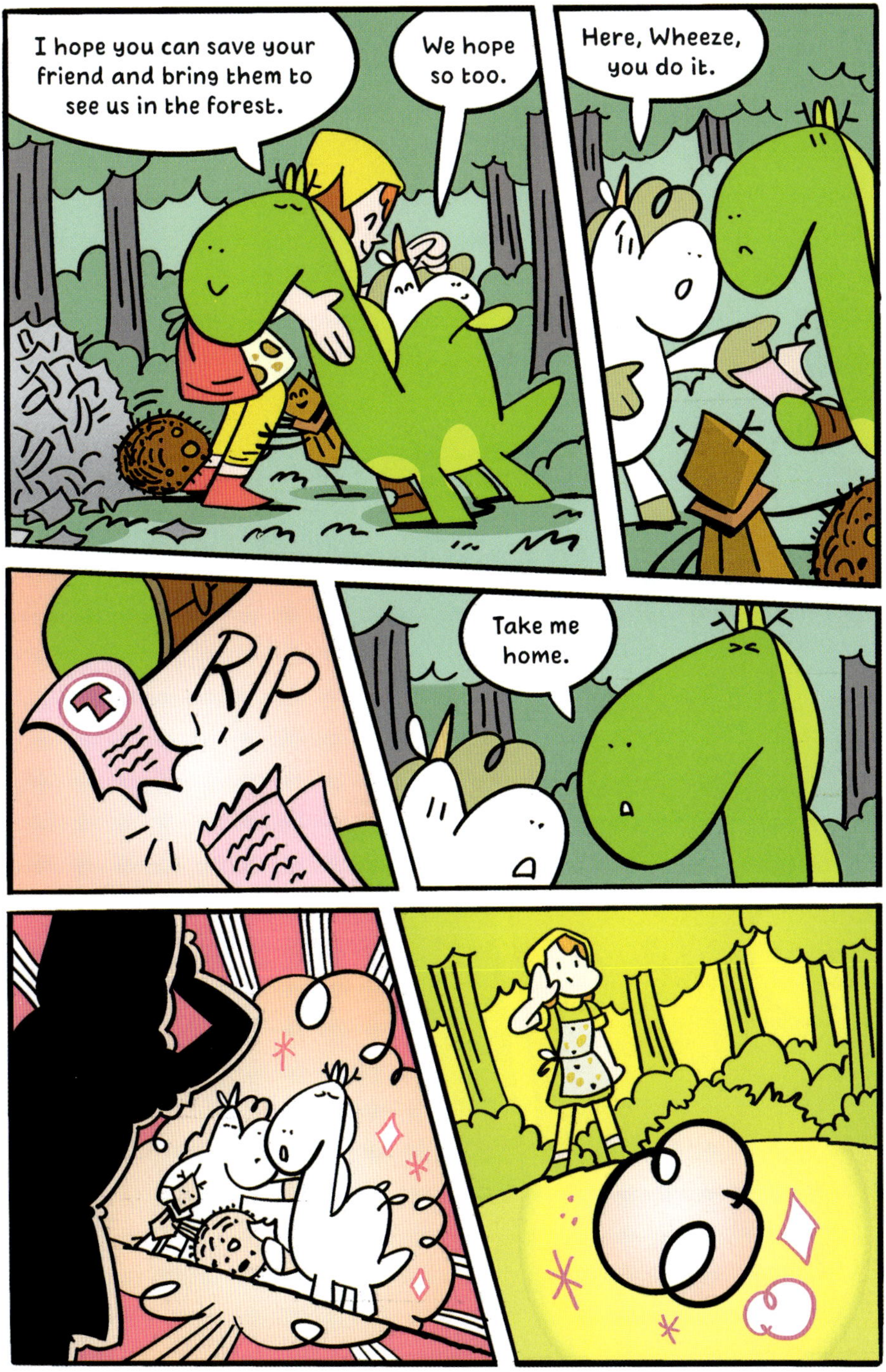
I hope you can save your friend and bring them to see us in the forest.
We hope so too.
Here, Wheeze, you do it.
RIP
Take me home.

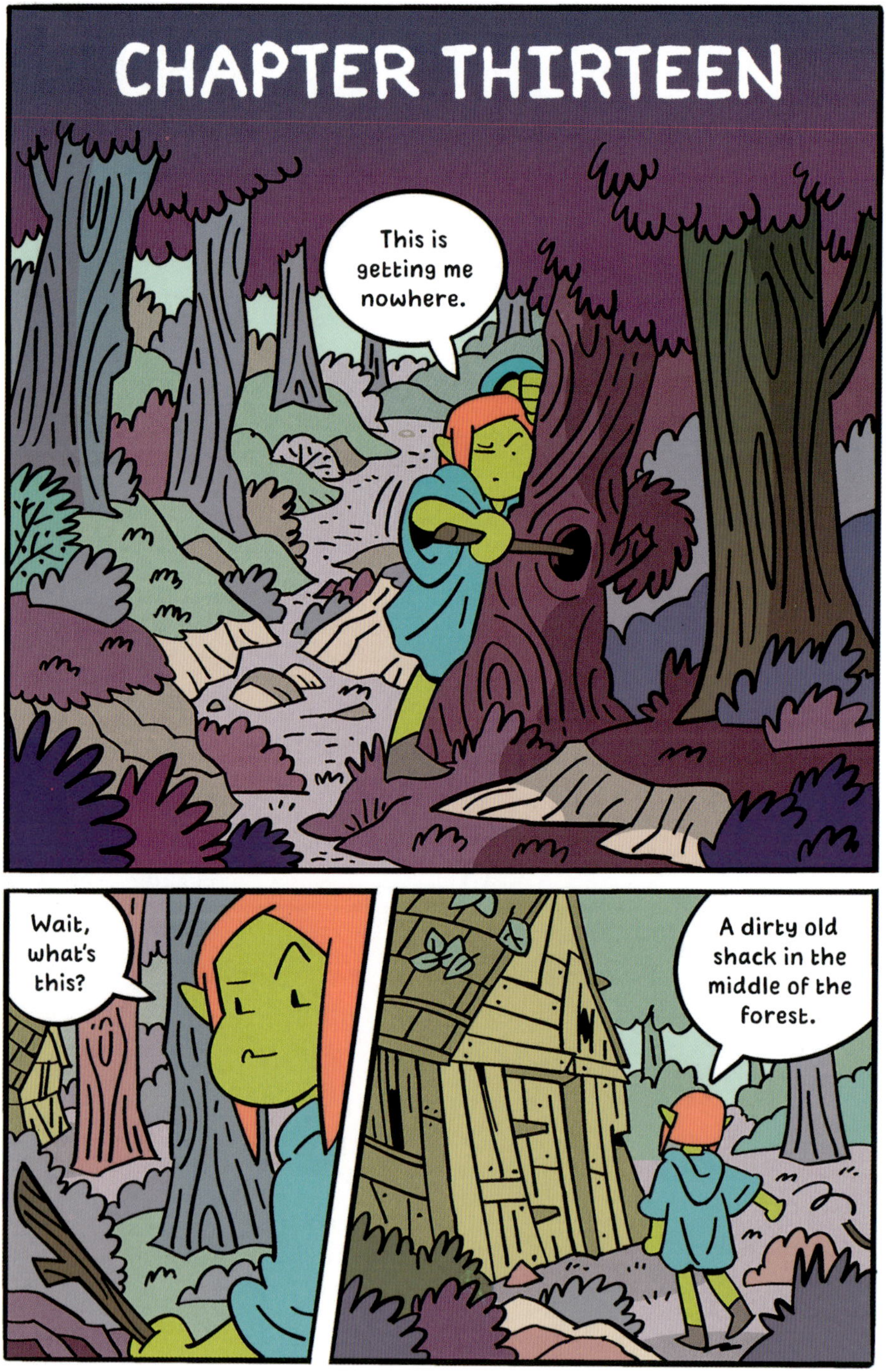
CHAPTER THIRTEEN
This is getting me nowhere.
Wait, what's this?
A dirty old shack in the middle of the forest.

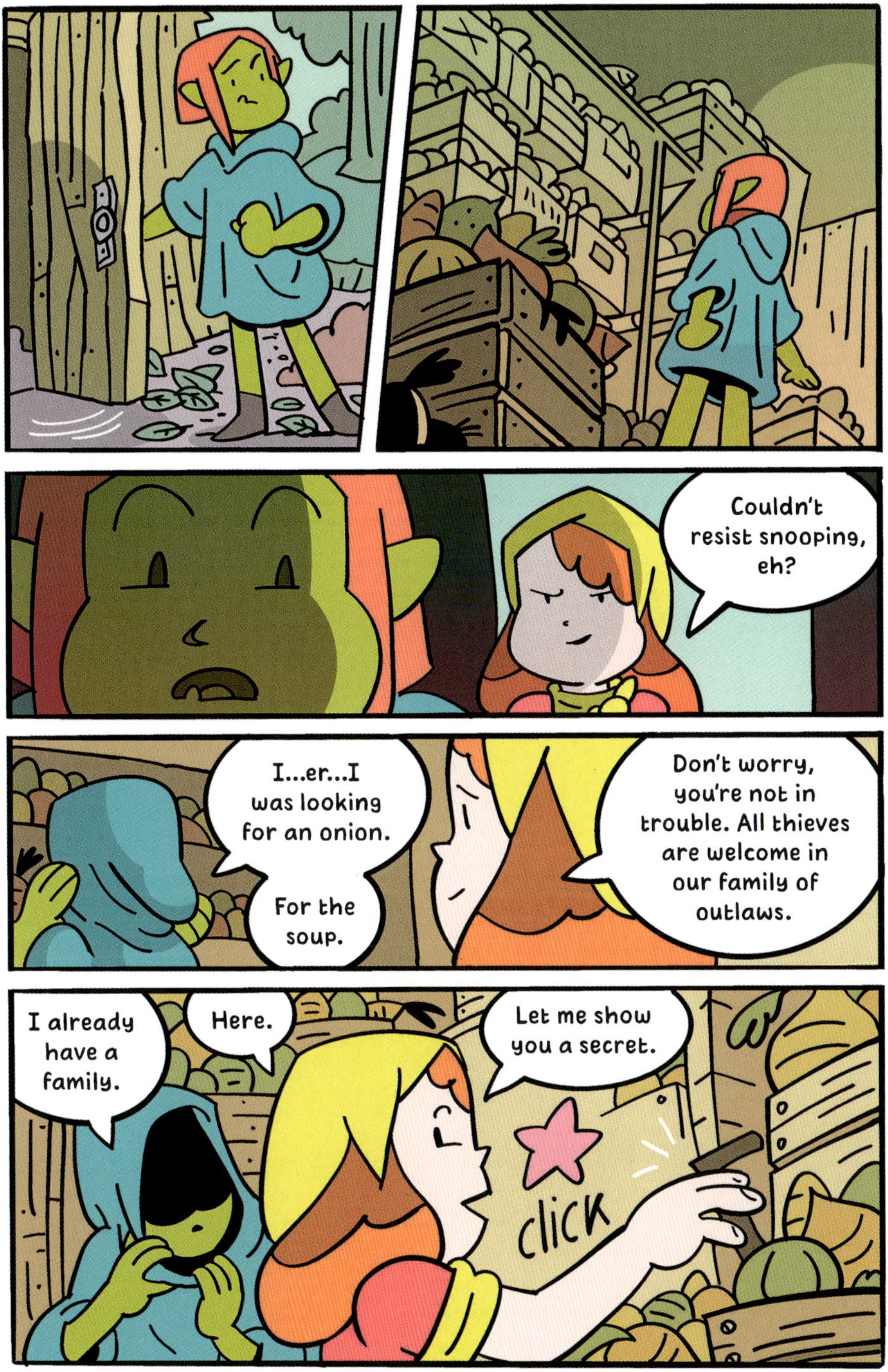
Couldn't resist snooping, eh?
I...er...I was looking for an onion.
For the soup.
Don't worry, you're not in trouble. All thieves are welcome in our family of outlaws.
I already have a family.
Here.
Let me show you a secret.
click

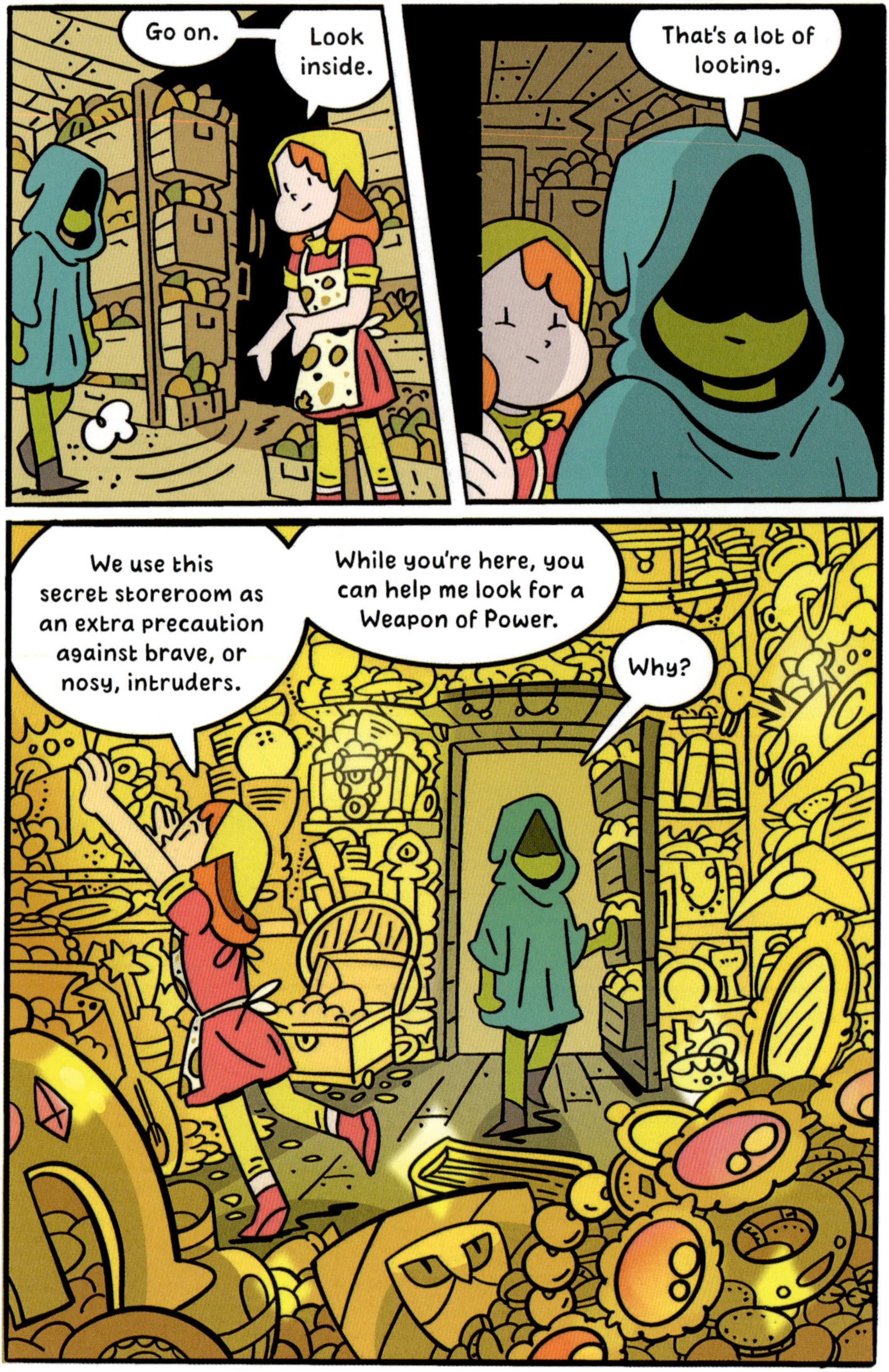
Go on.
Look inside.
That's a lot of looting.
We use this secret storeroom as an extra precaution against brave, or nosy, intruders.
While you're here, you can help me look for a Weapon of Power.
Why?

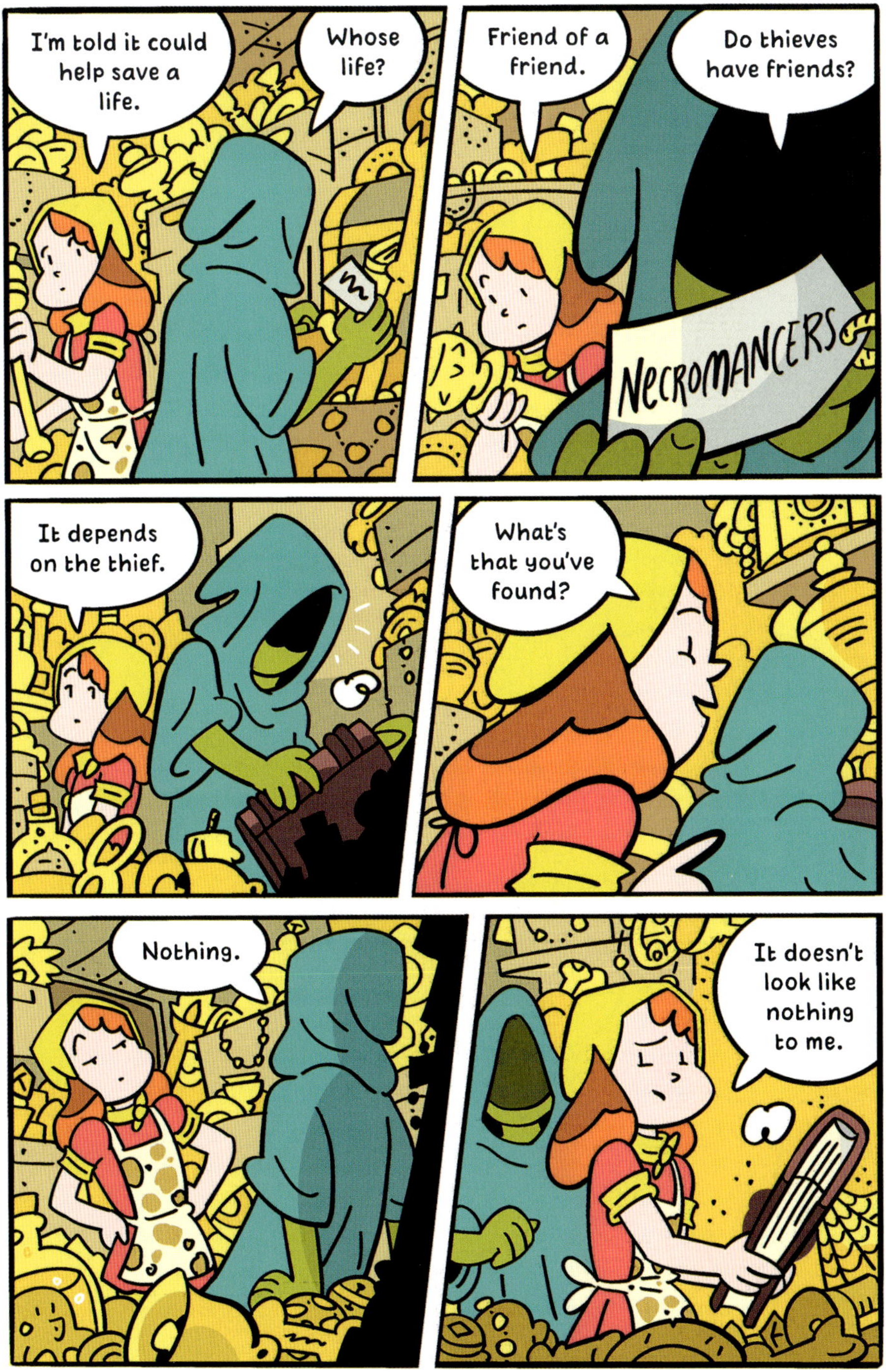
I'm told it could help save a life.
Whose life?
Friend of a friend.
Do thieves have friends?
NECROMANCERS
It depends on the thief.
What's that you've found?
Nothing.
It doesn't look like nothing to me.

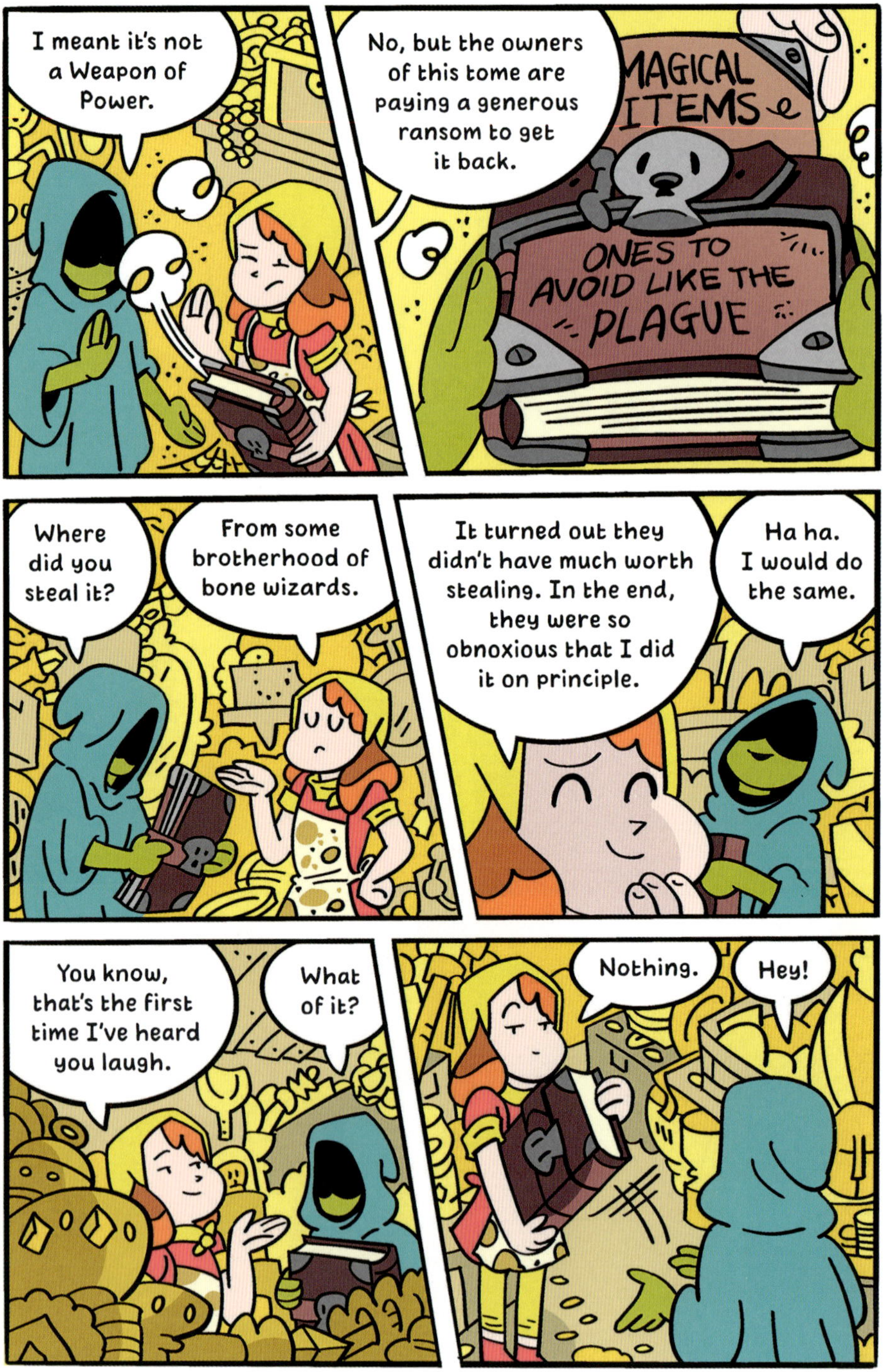
I meant it's not a Weapon of Power.
No, but the owners of this tome are paying a generous ransom to get it back.
MAGICAL ITEMS
ONES TO AVOID LIKE THE PLAGUE
Where did you steal it?
From some brotherhood of bone wizards.
It turned out they didn't have much worth stealing. In the end, they were so obnoxious that I did it on principle.
Ha ha. I would do the same.
You know, that's the first time I've heard you laugh.
What of it?
Nothing.
Hey!

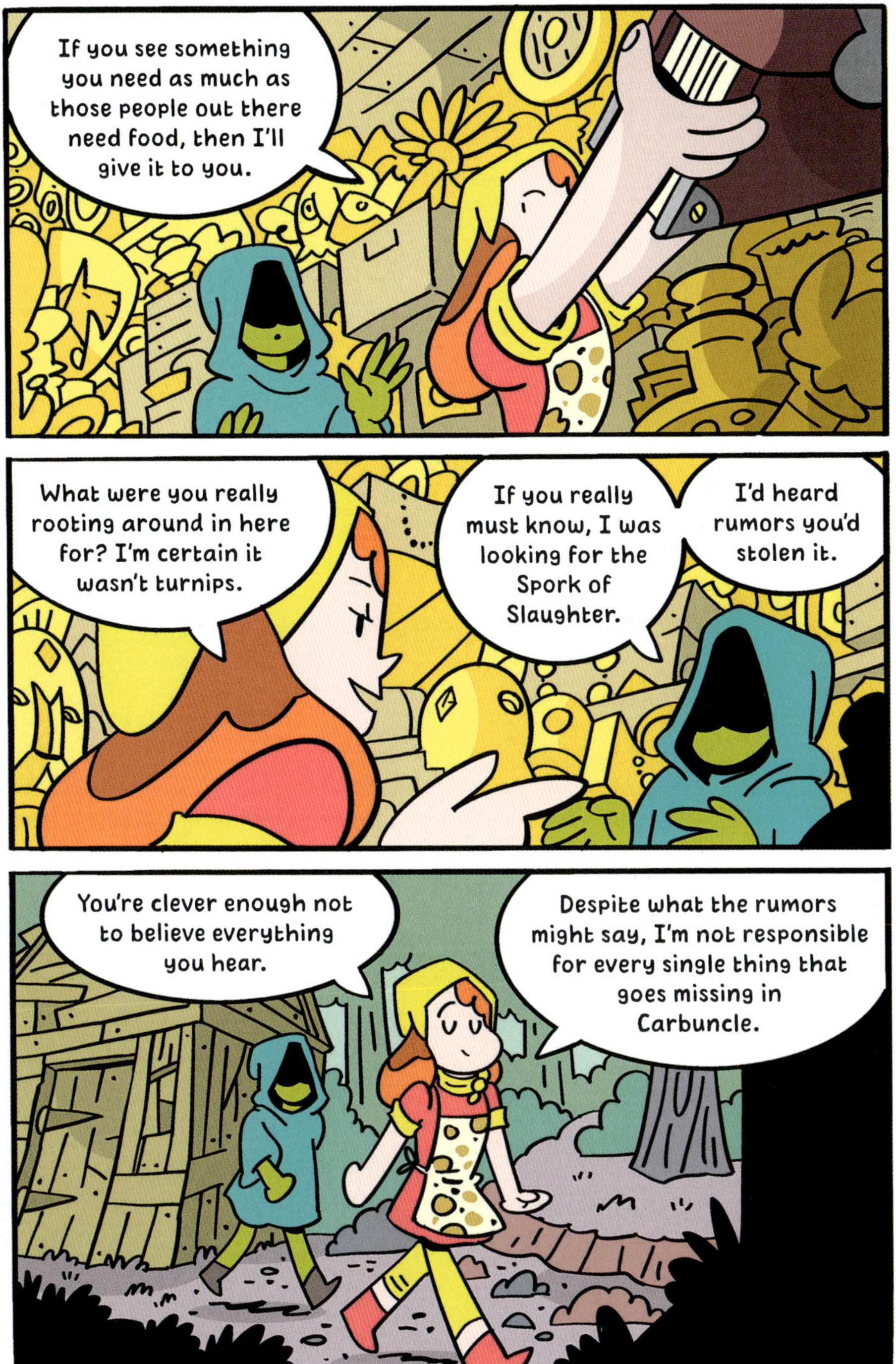
If you see something you need as much as those people out there need food, then I'll give it to you.
What were you really rooting around in here for? I'm certain it wasn't turnips.
If you really must know, I was looking for the Spork of Slaughter.
I'd heard rumors you'd stolen it.
You're clever enough not to believe everything you hear.
Despite what the rumors might say, I'm not responsible for every single thing that goes missing in Carbuncle.

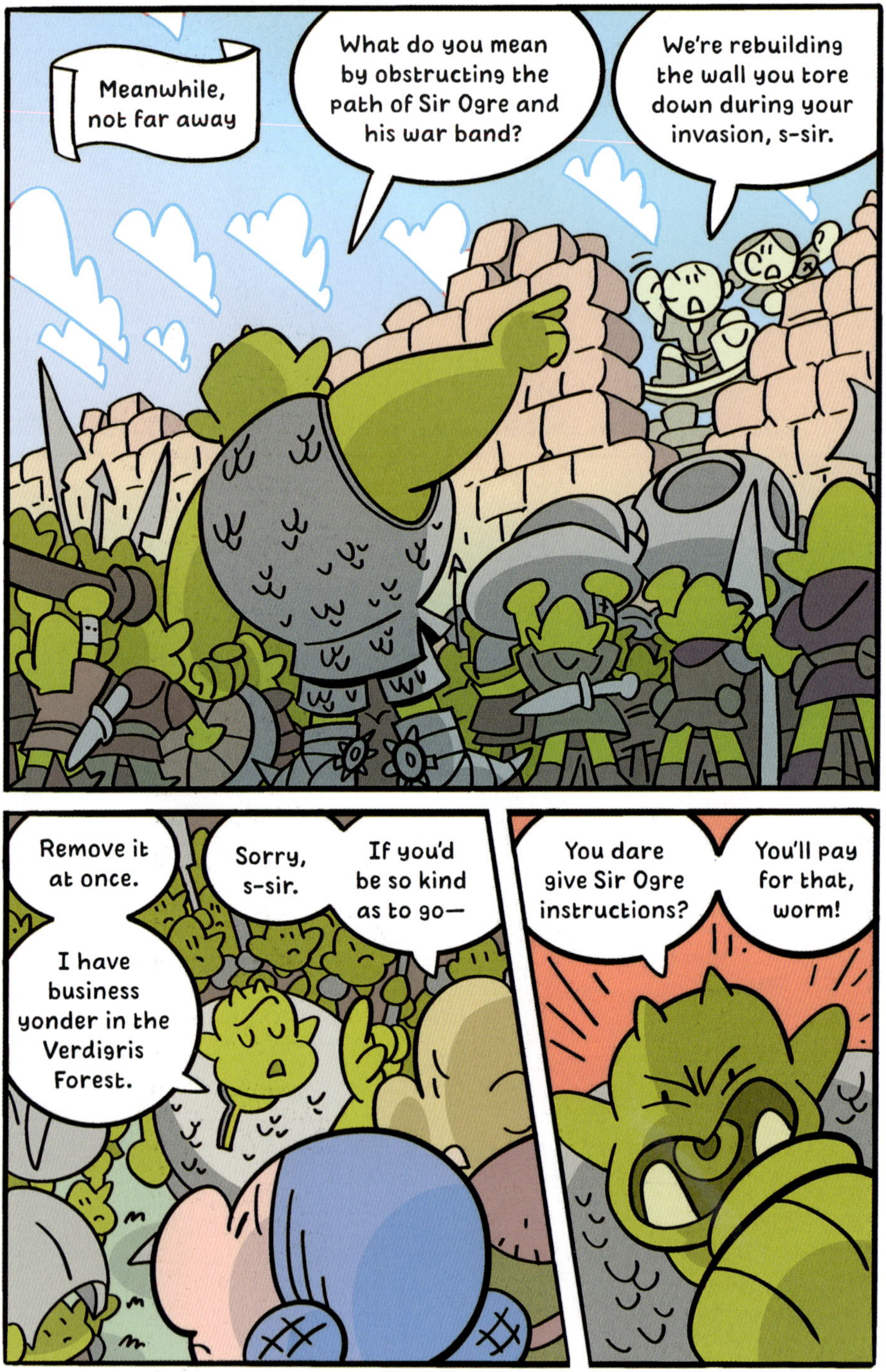
Meanwhile, not far away
What do you mean by obstructing the path of Sir Ogre and his war band?
We're rebuilding the wall you tore down during your invasion, s-sir.
Remove it at once.
I have business yonder in the Verdigris Forest.
Sorry, s-sir.
If you'd be so kind as to go—
You dare give Sir Ogre instructions?
You'll pay for that, worm!

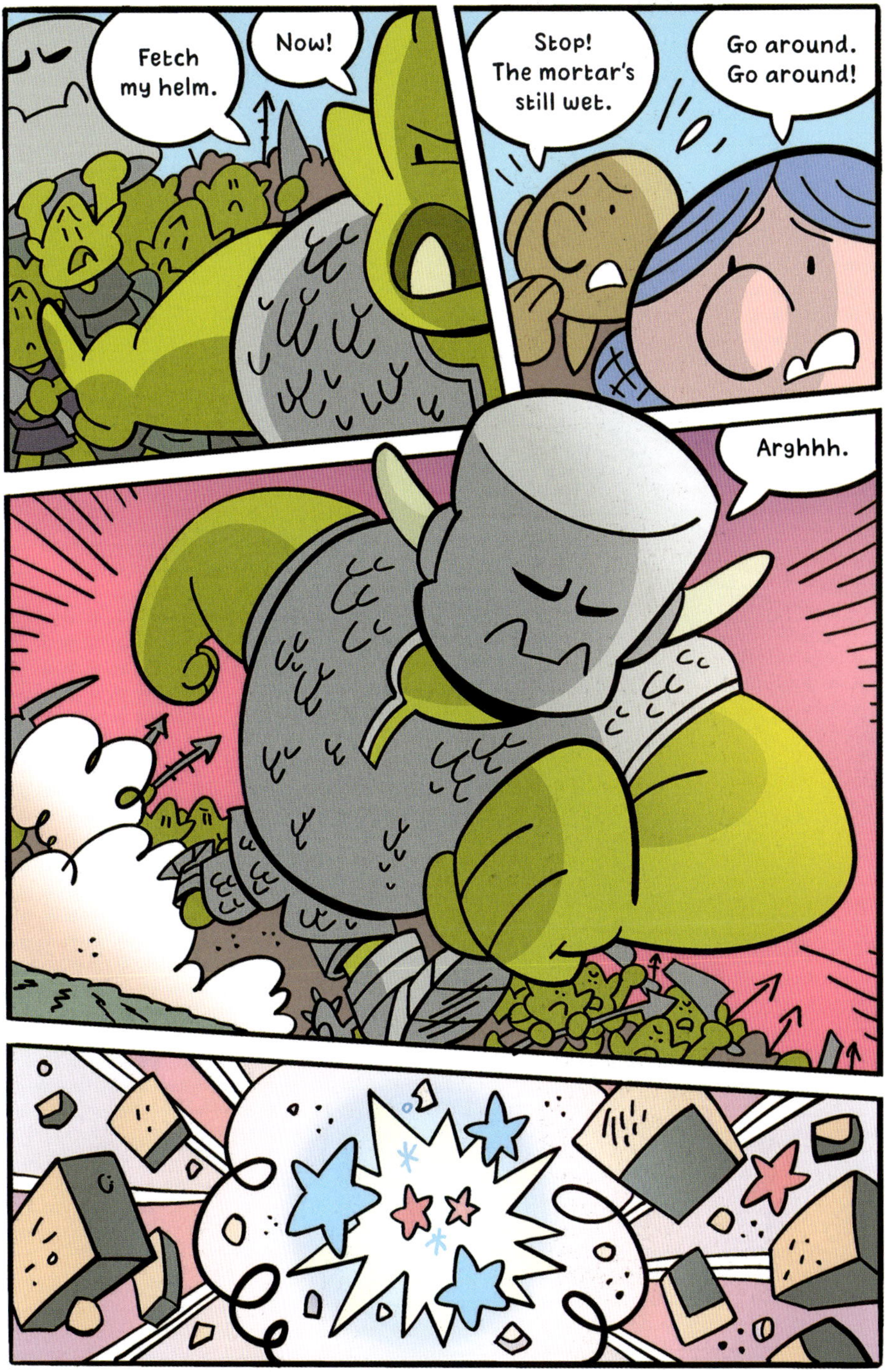
Fetch my helm.
Now!
Stop! The mortar's still wet.
Go around. Go around!
Arghhh.

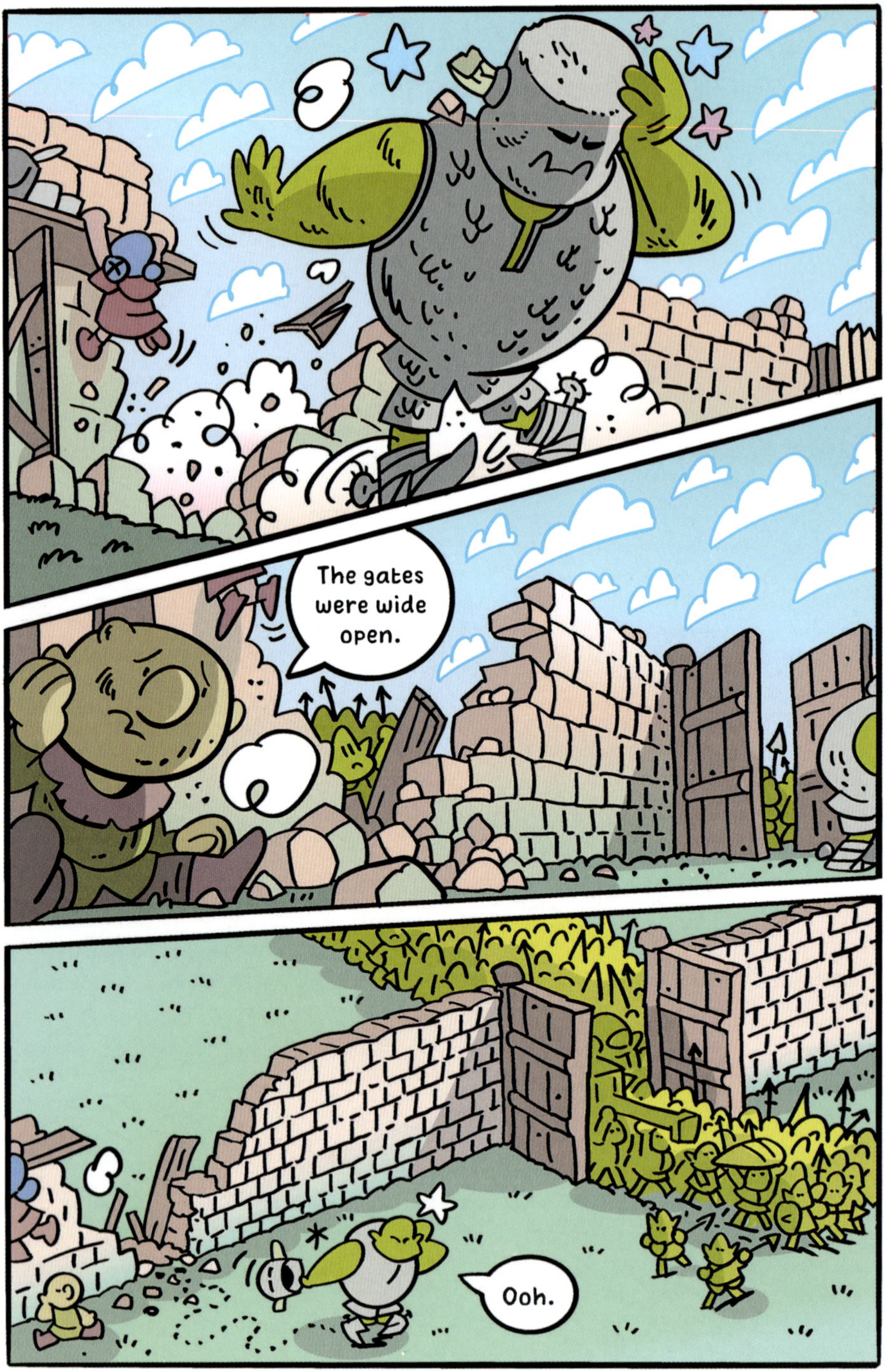
The gates were wide open.
Ooh.

CHAPTER FOURTEEN

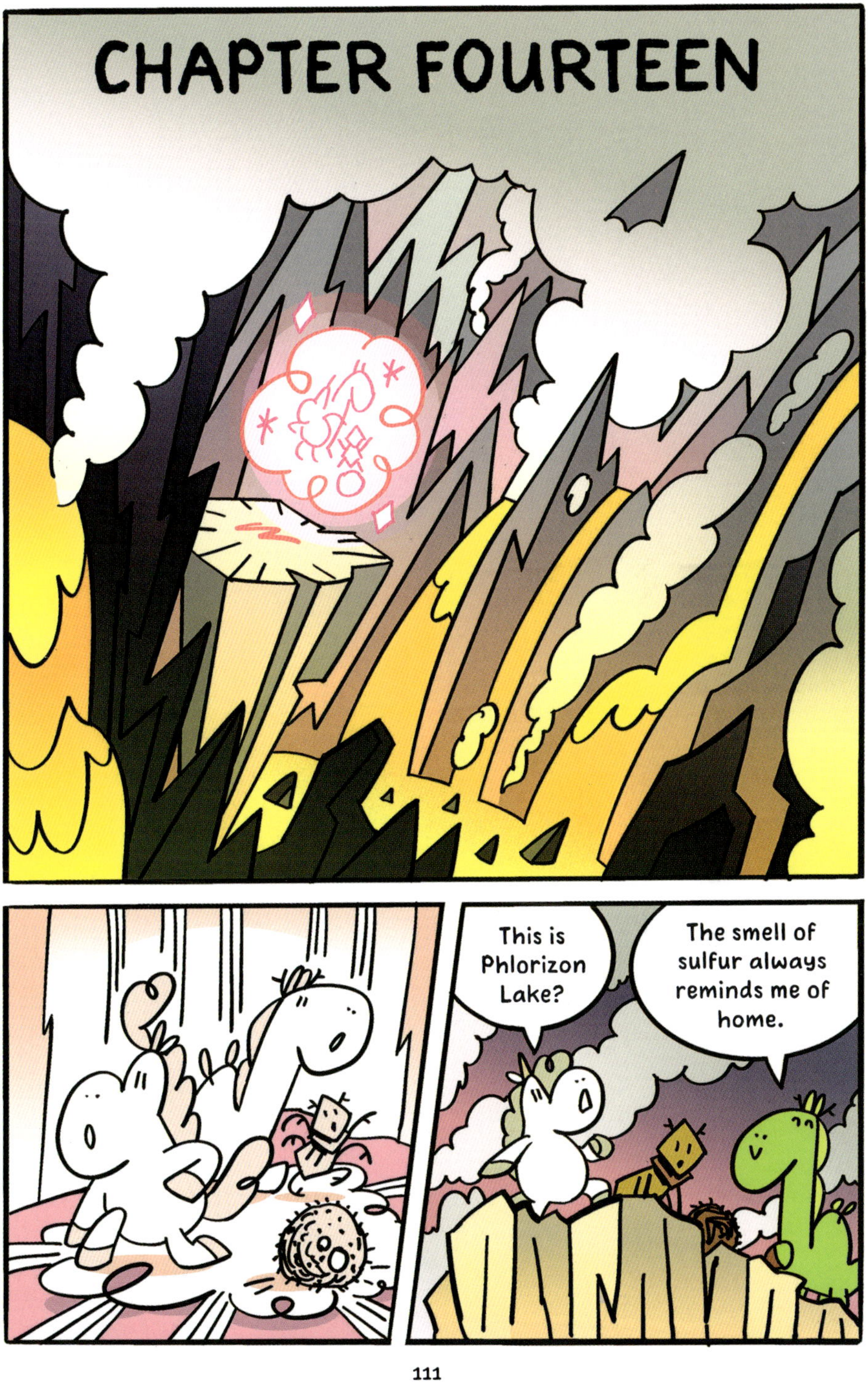
This is Phlorizon Lake?
The smell of sulfur always reminds me of home.

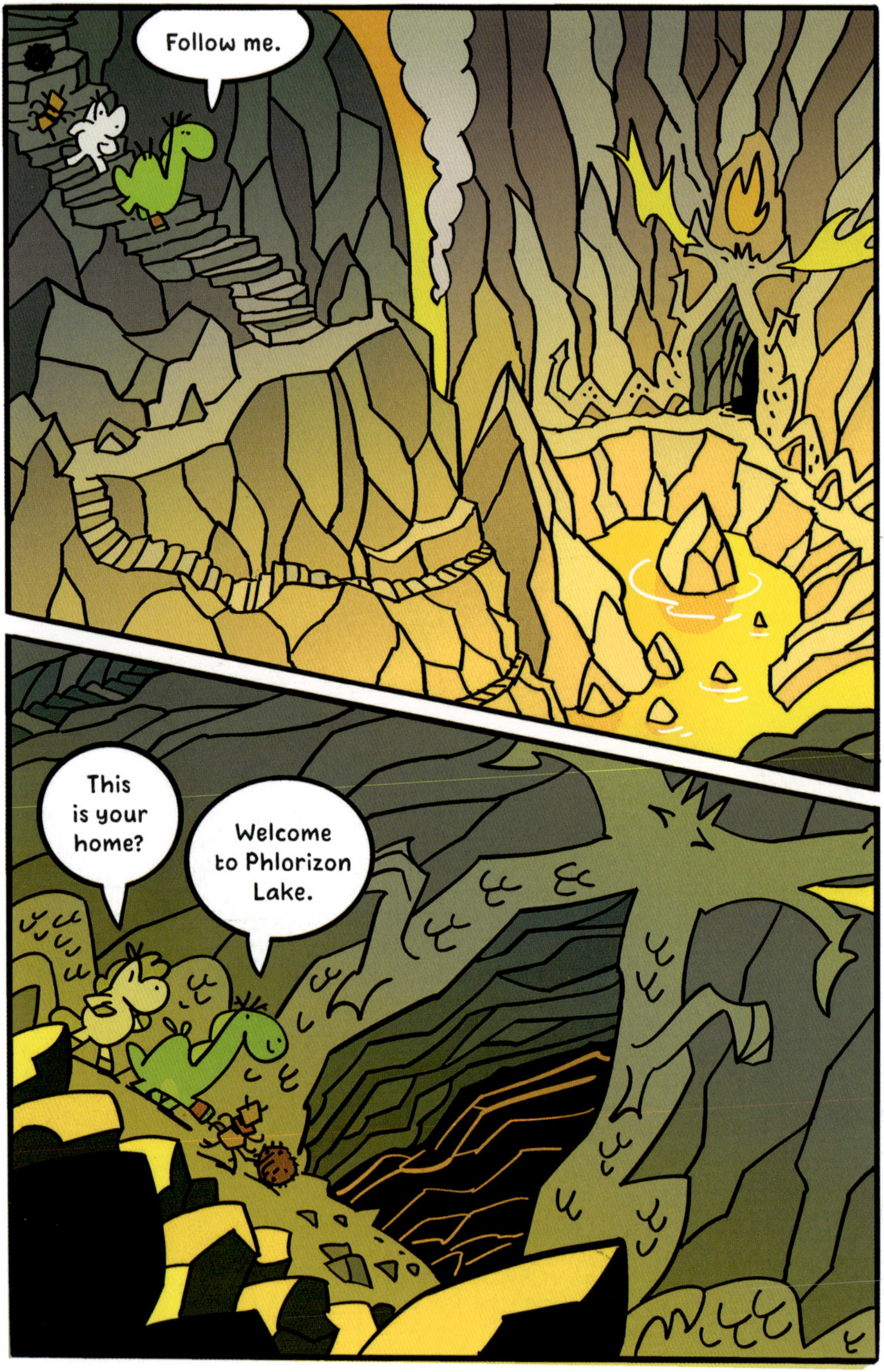
Follow me.
This is your home?
Welcome to Phlorizon Lake.

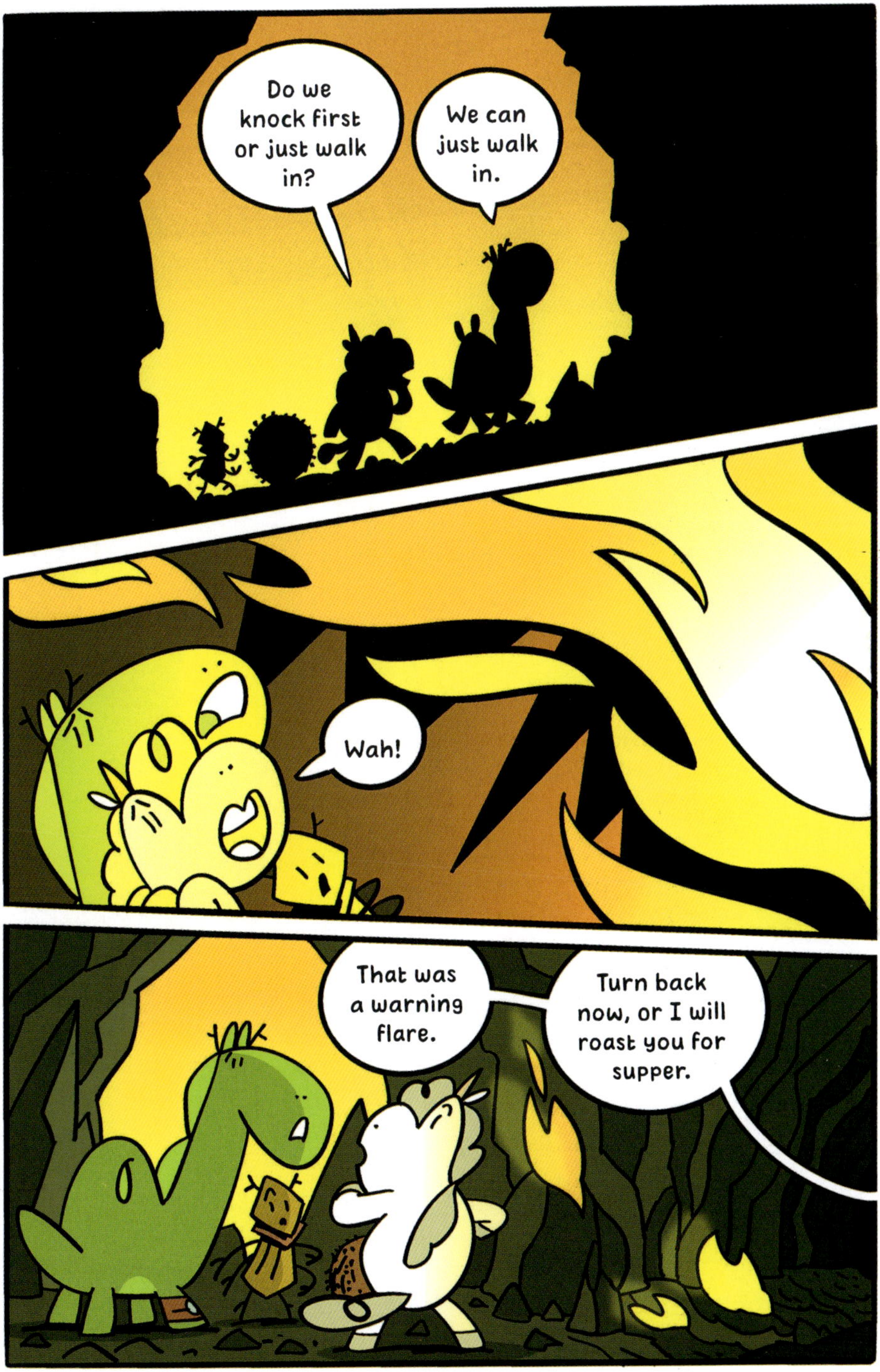
Do we knock first or just walk in?
We can just walk in.
Wah!
That was a warning flare.
Turn back now, or I will roast you for supper.

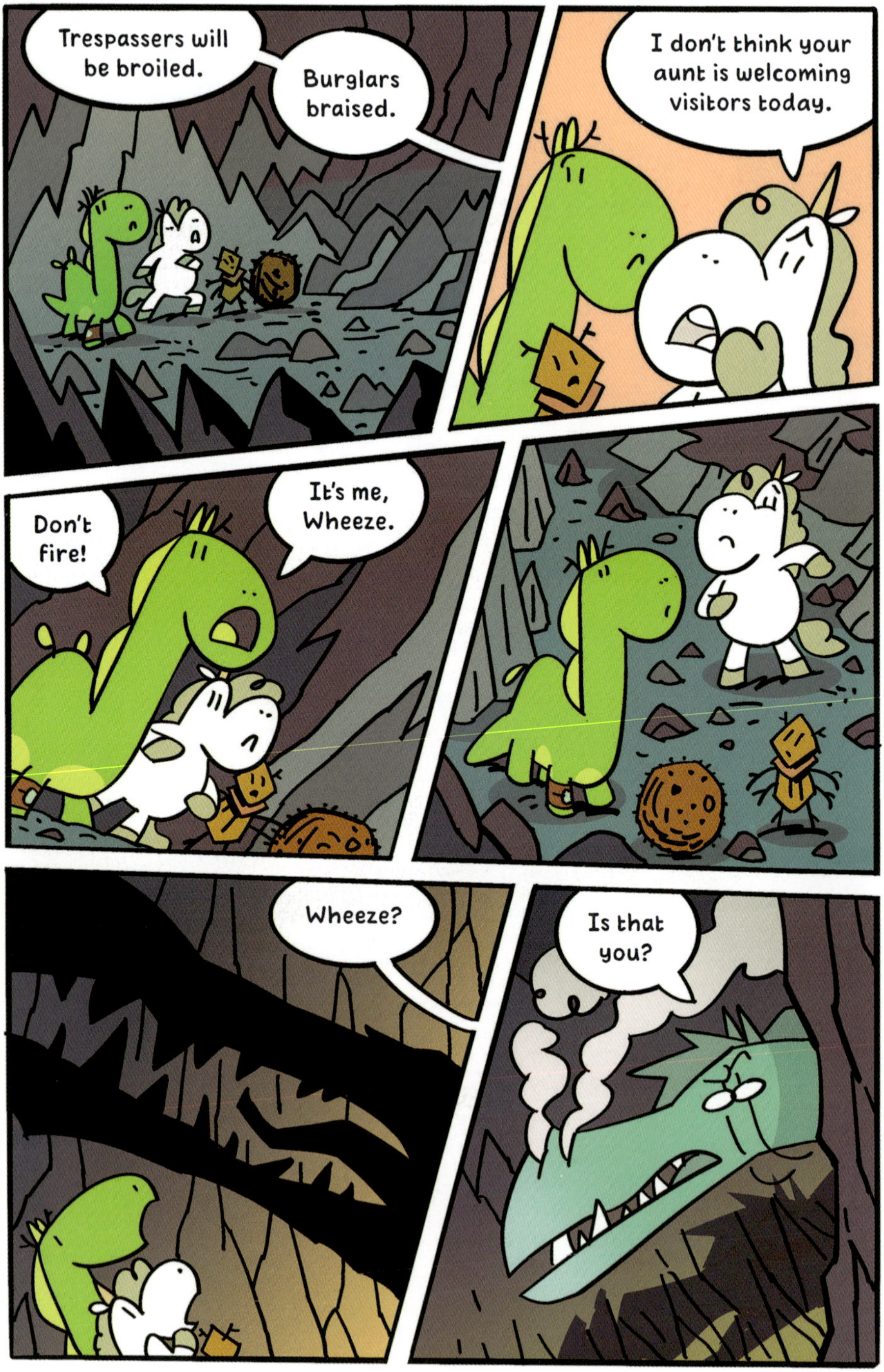
Trespassers will be broiled.
Burglars braised.
I don't think your aunt is welcoming visitors today.
Don't fire!
It's me, Wheeze.
Wheeze?
Is that you?

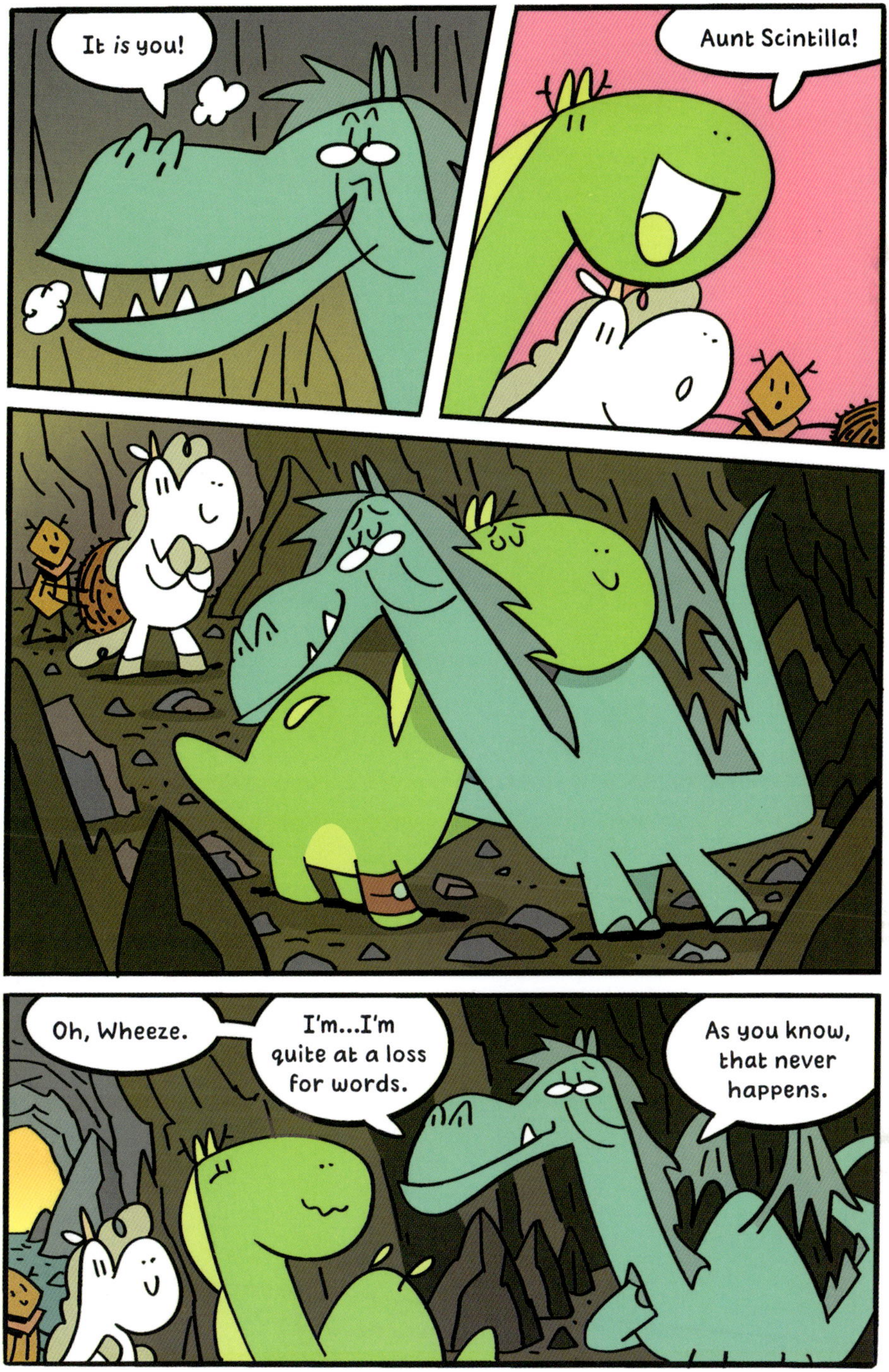
It *is* you!
Aunt Scintilla!
Oh, Wheeze.
I'm...I'm quite at a loss for words.
As you know, that never happens.

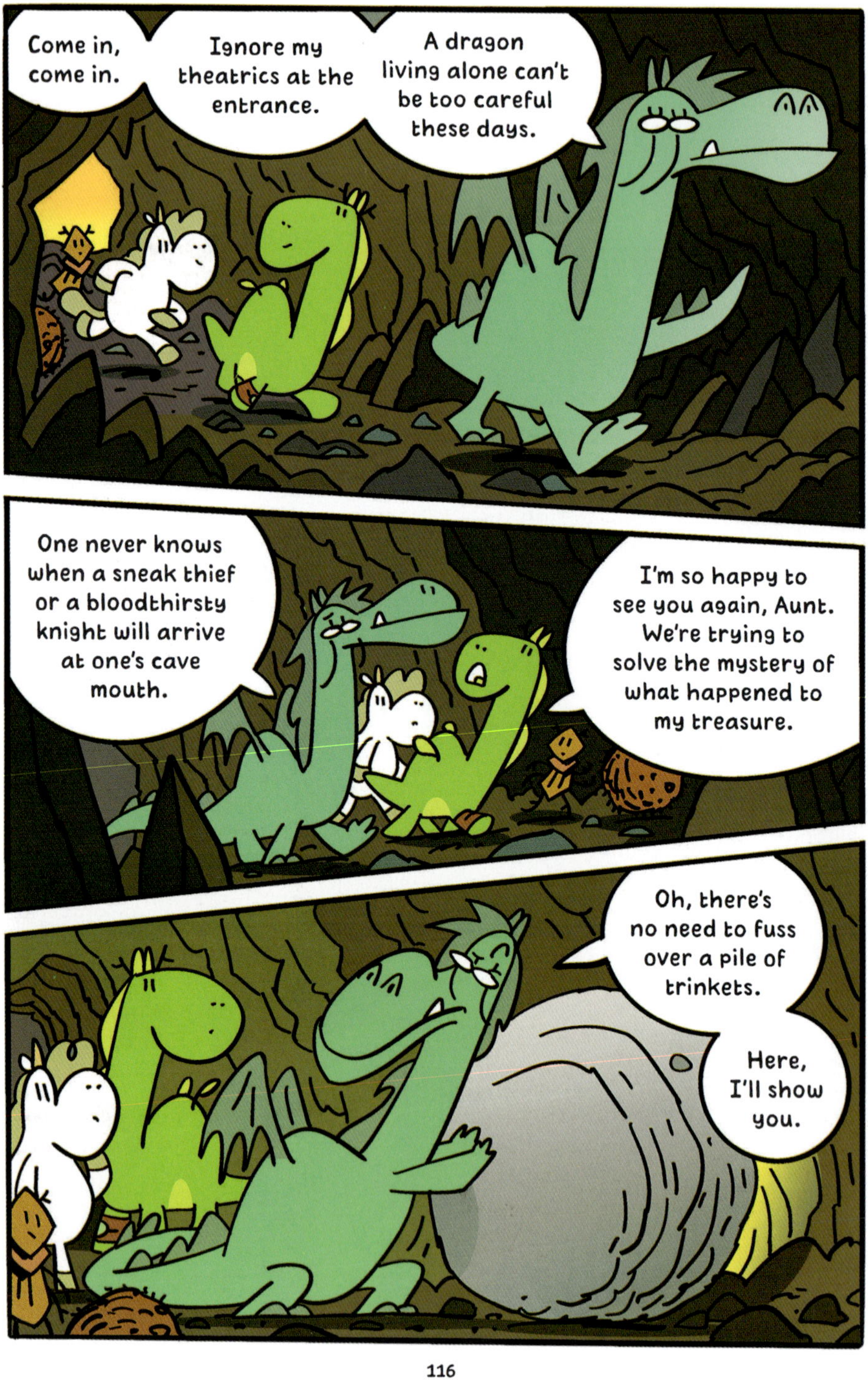

Come in, come in.
Ignore my theatrics at the entrance.
A dragon living alone can't be too careful these days.
One never knows when a sneak thief or a bloodthirsty knight will arrive at one's cave mouth.
I'm so happy to see you again, Aunt. We're trying to solve the mystery of what happened to my treasure.
Oh, there's no need to fuss over a pile of trinkets.
Here, I'll show you.

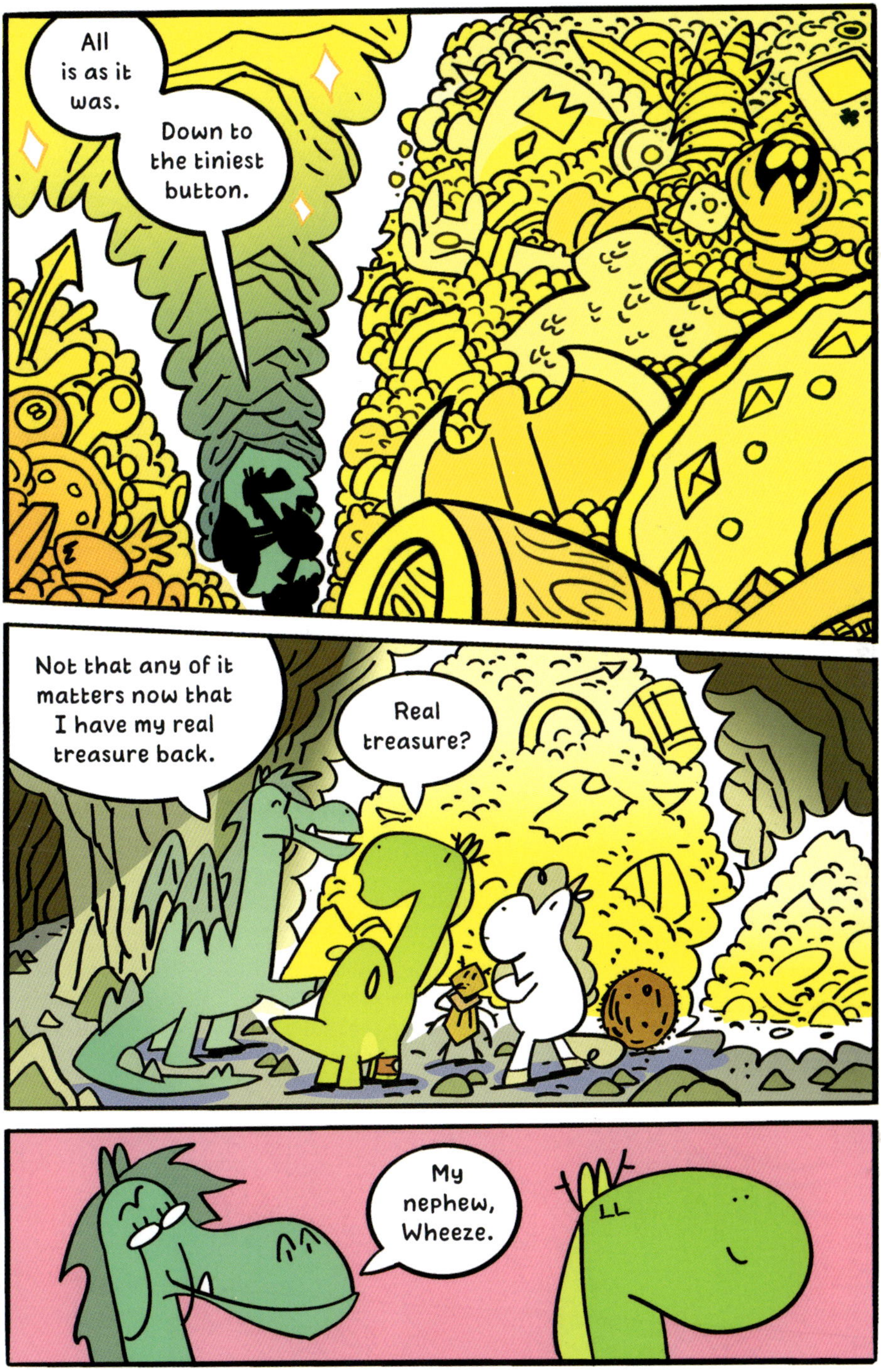
All is as it was.
Down to the tiniest button.
Not that any of it matters now that I have my real treasure back.
Real treasure?
My nephew, Wheeze.

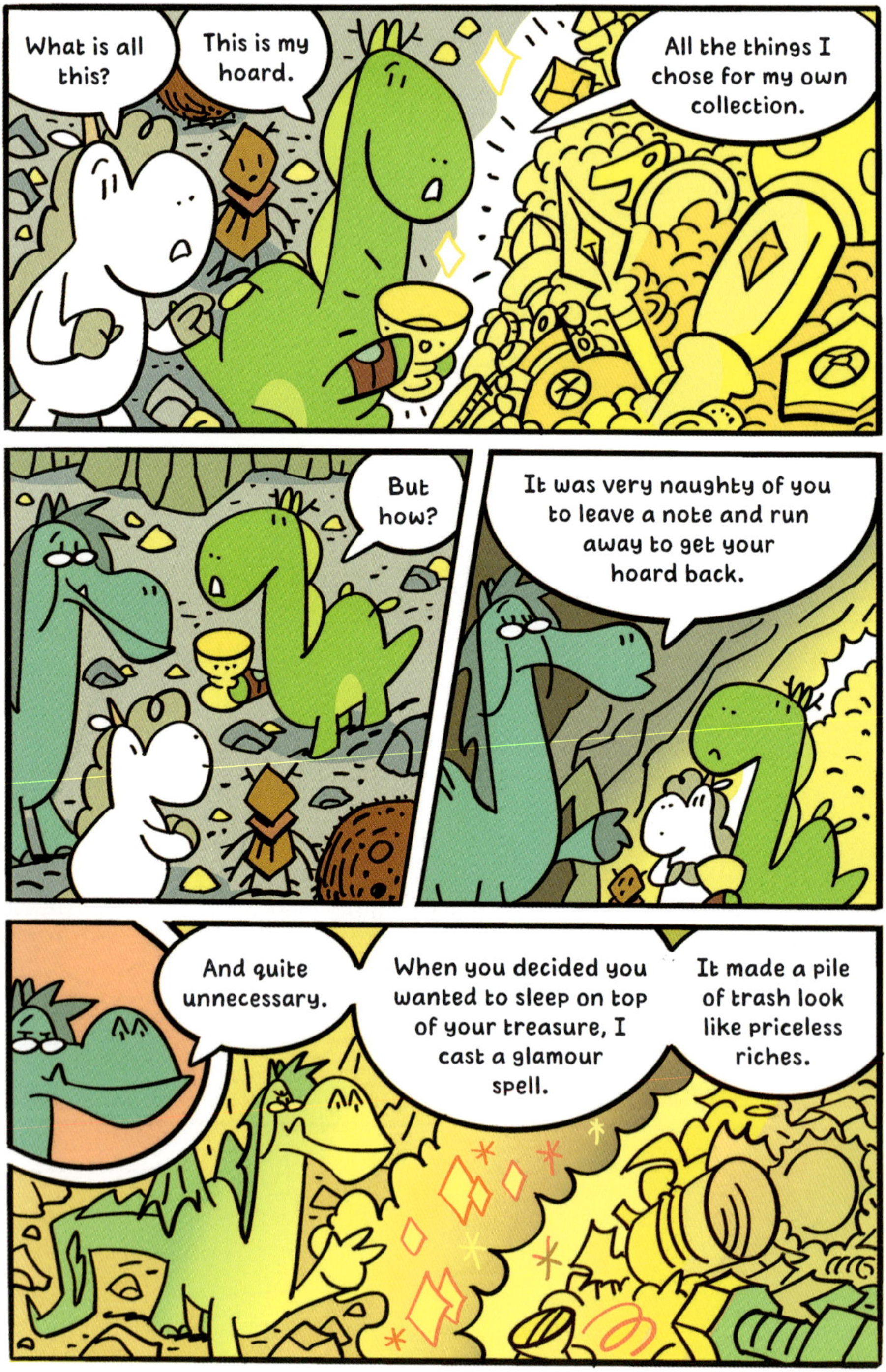
What is all this?
This is my hoard.
All the things I chose for my own collection.
But how?
It was very naughty of you to leave a note and run away to get your hoard back.
And quite unnecessary.
When you decided you wanted to sleep on top of your treasure, I cast a glamour spell.
It made a pile of trash look like priceless riches.

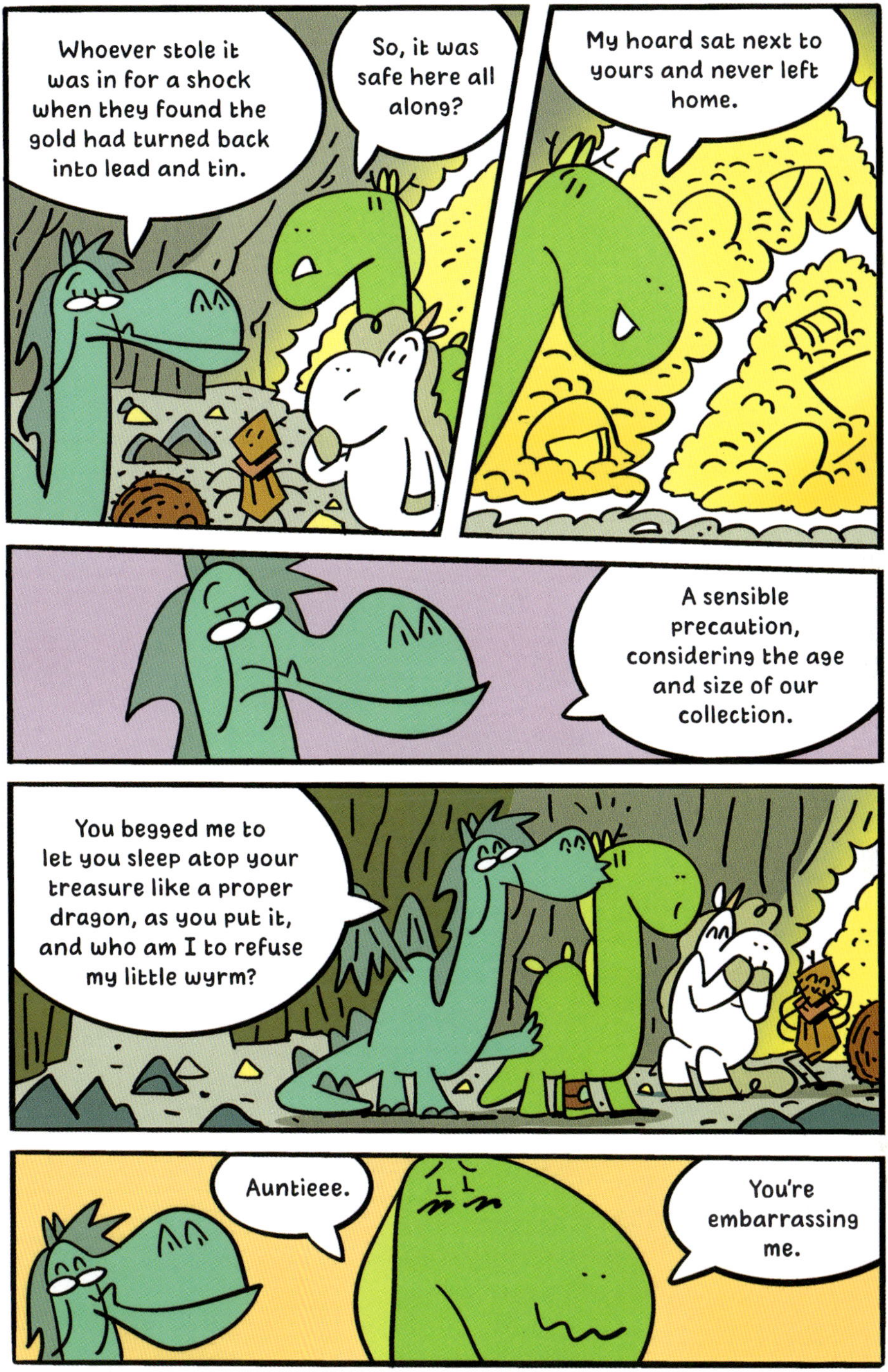

Whoever stole it was in for a shock when they found the gold had turned back into lead and tin.
So, it was safe here all along?
My hoard sat next to yours and never left home.
A sensible precaution, considering the age and size of our collection.
You begged me to let you sleep atop your treasure like a proper dragon, as you put it, and who am I to refuse my little wyrm?
Auntieee.
You're embarrassing me.

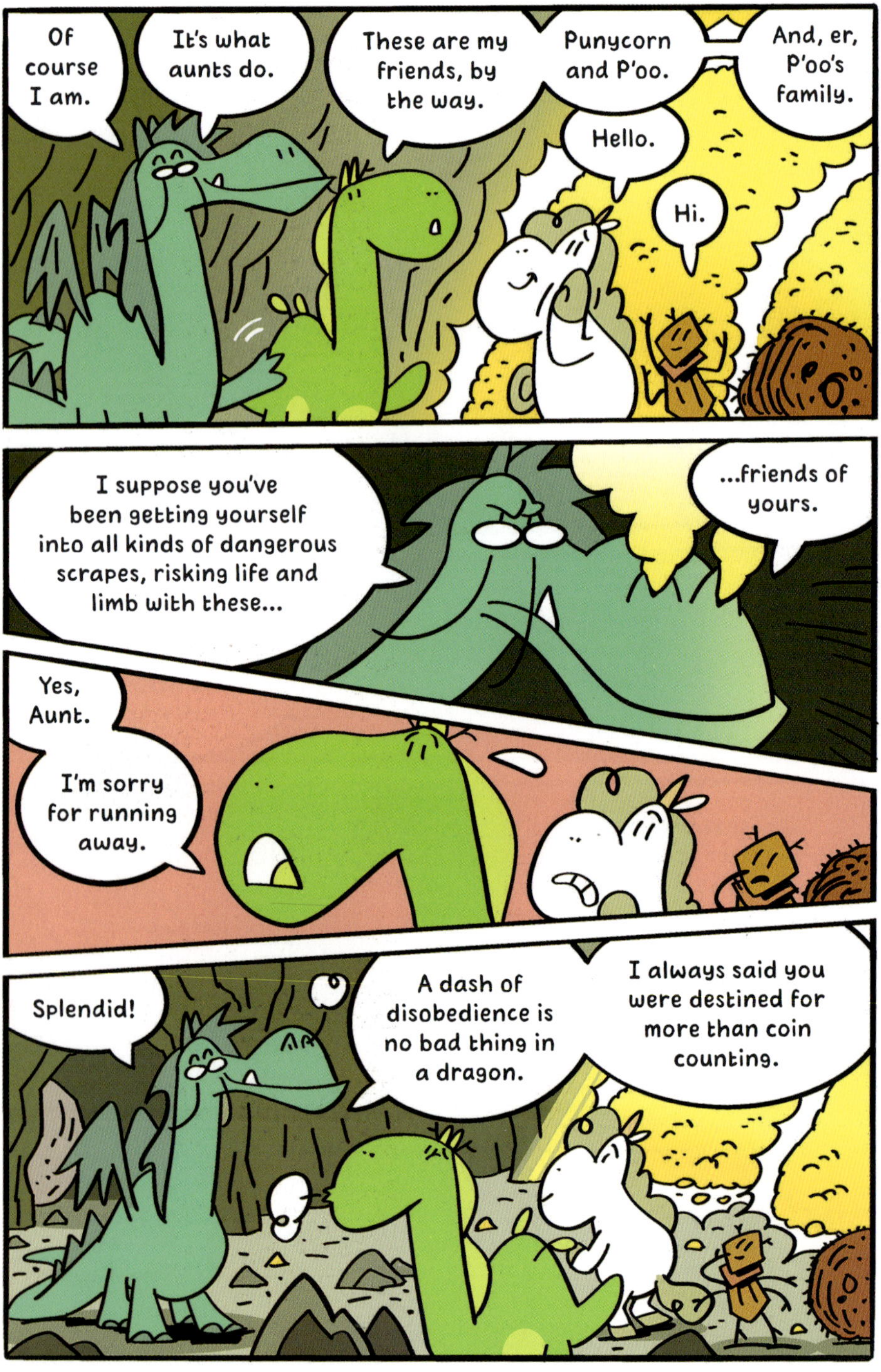

Of course I am.
It's what aunts do.
These are my friends, by the way.
Punycorn and P'oo.
And, er, P'oo's family.
Hello.
Hi.
I suppose you've been getting yourself into all kinds of dangerous scrapes, risking life and limb with these...
...friends of yours.
Yes, Aunt.
I'm sorry for running away.
Splendid!
A dash of disobedience is no bad thing in a dragon.
I always said you were destined for more than coin counting.

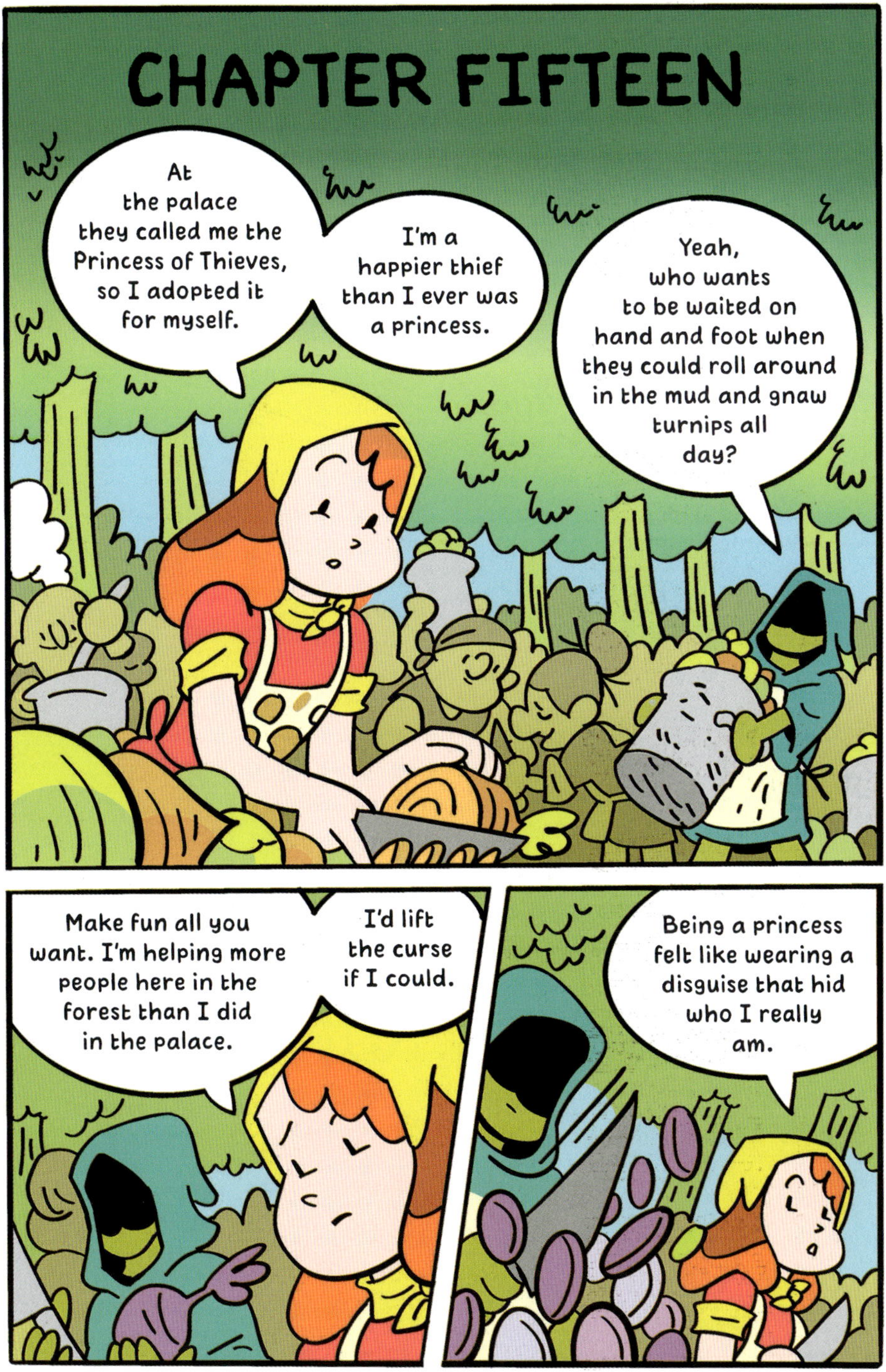
CHAPTER FIFTEEN
At the palace they called me the Princess of Thieves, so I adopted it for myself.
I'm a happier thief than I ever was a princess.
Yeah, who wants to be waited on hand and foot when they could roll around in the mud and gnaw turnips all day?
Make fun all you want. I'm helping more people here in the forest than I did in the palace.
I'd lift the curse if I could.
Being a princess felt like wearing a disguise that hid who I really am.

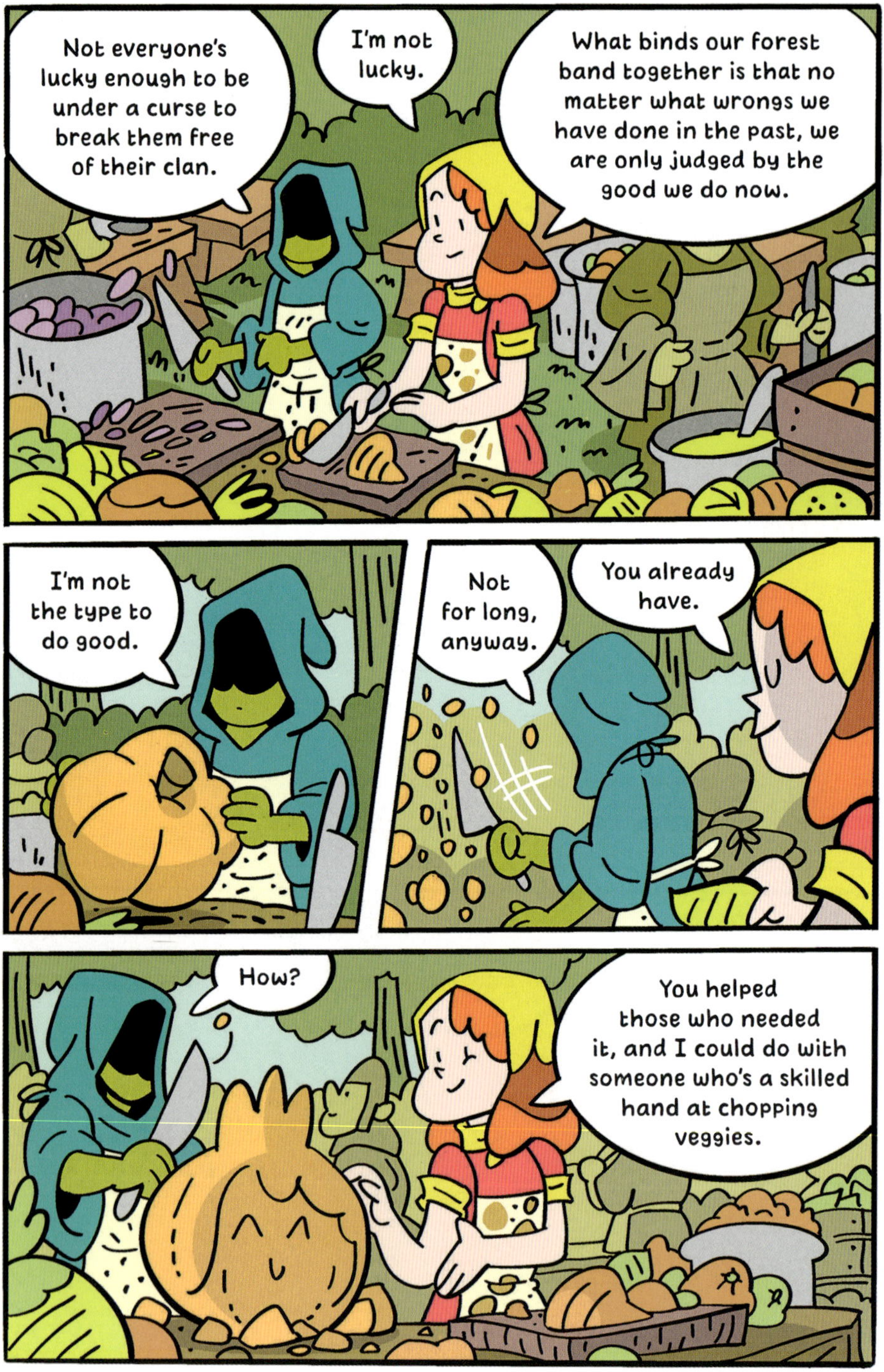
Not everyone's lucky enough to be under a curse to break them free of their clan.
I'm not lucky.
What binds our forest band together is that no matter what wrongs we have done in the past, we are only judged by the good we do now.
I'm not the type to do good.
Not for long, anyway.
You already have.
How?
You helped those who needed it, and I could do with someone who's a skilled hand at chopping veggies.

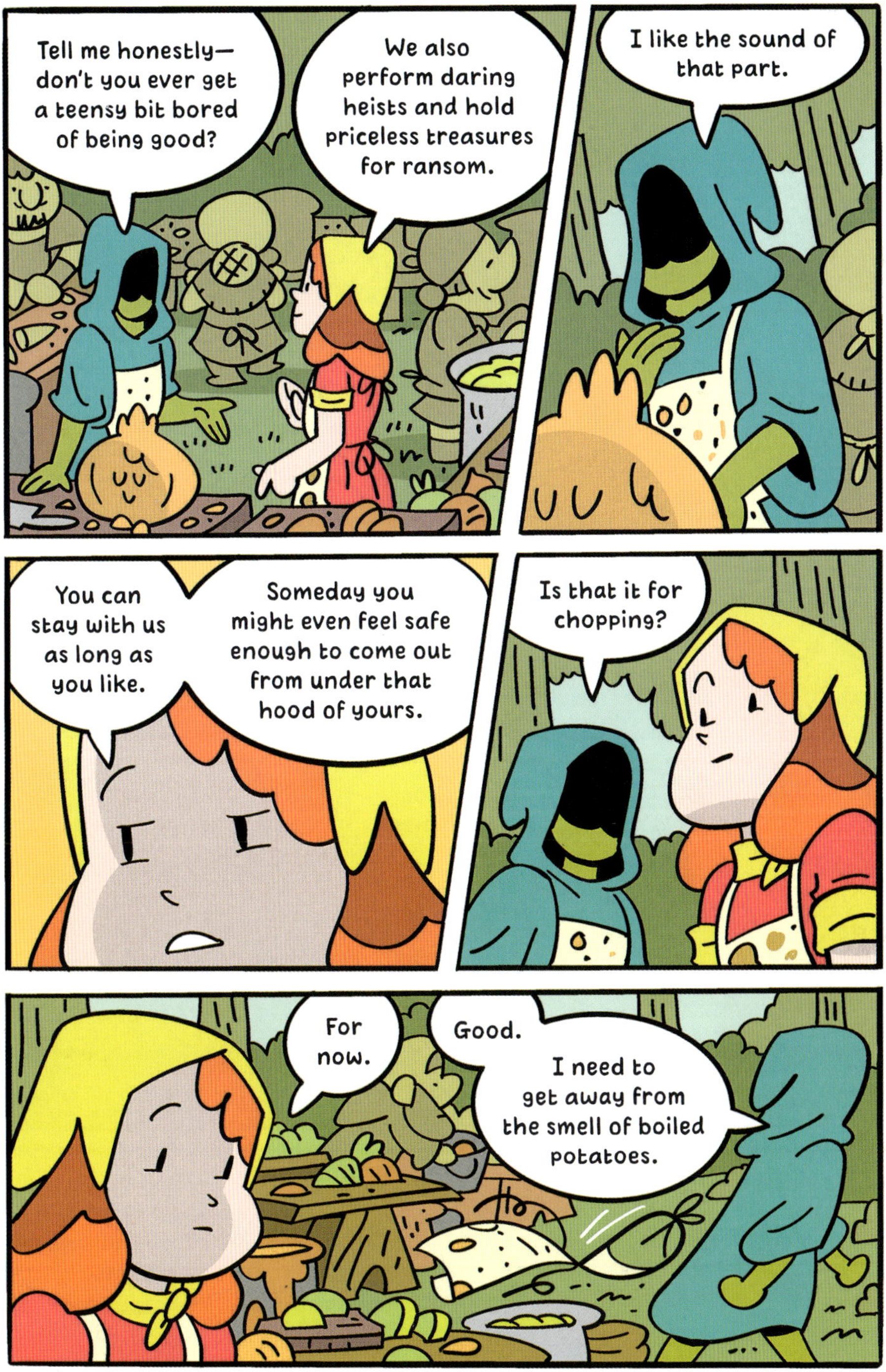
Tell me honestly— don't you ever get a teensy bit bored of being good?
We also perform daring heists and hold priceless treasures for ransom.
I like the sound of that part.
You can stay with us as long as you like.
Someday you might even feel safe enough to come out from under that hood of yours.
Is that it for chopping?
For now.
Good.
I need to get away from the smell of boiled potatoes.

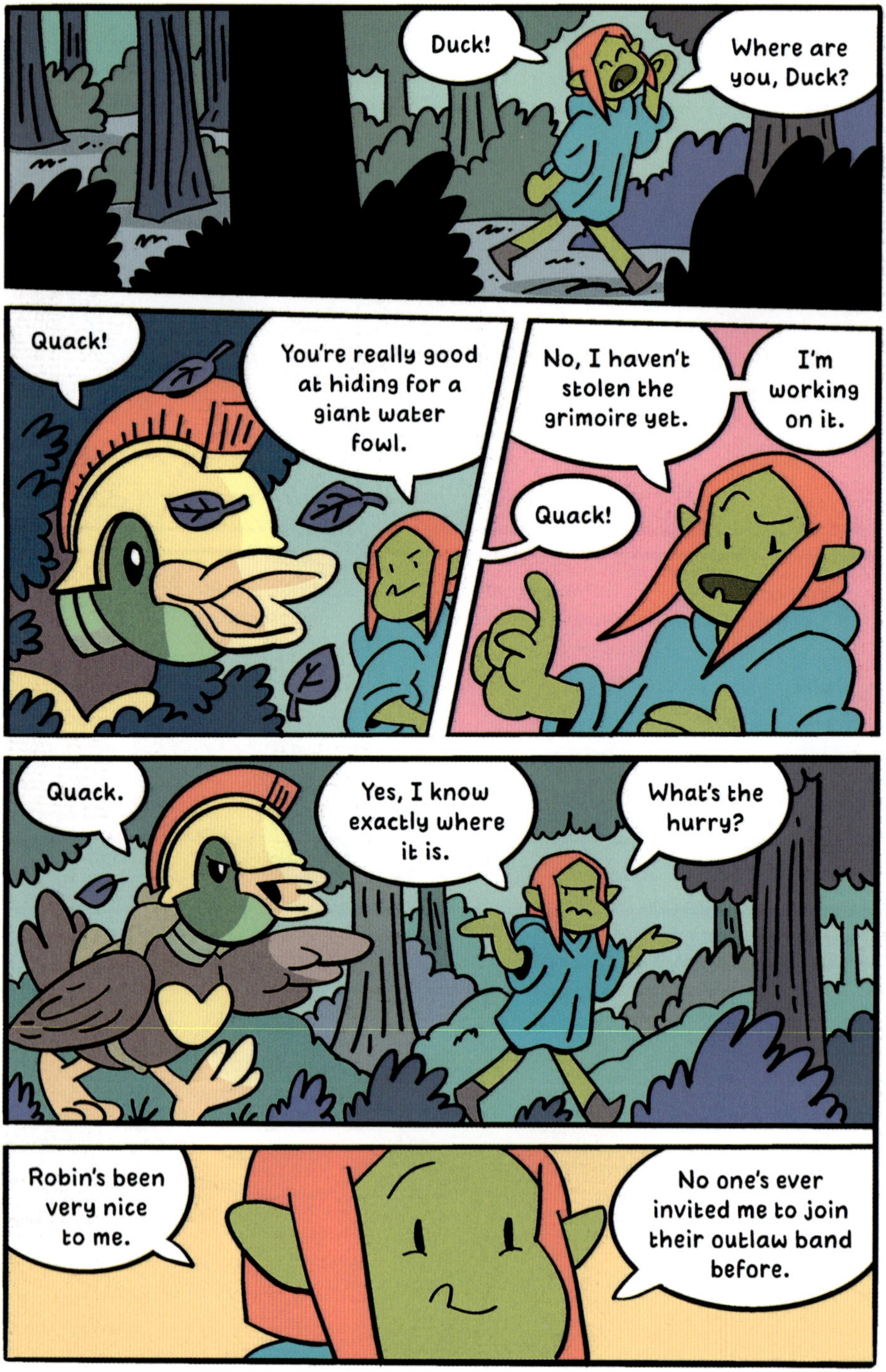
Duck!
Where are you, Duck?
Quack!
You're really good at hiding for a giant water fowl.
No, I haven't stolen the grimoire yet.
I'm working on it.
Quack!
Quack.
Yes, I know exactly where it is.
What's the hurry?
Robin's been very nice to me.
No one's ever invited me to join their outlaw band before.

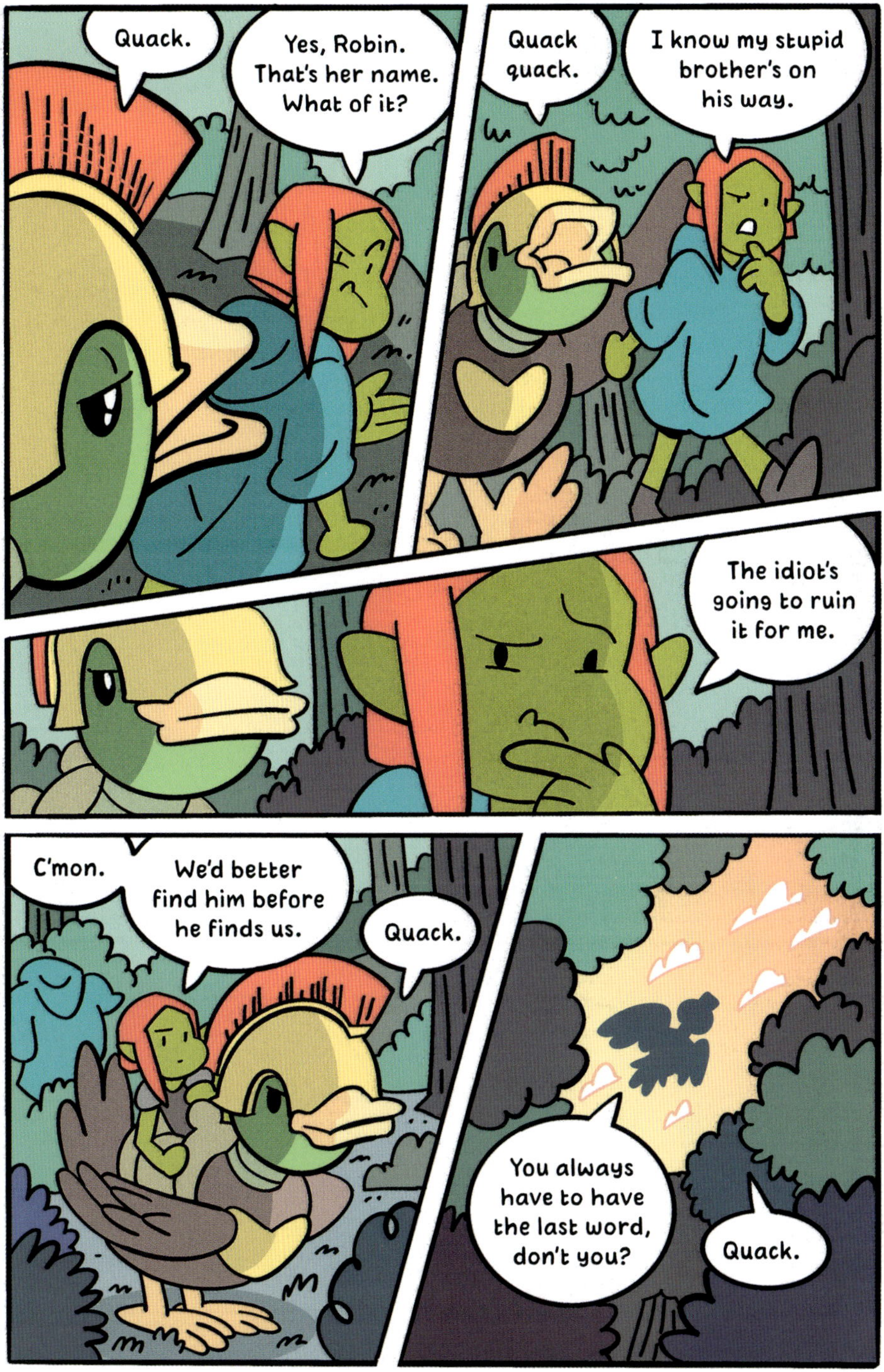
Quack.
Yes, Robin.
That's her name.
What of it?
Quack
quack.
I know my stupid
brother's on
his way.
The idiot's
going to ruin
it for me.
C'mon.
We'd better
find him before
he finds us.
Quack.
You always
have to have
the last word,
don't you?
Quack.

CHAPTER SIXTEEN

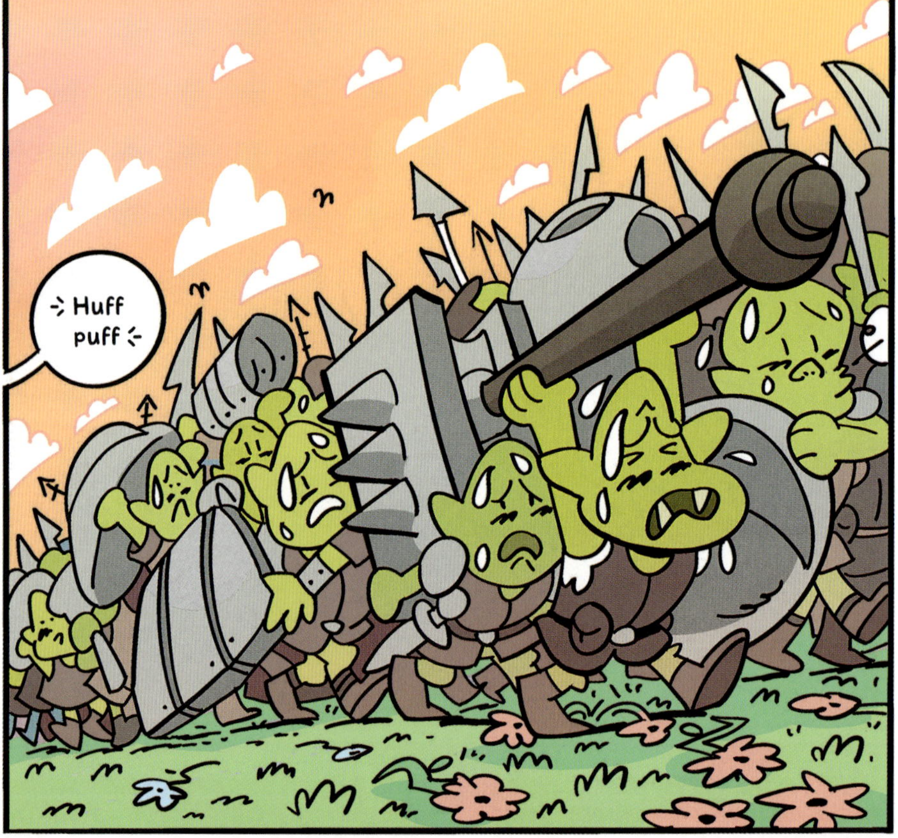
Huff puff

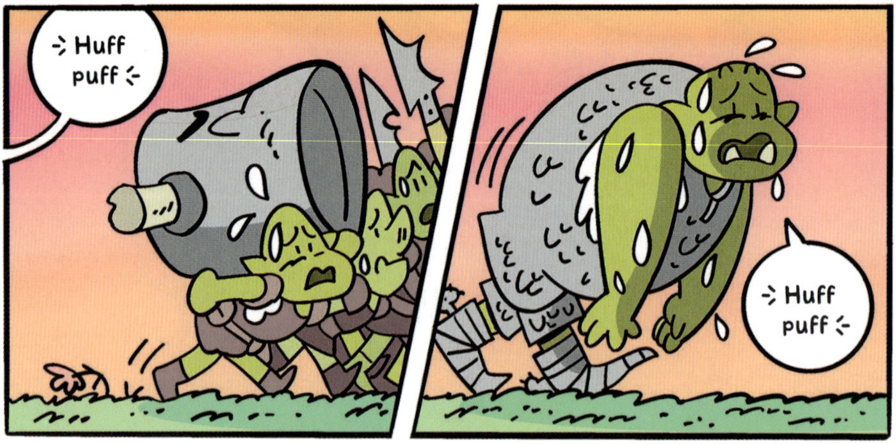
Huff puff
Huff puff

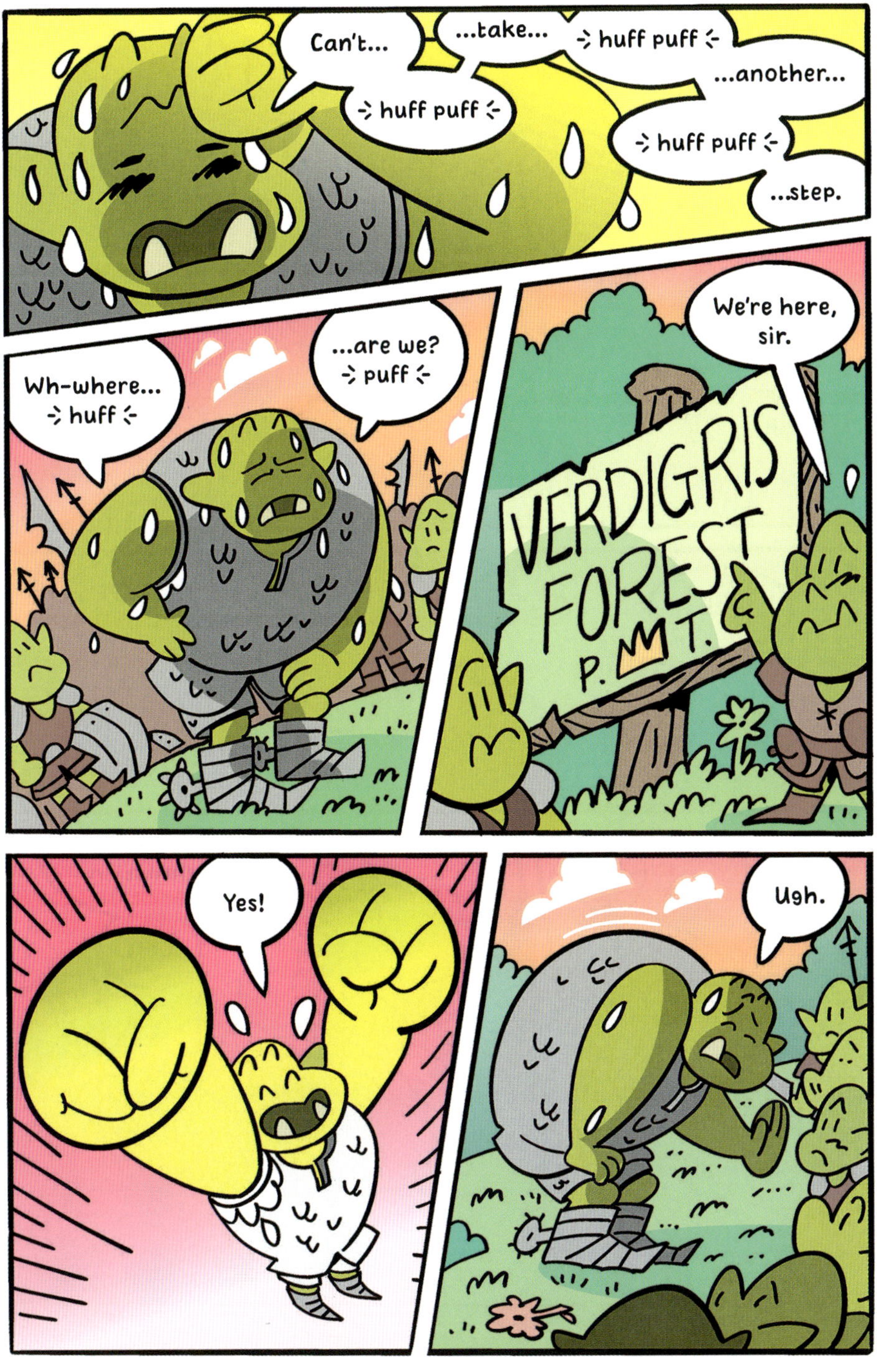
Can't...
⁘ huff puff ⁘
...take...
⁘ huff puff ⁘
...another...
⁘ huff puff ⁘
...step.
Wh-where... ⁘ huff ⁘
...are we? ⁘ puff ⁘
We're here, sir.
VERDIGRIS FOREST
P. T.
Yes!
Ugh.

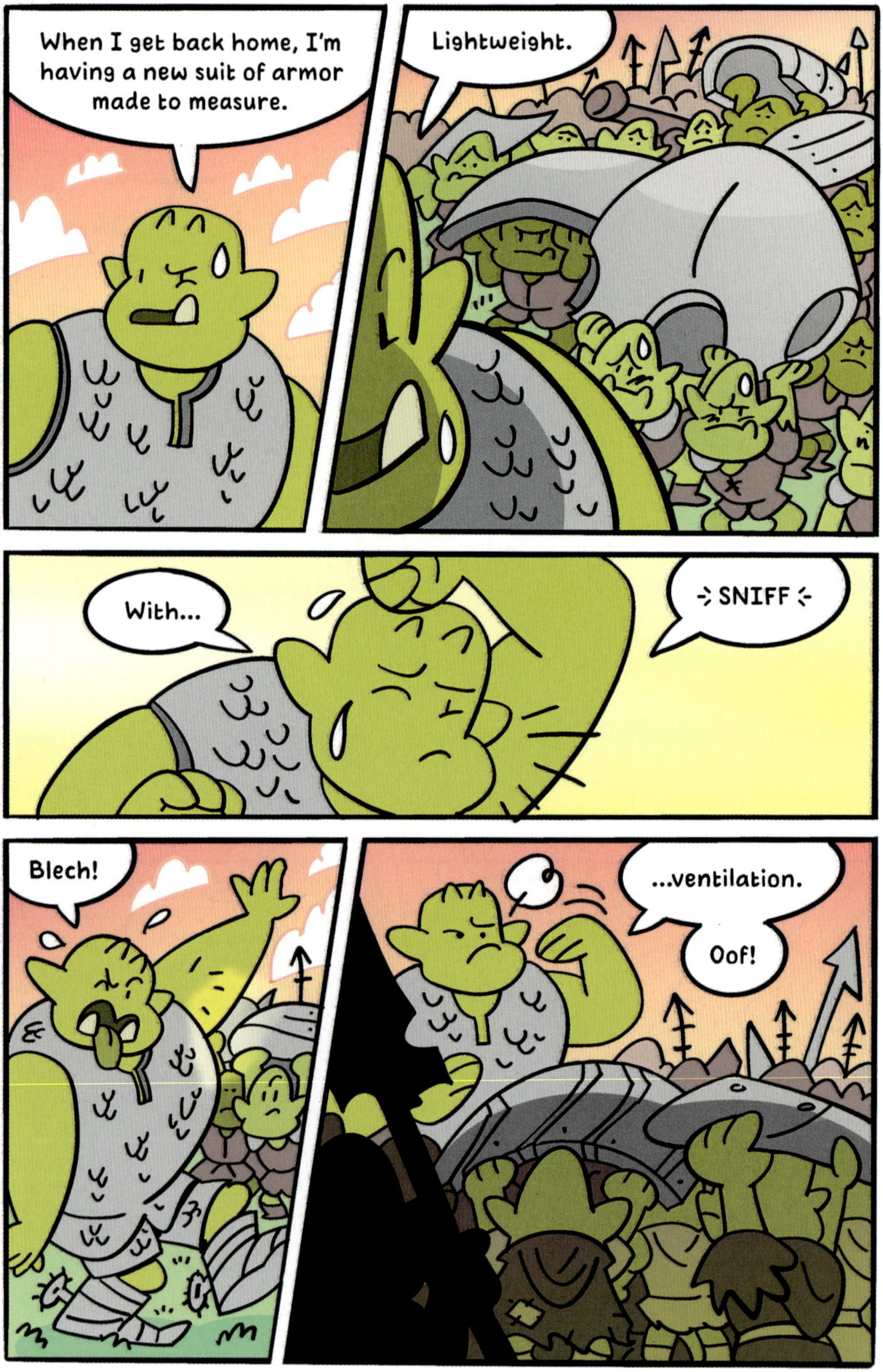
When I get back home, I'm having a new suit of armor made to measure.
Lightweight.
With...
SNIFF
Blech!
...ventilation.
Oof!

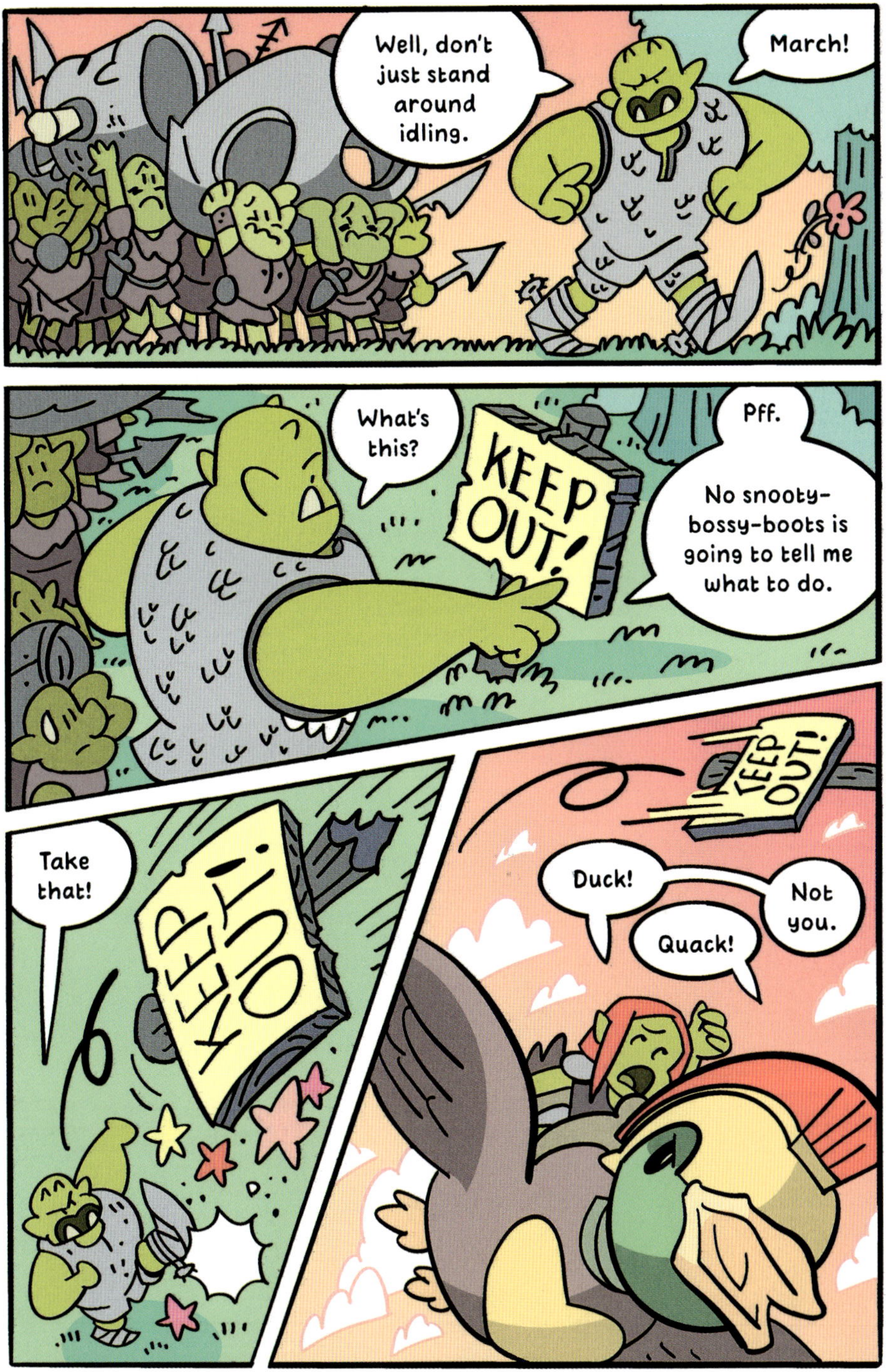
Well, don't just stand around idling.
March!
What's this?
KEEP OUT!
Pff.
No snooty-bossy-boots is going to tell me what to do.
Take that!
KEEP OUT!
KEEP OUT!
Duck!
Not you.
Quack!

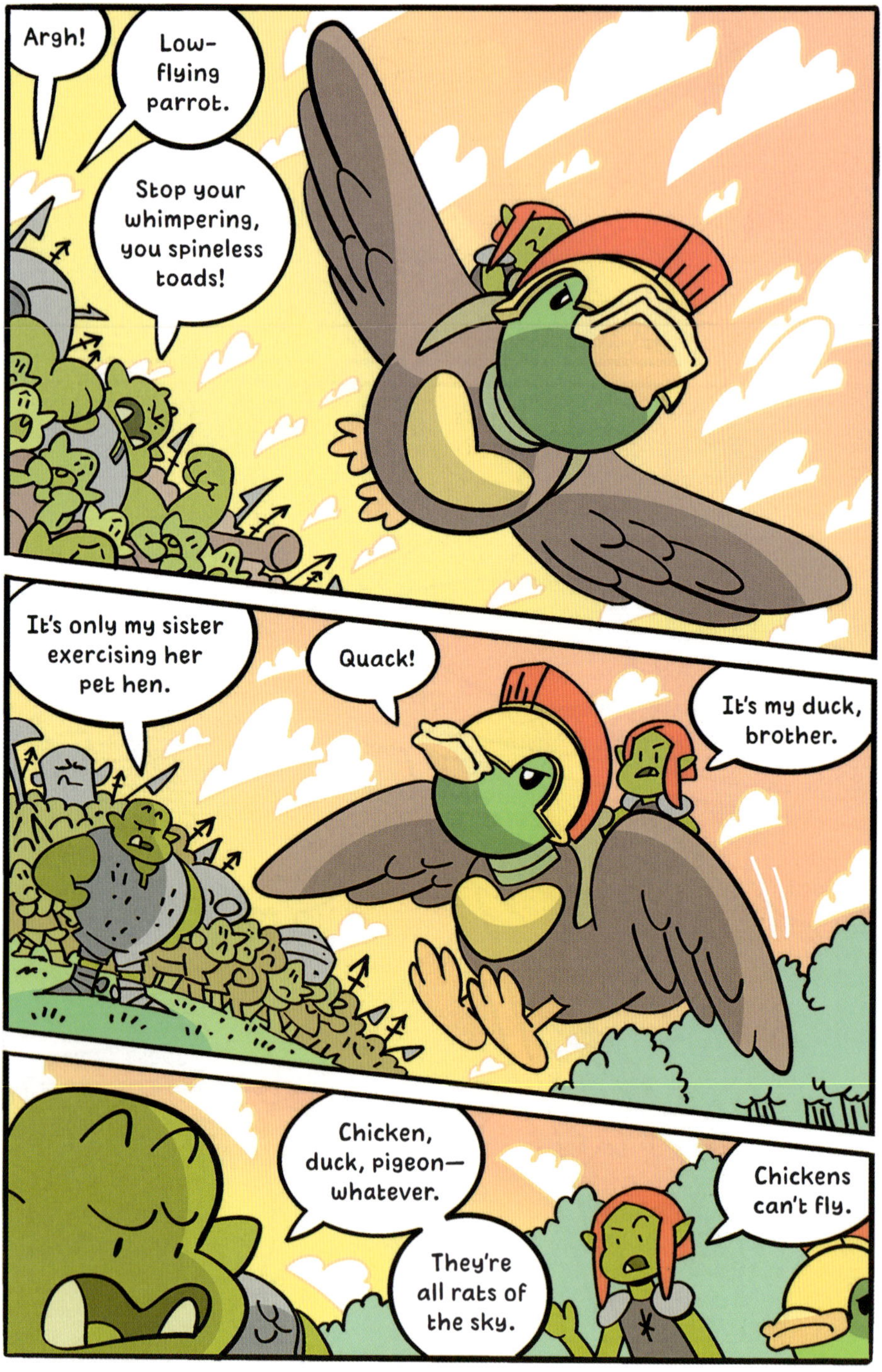
Argh!
Low-flying parrot.
Stop your whimpering, you spineless toads!
It's only my sister exercising her pet hen.
Quack!
It's my duck, brother.
Chicken, duck, pigeon—whatever.
They're all rats of the sky.
Chickens can't fly.

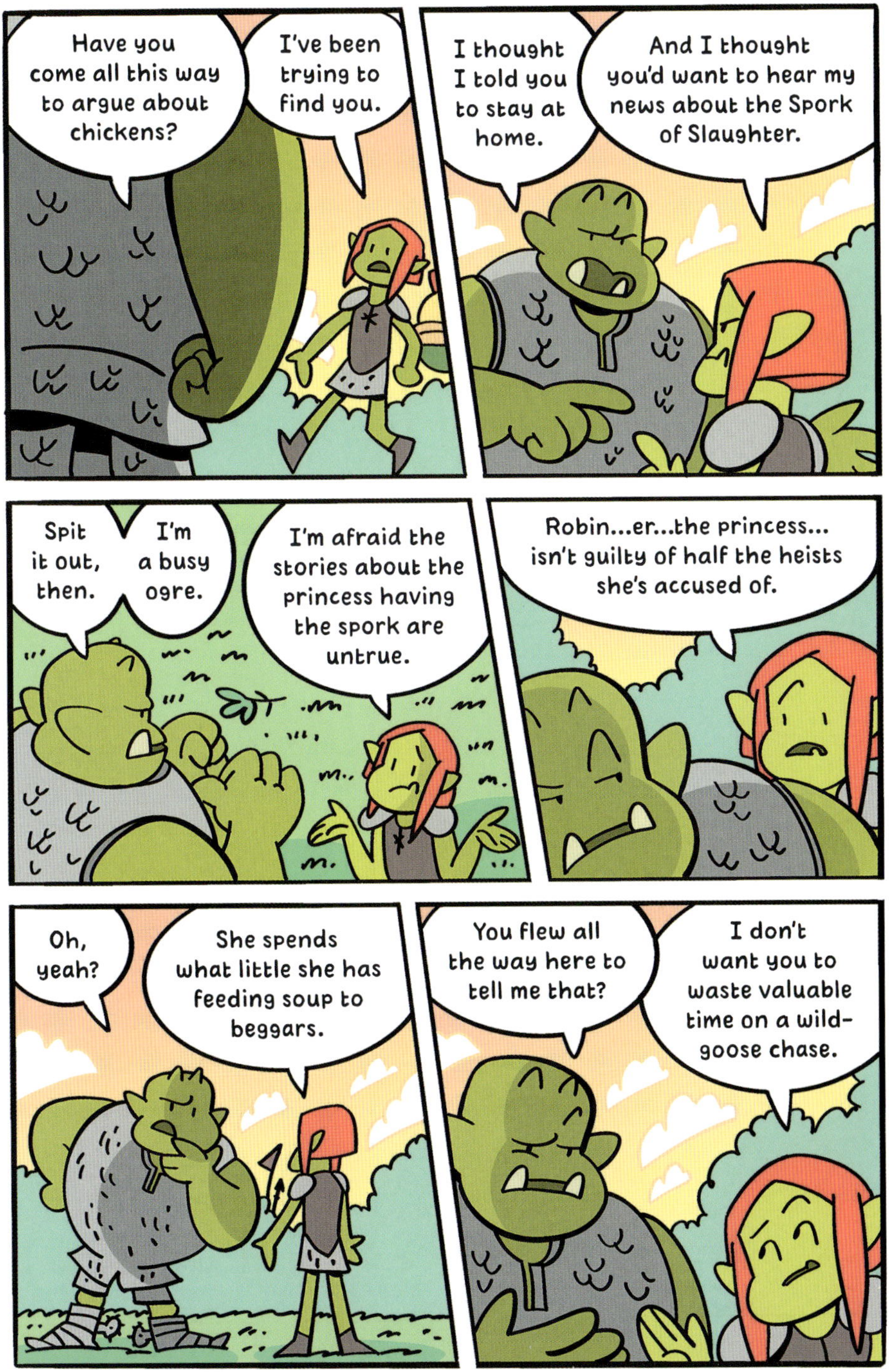

Have you come all this way to argue about chickens?
I've been trying to find you.
I thought I told you to stay at home.
And I thought you'd want to hear my news about the Spork of Slaughter.
Spit it out, then.
I'm a busy ogre.
I'm afraid the stories about the princess having the spork are untrue.
Robin...er...the princess... isn't guilty of half the heists she's accused of.
Oh, yeah?
She spends what little she has feeding soup to beggars.
You flew all the way here to tell me that?
I don't want you to waste valuable time on a wild-goose chase.

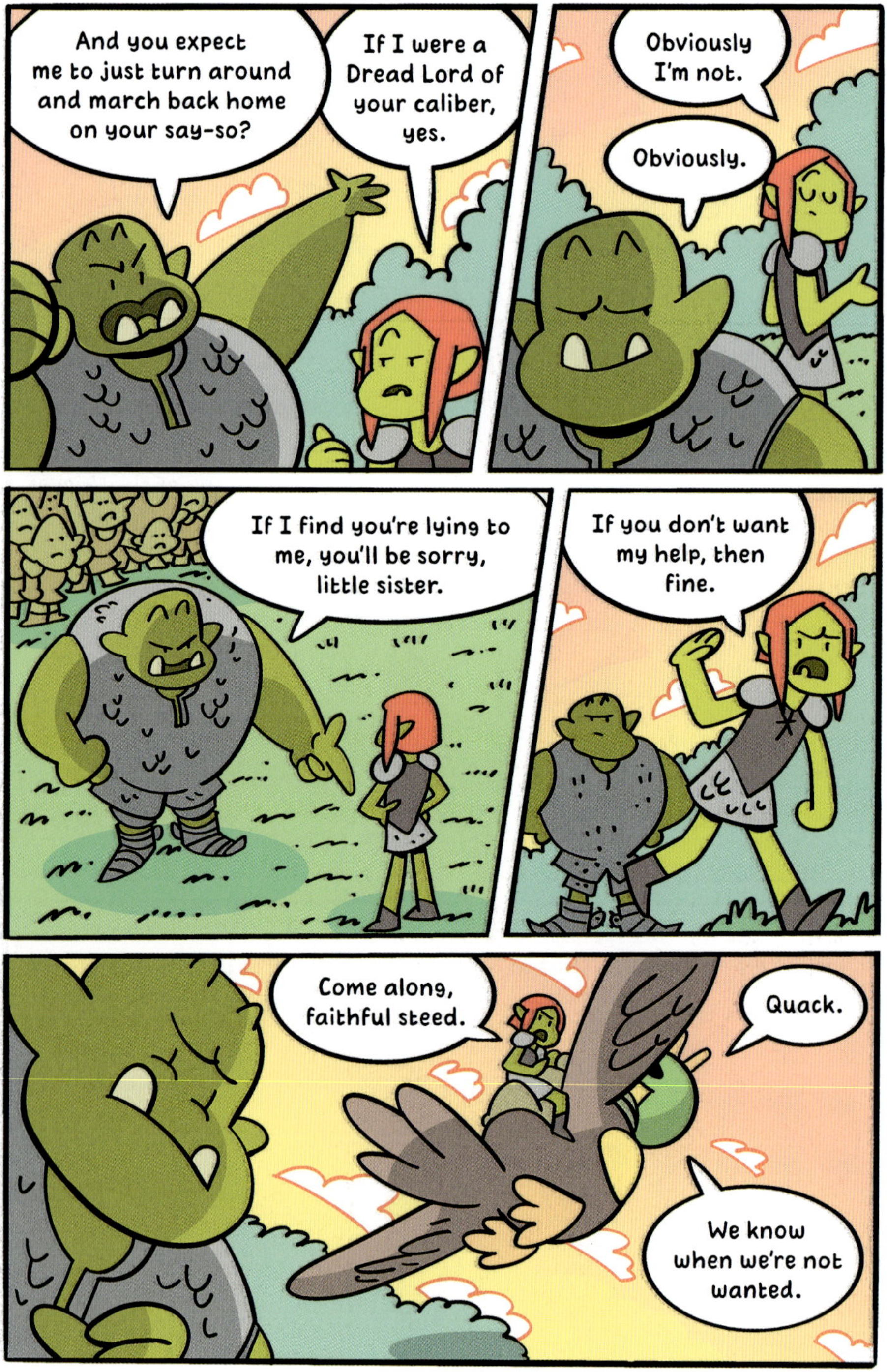
And you expect me to just turn around and march back home on your say-so?
If I were a Dread Lord of your caliber, yes.
Obviously I'm not.
Obviously.
If I find you're lying to me, you'll be sorry, little sister.
If you don't want my help, then fine.
Come along, faithful steed.
Quack.
We know when we're not wanted.

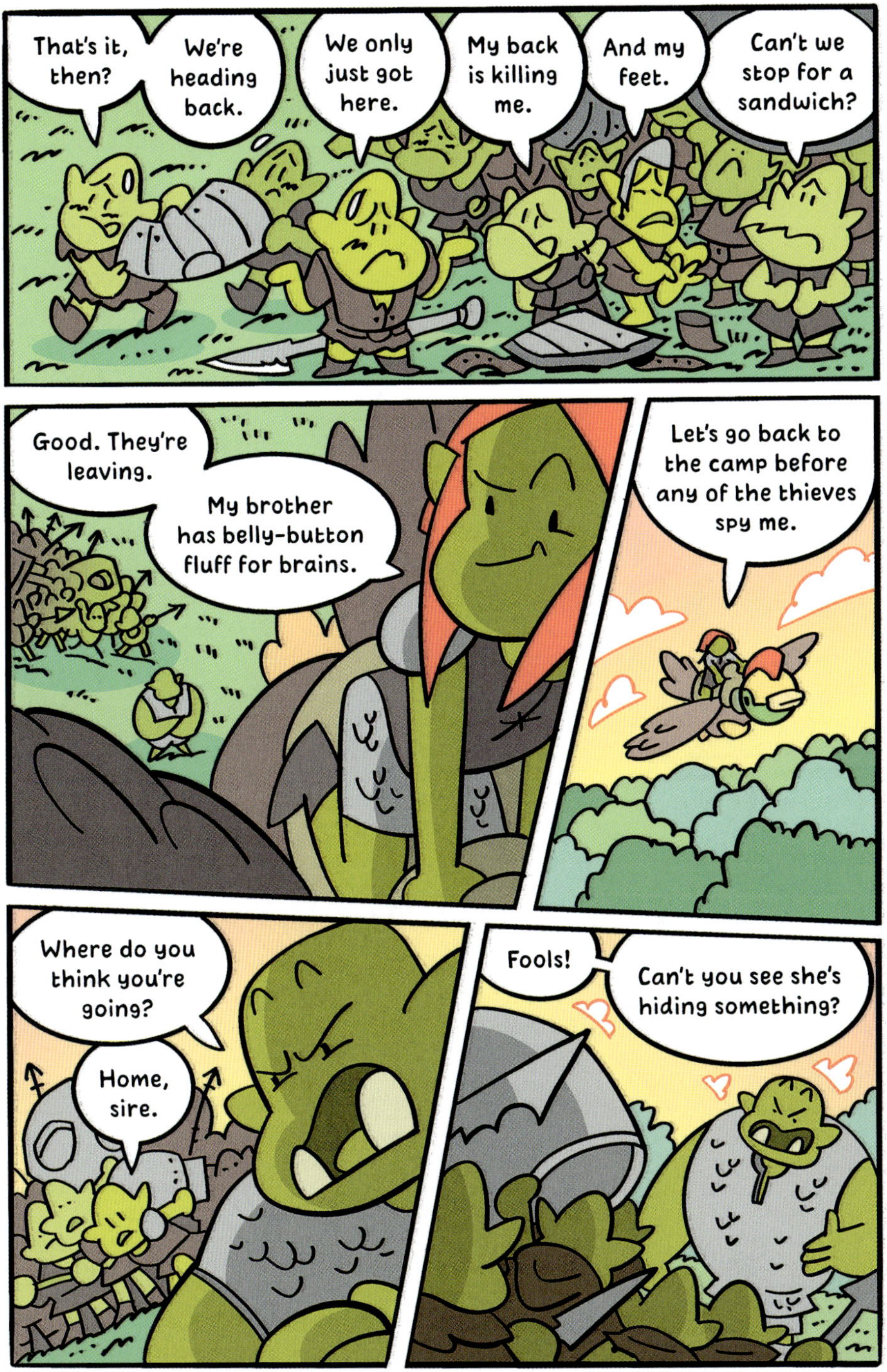
That's it, then?
We're heading back.
We only just got here.
My back is killing me.
And my feet.
Can't we stop for a sandwich?
Good. They're leaving.
My brother has belly-button fluff for brains.
Let's go back to the camp before any of the thieves spy me.
Where do you think you're going?
Home, sire.
Fools!
Can't you see she's hiding something?

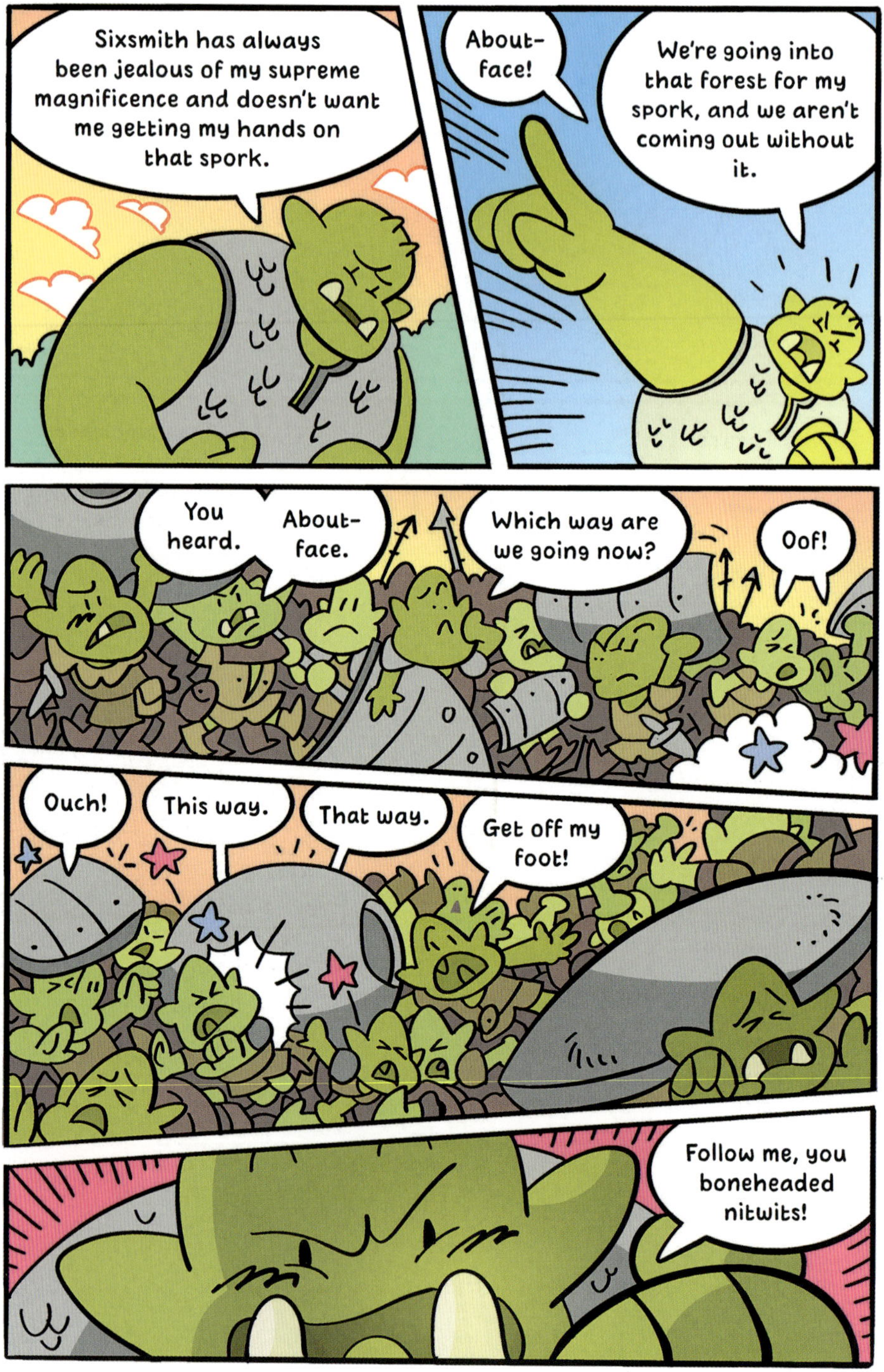

Sixsmith has always been jealous of my supreme magnificence and doesn't want me getting my hands on that spork.
About-face!
We're going into that forest for my spork, and we aren't coming out without it.
You heard.
About-face.
Which way are we going now?
Oof!
Ouch!
This way.
That way.
Get off my foot!
Follow me, you boneheaded nitwits!

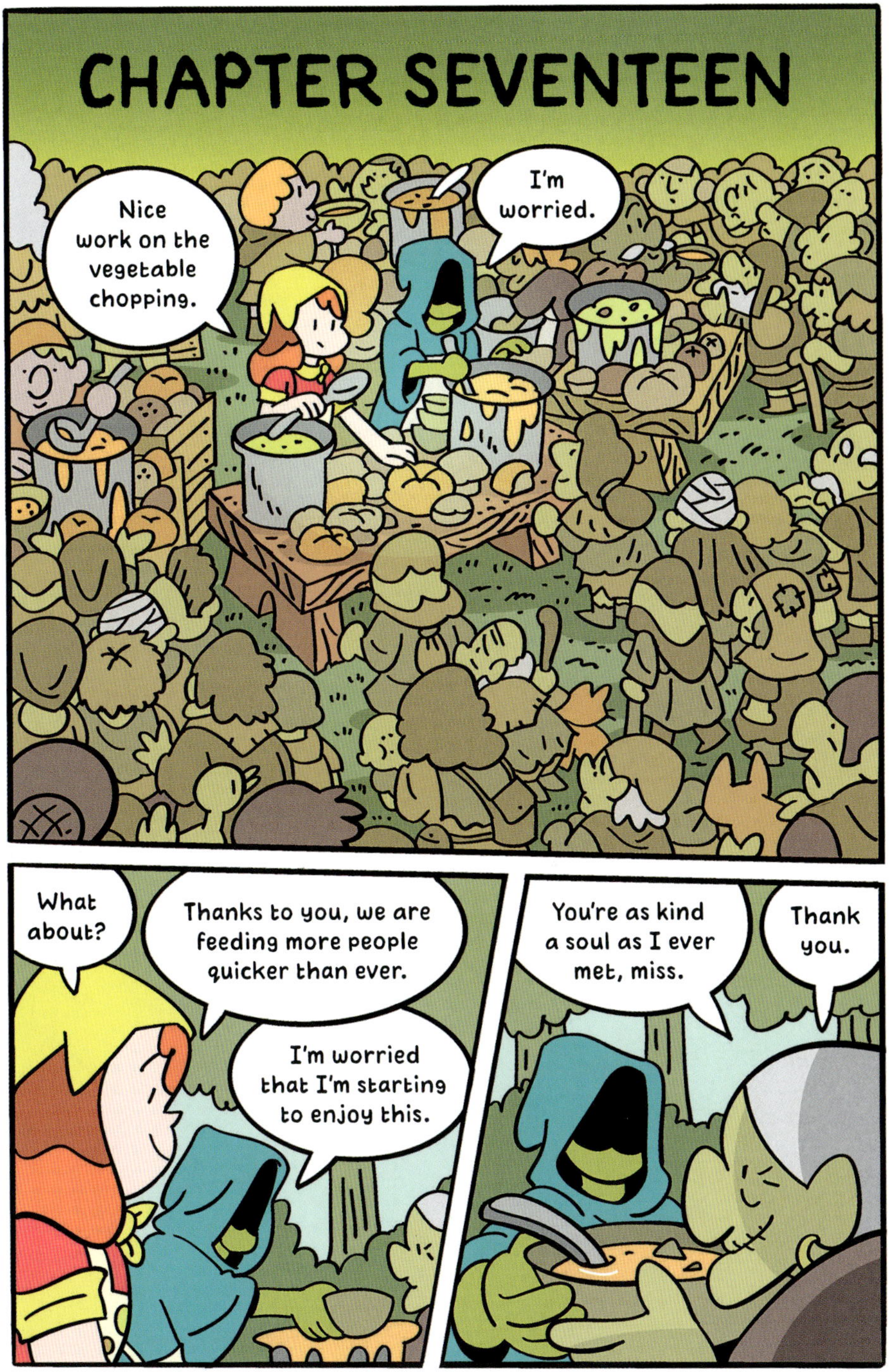
CHAPTER SEVENTEEN
Nice work on the vegetable chopping.
I'm worried.
What about?
Thanks to you, we are feeding more people quicker than ever.
I'm worried that I'm starting to enjoy this.
You're as kind a soul as I ever met, miss.
Thank you.

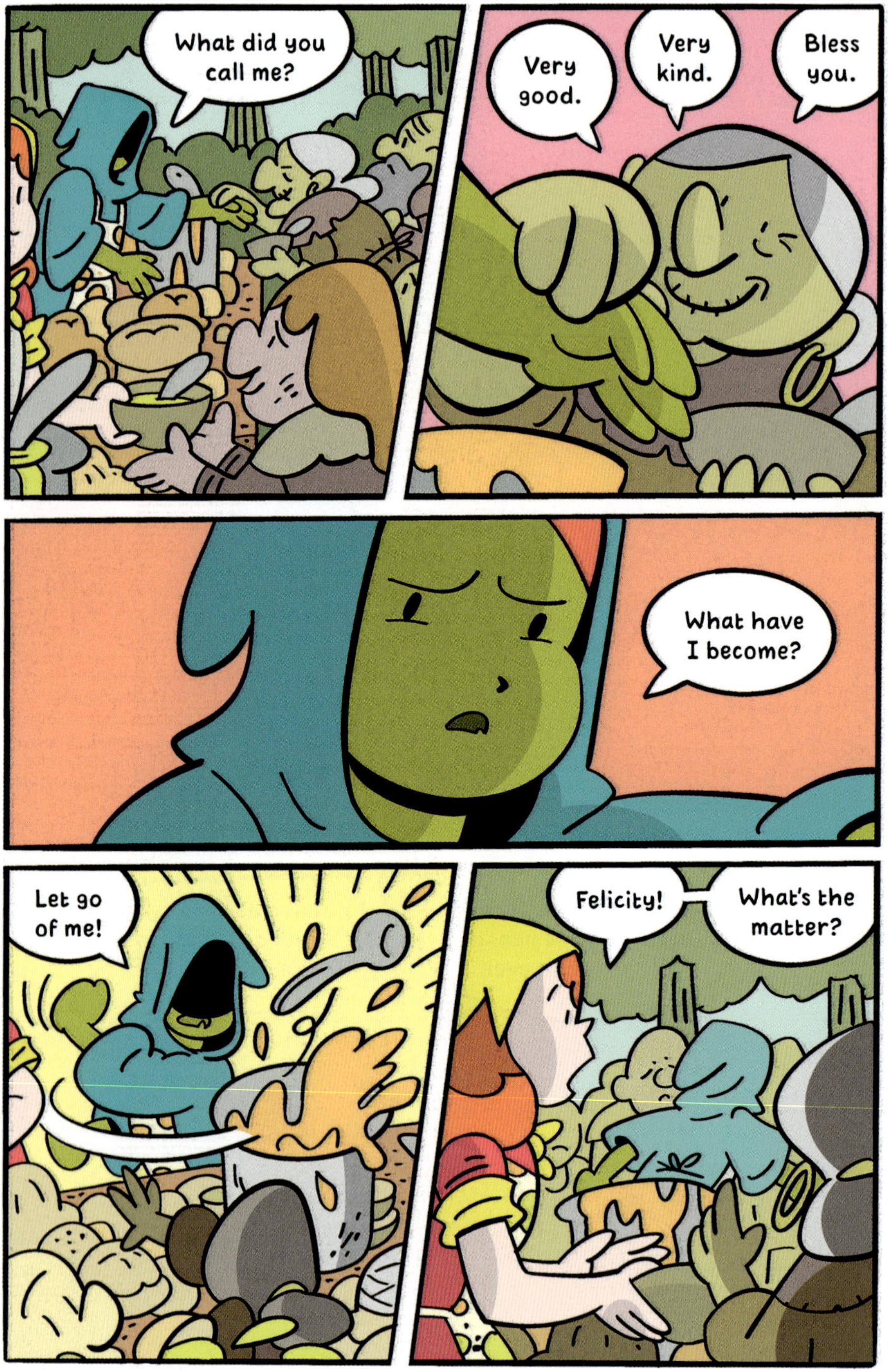
What did you call me?
Very good.
Very kind.
Bless you.
What have I become?
Let go of me!
Felicity!
What's the matter?

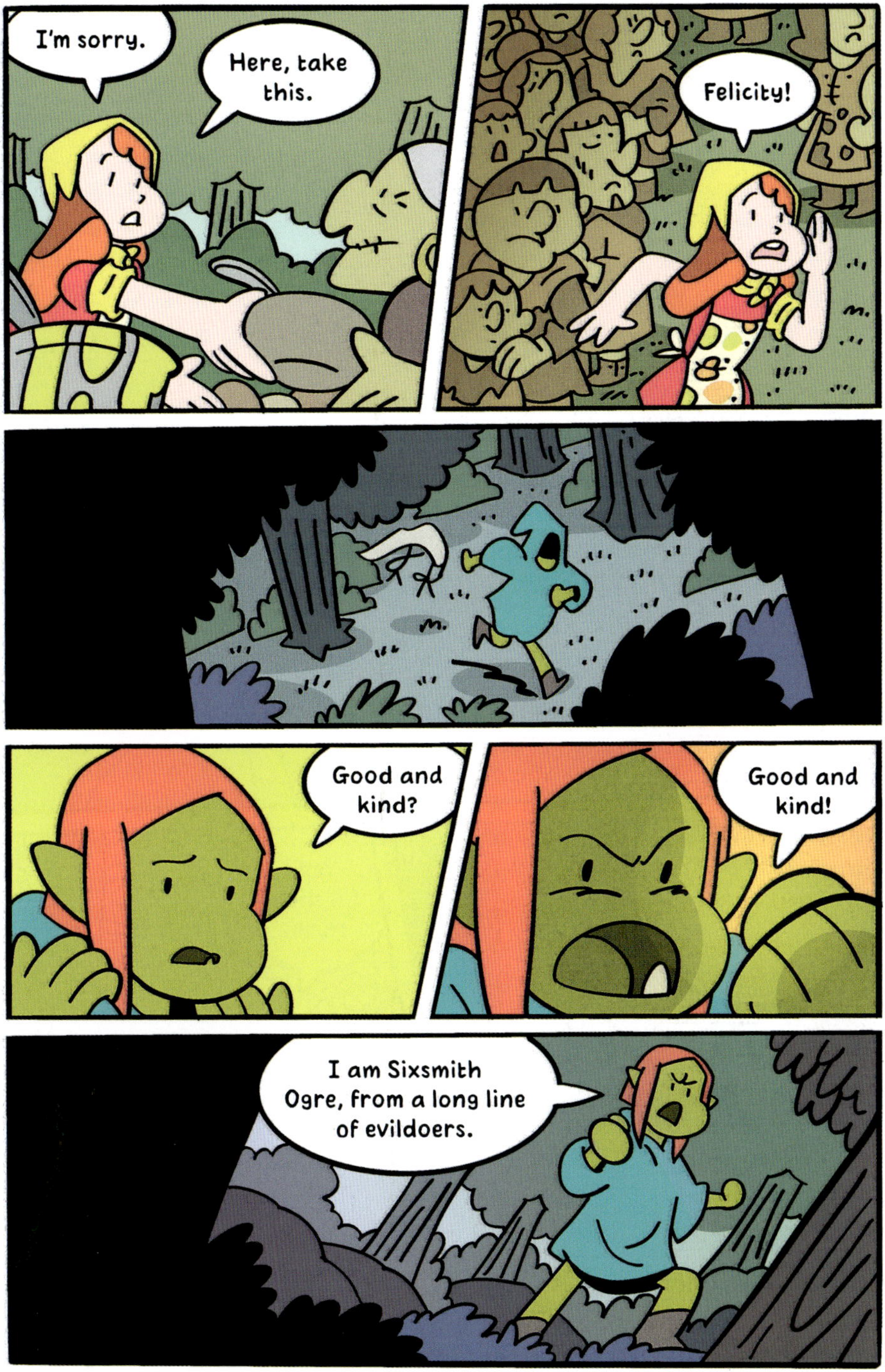
I'm sorry.
Here, take this.
Felicity!
Good and kind?
Good and kind!
I am Sixsmith Ogre, from a long line of evildoers.

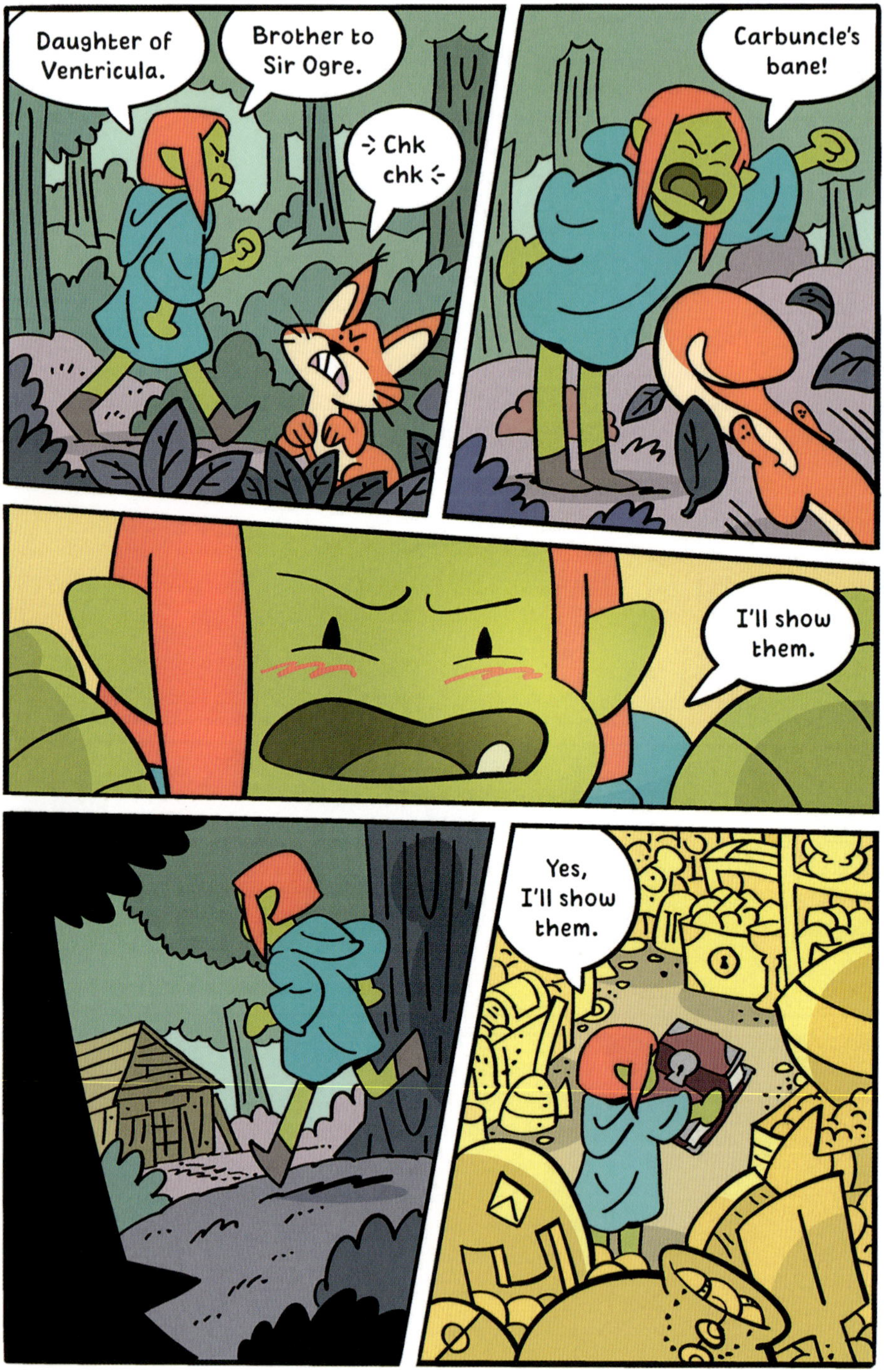
Daughter of Ventricula.
Brother to Sir Ogre.
Chk chk
Carbuncle's bane!
I'll show them.
Yes, I'll show them.

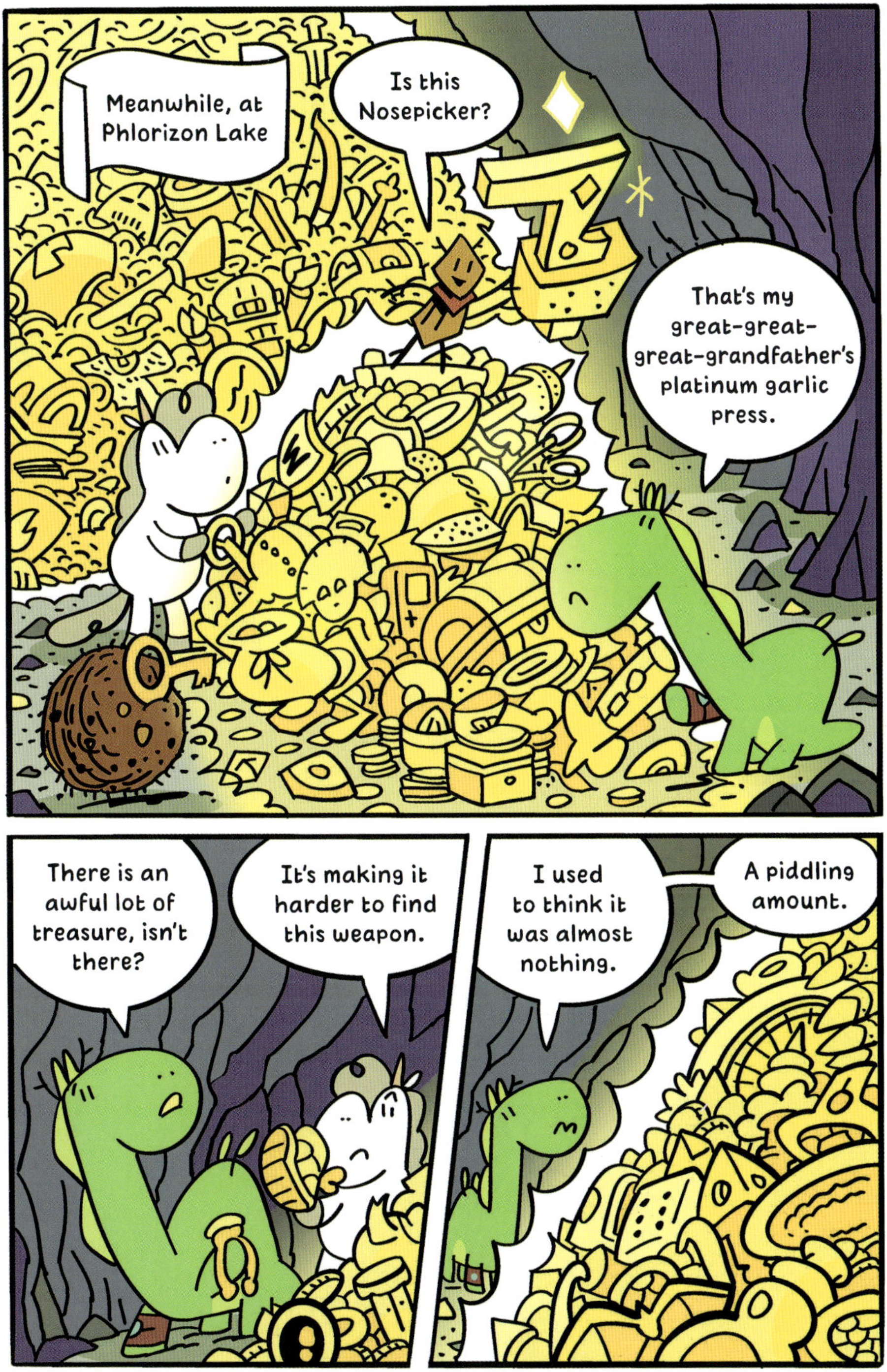
Meanwhile, at Phlorizon Lake
Is this Nosepicker?
That's my great-great-great-grandfather's platinum garlic press.
There is an awful lot of treasure, isn't there?
It's making it harder to find this weapon.
I used to think it was almost nothing.
A piddling amount.

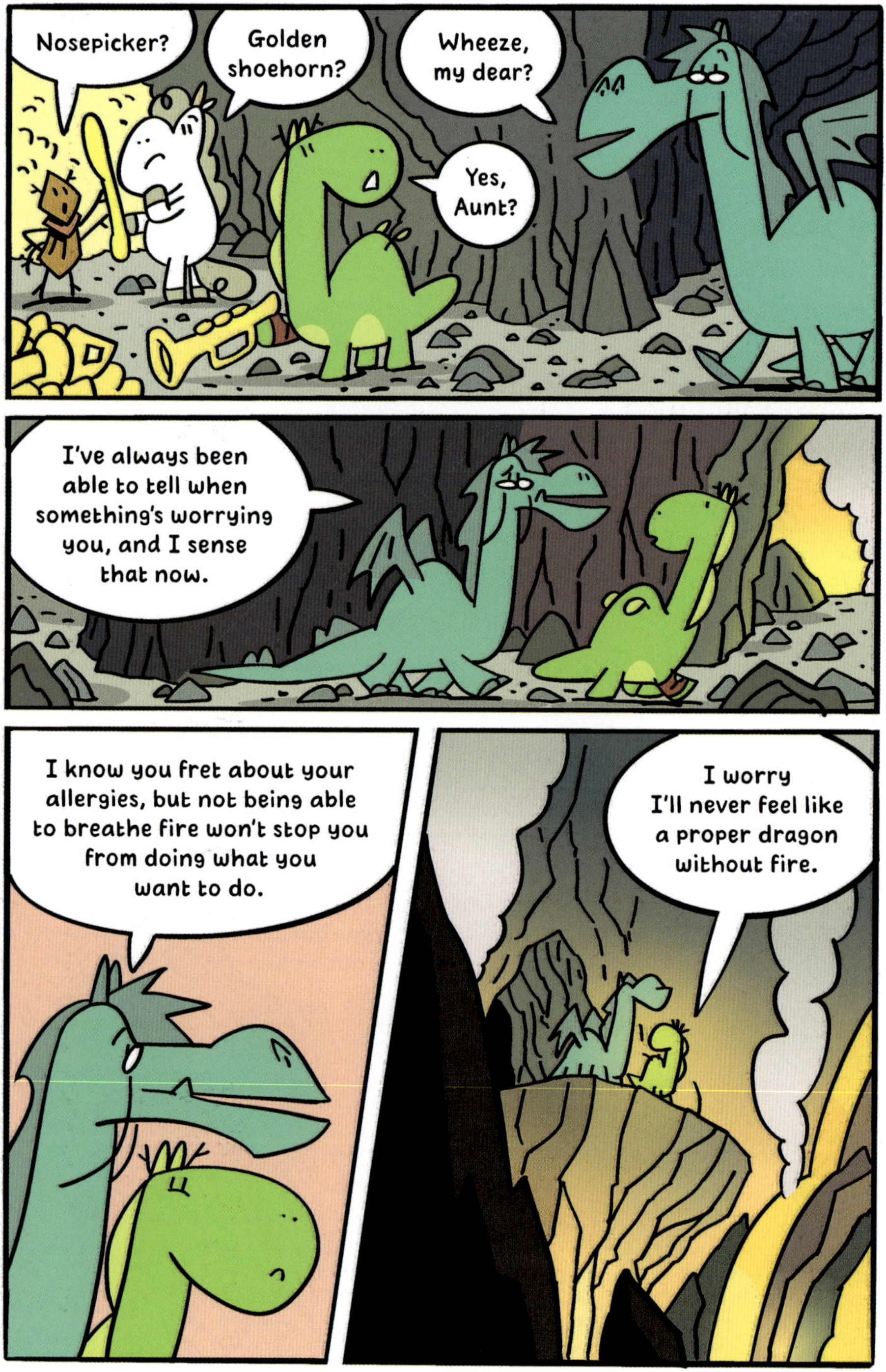
Nosepicker?
Golden shoehorn?
Wheeze, my dear?
Yes, Aunt?
I've always been able to tell when something's worrying you, and I sense that now.
I know you fret about your allergies, but not being able to breathe fire won't stop you from doing what you want to do.
I worry I'll never feel like a proper dragon without fire.

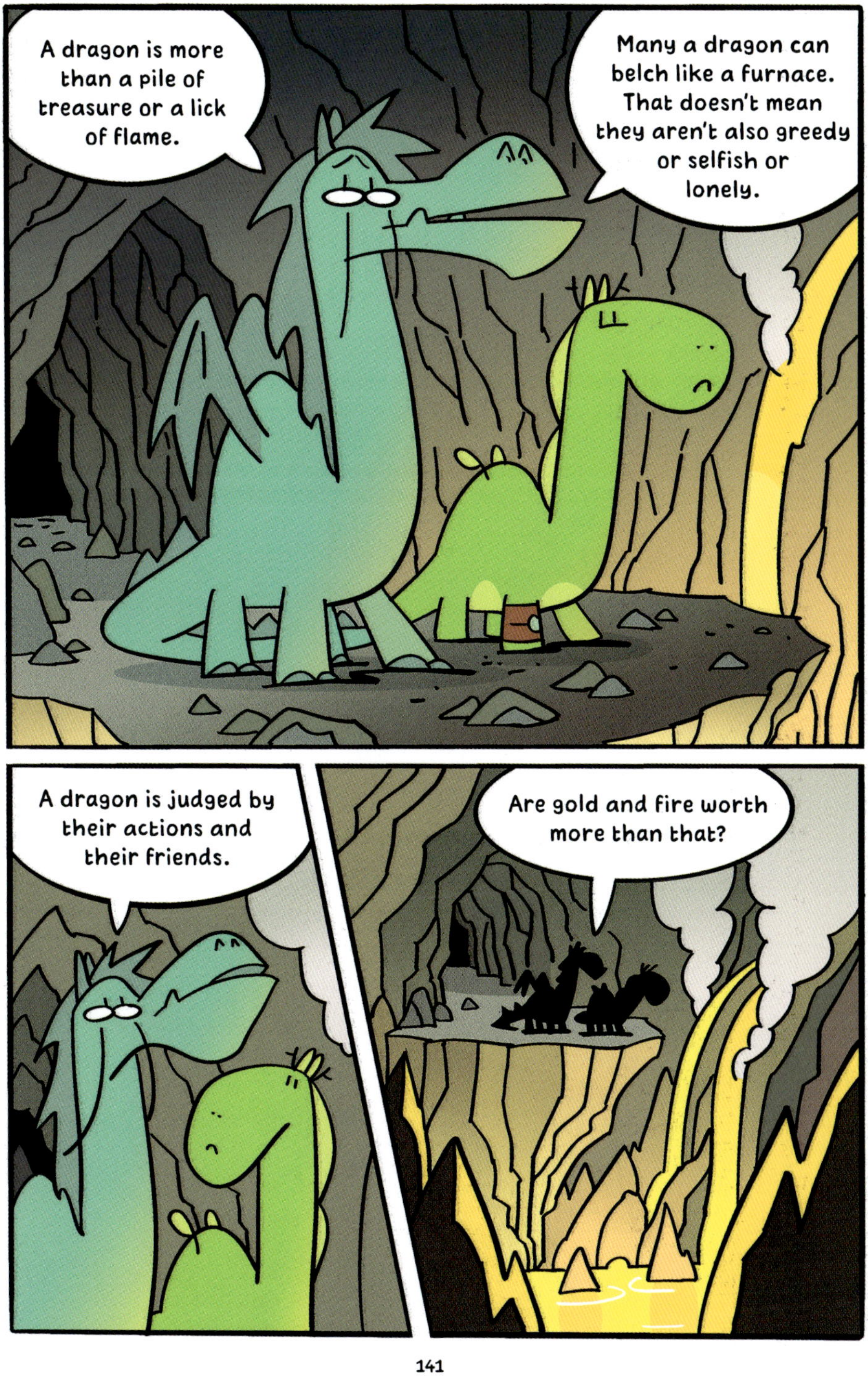
A dragon is more than a pile of treasure or a lick of flame.
Many a dragon can belch like a furnace. That doesn't mean they aren't also greedy or selfish or lonely.
A dragon is judged by their actions and their friends.
Are gold and fire worth more than that?

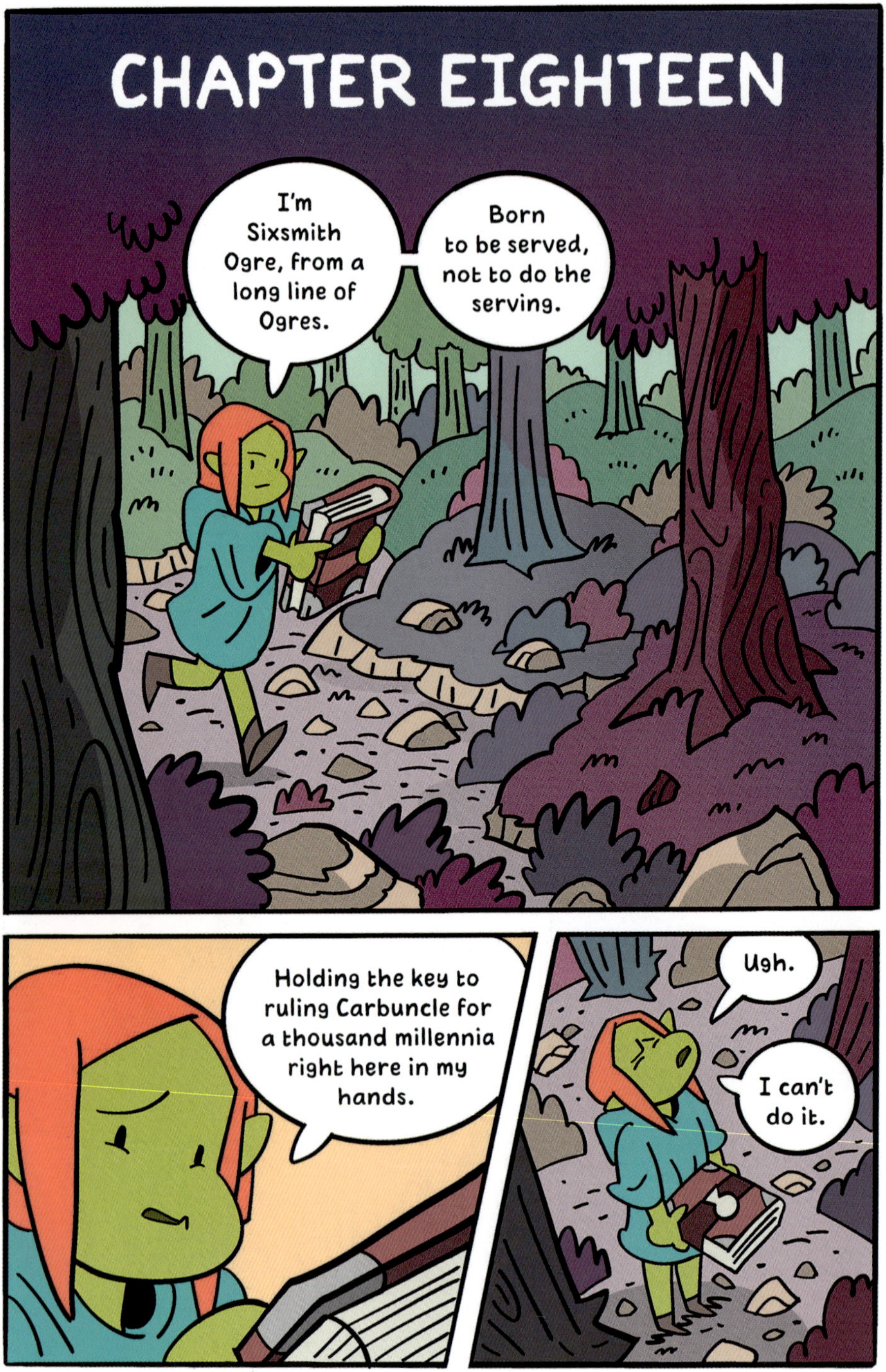
CHAPTER EIGHTEEN
I'm Sixsmith Ogre, from a long line of Ogres.
Born to be served, not to do the serving.
Holding the key to ruling Carbuncle for a thousand millennia right here in my hands.
Ugh.
I can't do it.

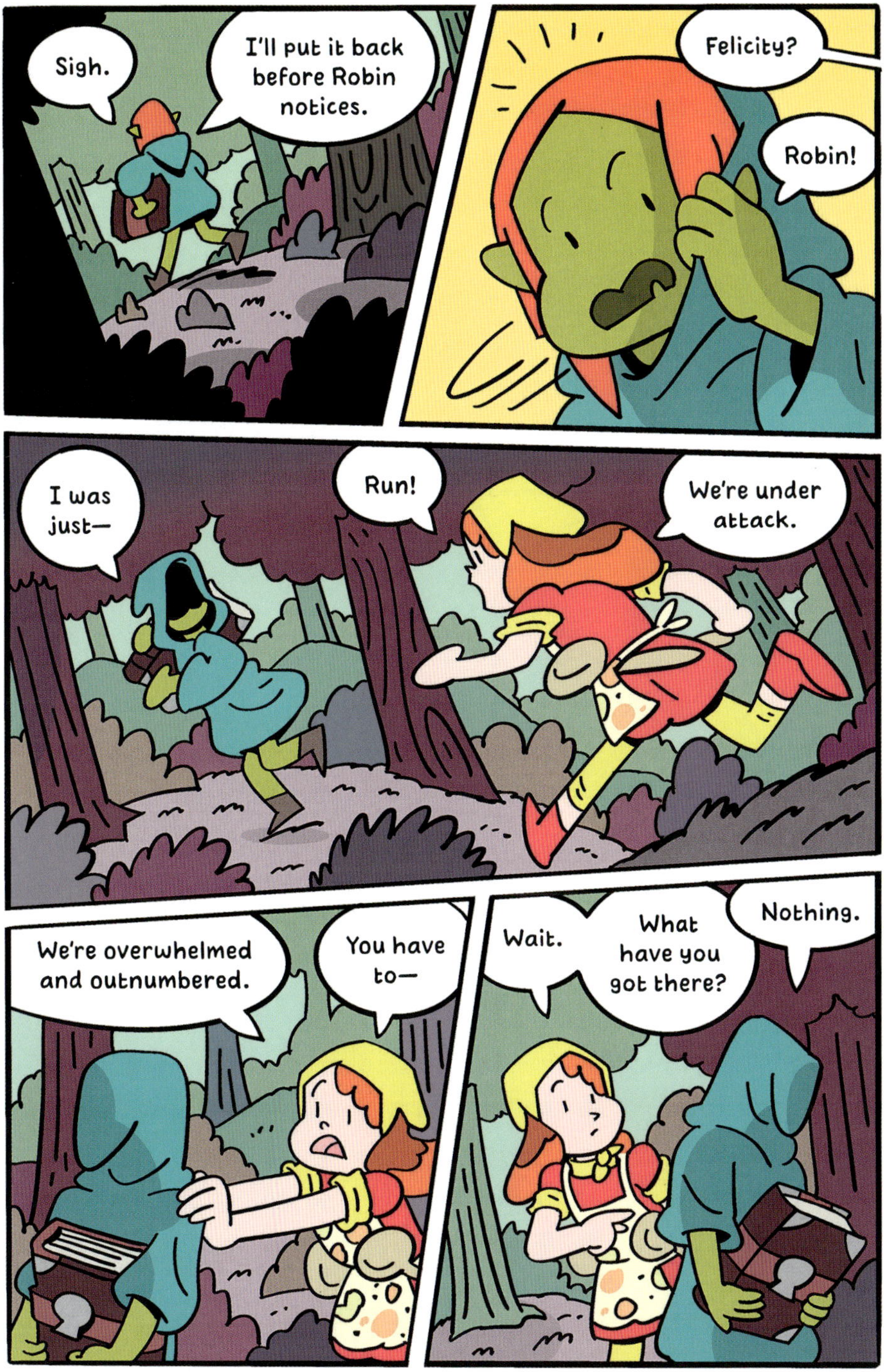
Sigh.
I'll put it back before Robin notices.
Felicity?
Robin!
I was just—
Run!
We're under attack.
We're overwhelmed and outnumbered.
You have to—
Wait.
What have you got there?
Nothing.

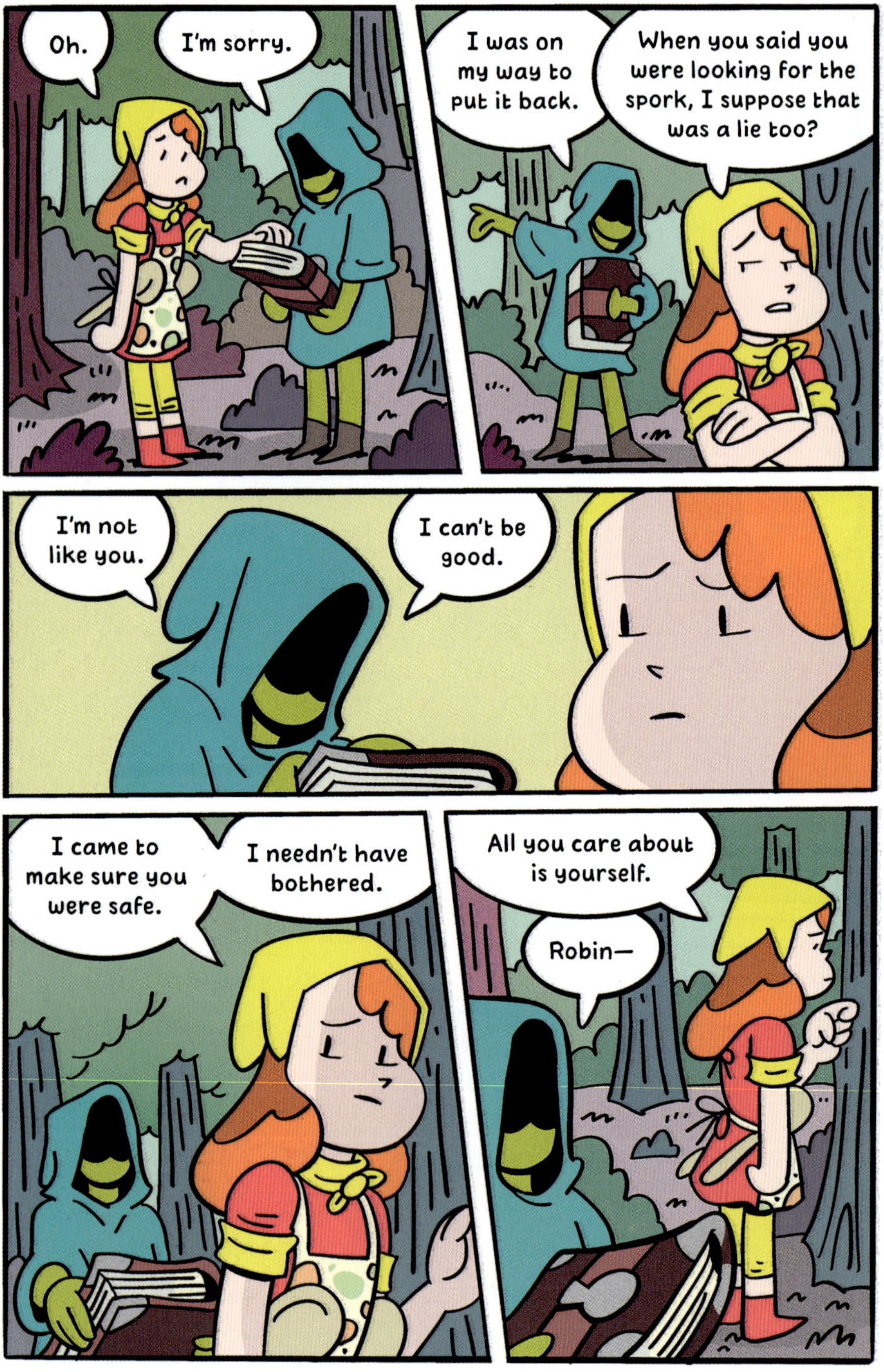
Oh.
I'm sorry.
I was on my way to put it back.
When you said you were looking for the spork, I suppose that was a lie too?
I'm not like you.
I can't be good.
I came to make sure you were safe.
I needn't have bothered.
All you care about is yourself.
Robin—

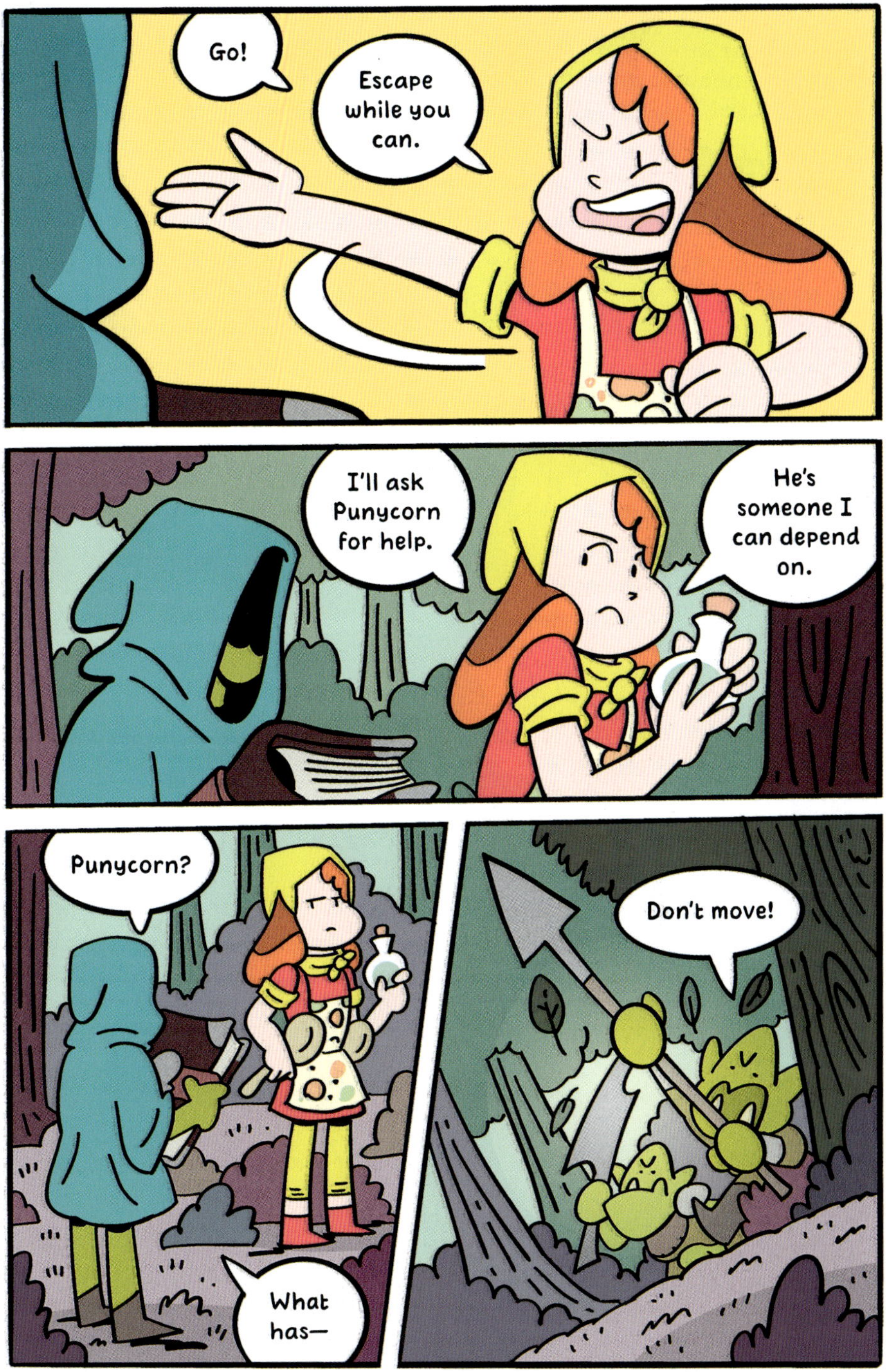
Go!
Escape while you can.
I'll ask Punycorn for help.
He's someone I can depend on.
Punycorn?
What has—
Don't move!

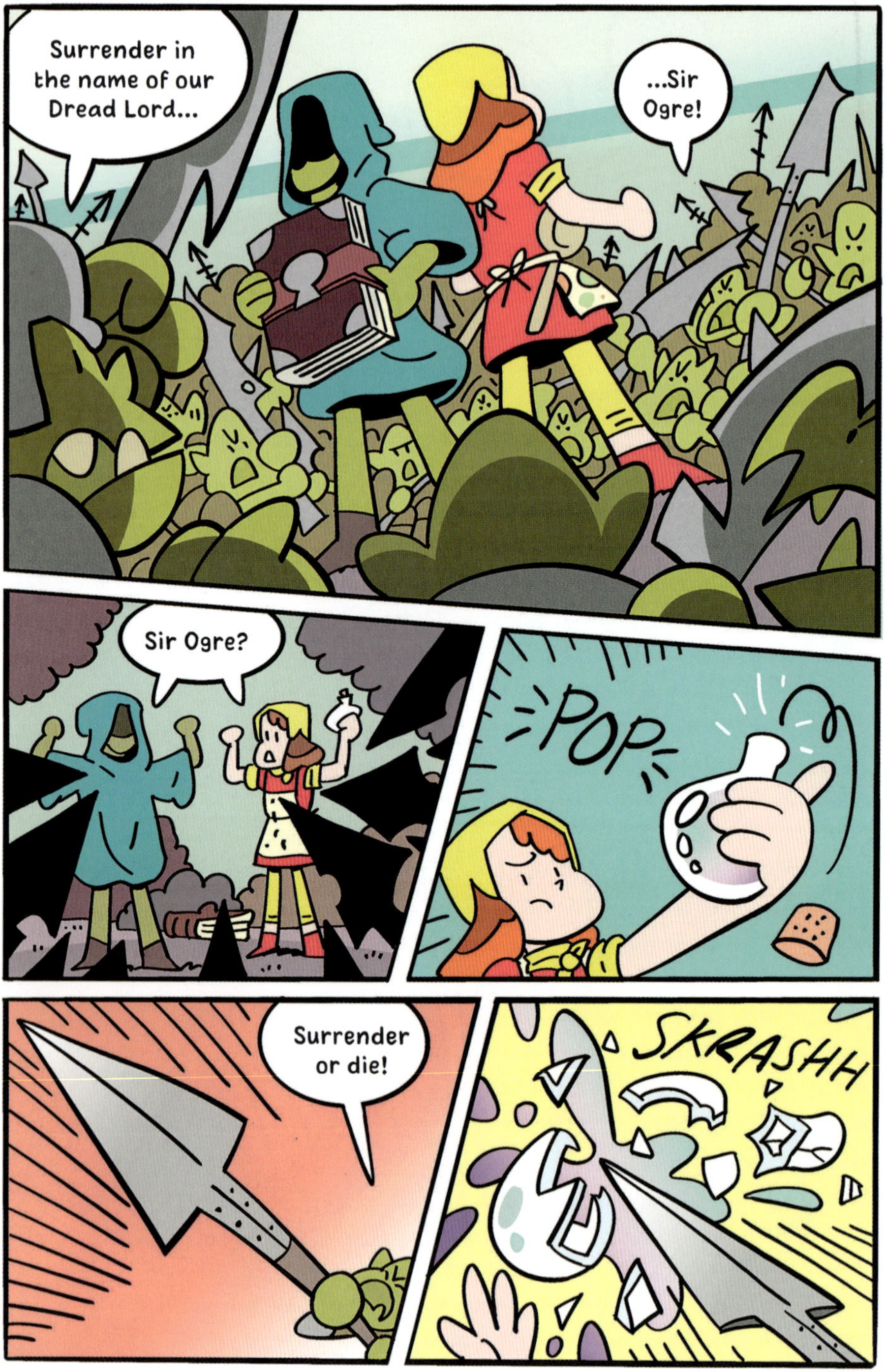
Surrender in the name of our Dread Lord...
...Sir Ogre!
Sir Ogre?
POP
Surrender or die!
SKRASHH

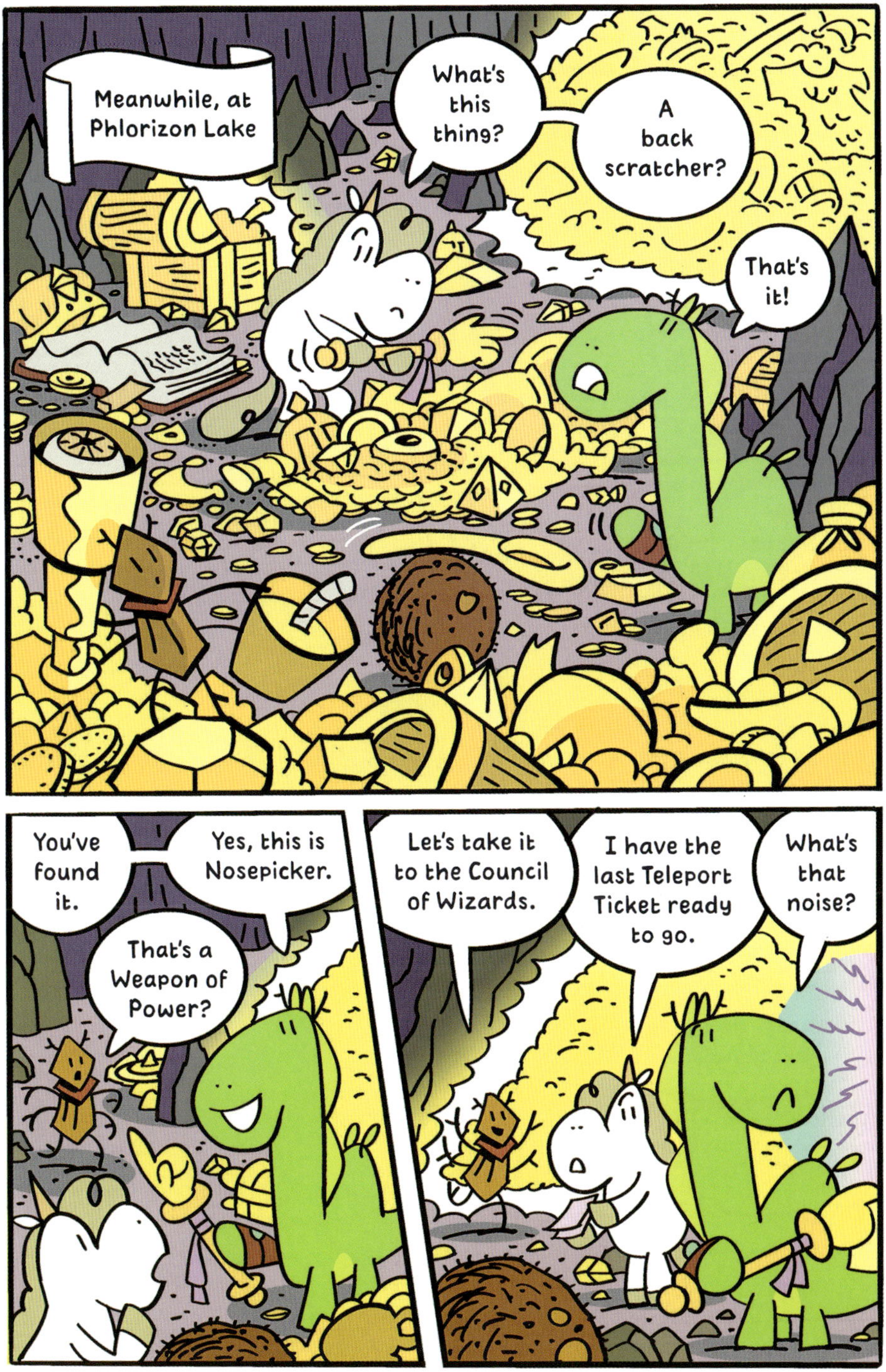

Meanwhile, at Phlorizon Lake
What's this thing?
A back scratcher?
That's it!
You've found it.
Yes, this is Nosepicker.
That's a Weapon of Power?
Let's take it to the Council of Wizards.
I have the last Teleport Ticket ready to go.
What's that noise?

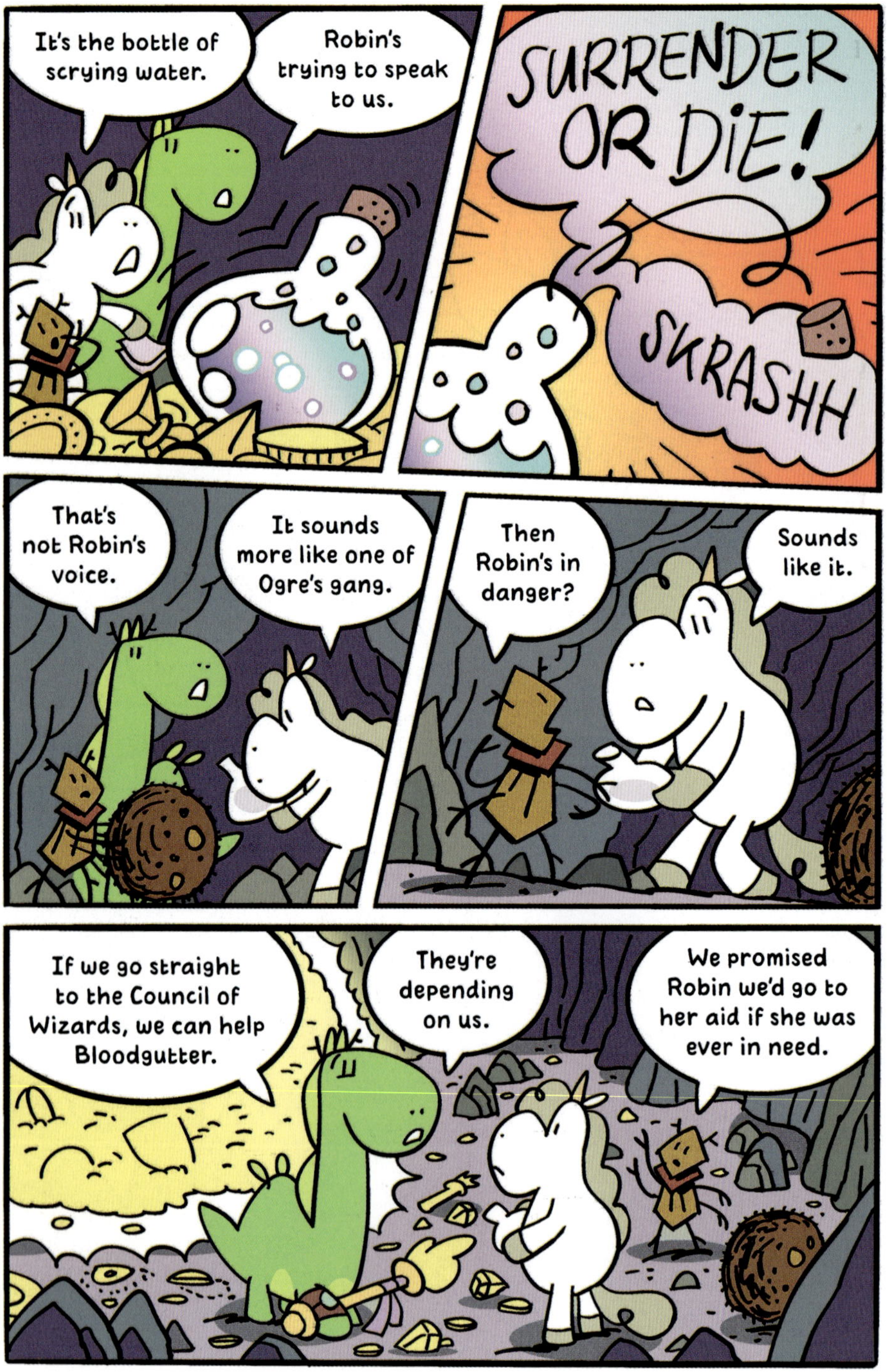
It's the bottle of scrying water.
Robin's trying to speak to us.
SURRENDER OR DIE!
SKRASHH
That's not Robin's voice.
It sounds more like one of Ogre's gang.
Then Robin's in danger?
Sounds like it.
If we go straight to the Council of Wizards, we can help Bloodgutter.
They're depending on us.
We promised Robin we'd go to her aid if she was ever in need.

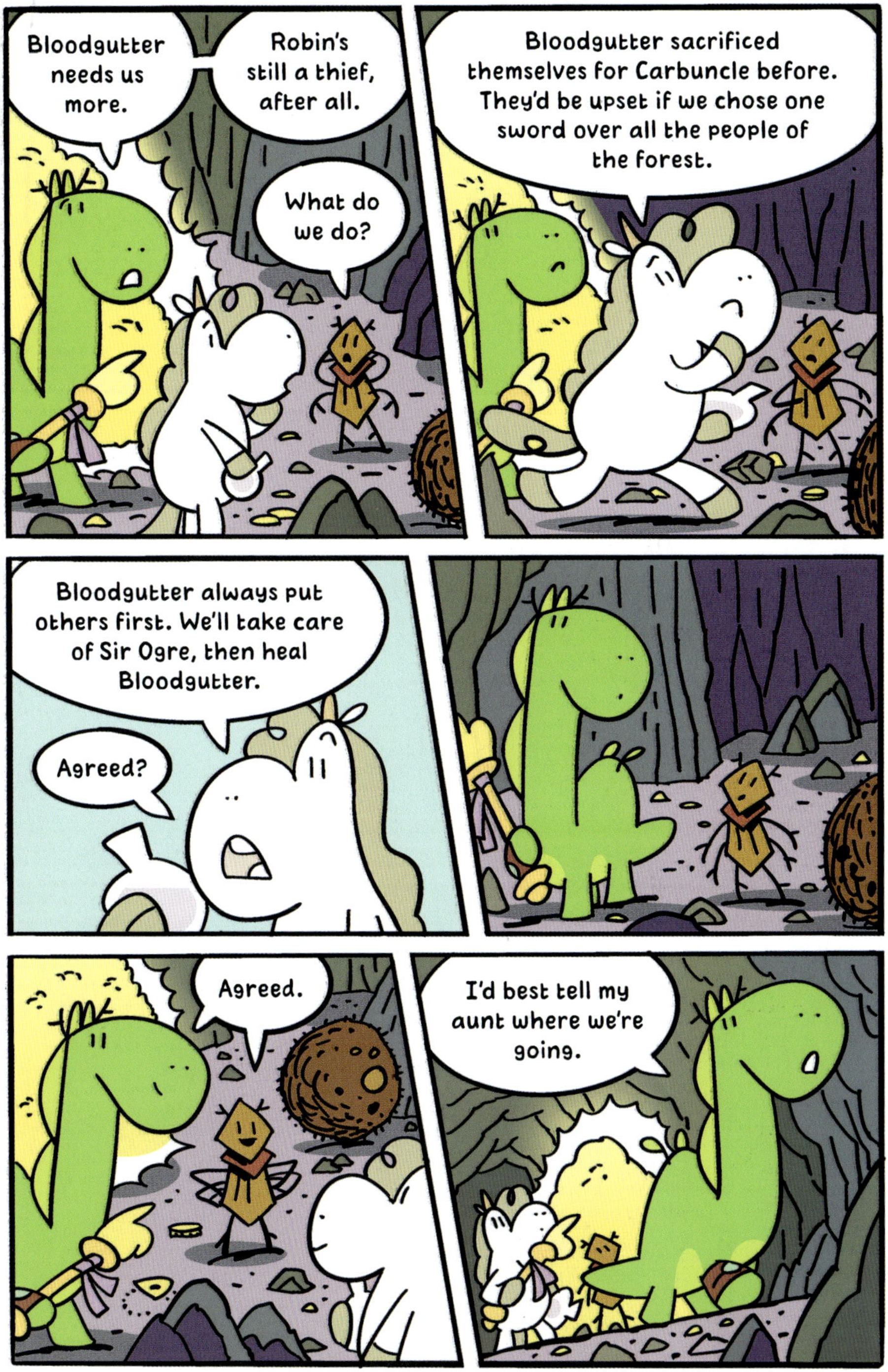
Bloodgutter needs us more.
Robin's still a thief, after all.
What do we do?
Bloodgutter sacrificed themselves for Carbuncle before. They'd be upset if we chose one sword over all the people of the forest.
Bloodgutter always put others first. We'll take care of Sir Ogre, then heal Bloodgutter.
Agreed?
Agreed.
I'd best tell my aunt where we're going.

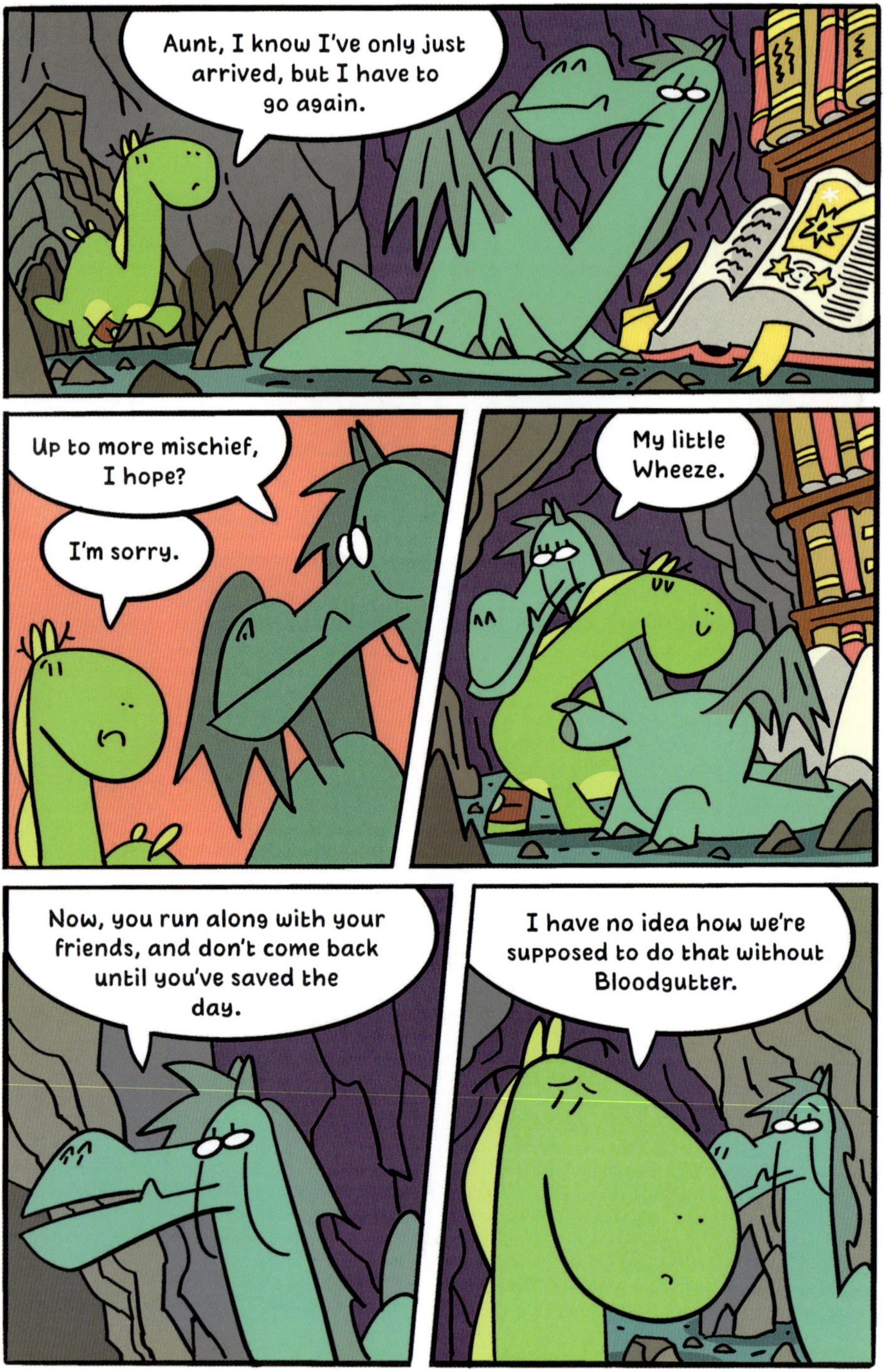
Aunt, I know I've only just arrived, but I have to go again.
Up to more mischief, I hope?
I'm sorry.
My little Wheeze.
Now, you run along with your friends, and don't come back until you've saved the day.
I have no idea how we're supposed to do that without Bloodgutter.

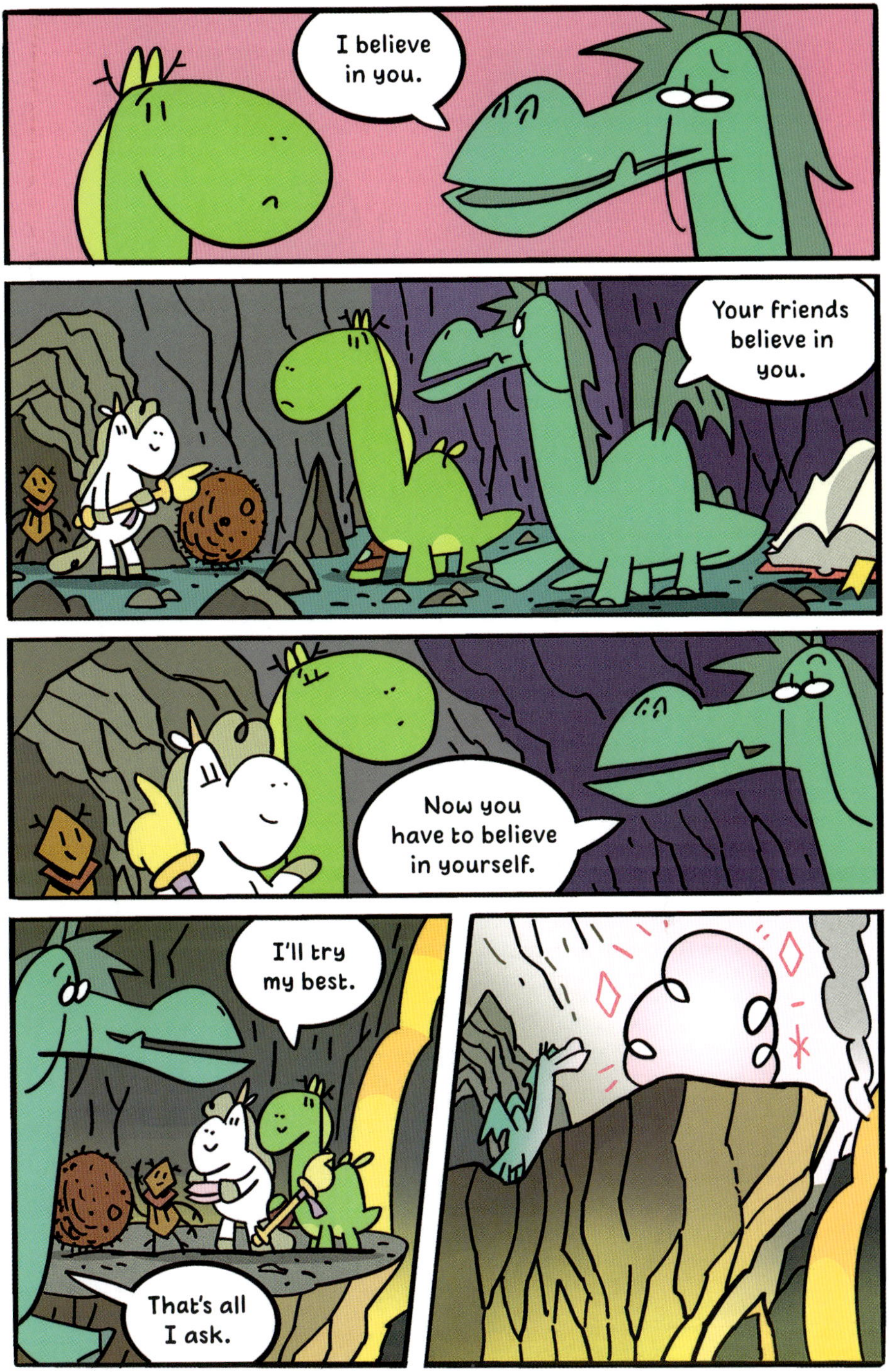
I believe in you.
Your friends believe in you.
Now you have to believe in yourself.
I'll try my best.
That's all I ask.

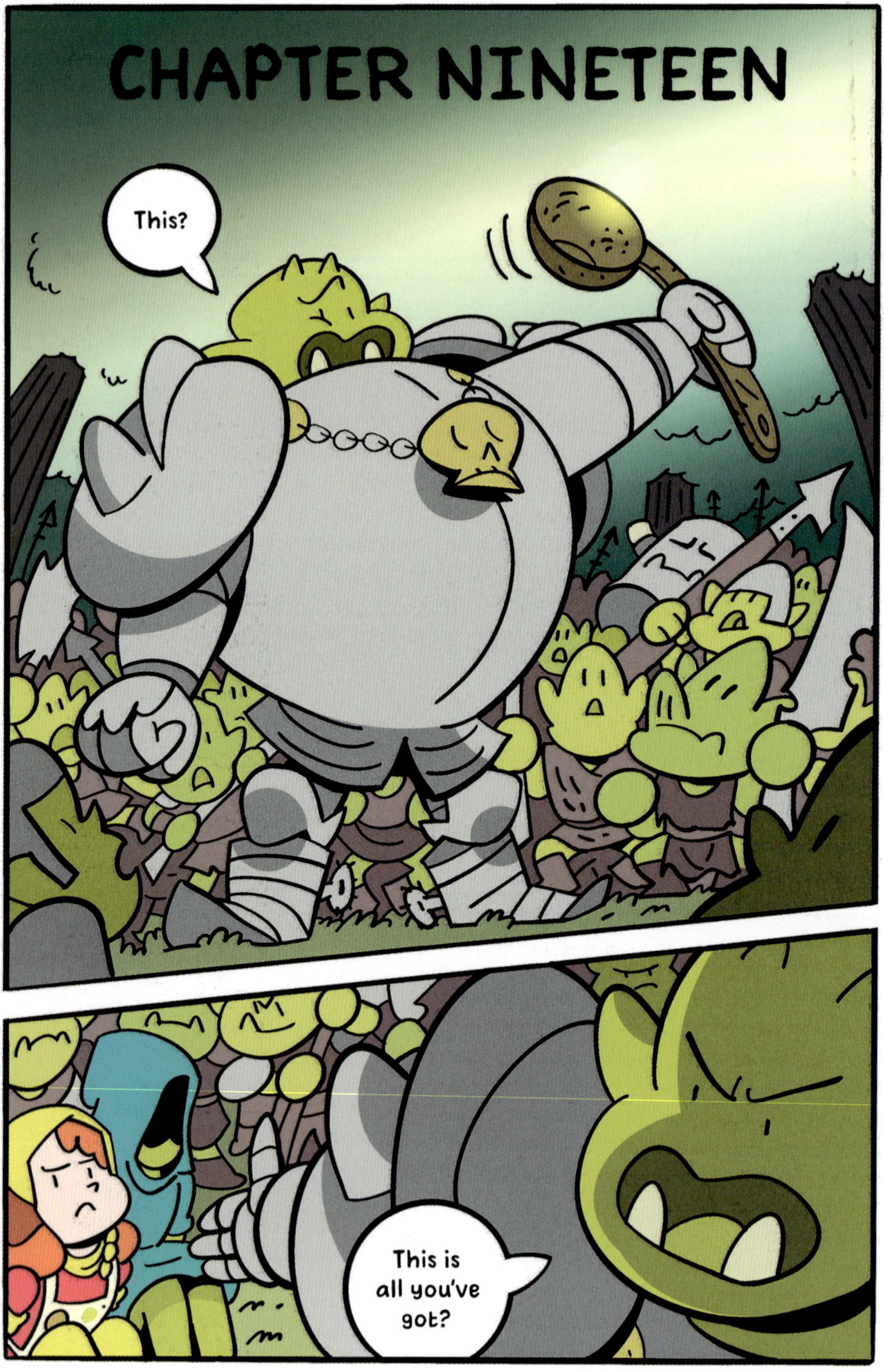
CHAPTER NINETEEN
This?
This is all you've got?

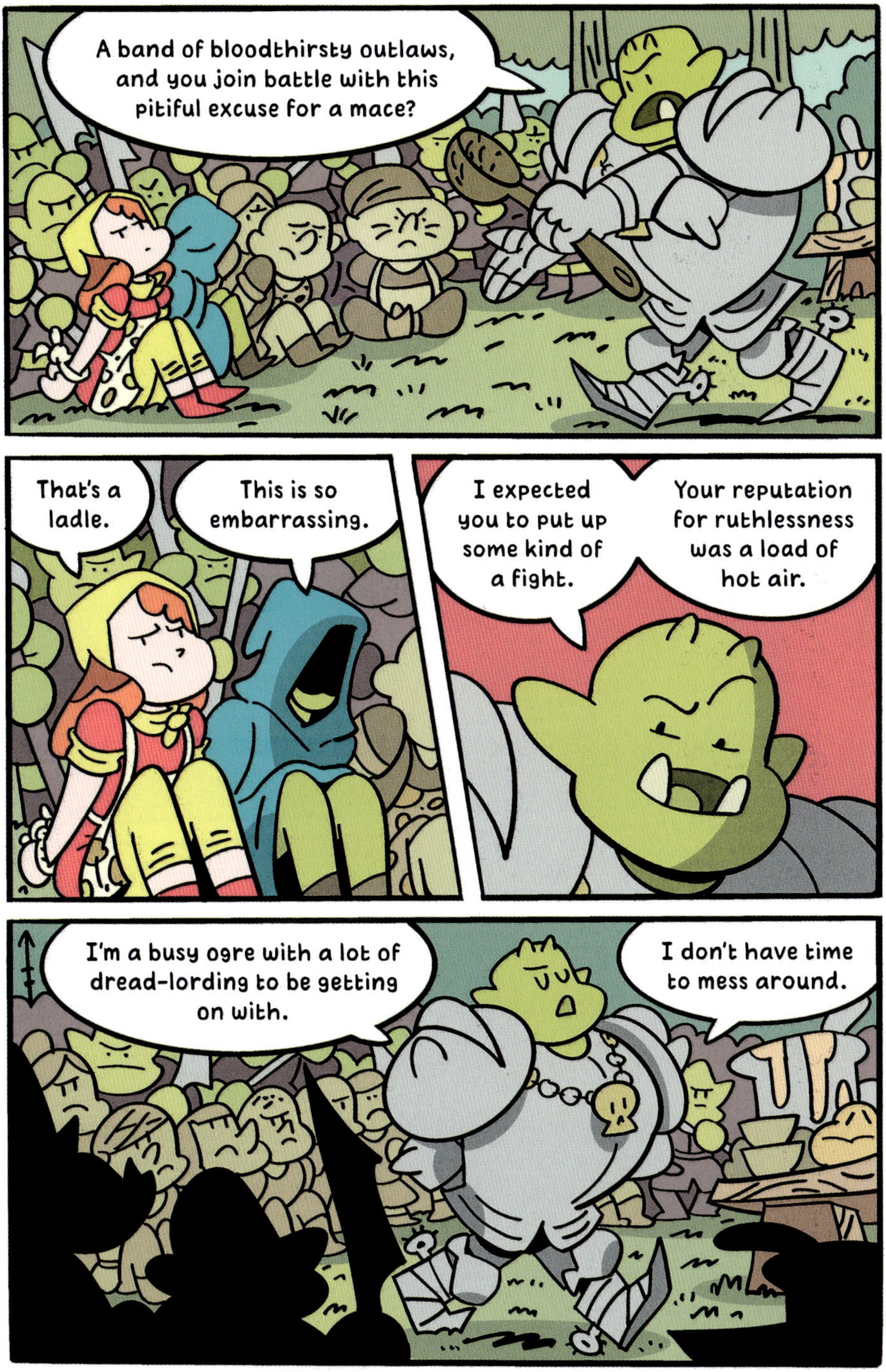
A band of bloodthirsty outlaws, and you join battle with this pitiful excuse for a mace?
That's a ladle.
This is so embarrassing.
I expected you to put up some kind of a fight.
Your reputation for ruthlessness was a load of hot air.
I'm a busy ogre with a lot of dread-lording to be getting on with.
I don't have time to mess around.

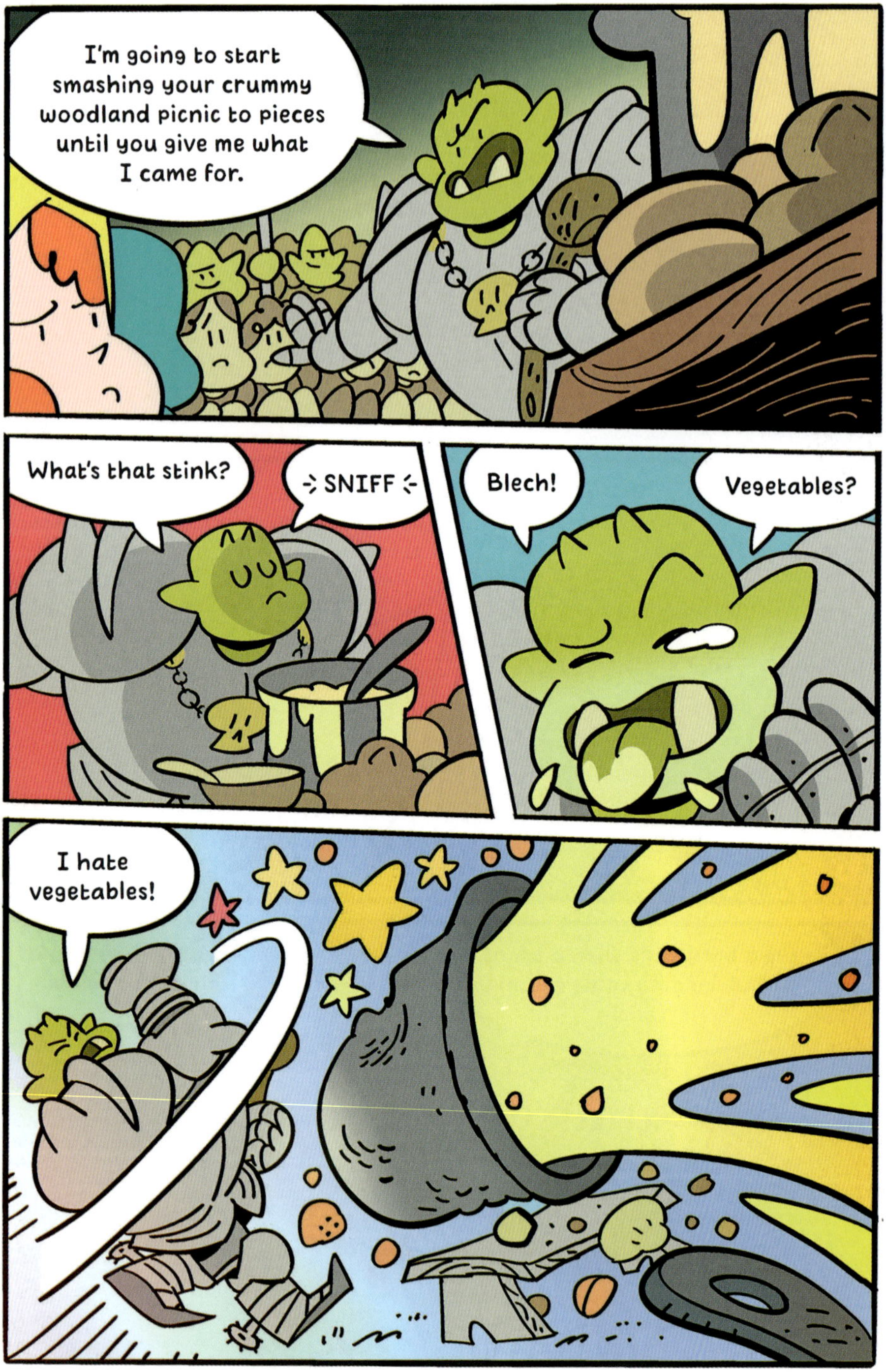

I'm going to start smashing your crummy woodland picnic to pieces until you give me what I came for.
What's that stink?
SNIFF
Blech!
Vegetables?
I hate vegetables!

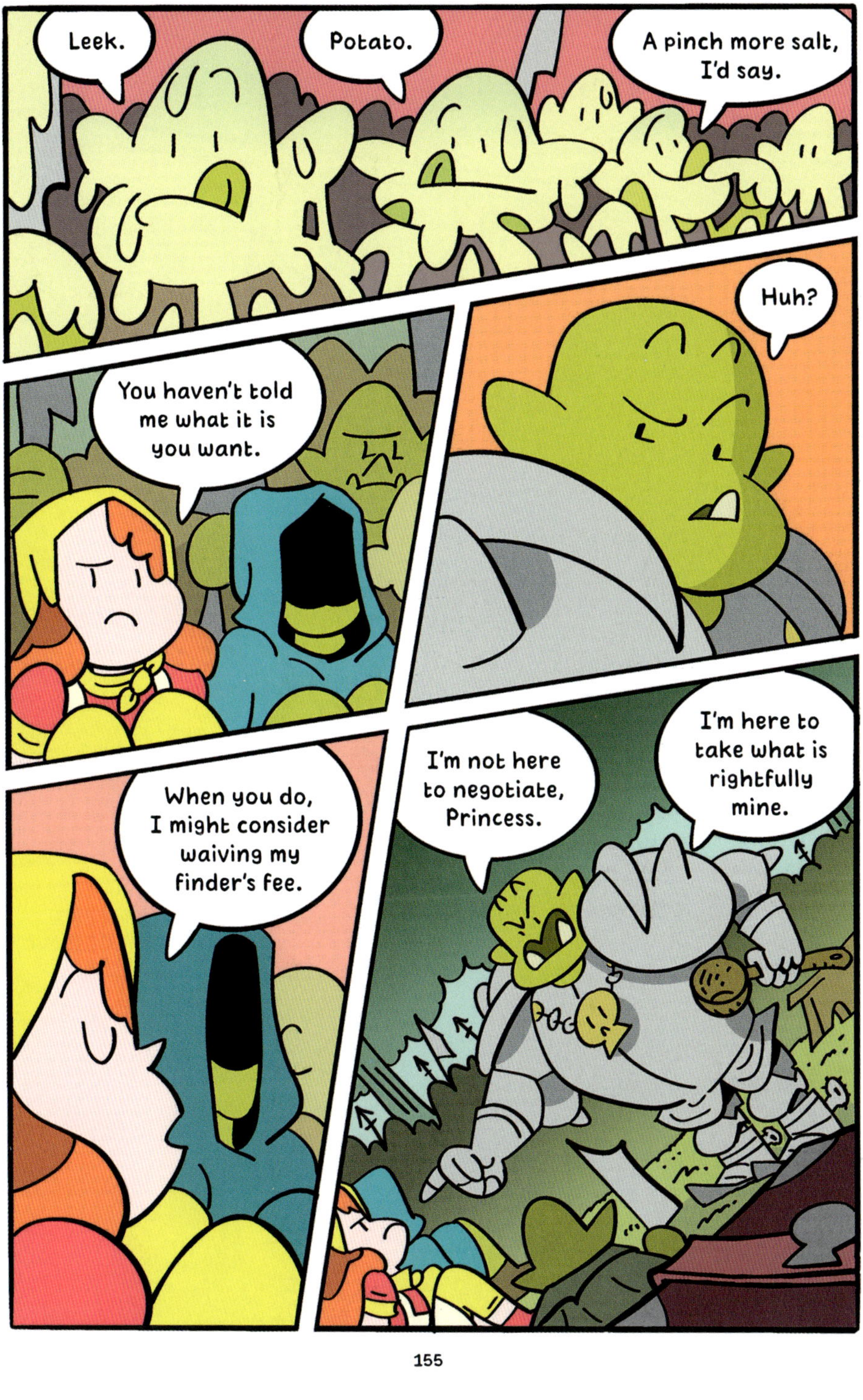
Leek.
Potato.
A pinch more salt, I'd say.
Huh?
You haven't told me what it is you want.
When you do, I might consider waiving my finder's fee.
I'm not here to negotiate, Princess.
I'm here to take what is rightfully mine.

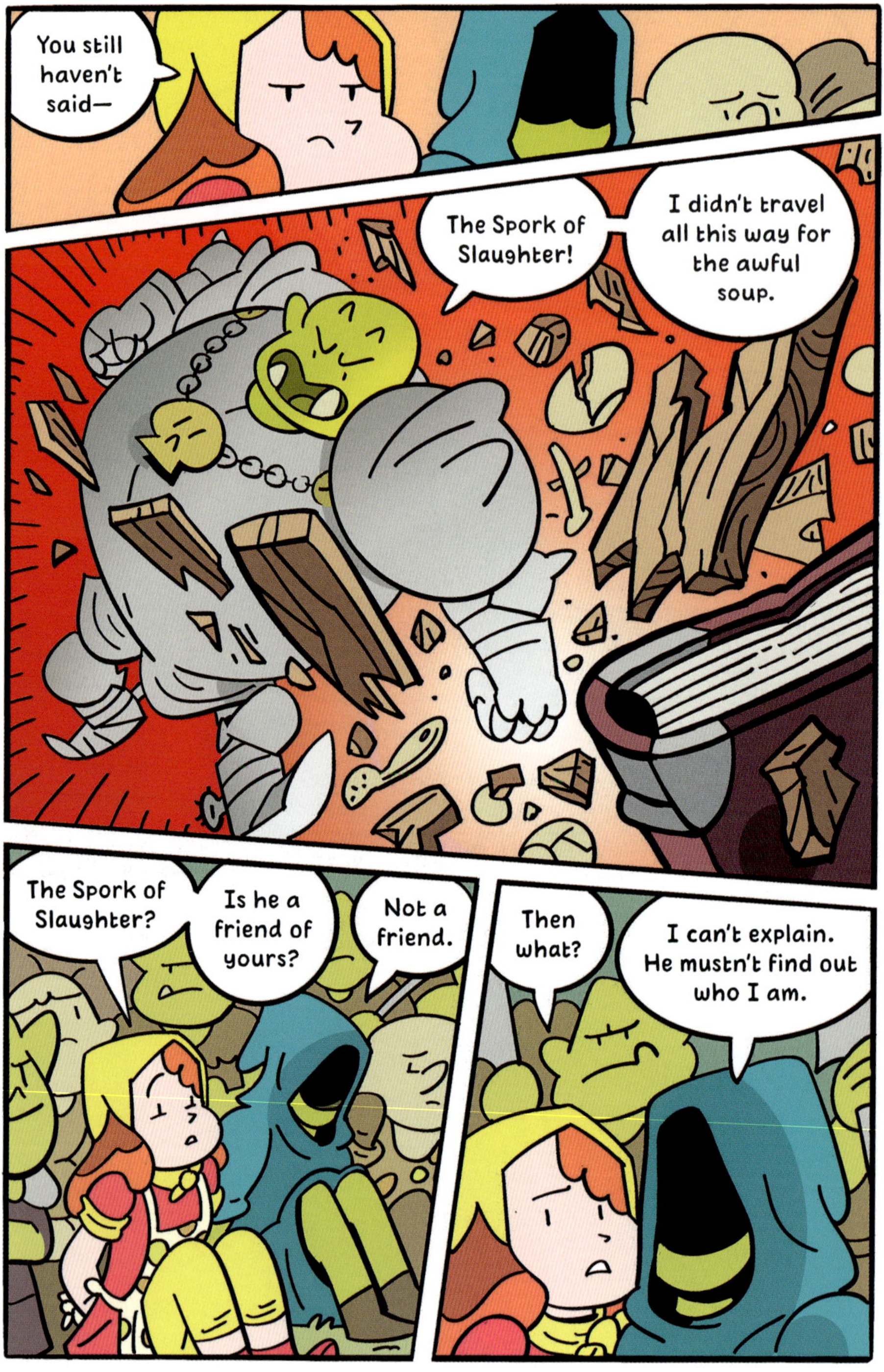
You still haven't said—
The Spork of Slaughter!
I didn't travel all this way for the awful soup.
The Spork of Slaughter?
Is he a friend of yours?
Not a friend.
Then what?
I can't explain. He mustn't find out who I am.

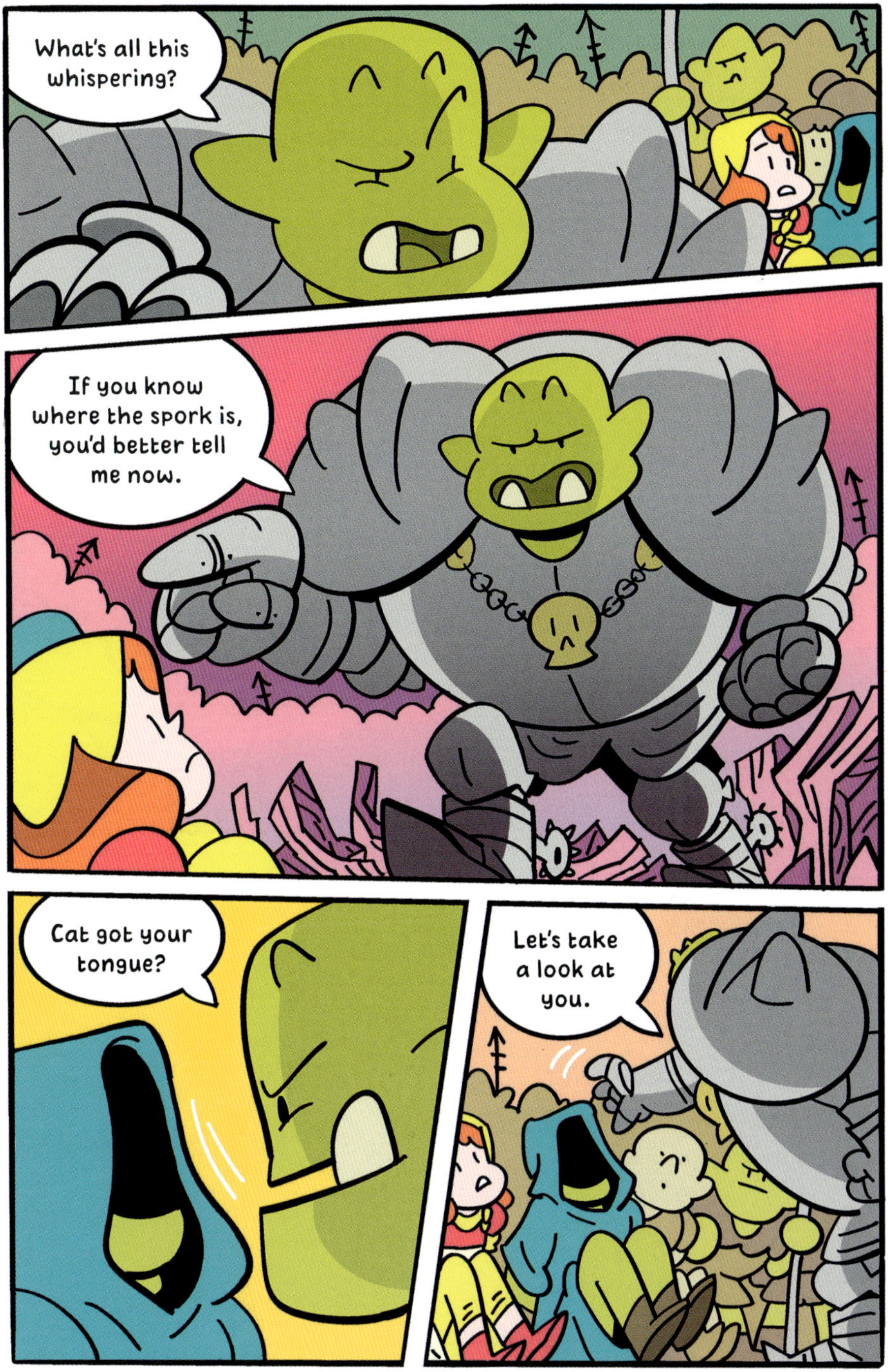
What's all this whispering?
If you know where the spork is, you'd better tell me now.
Cat got your tongue?
Let's take a look at you.

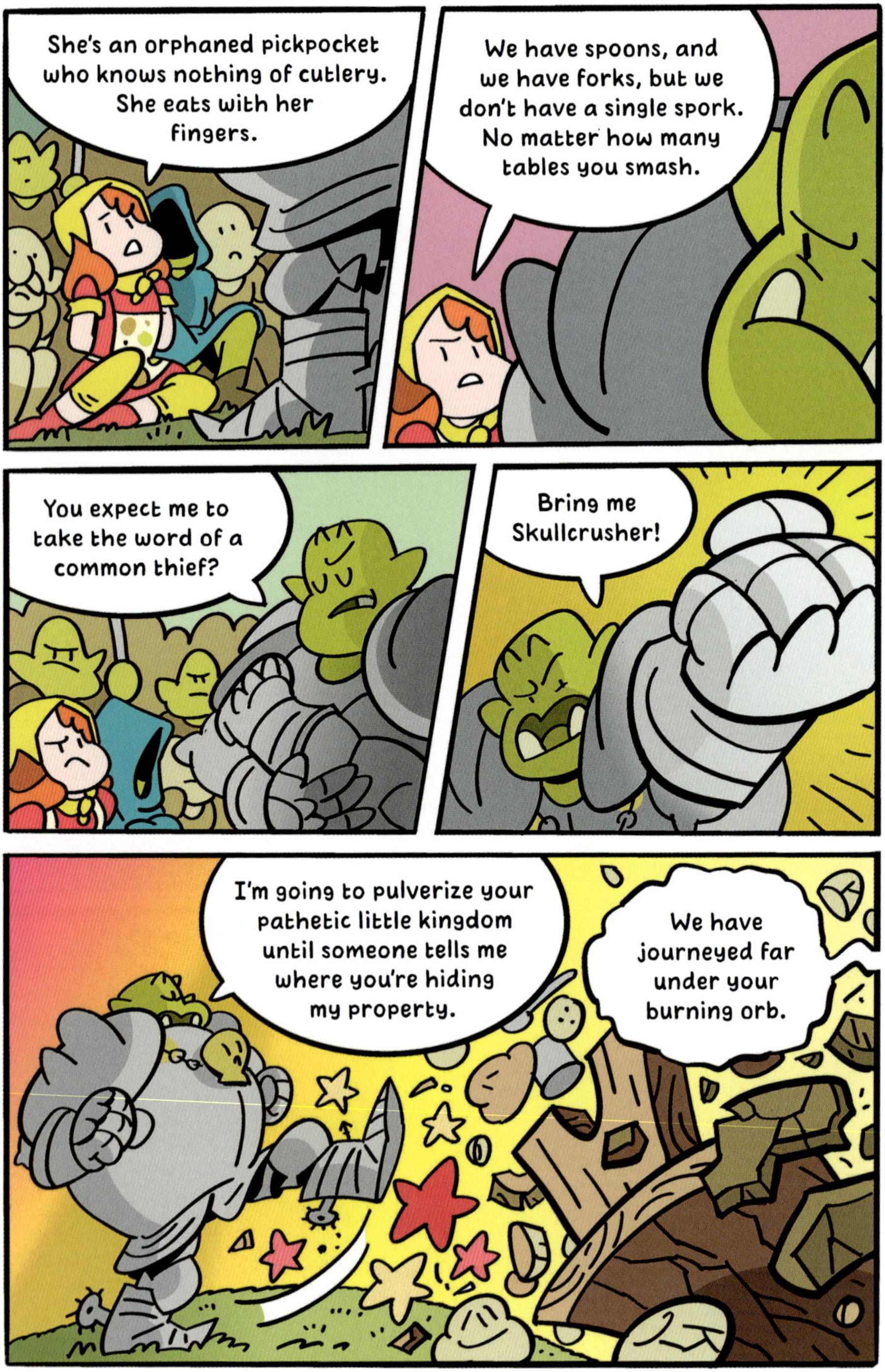
She's an orphaned pickpocket who knows nothing of cutlery. She eats with her fingers.
We have spoons, and we have forks, but we don't have a single spork. No matter how many tables you smash.
You expect me to take the word of a common thief?
Bring me Skullcrusher!
I'm going to pulverize your pathetic little kingdom until someone tells me where you're hiding my property.
We have journeyed far under your burning orb.

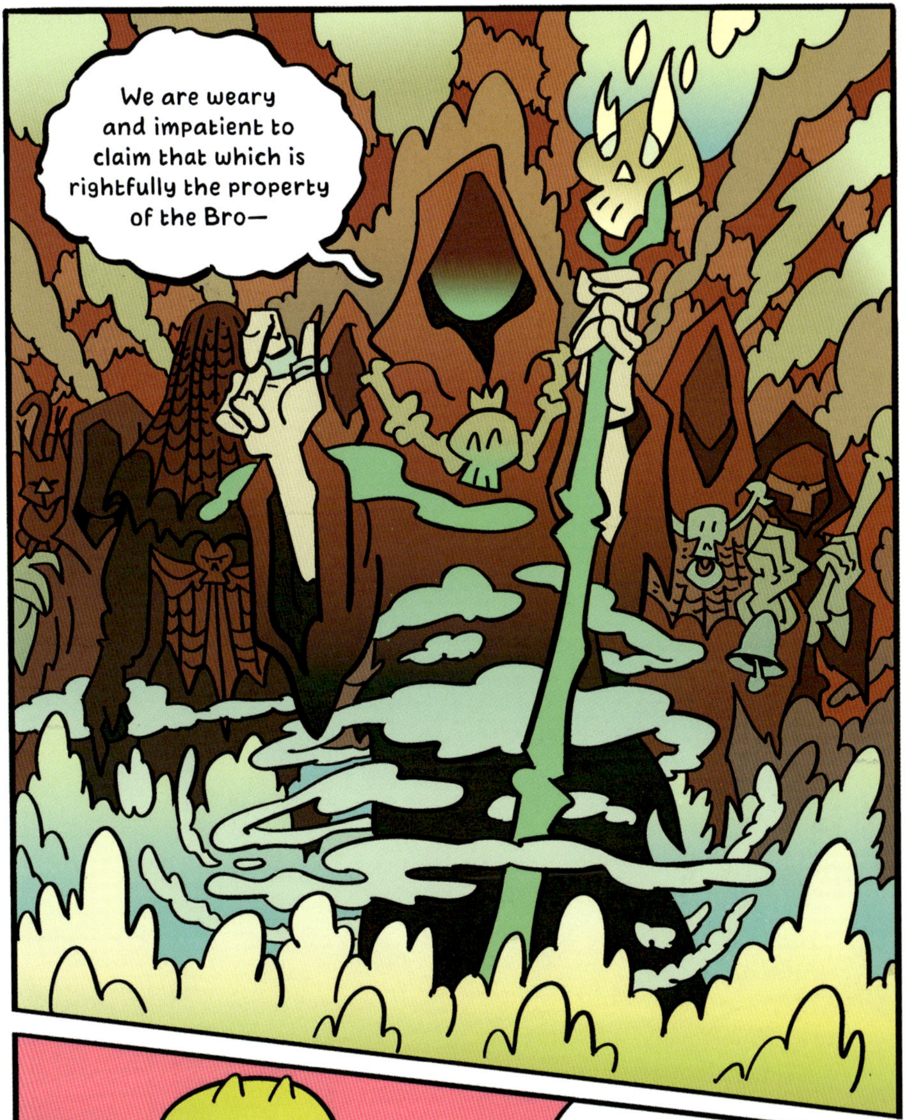
We are weary and impatient to claim that which is rightfully the property of the Bro—

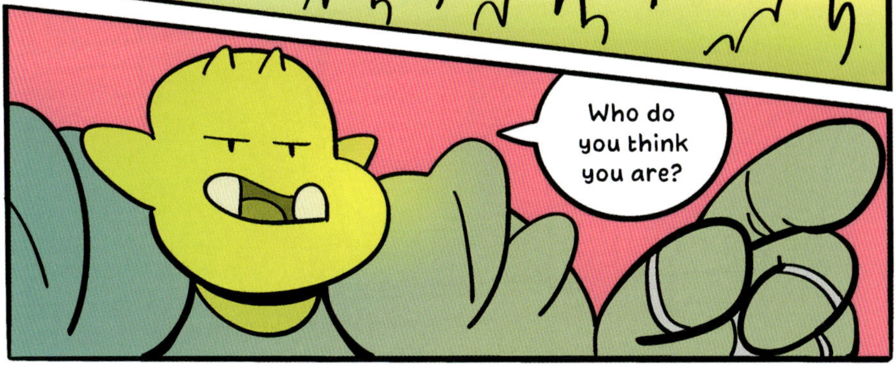
Who do you think you are?

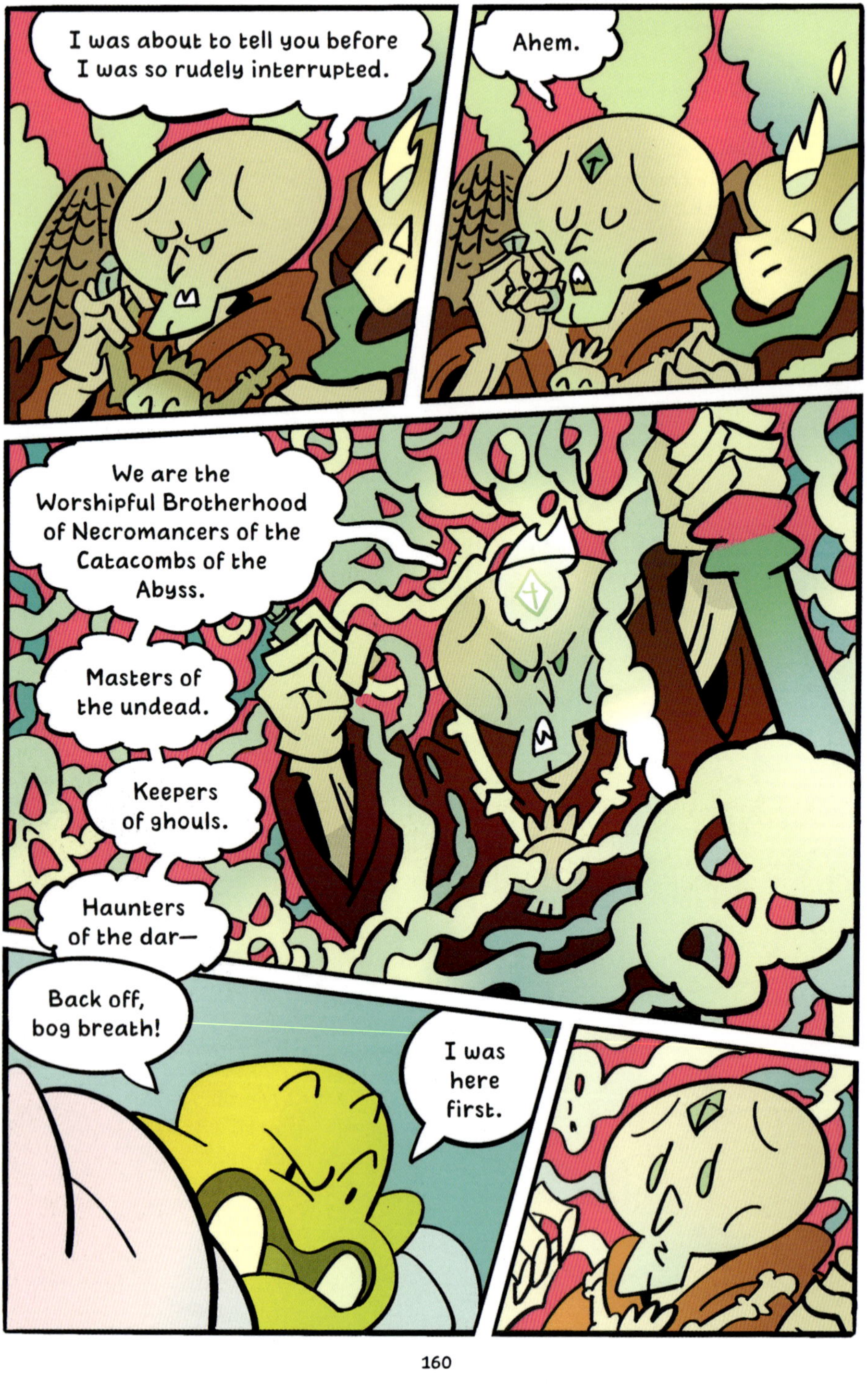
I was about to tell you before I was so rudely interrupted.
Ahem.
We are the Worshipful Brotherhood of Necromancers of the Catacombs of the Abyss.
Masters of the undead.
Keepers of ghouls.
Haunters of the dar—
Back off, bog breath!
I was here first.

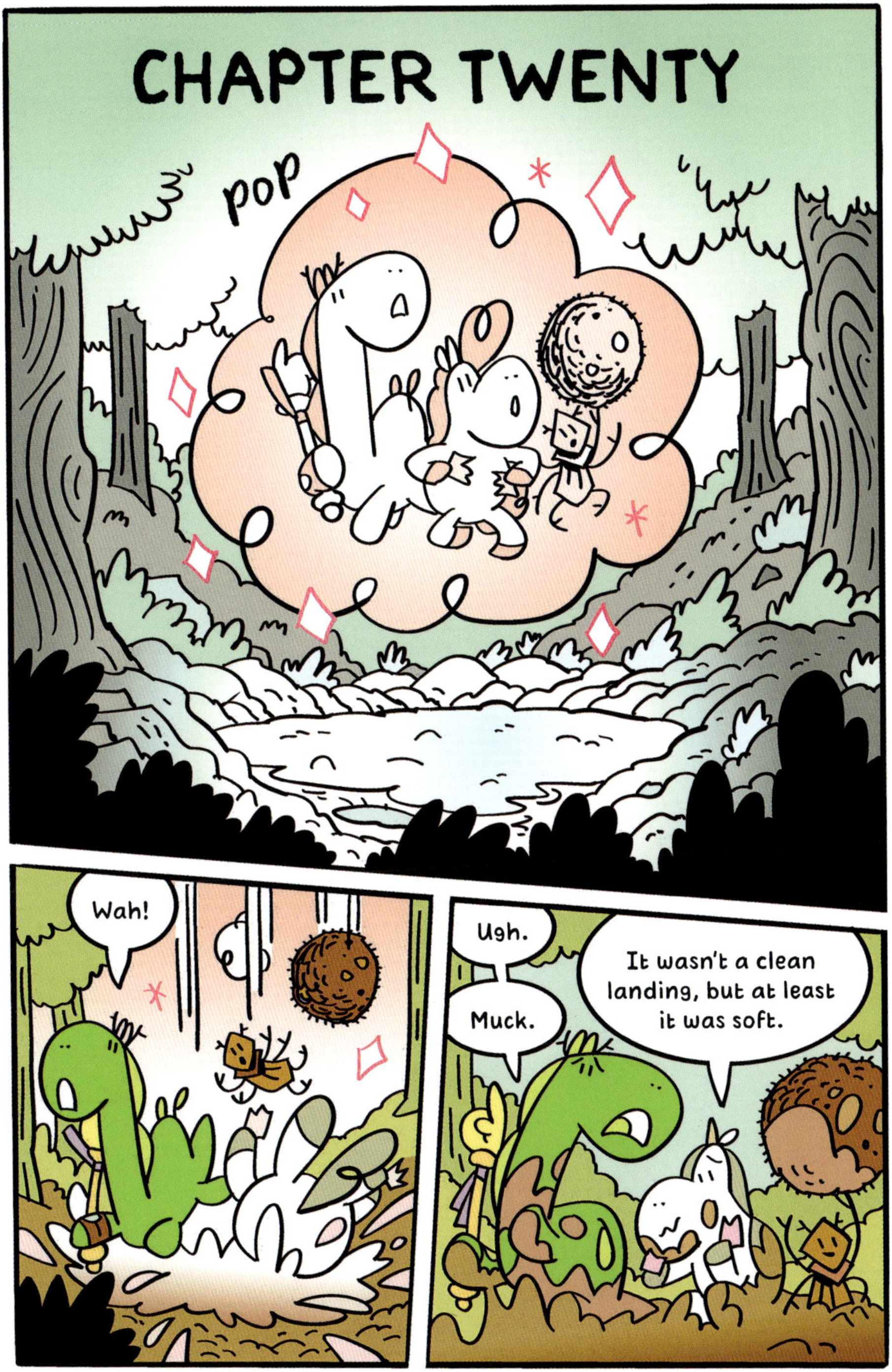
CHAPTER TWENTY
pop
Wah!
Ugh.
Muck.
It wasn't a clean landing, but at least it was soft.

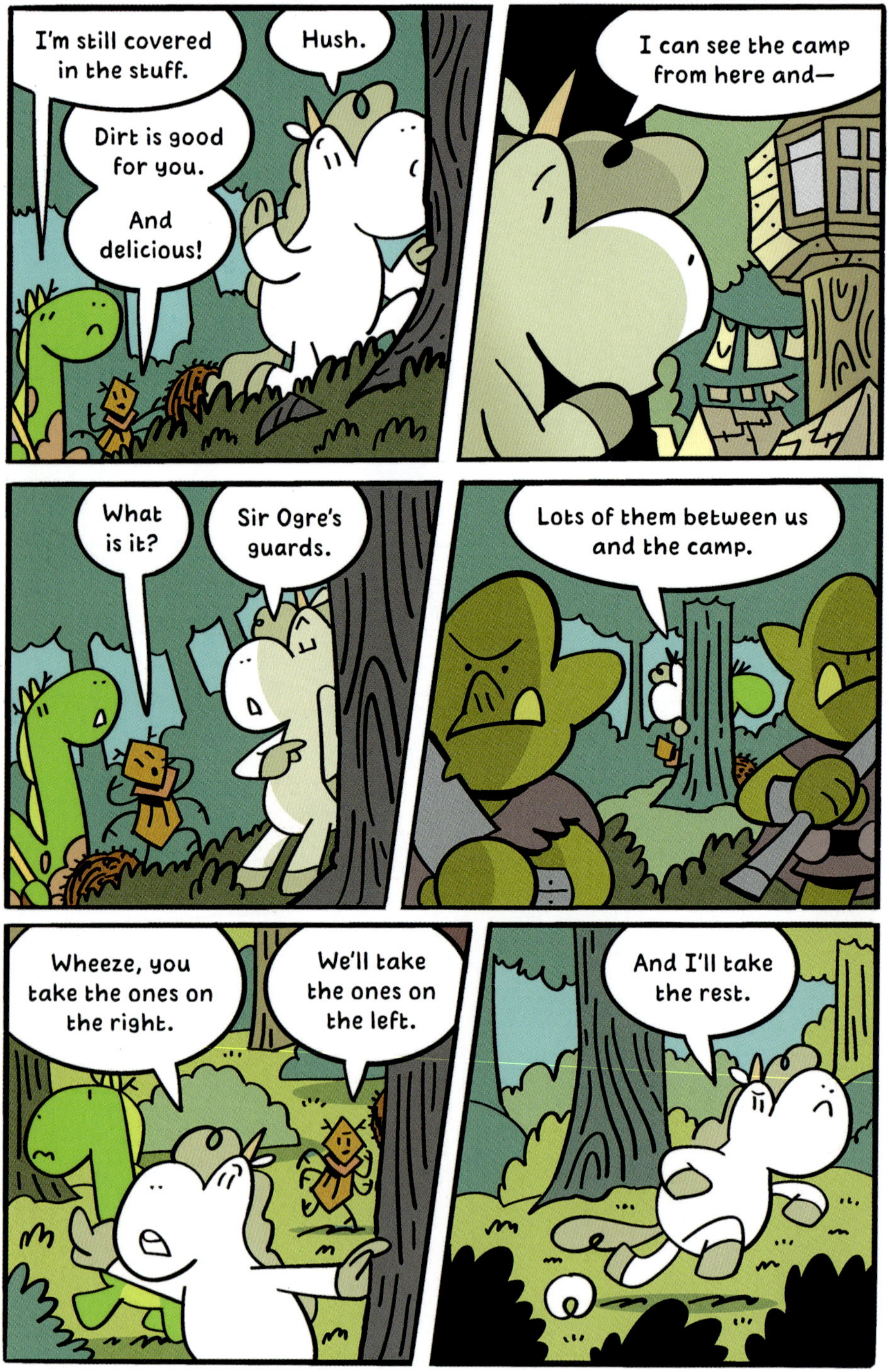
I'm still covered in the stuff.
Hush.
Dirt is good for you.
And delicious!
I can see the camp from here and—
What is it?
Sir Ogre's guards.
Lots of them between us and the camp.
Wheeze, you take the ones on the right.
We'll take the ones on the left.
And I'll take the rest.

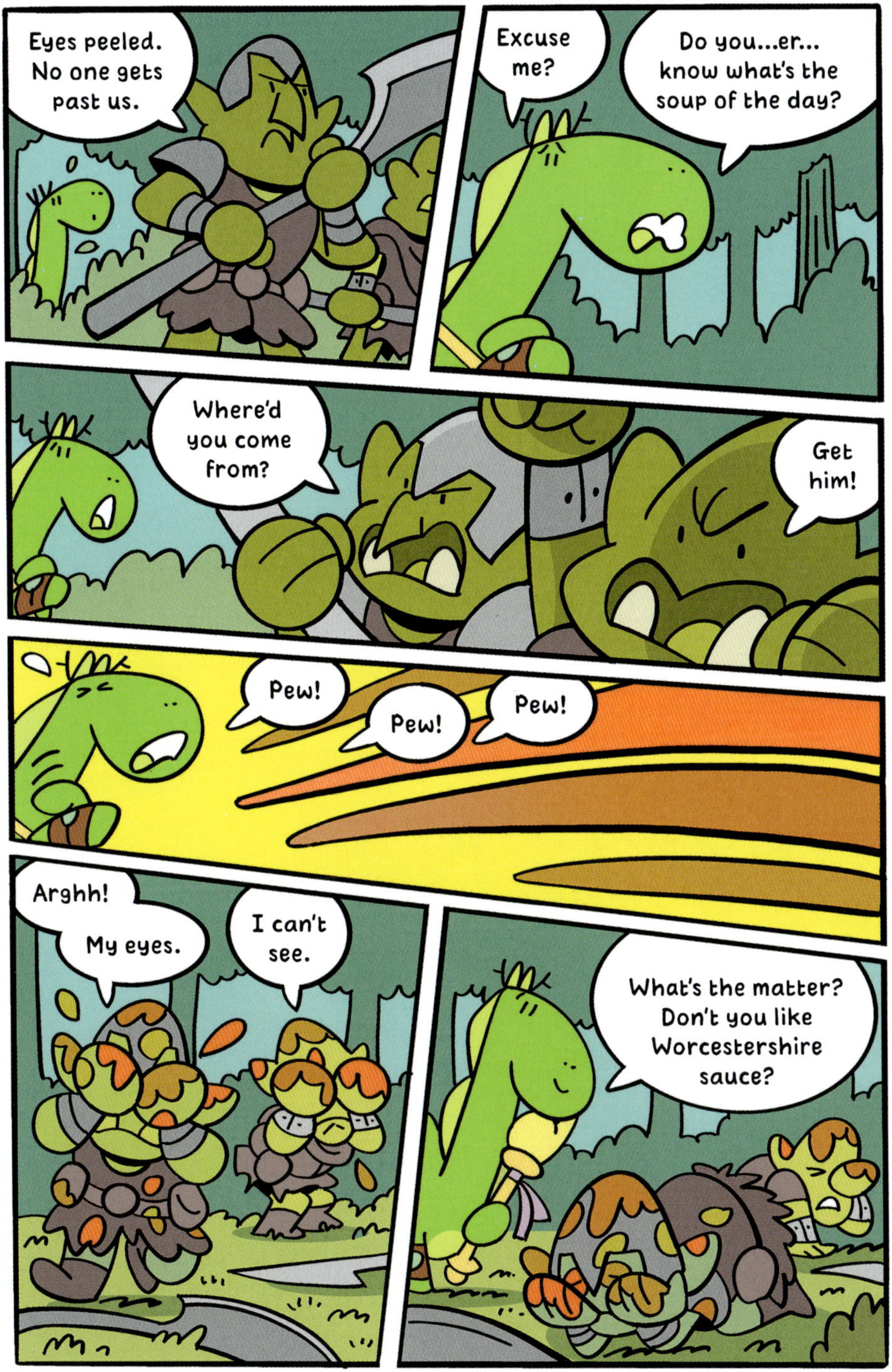
Eyes peeled. No one gets past us.
Excuse me?
Do you...er... know what's the soup of the day?
Where'd you come from?
Get him!
Pew!
Pew!
Pew!
Arghh!
My eyes.
I can't see.
What's the matter? Don't you like Worcestershire sauce?

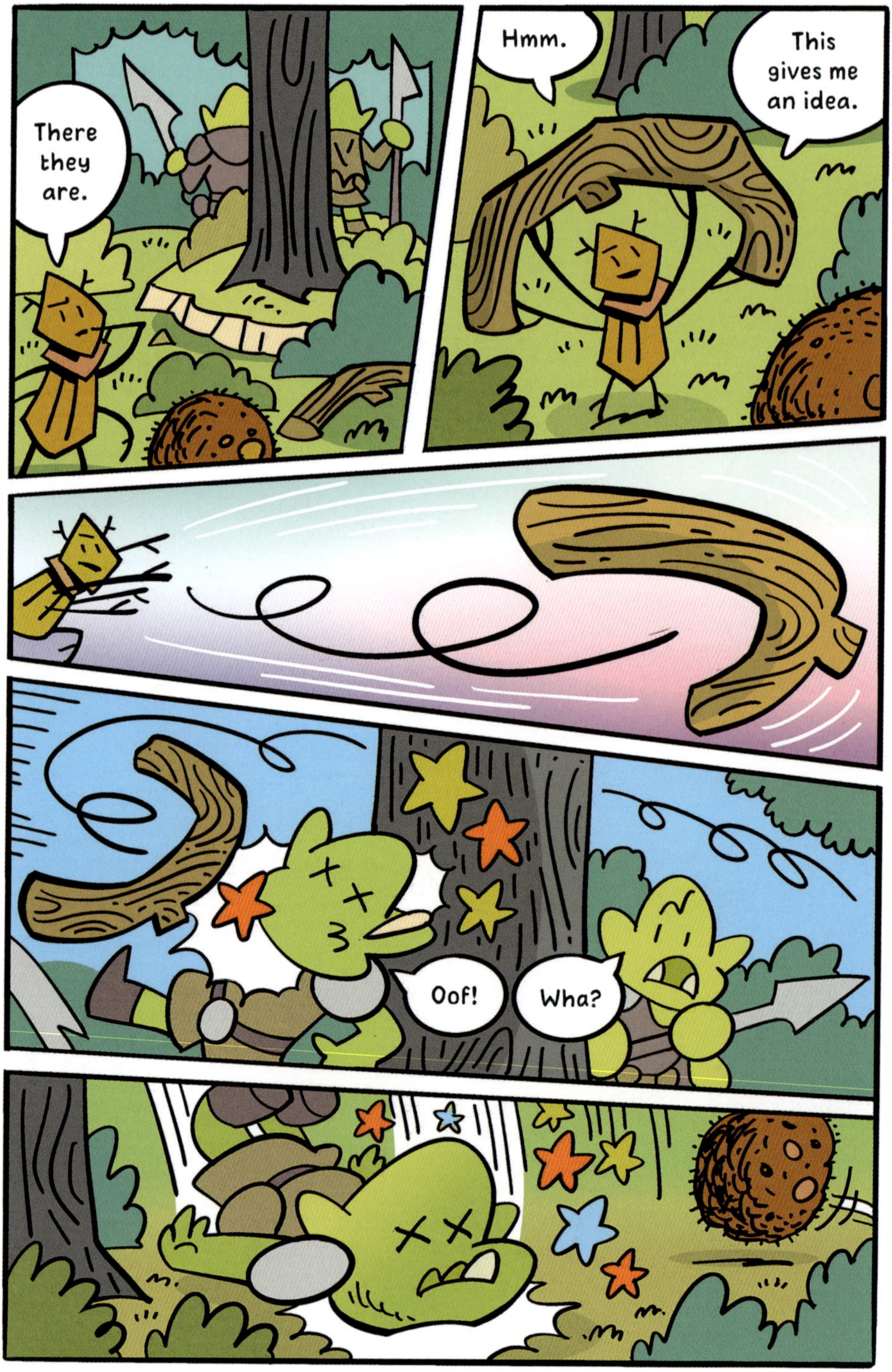
There they are.
Hmm.
This gives me an idea.
Oof!
Wha?

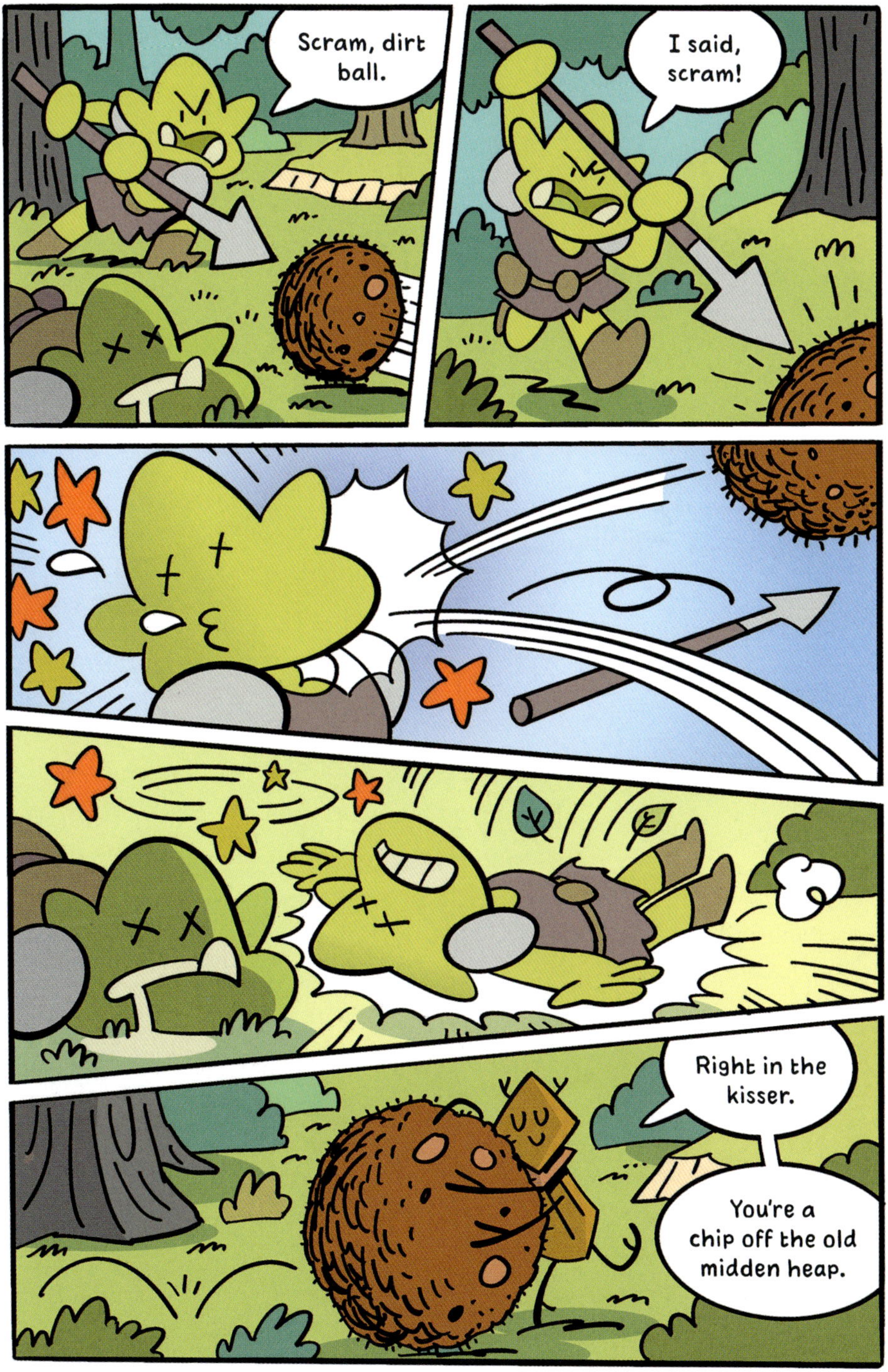
Scram, dirt ball.
I said, scram!
Right in the kisser.
You're a chip off the old midden heap.

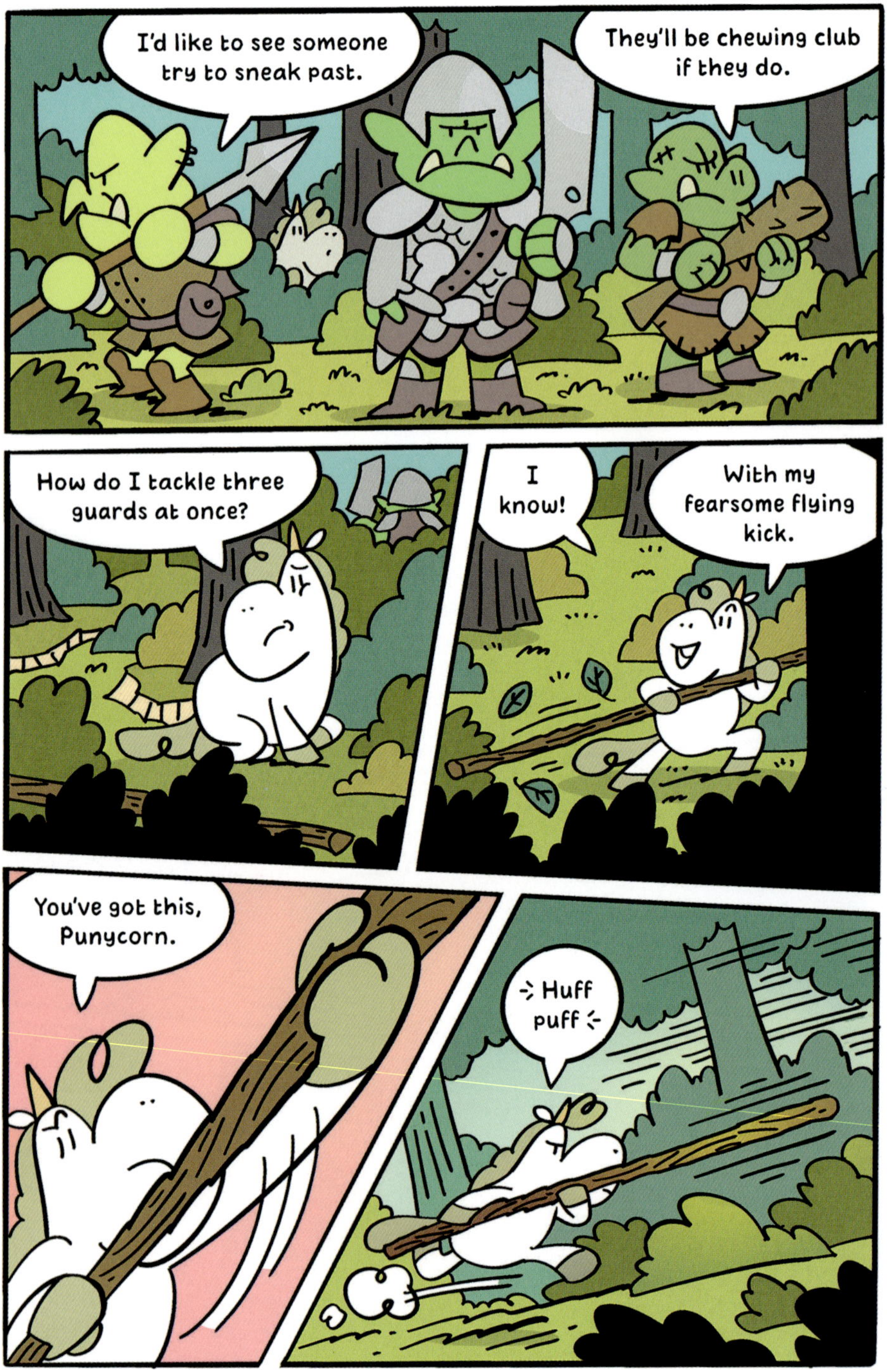
I'd like to see someone try to sneak past.
They'll be chewing club if they do.
How do I tackle three guards at once?
I know!
With my fearsome flying kick.
You've got this, Punycorn.
Huff puff

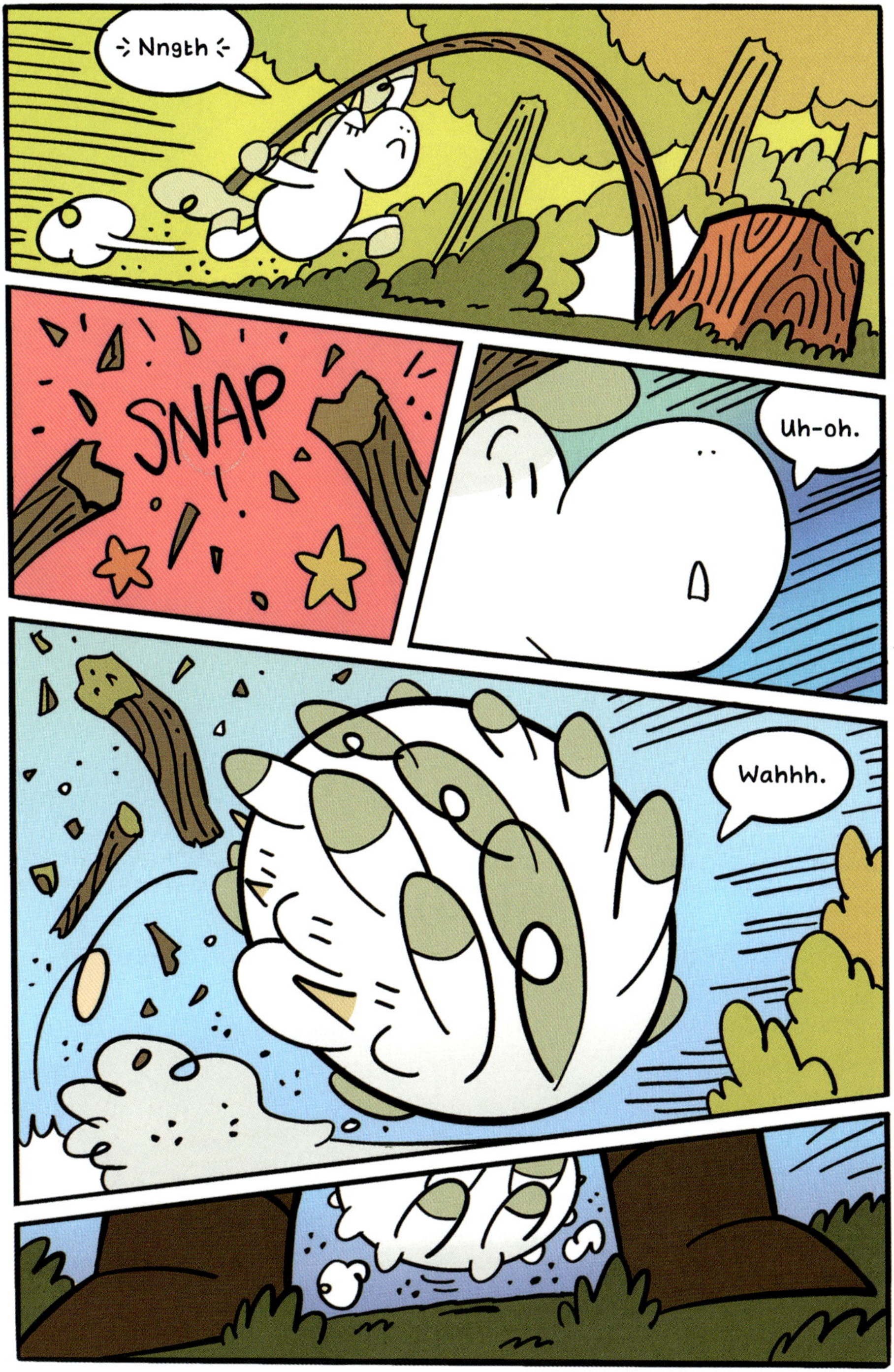
Nngth
SNAP
Uh-oh.
Wahhh.

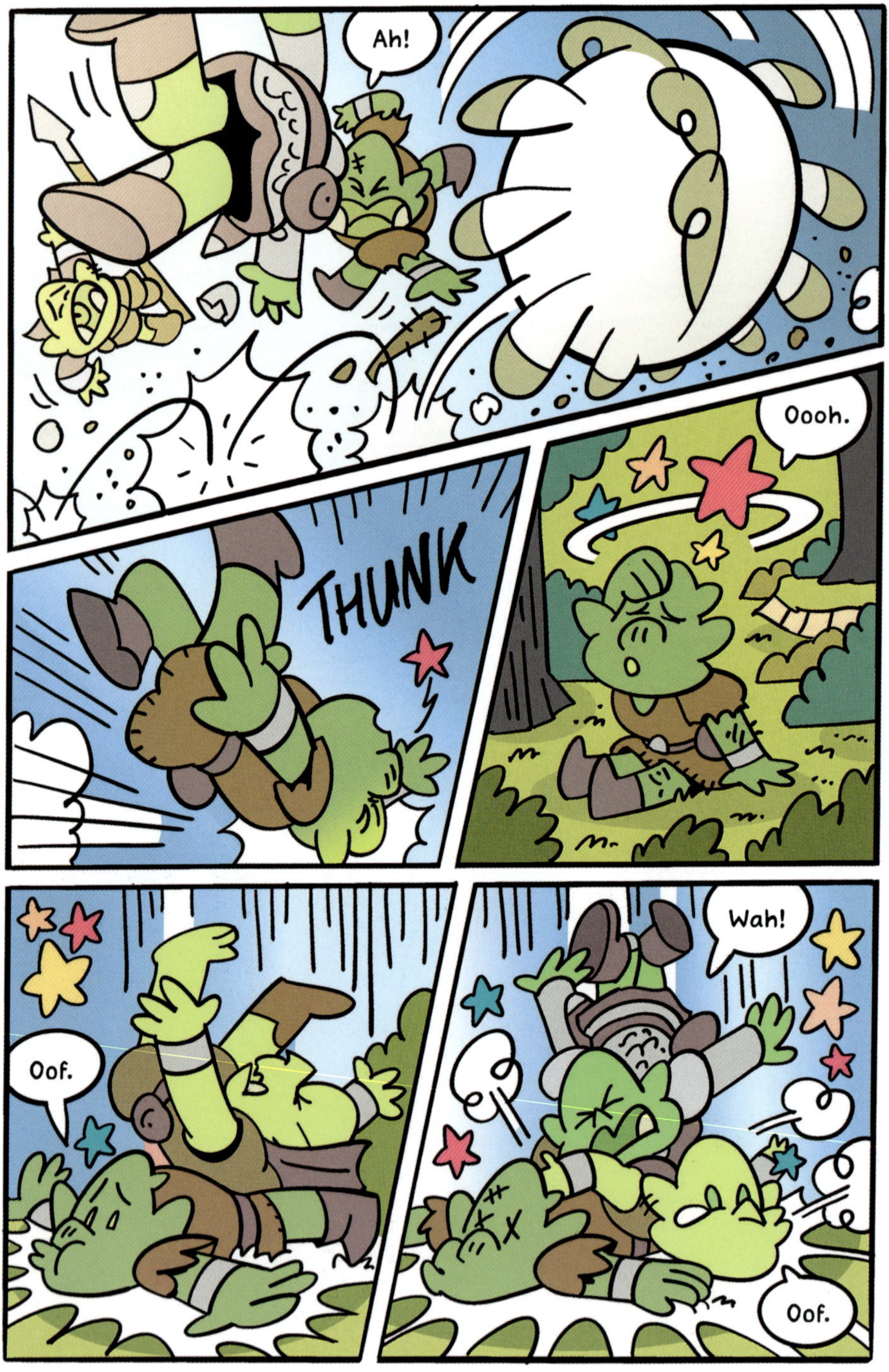
Ah!
THUNK
Oooh.
Oof.
Wah!
Oof.

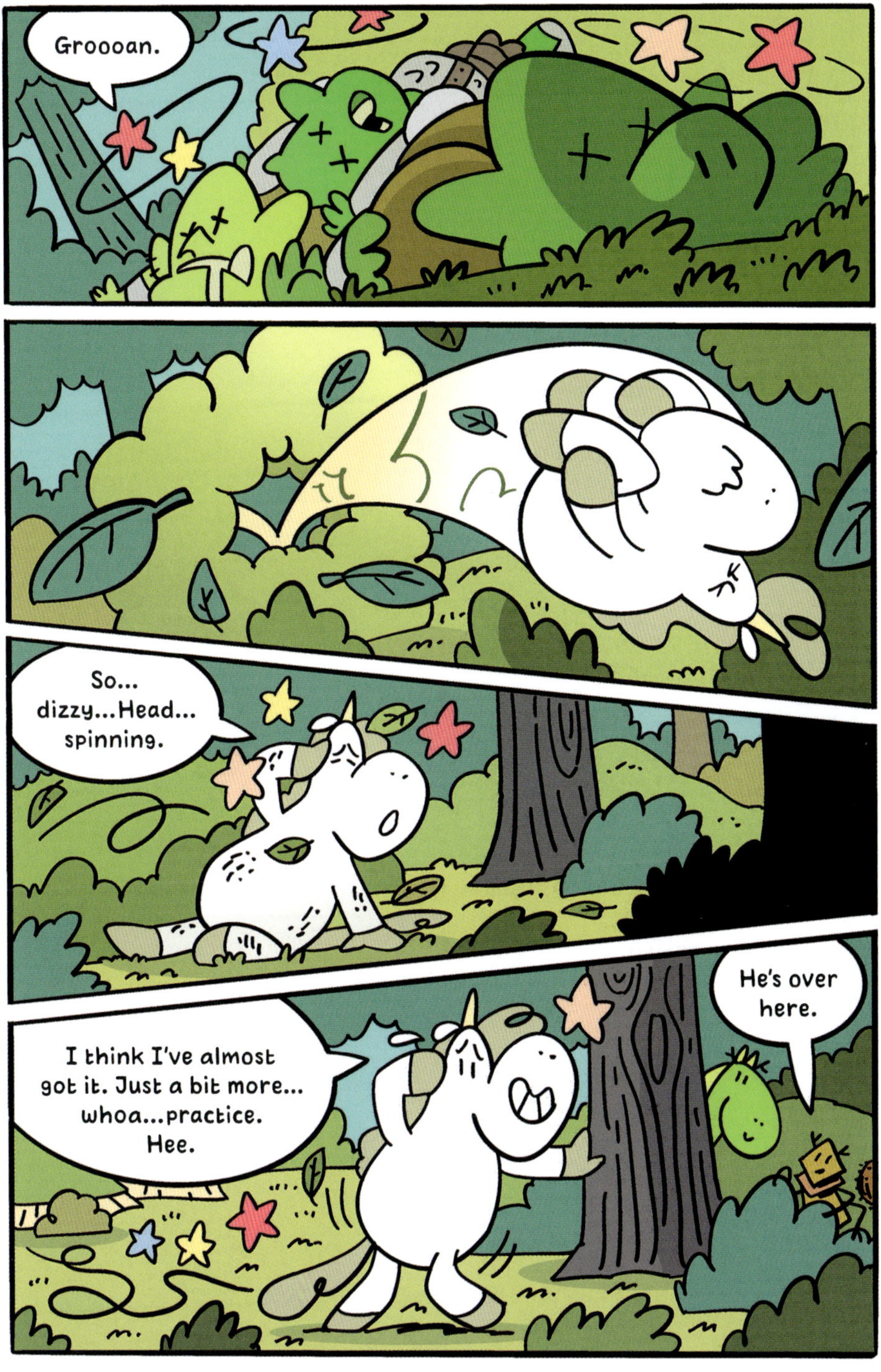
Groooan.
So... dizzy...Head... spinning.
I think I've almost got it. Just a bit more... whoa...practice. Hee.
He's over here.

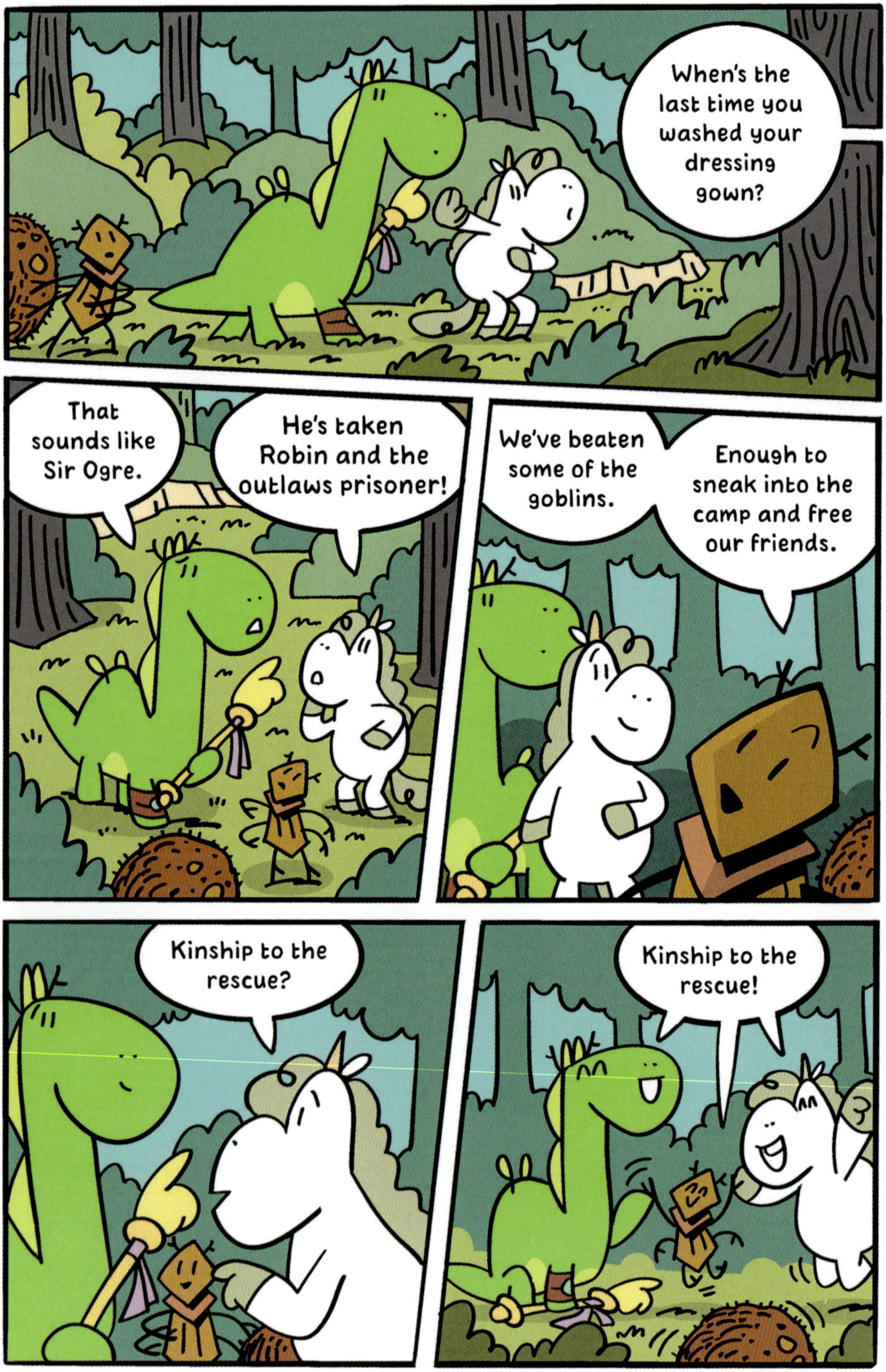
When's the last time you washed your dressing gown?
That sounds like Sir Ogre.
He's taken Robin and the outlaws prisoner!
We've beaten some of the goblins.
Enough to sneak into the camp and free our friends.
Kinship to the rescue?
Kinship to the rescue!

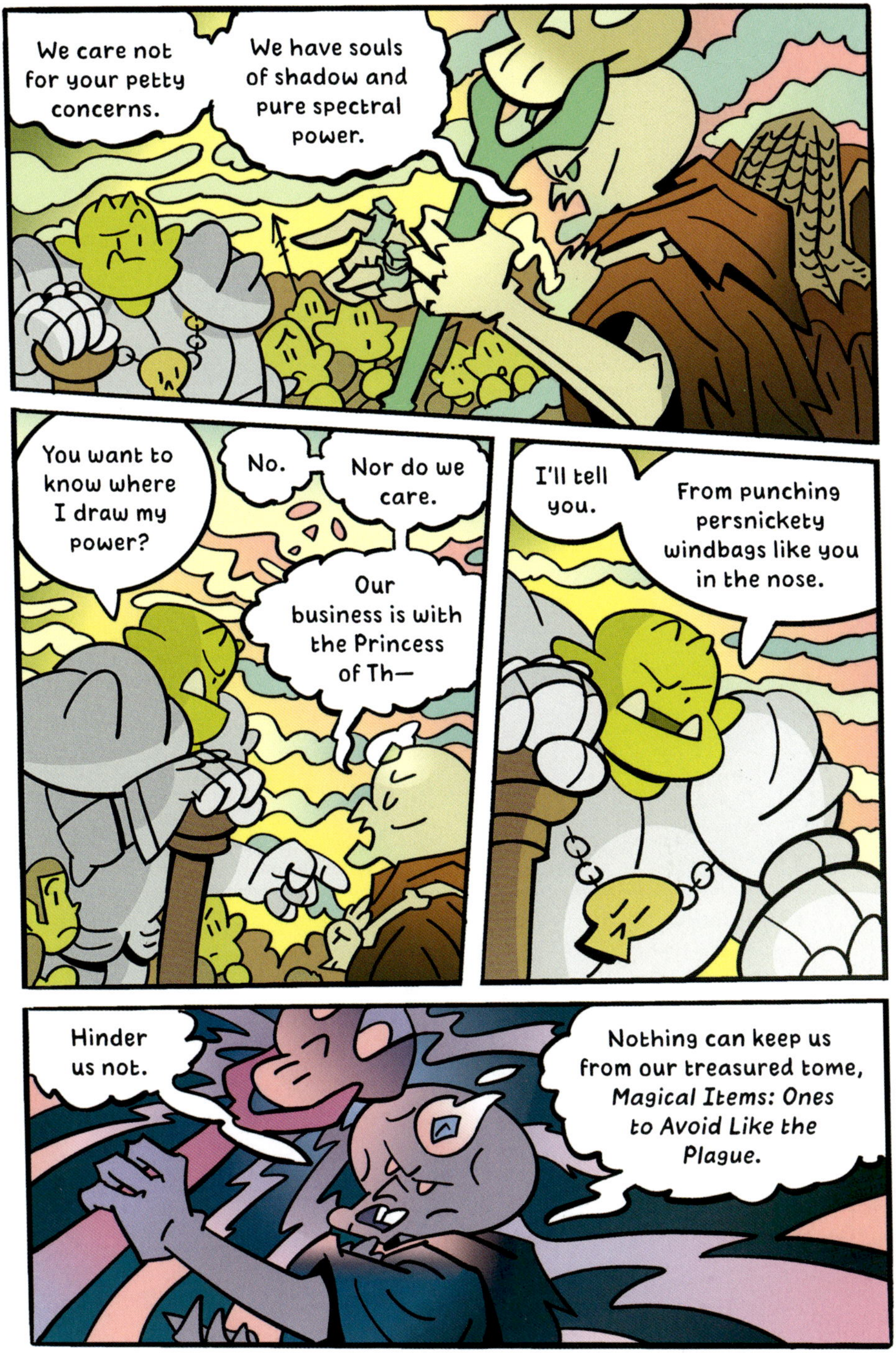
We care not for your petty concerns.
We have souls of shadow and pure spectral power.
You want to know where I draw my power?
No.
Nor do we care.
Our business is with the Princess of Th—
I'll tell you.
From punching persnickety windbags like you in the nose.
Hinder us not.
Nothing can keep us from our treasured tome, *Magical Items: Ones to Avoid Like the Plague*.

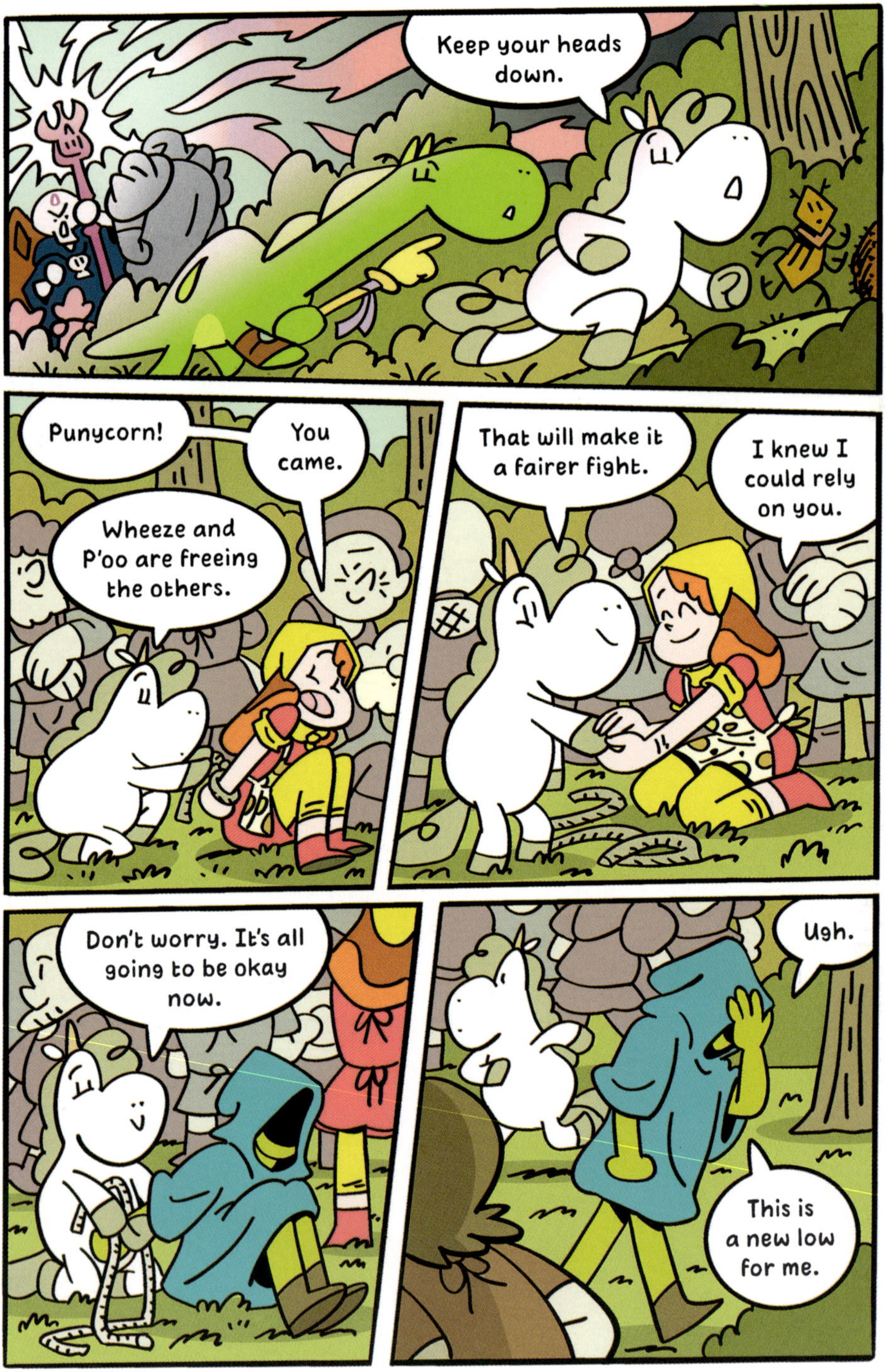
Keep your heads down.
Punycorn!
You came.
Wheeze and P'oo are freeing the others.
That will make it a fairer fight.
I knew I could rely on you.
Don't worry. It's all going to be okay now.
Ugh.
This is a new low for me.

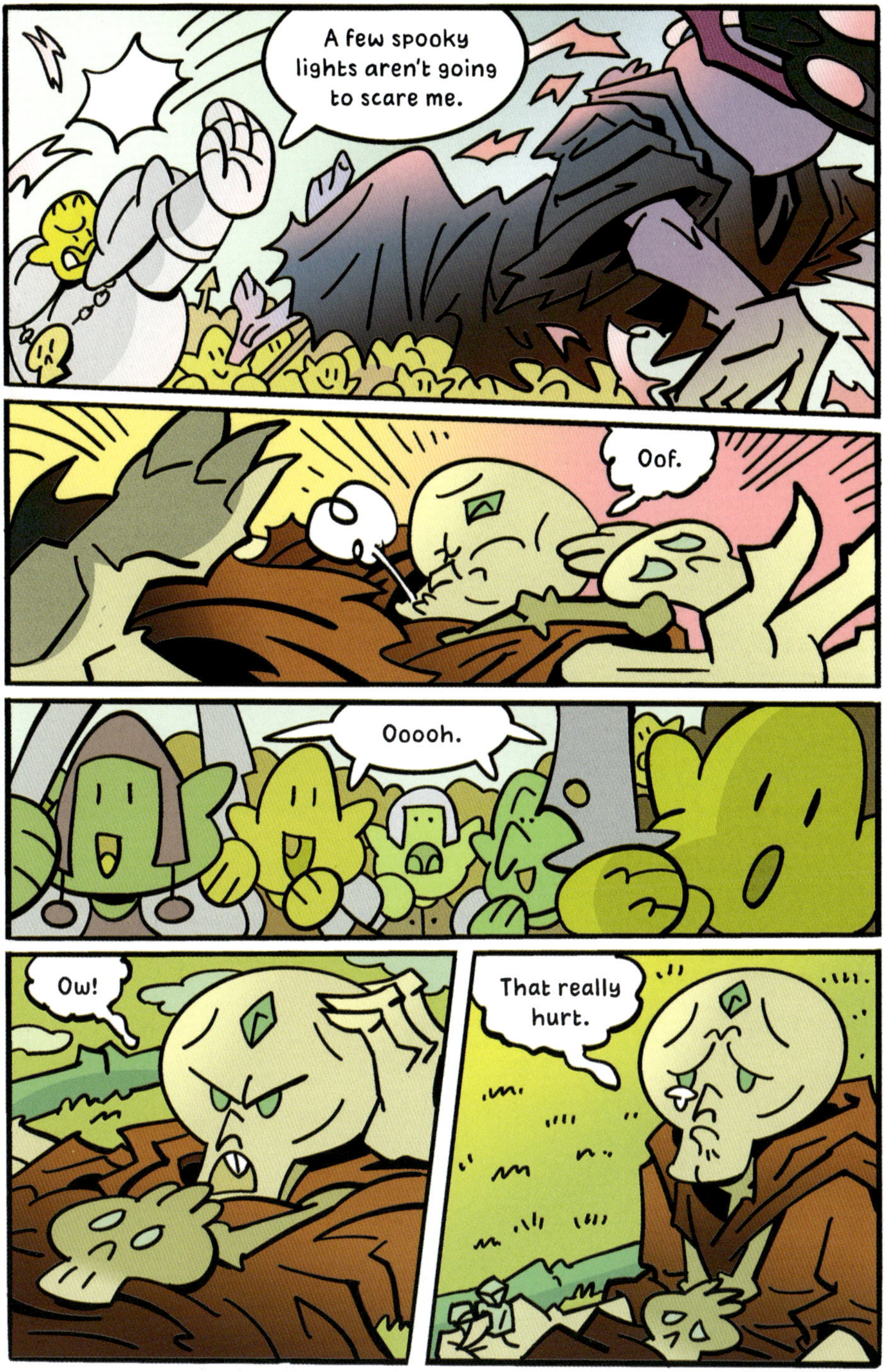
A few spooky lights aren't going to scare me.
Oof.
Ooooh.
Ow!
That really hurt.

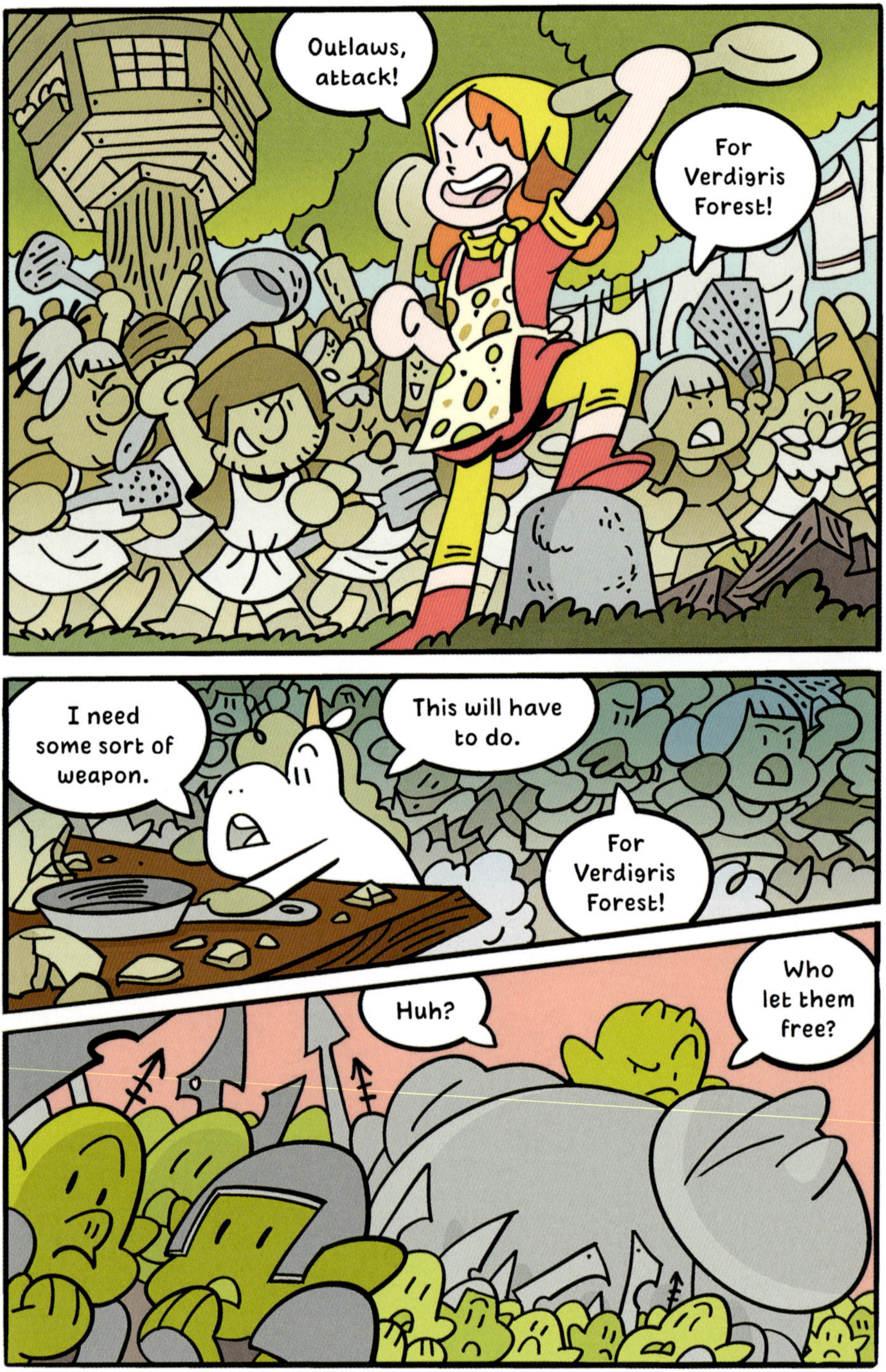
Outlaws, attack!
For Verdigris Forest!
I need some sort of weapon.
This will have to do.
For Verdigris Forest!
Huh?
Who let them free?

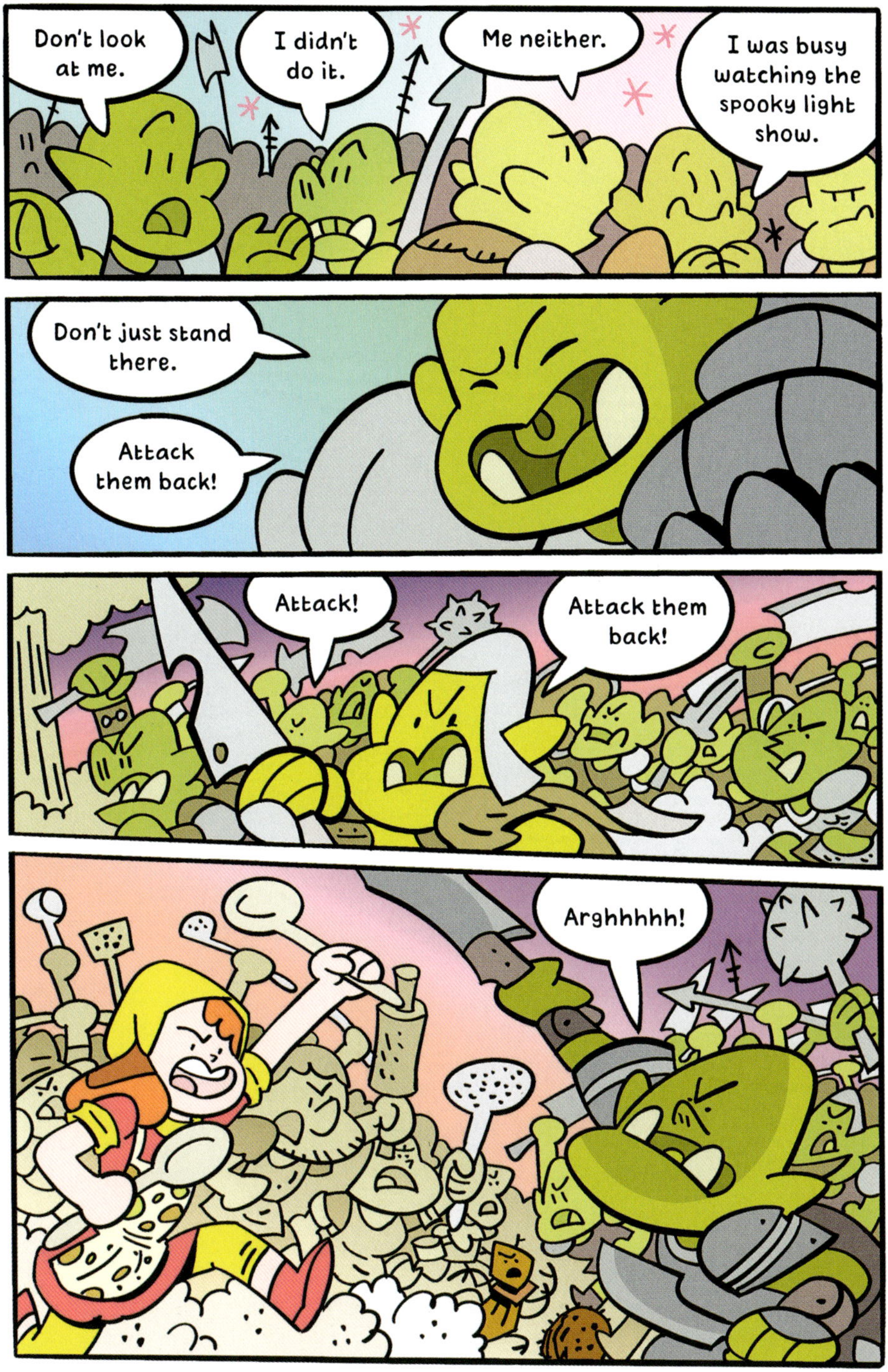
Don't look at me.
I didn't do it.
Me neither.
I was busy watching the spooky light show.
Don't just stand there.
Attack them back!
Attack!
Attack them back!
Arghhhhh!

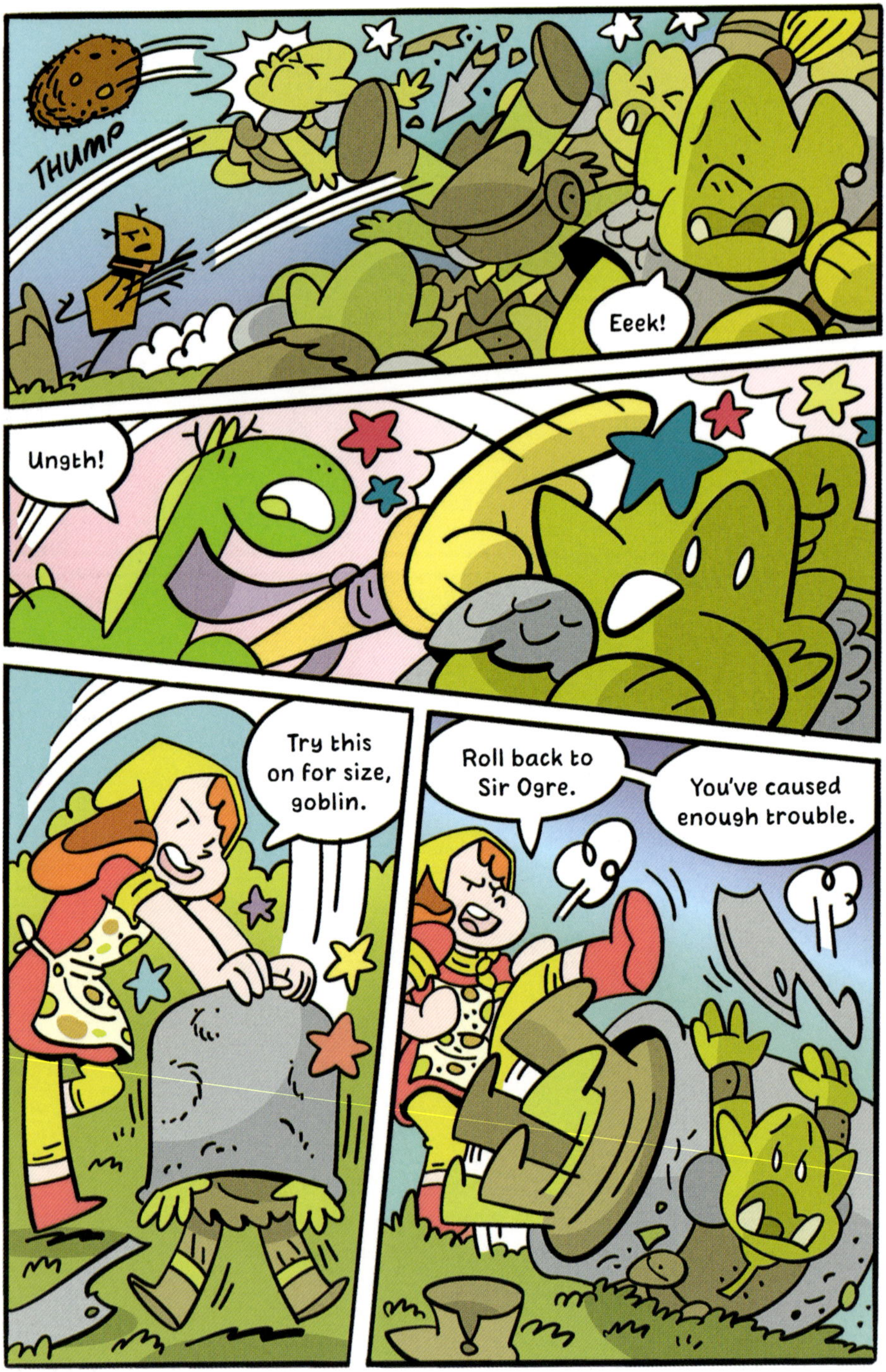
THUMP
Eeek!
Ungth!
Try this on for size, goblin.
Roll back to Sir Ogre.
You've caused enough trouble.

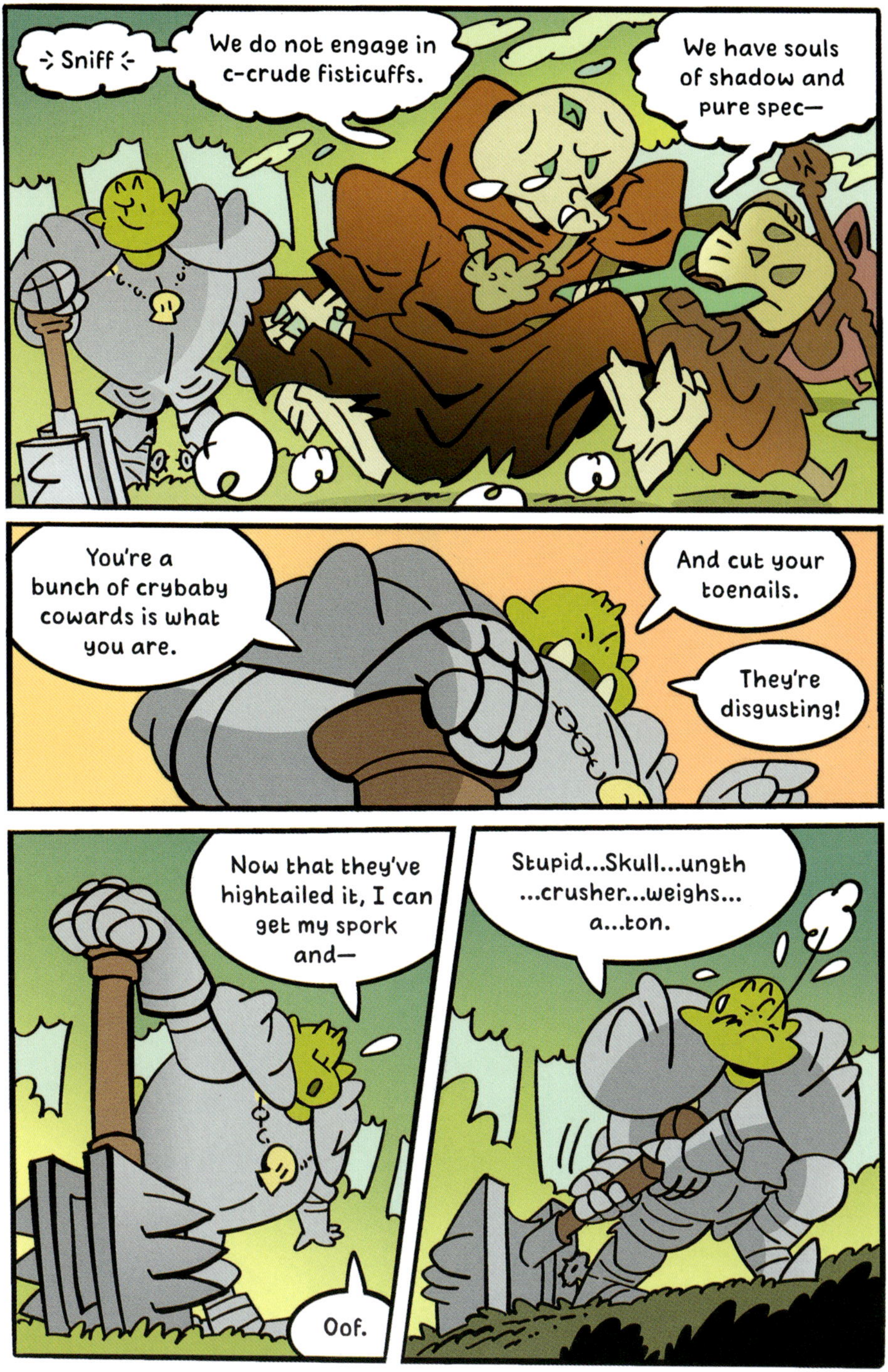

-: Sniff :-
We do not engage in c-crude fisticuffs.
We have souls of shadow and pure spec—
You're a bunch of crybaby cowards is what you are.
And cut your toenails.
They're disgusting!
Now that they've hightailed it, I can get my spork and—
Oof.
Stupid...Skull...ungth ...crusher...weighs... a...ton.

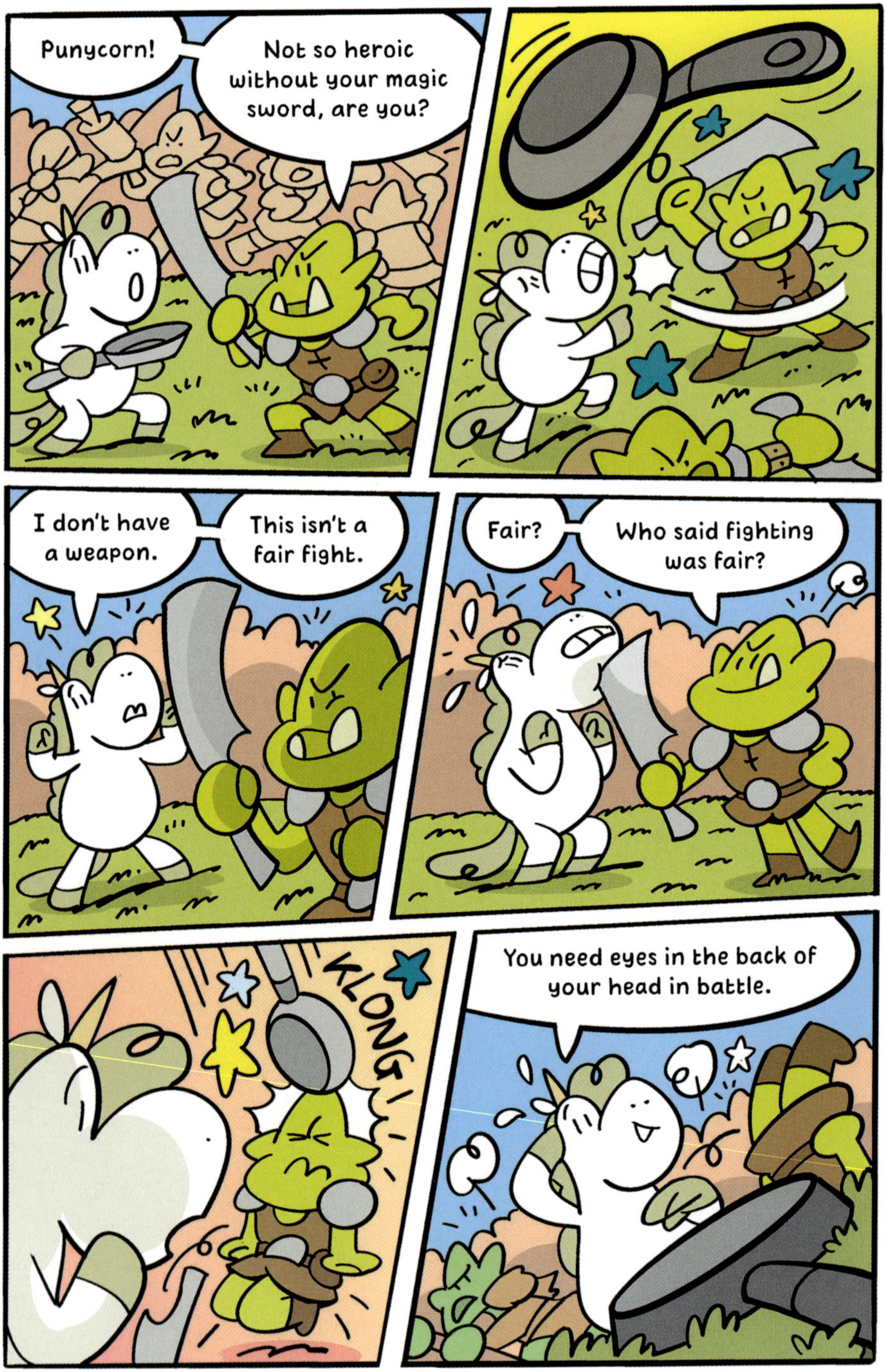
Punycorn!
Not so heroic without your magic sword, are you?
I don't have a weapon.
This isn't a fair fight.
Fair?
Who said fighting was fair?
KLONG
You need eyes in the back of your head in battle.

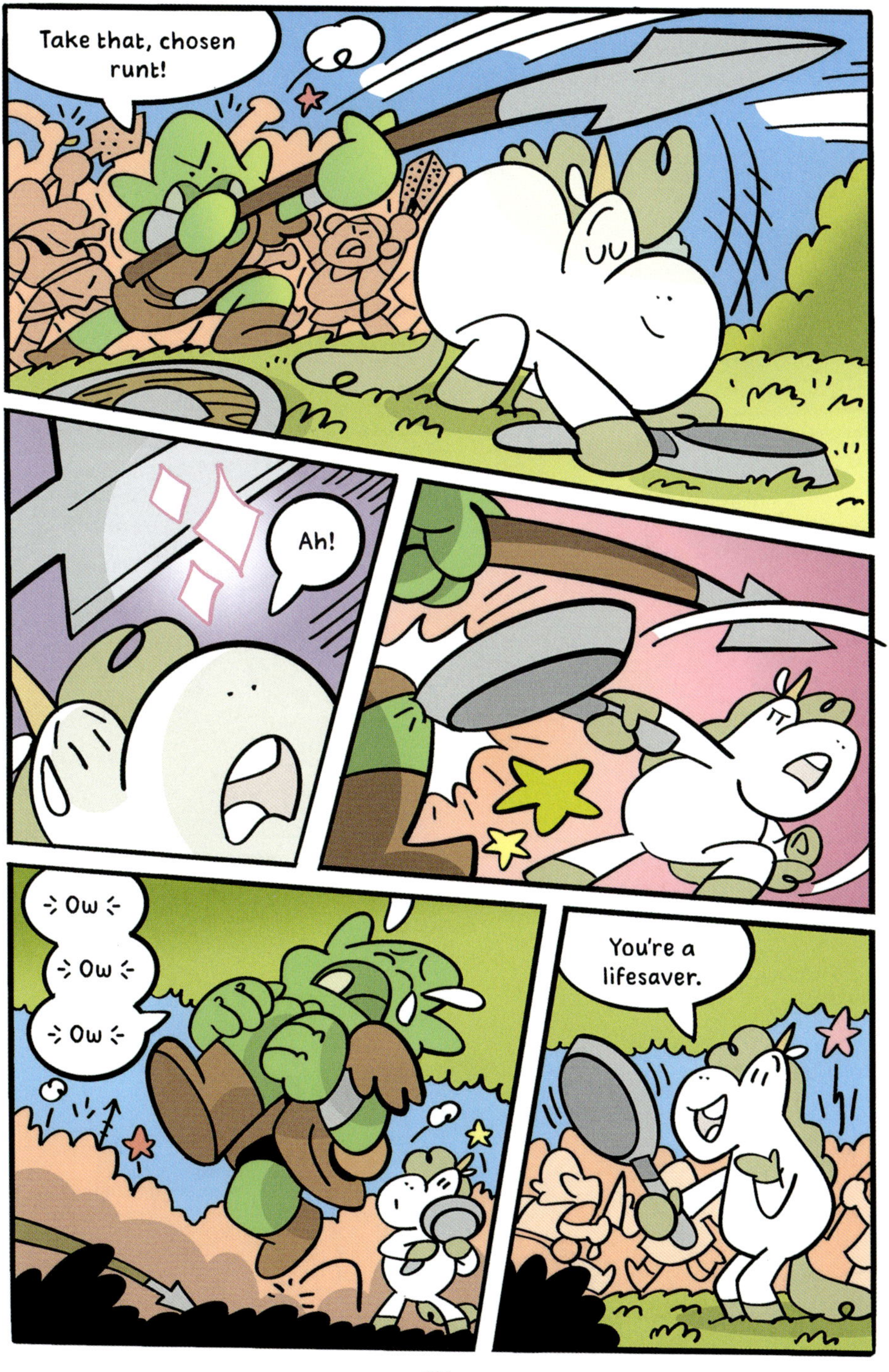
Take that, chosen runt!
Ah!
Ow
Ow
Ow
You're a lifesaver.

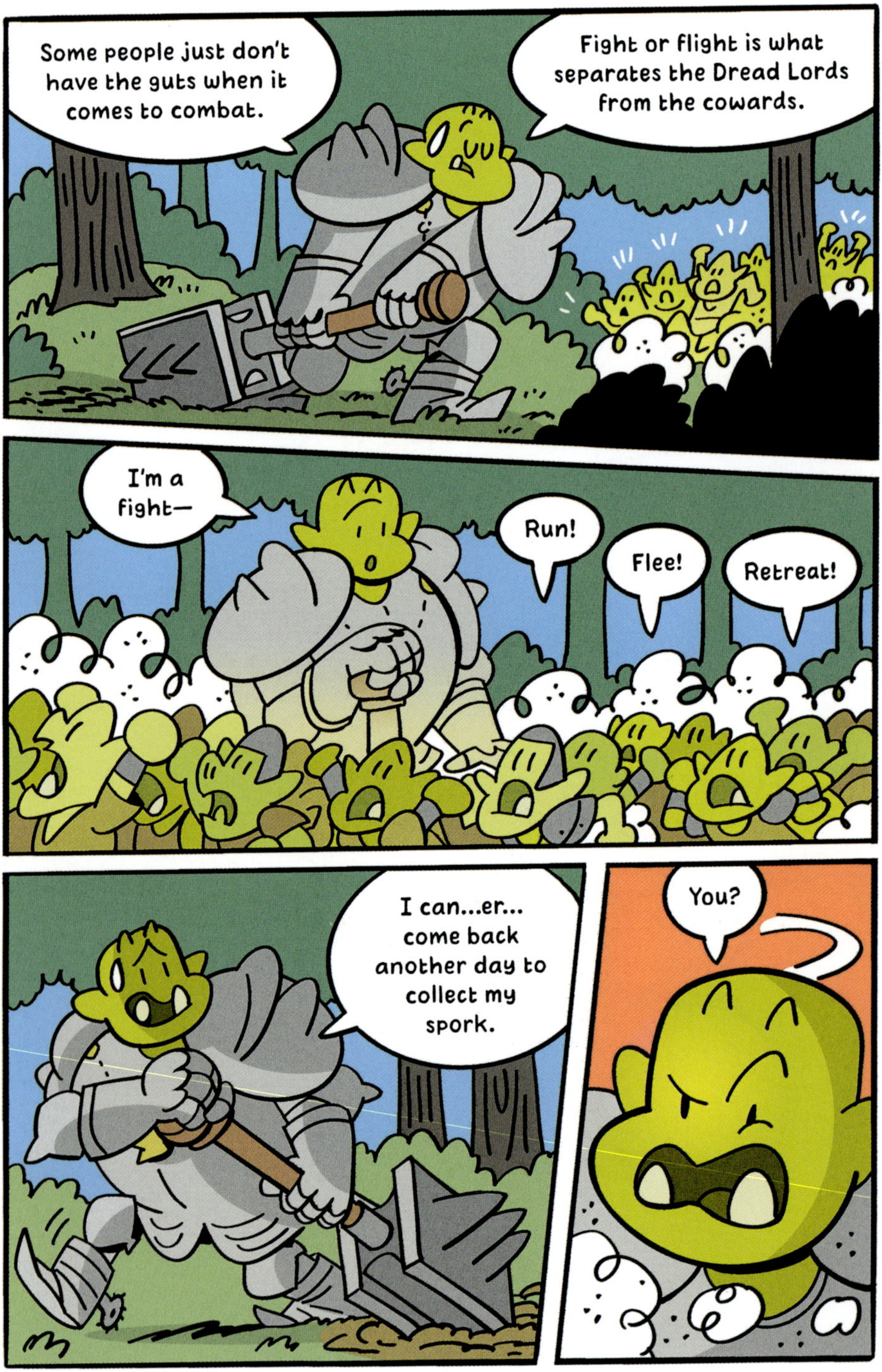
Some people just don't have the guts when it comes to combat.
Fight or flight is what separates the Dread Lords from the cowards.
I'm a fight—
Run!
Flee!
Retreat!
I can...er... come back another day to collect my spork.
You?

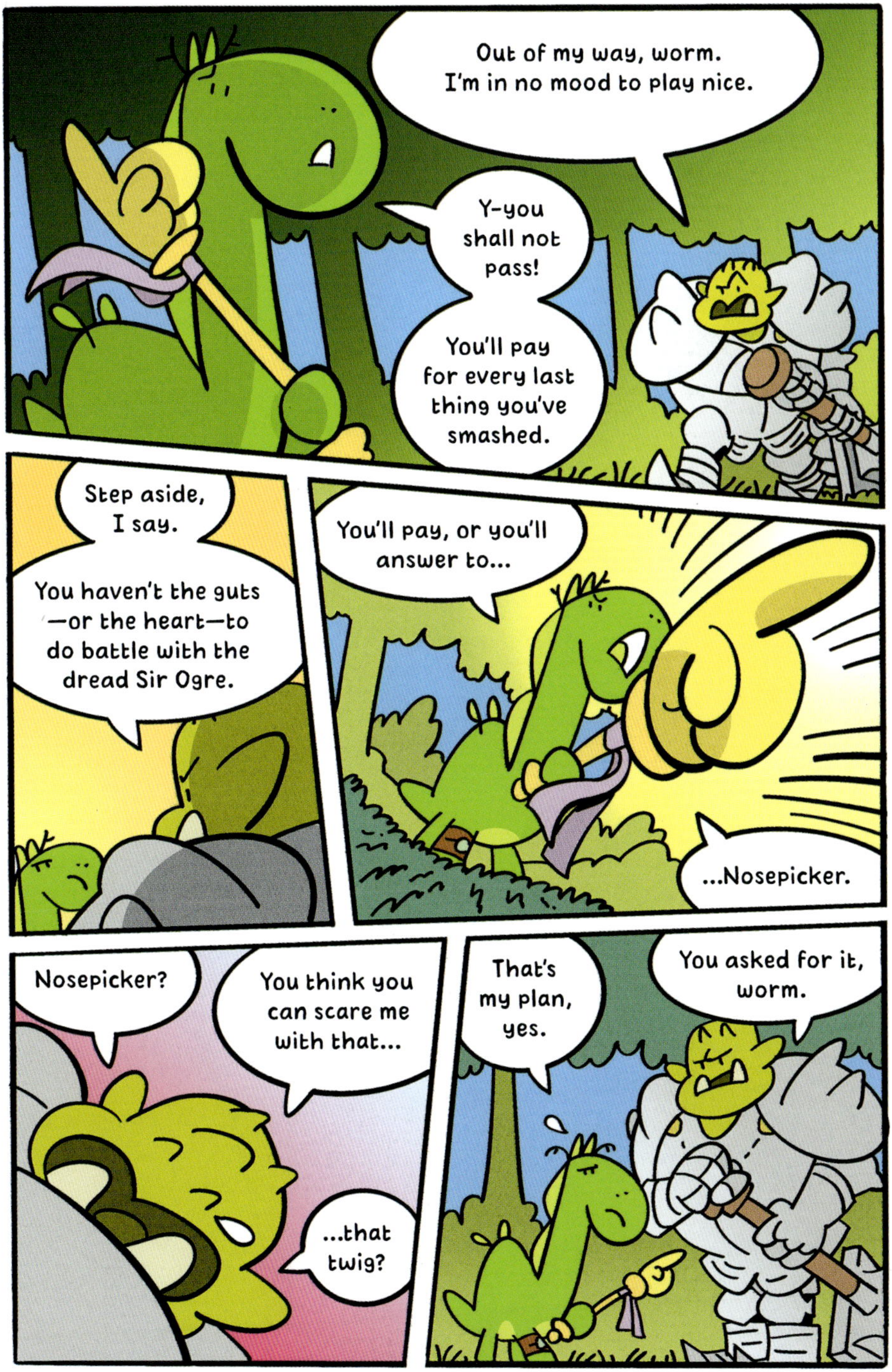
Out of my way, worm. I'm in no mood to play nice.
Y-you shall not pass!
You'll pay for every last thing you've smashed.
Step aside, I say.
You haven't the guts —or the heart—to do battle with the dread Sir Ogre.
You'll pay, or you'll answer to...
...Nosepicker.
Nosepicker?
You think you can scare me with that...
...that twig?
That's my plan, yes.
You asked for it, worm.

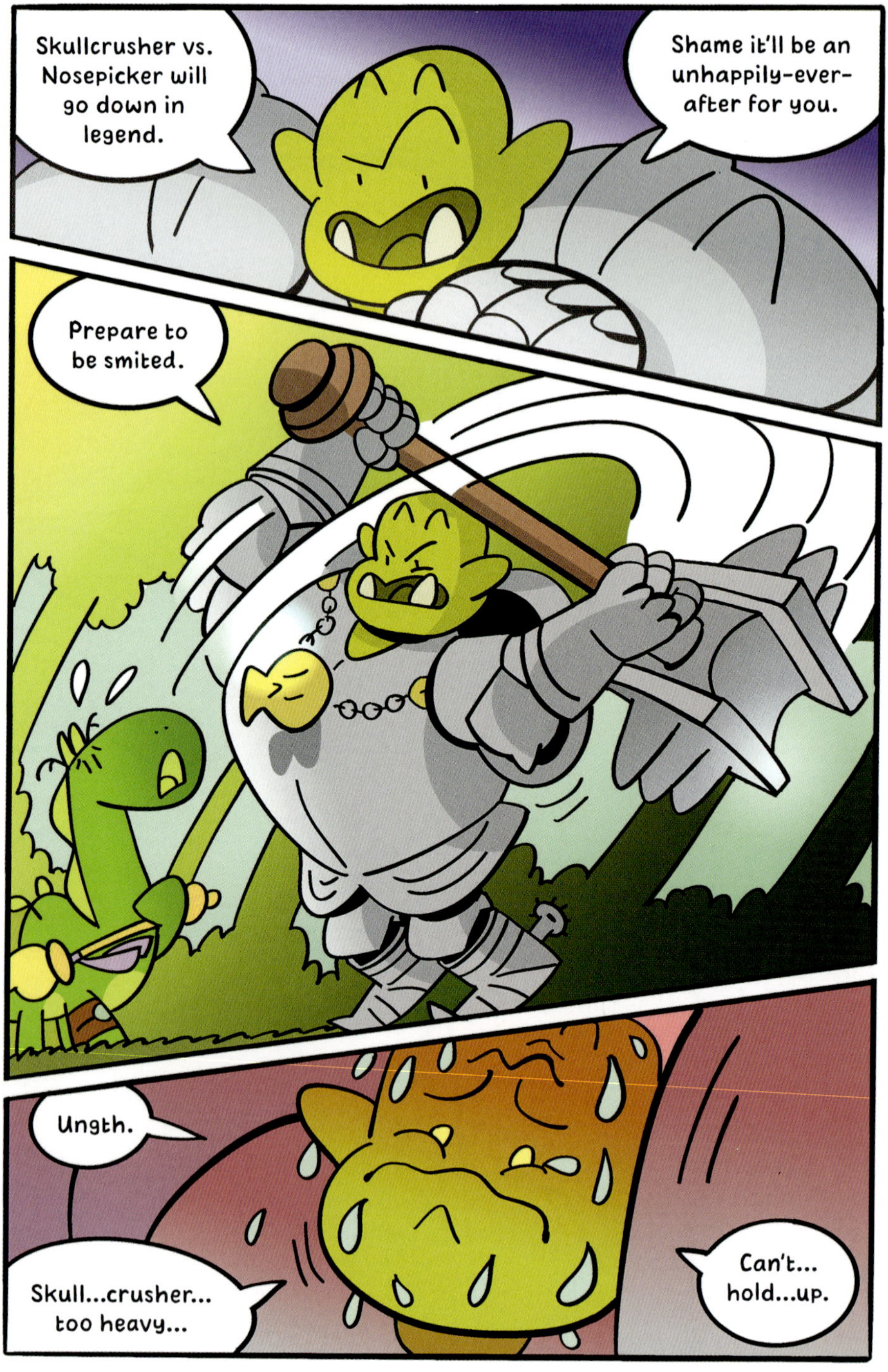
Skullcrusher vs. Nosepicker will go down in legend.
Shame it'll be an unhappily-ever-after for you.
Prepare to be smited.
Ungth.
Skull...crusher... too heavy...
Can't... hold...up.

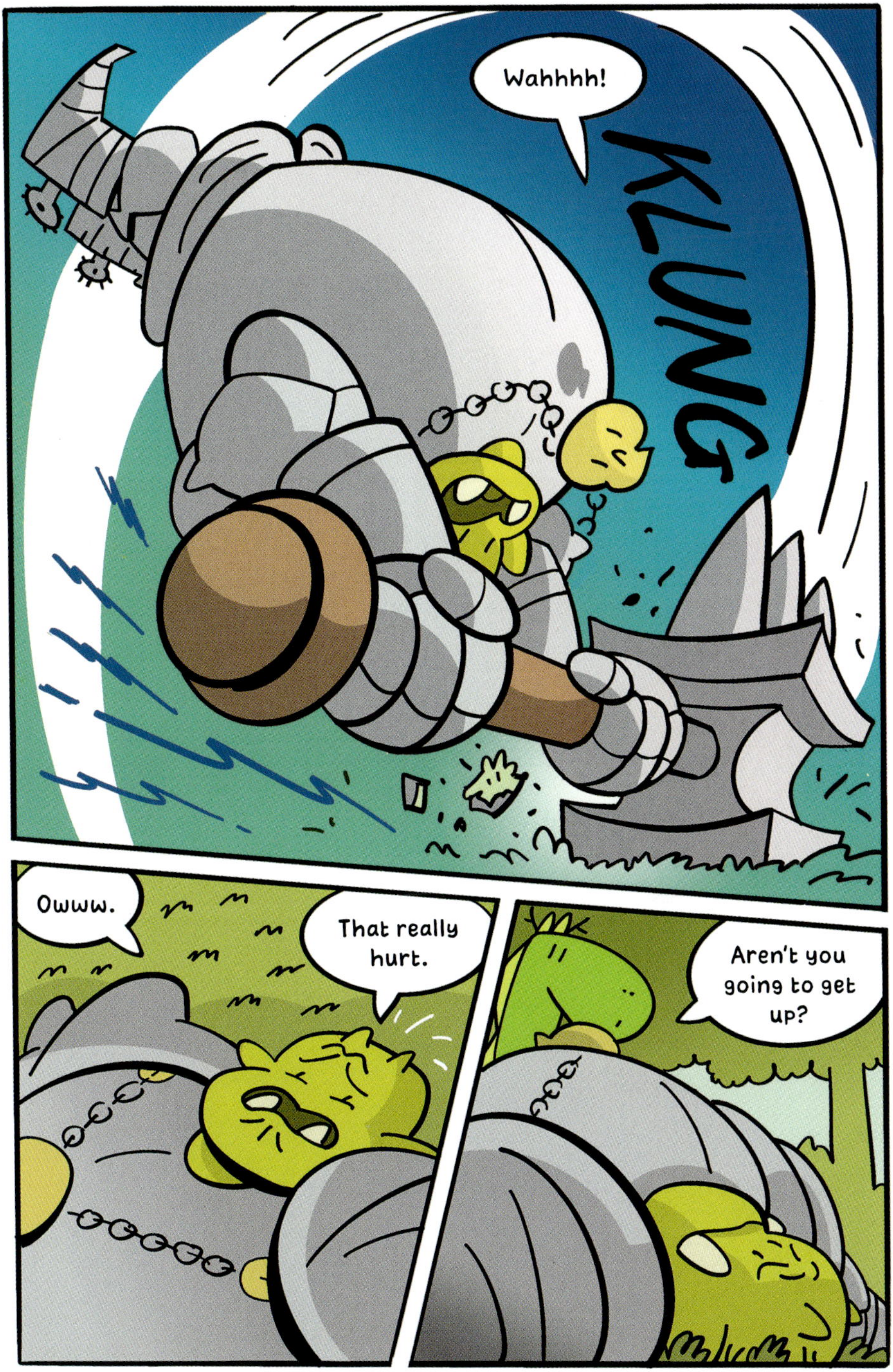
Wahhhh!
KLUNG
Owww.
That really hurt.
Aren't you going to get up?

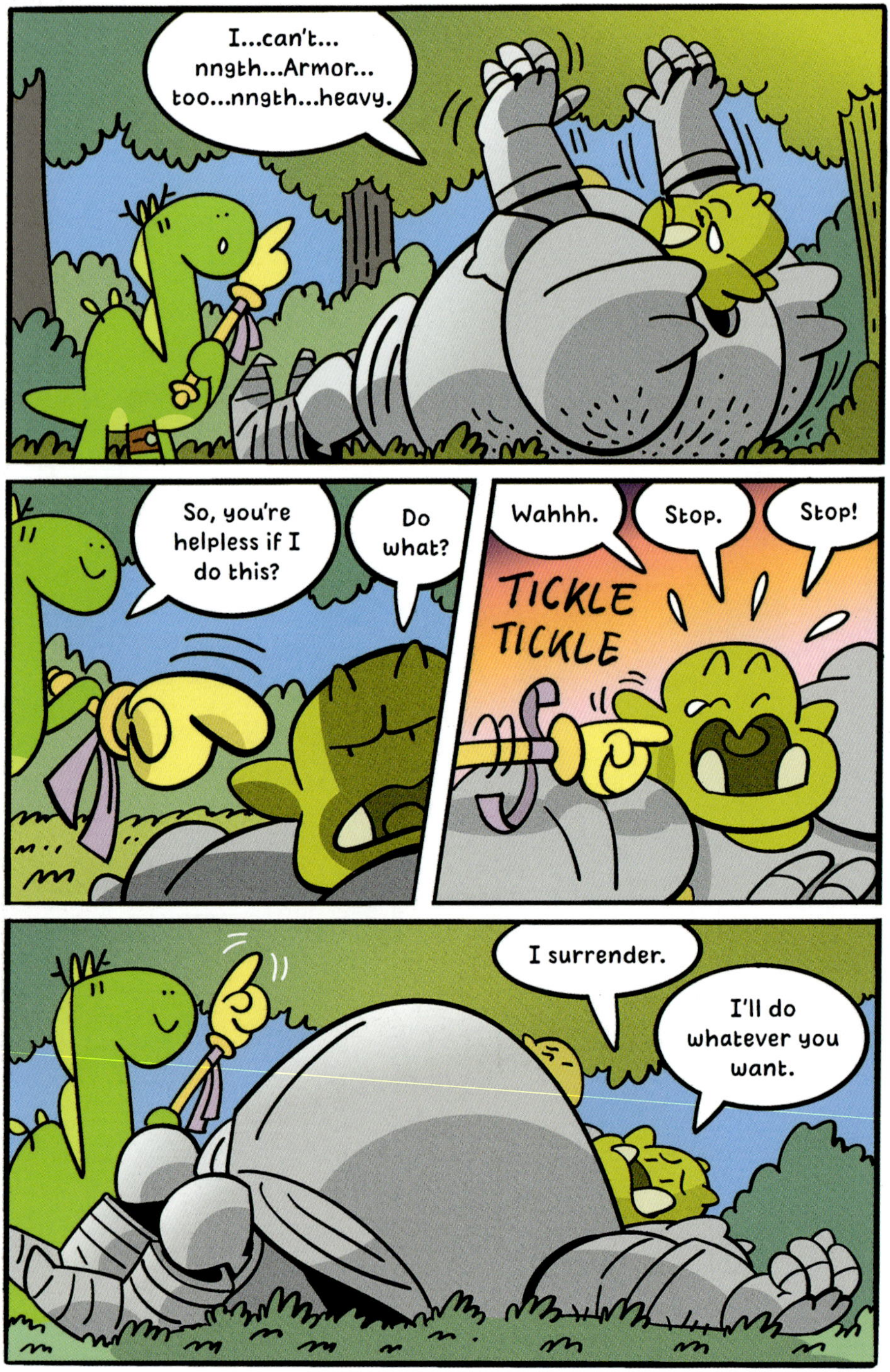
I...can't...
nngth...Armor...
too...nngth...heavy.
So, you're helpless if I do this?
Do what?
Wahhh.
Stop.
Stop!
TICKLE
TICKLE
I surrender.
I'll do whatever you want.

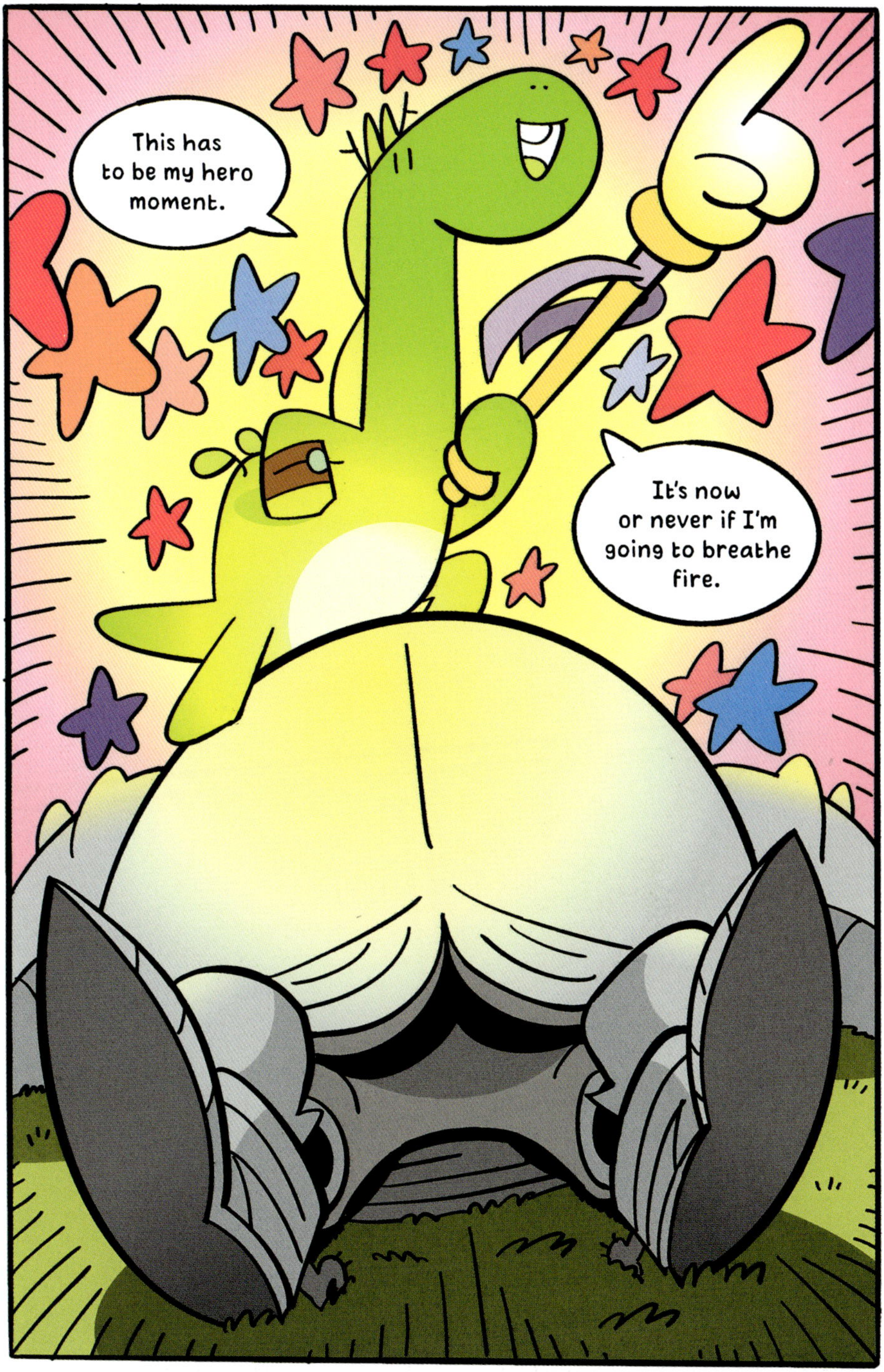
This has to be my hero moment.
It's now or never if I'm going to breathe fire.

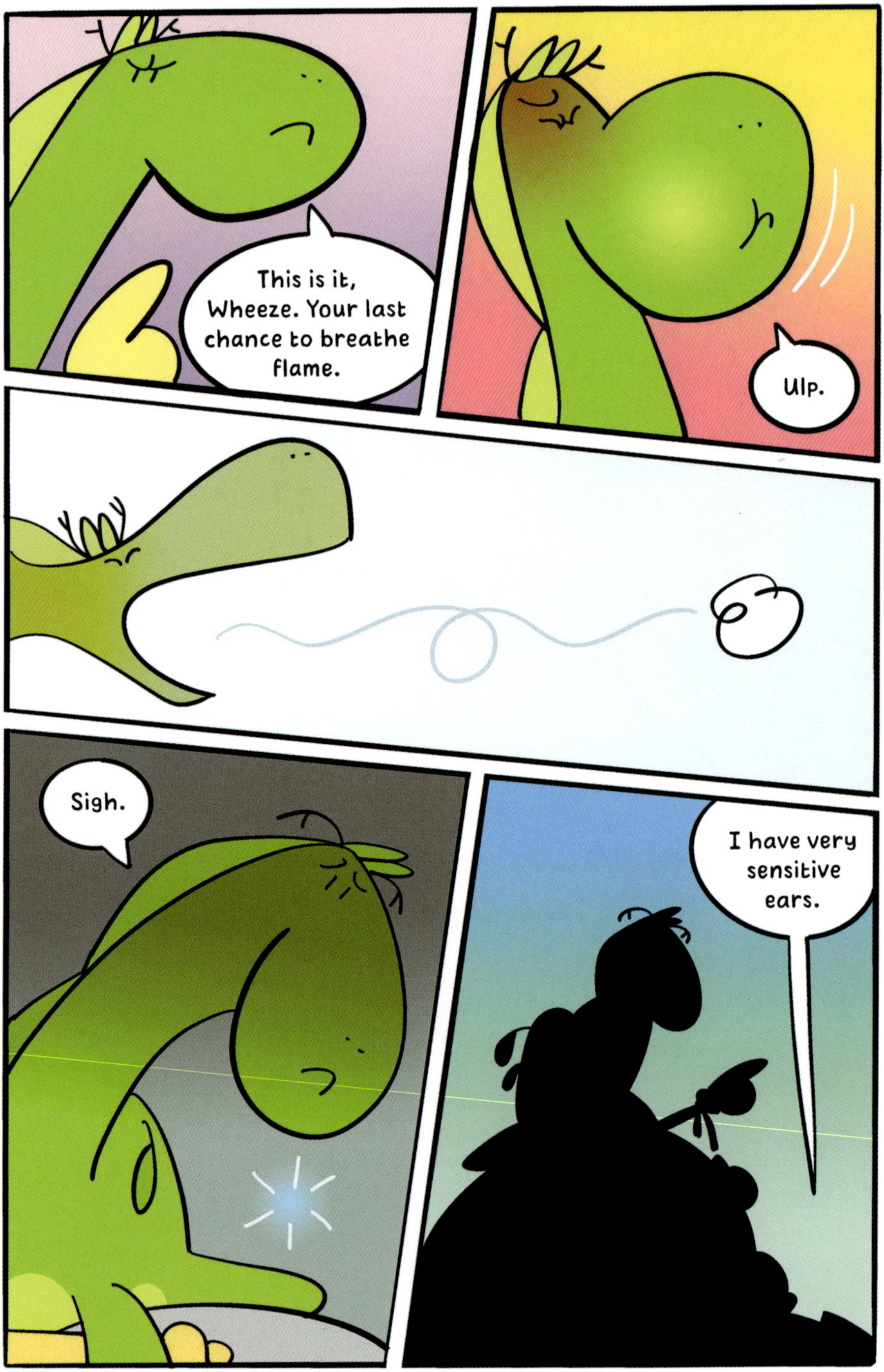
This is it, Wheeze. Your last chance to breathe flame.
Ulp.
Sigh.
I have very sensitive ears.

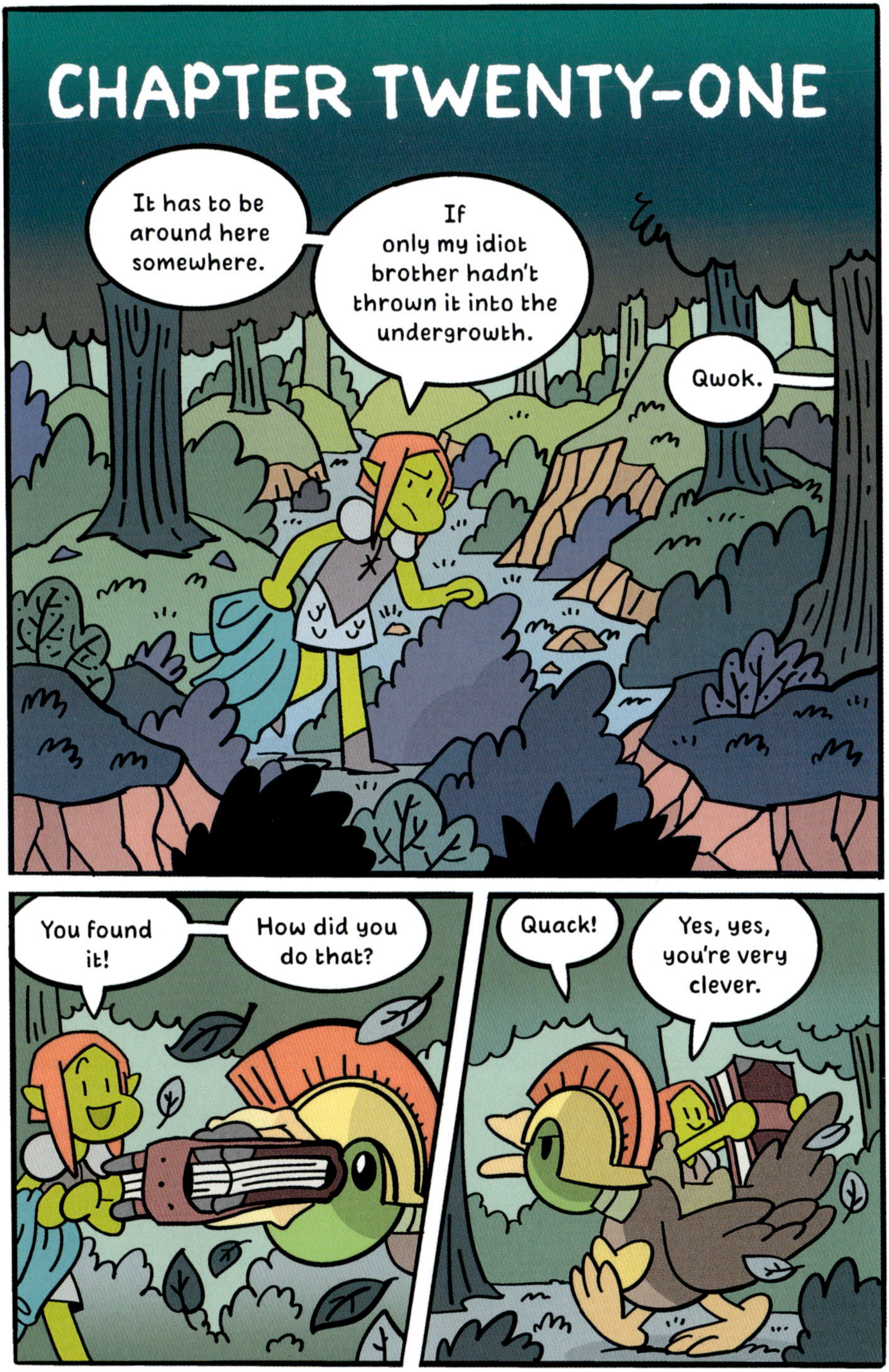
CHAPTER TWENTY-ONE
It has to be around here somewhere.
If only my idiot brother hadn't thrown it into the undergrowth.
Qwok.
You found it!
How did you do that?
Quack!
Yes, yes, you're very clever.

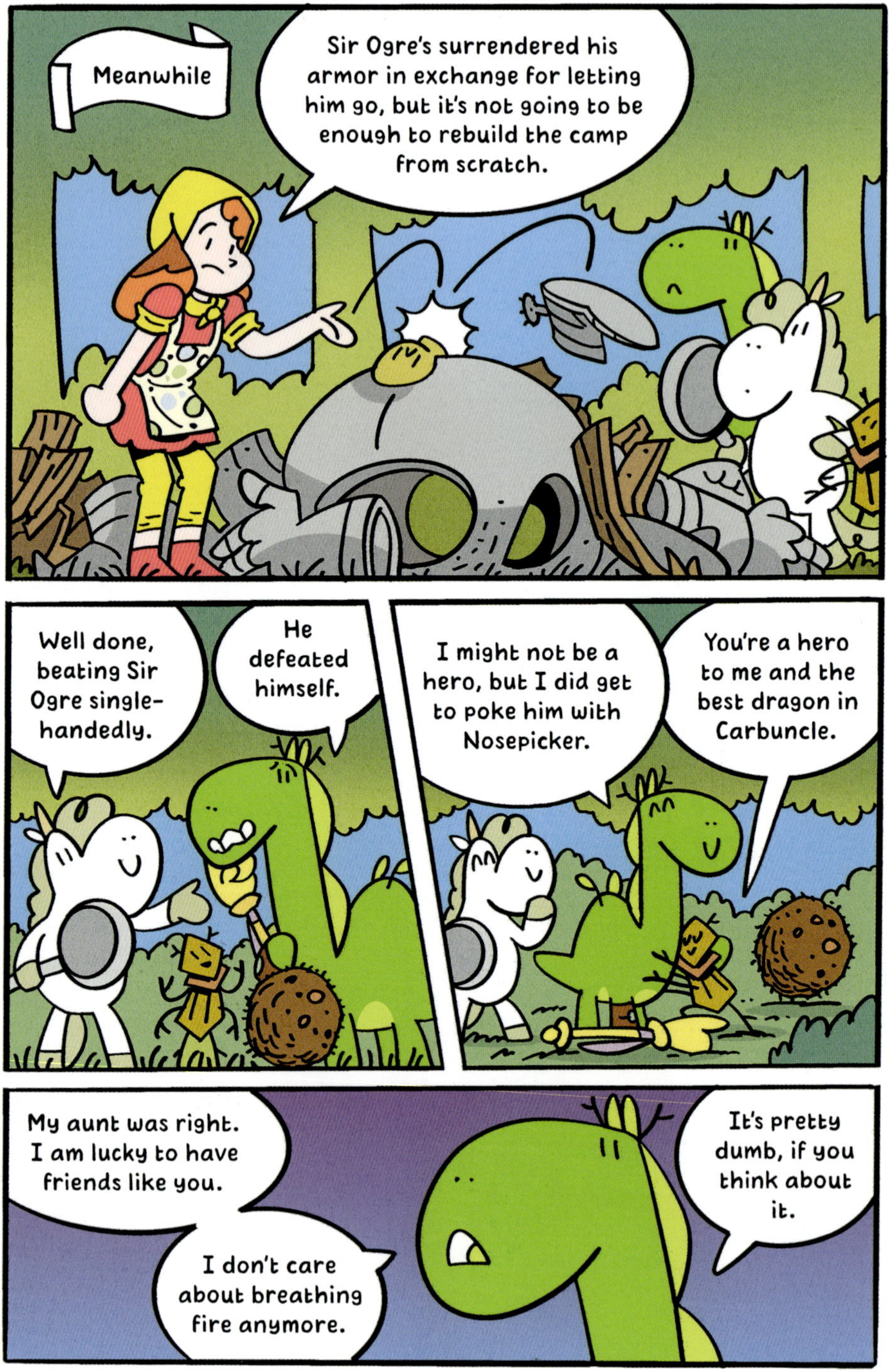
Meanwhile
Sir Ogre's surrendered his armor in exchange for letting him go, but it's not going to be enough to rebuild the camp from scratch.
Well done, beating Sir Ogre single-handedly.
He defeated himself.
I might not be a hero, but I did get to poke him with Nosepicker.
You're a hero to me and the best dragon in Carbuncle.
My aunt was right. I am lucky to have friends like you.
I don't care about breathing fire anymore.
It's pretty dumb, if you think about it.

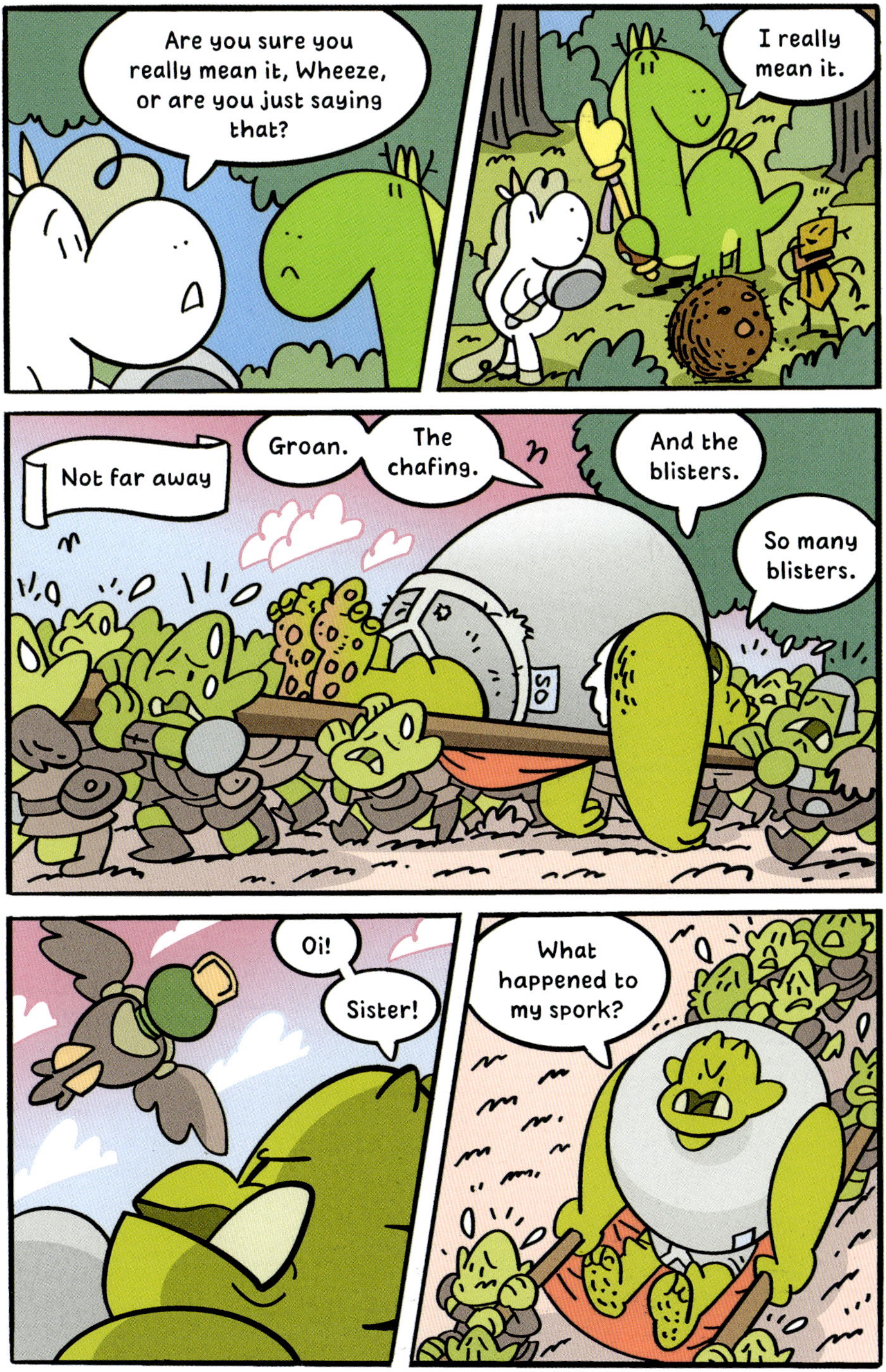
Are you sure you really mean it, Wheeze, or are you just saying that?
I really mean it.
Not far away
Groan.
The chafing.
And the blisters.
So many blisters.
Oi!
Sister!
What happened to my spork?

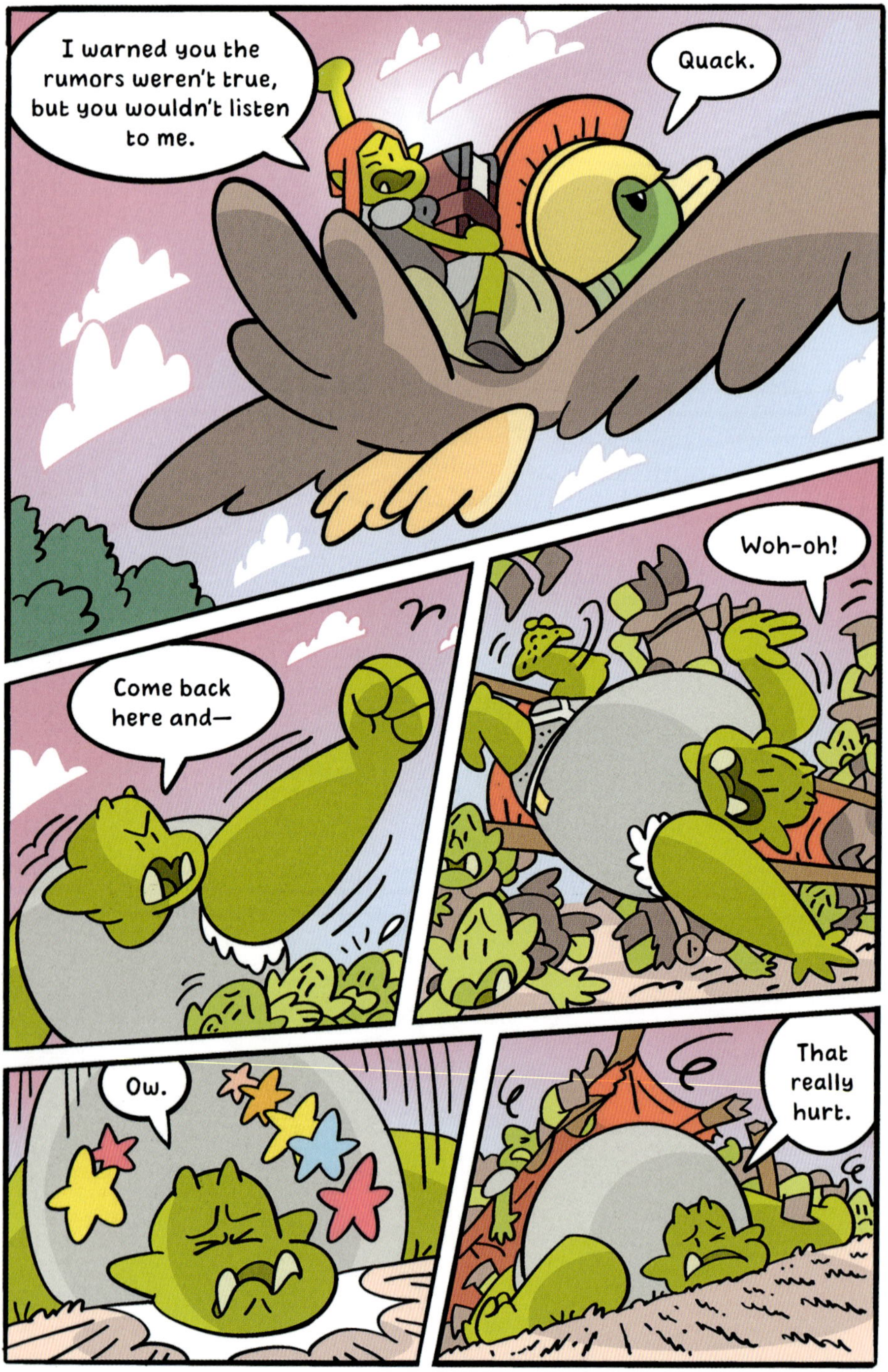
I warned you the rumors weren't true, but you wouldn't listen to me.
Quack.
Woh-oh!
Come back here and—
Ow.
That really hurt.

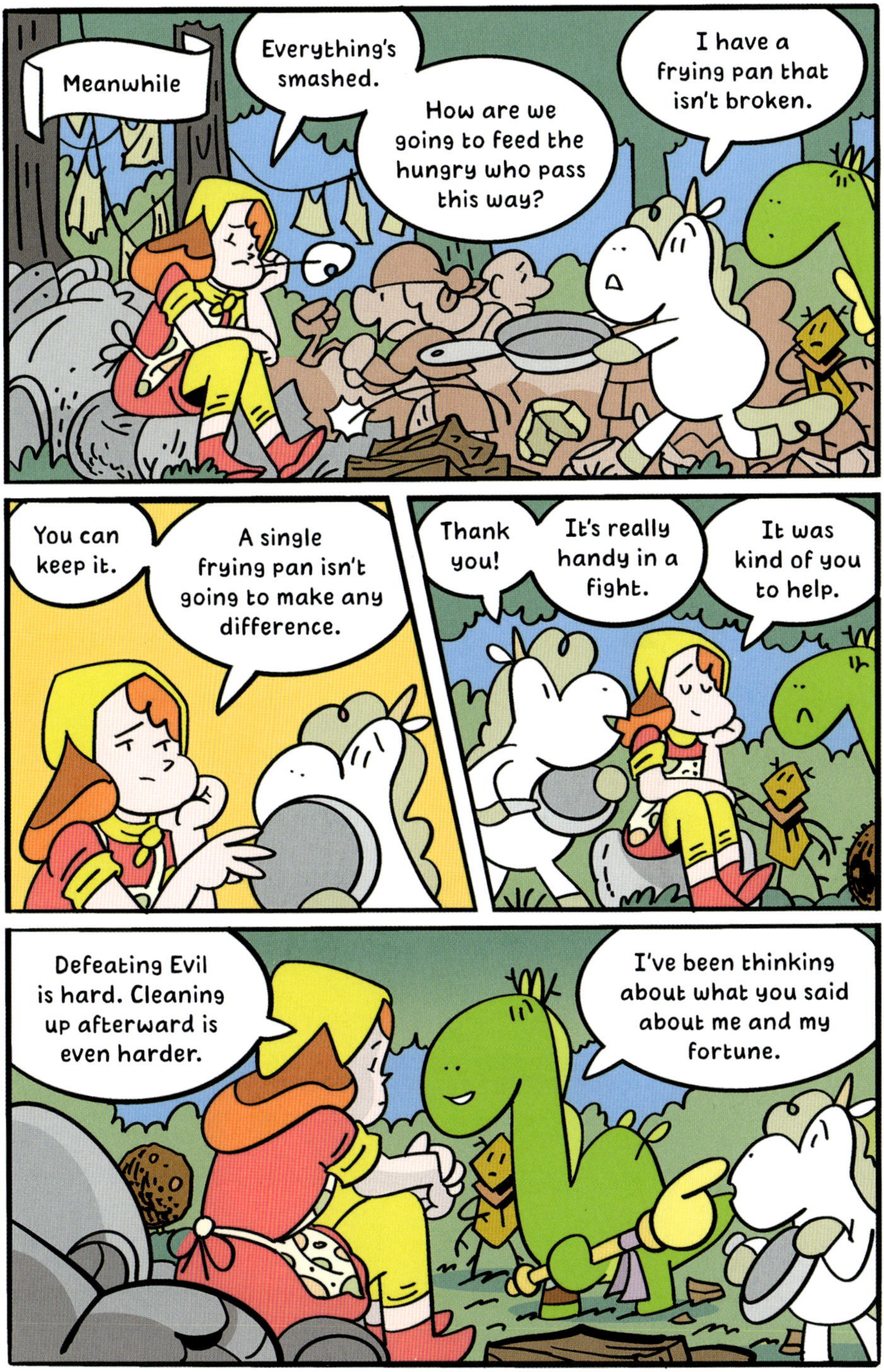
Meanwhile
Everything's smashed.
How are we going to feed the hungry who pass this way?
I have a frying pan that isn't broken.
You can keep it.
A single frying pan isn't going to make any difference.
Thank you!
It's really handy in a fight.
It was kind of you to help.
Defeating Evil is hard. Cleaning up afterward is even harder.
I've been thinking about what you said about me and my fortune.

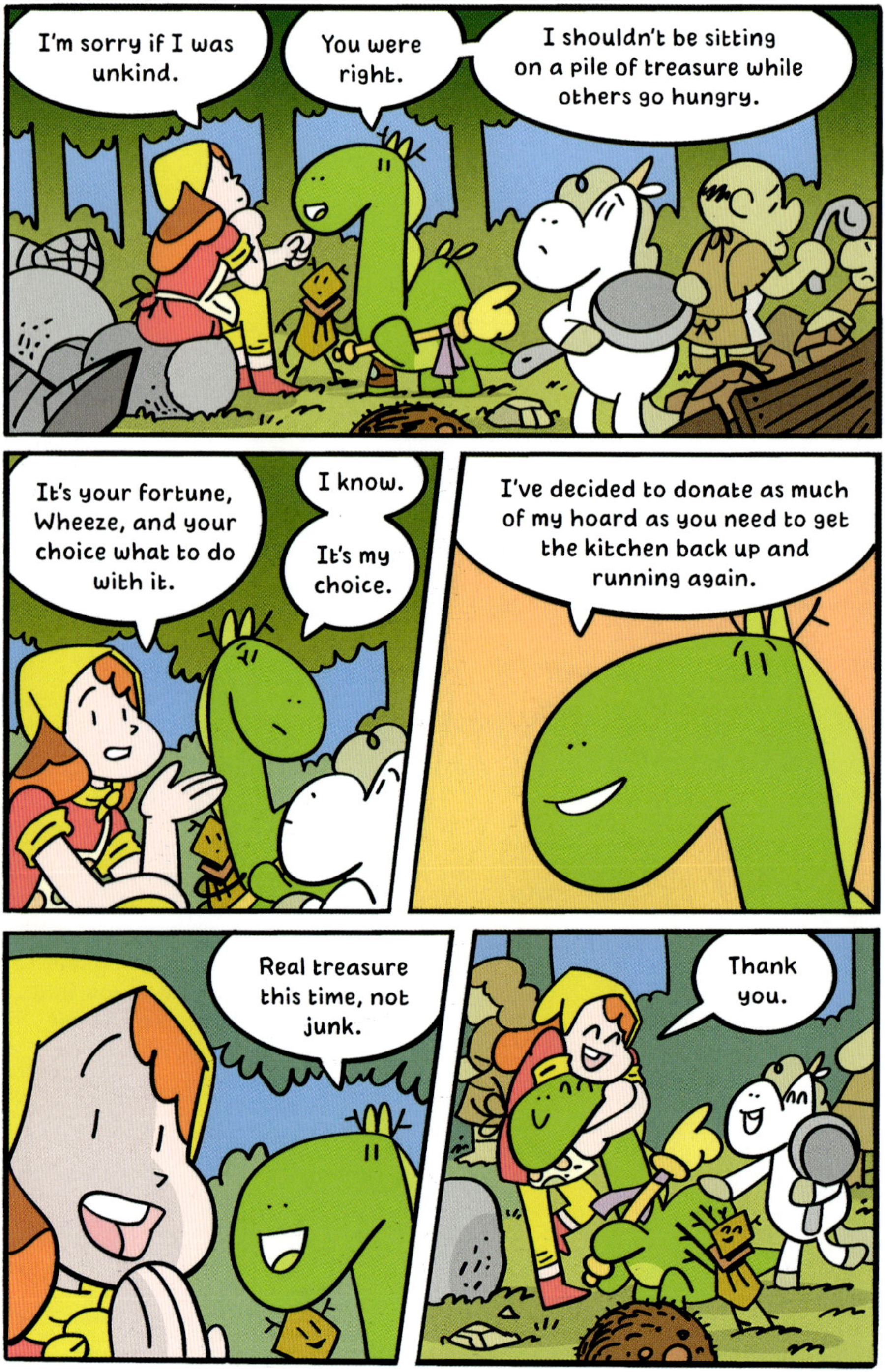
I'm sorry if I was unkind.
You were right.
I shouldn't be sitting on a pile of treasure while others go hungry.
It's your fortune, Wheeze, and your choice what to do with it.
I know.
It's my choice.
I've decided to donate as much of my hoard as you need to get the kitchen back up and running again.
Real treasure this time, not junk.
Thank you.

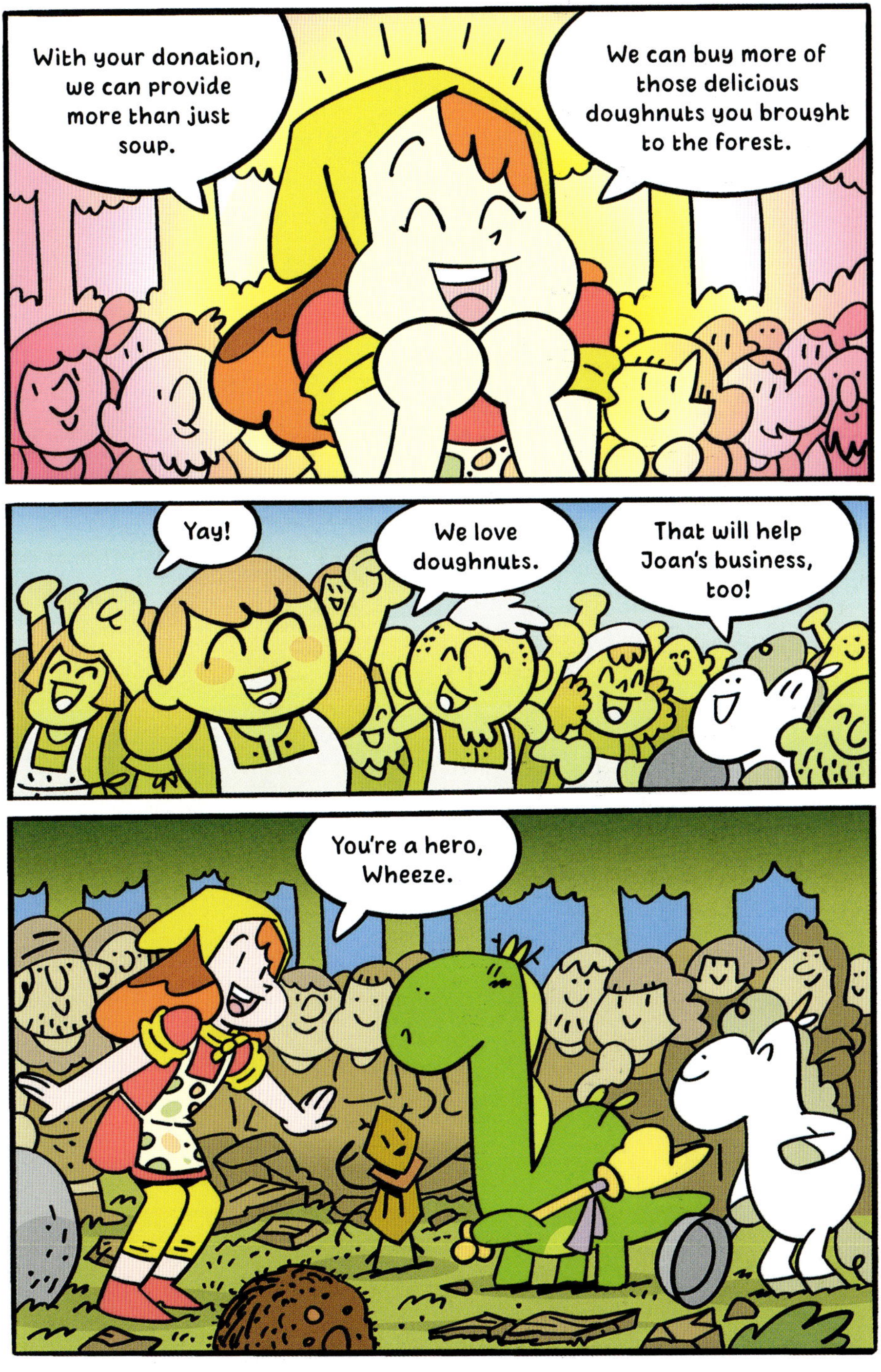
With your donation, we can provide more than just soup.
We can buy more of those delicious doughnuts you brought to the forest.
Yay!
We love doughnuts.
That will help Joan's business, too!
You're a hero, Wheeze.

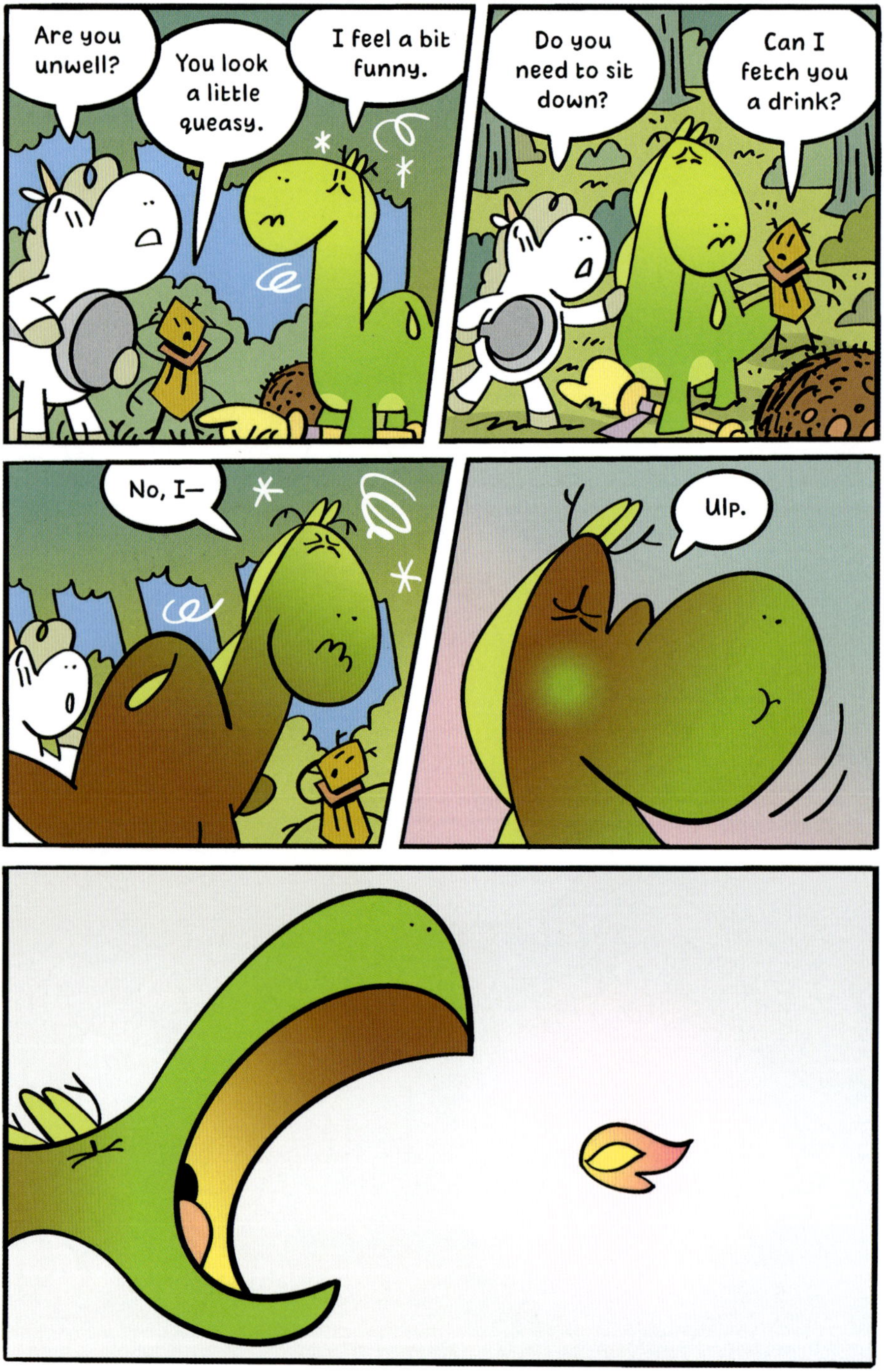
Are you unwell?
You look a little queasy.
I feel a bit funny.
Do you need to sit down?
Can I fetch you a drink?
No, I—
Ulp.

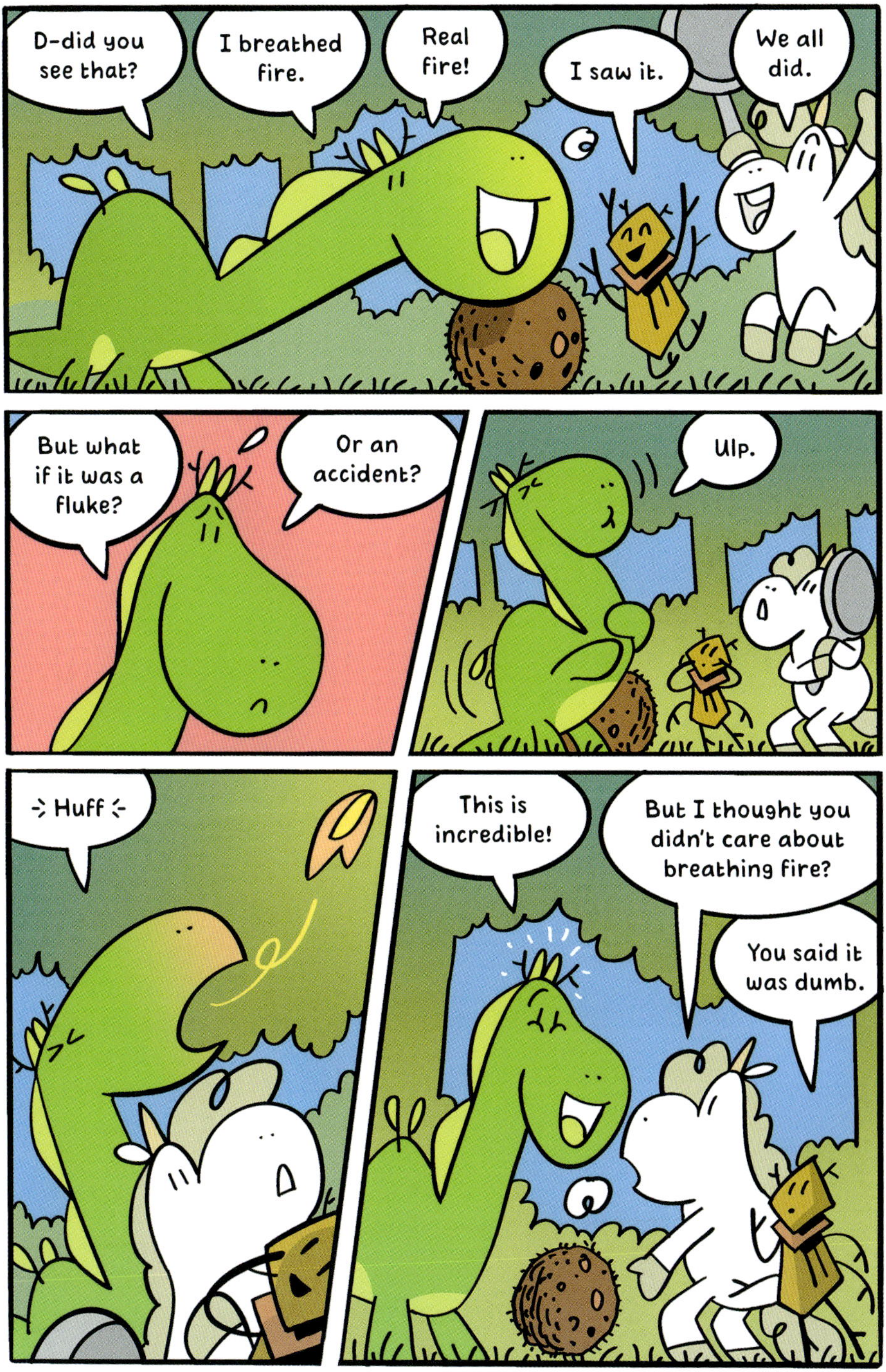
D-did you see that?
I breathed fire.
Real fire!
I saw it.
We all did.
But what if it was a fluke?
Or an accident?
Ulp.
Huff
This is incredible!
But I thought you didn't care about breathing fire?
You said it was dumb.

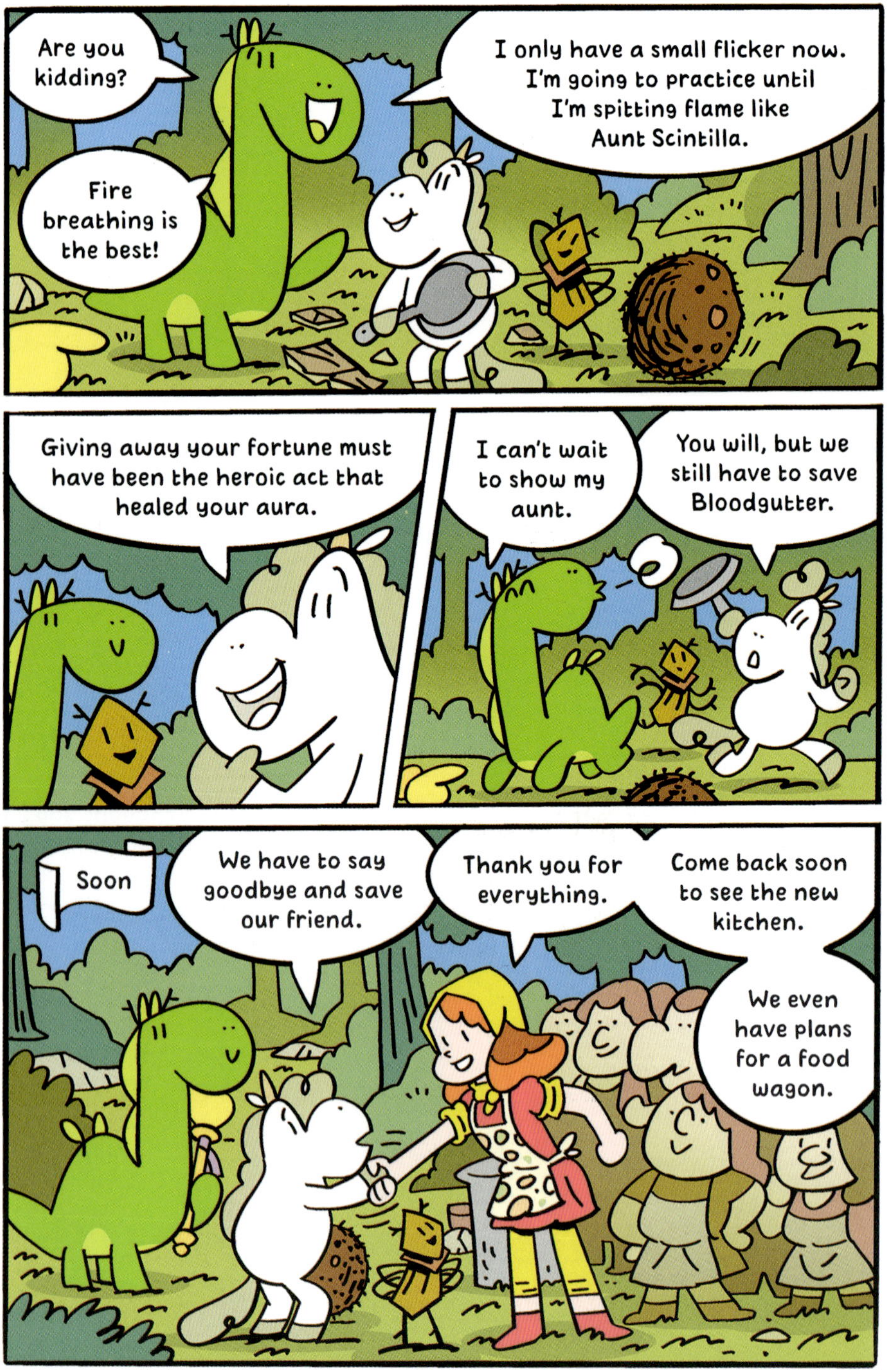
Are you kidding?
Fire breathing is the best!
I only have a small flicker now. I'm going to practice until I'm spitting flame like Aunt Scintilla.
Giving away your fortune must have been the heroic act that healed your aura.
I can't wait to show my aunt.
You will, but we still have to save Bloodgutter.
Soon
We have to say goodbye and save our friend.
Thank you for everything.
Come back soon to see the new kitchen.
We even have plans for a food wagon.

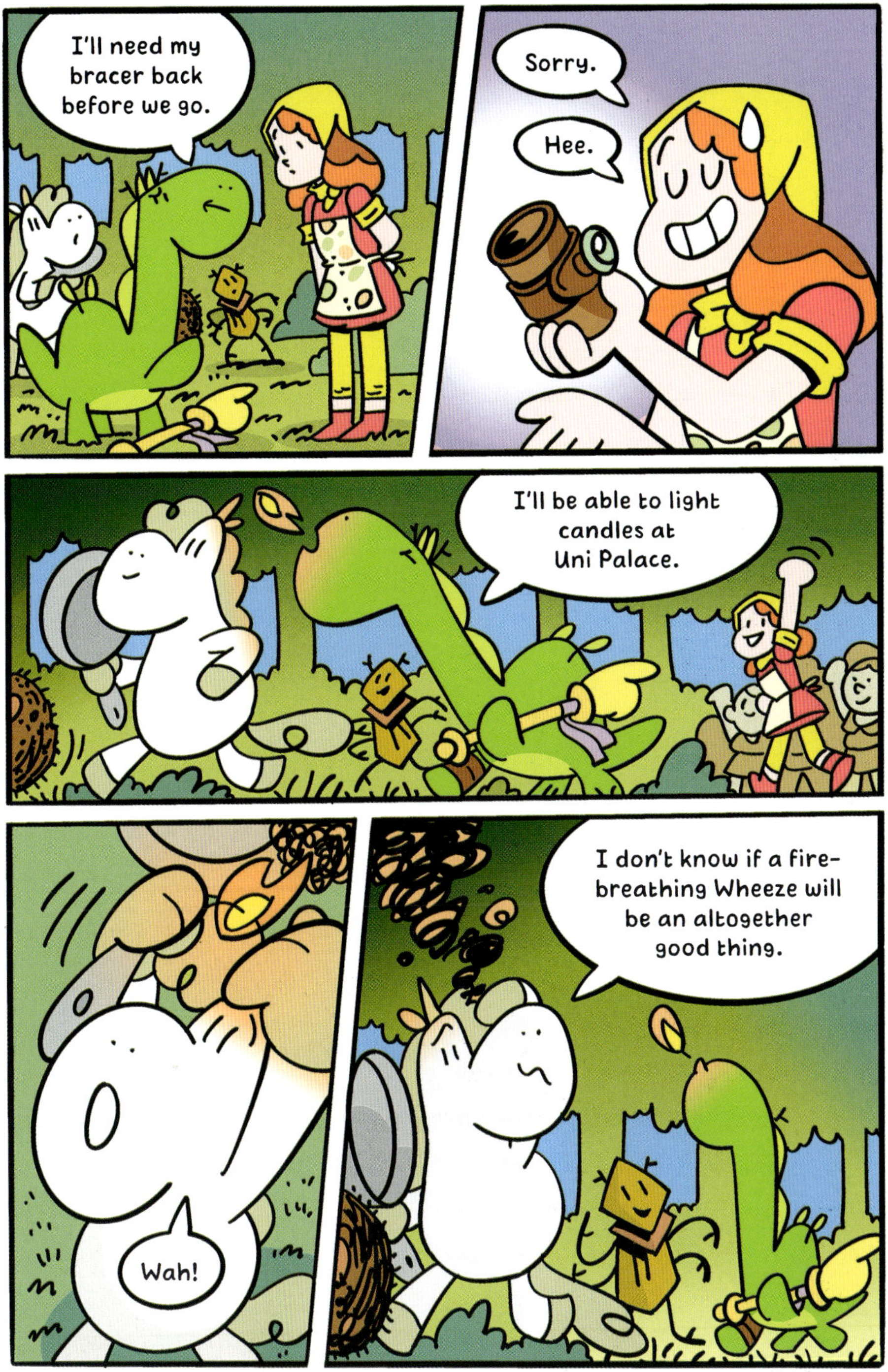
I'll need my bracer back before we go.
Sorry.
Hee.
I'll be able to light candles at Uni Palace.
Wah!
I don't know if a fire-breathing Wheeze will be an altogether good thing.

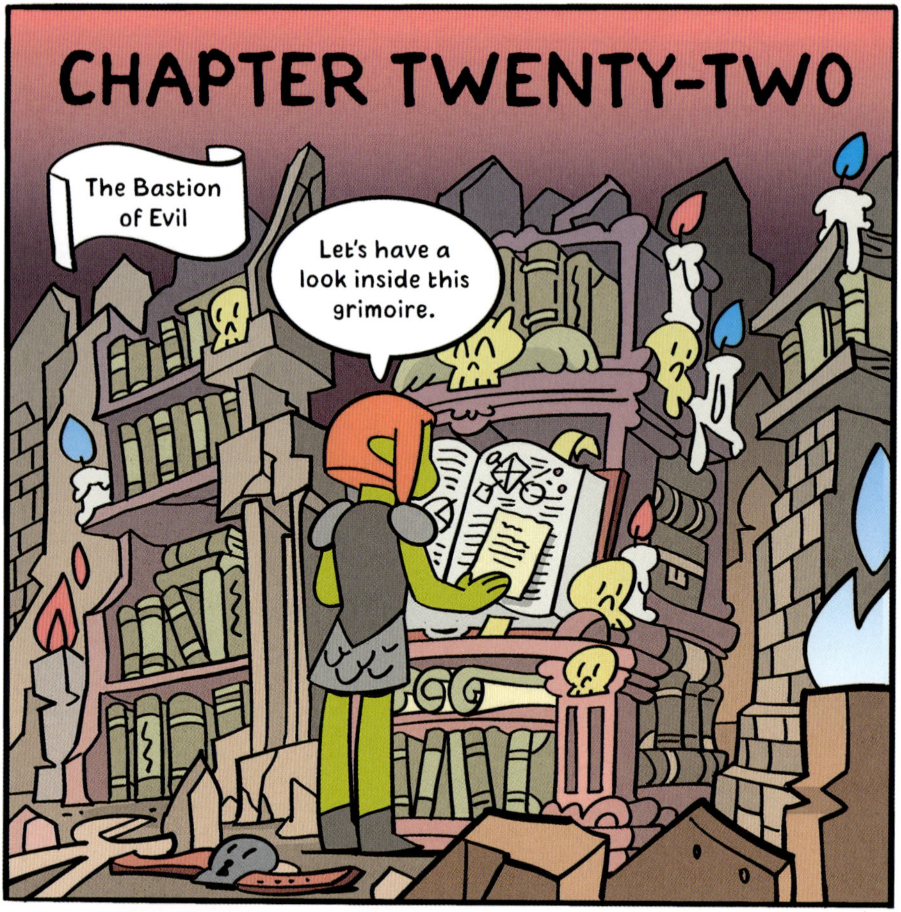
CHAPTER TWENTY-TWO
The Bastion of Evil
Let's have a look inside this grimoire.

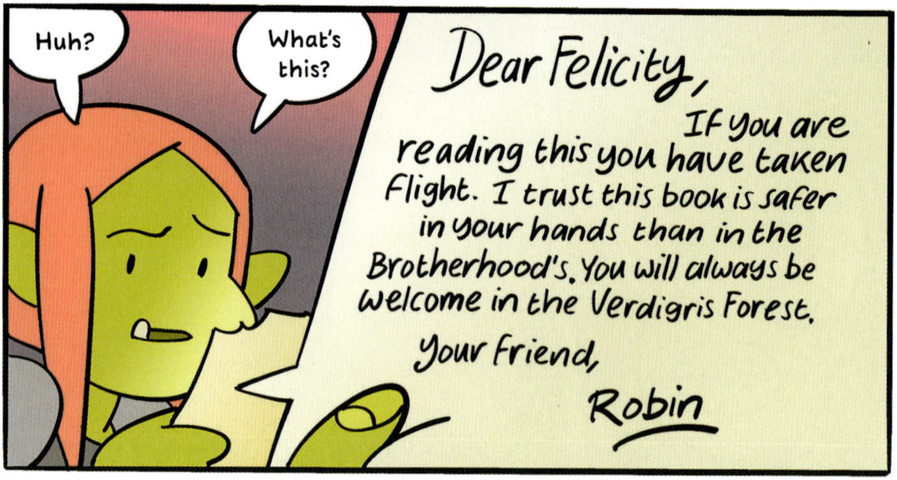
Huh?
What's this?
Dear Felicity,
If you are reading this you have taken flight. I trust this book is safer in your hands than in the Brotherhood's. You will always be welcome in the Verdigris Forest.
Your Friend,
Robin

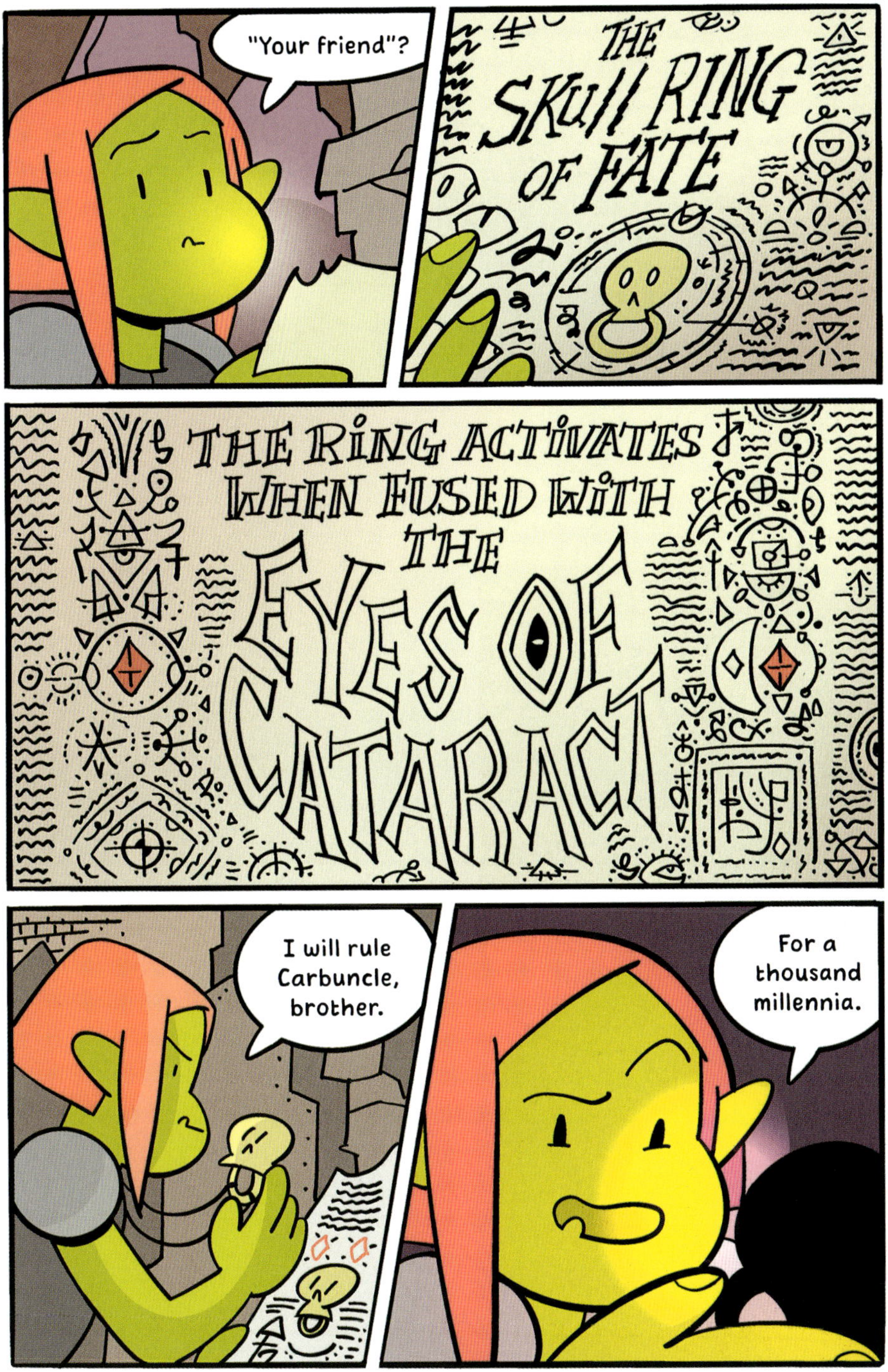
"Your friend"?
THE SKULL RING OF FATE
THE RING ACTIVATES WHEN FUSED WITH THE EYES OF CATARACT
I will rule Carbuncle, brother.
For a thousand millennia.

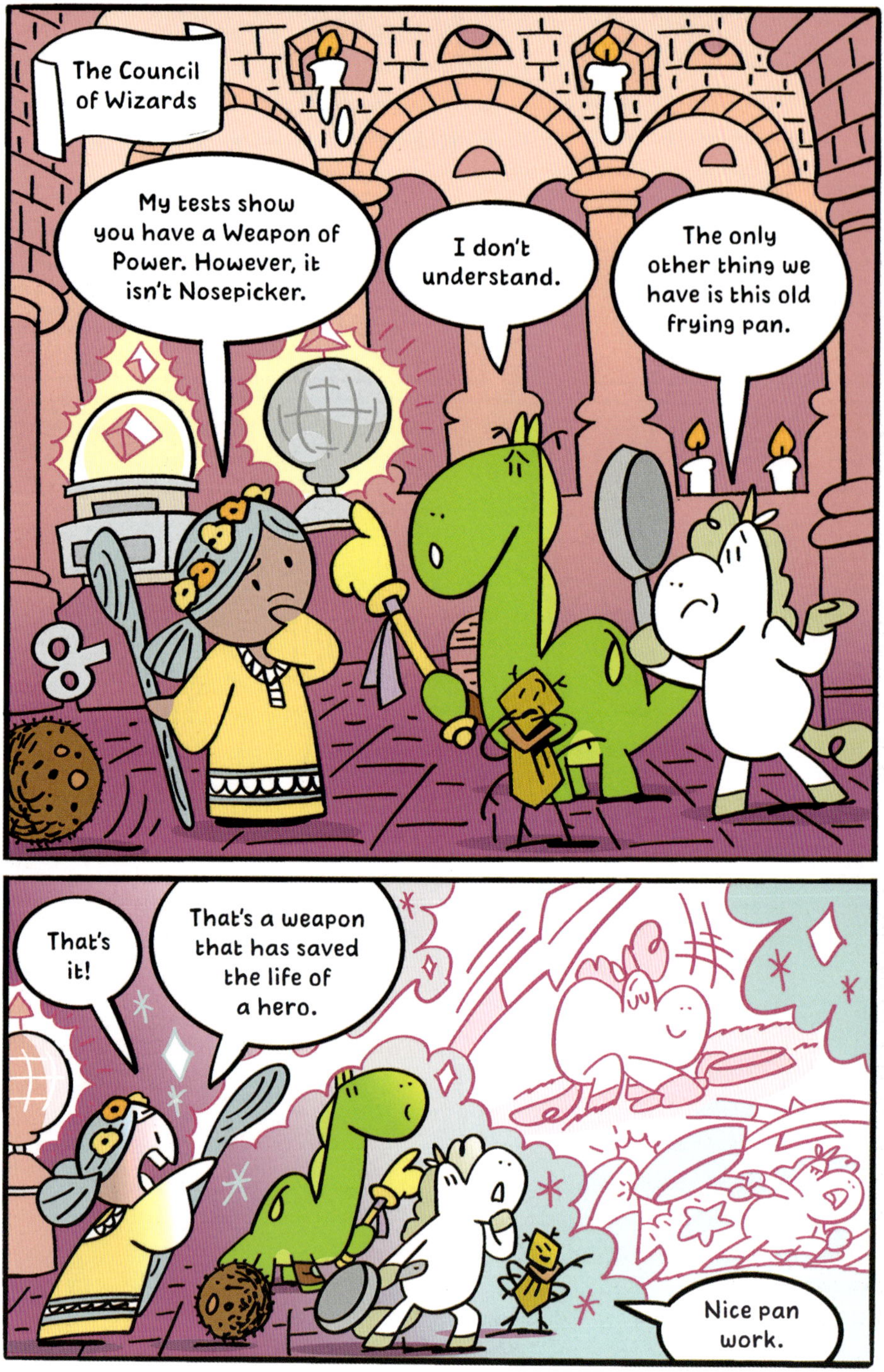
The Council of Wizards
My tests show you have a Weapon of Power. However, it isn't Nosepicker.
I don't understand.
The only other thing we have is this old frying pan.
That's it!
That's a weapon that has saved the life of a hero.
Nice pan work.

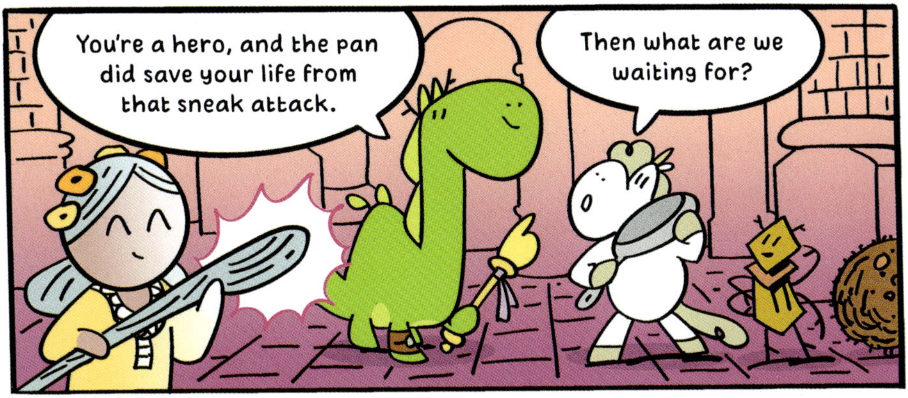
You're a hero, and the pan did save your life from that sneak attack.
Then what are we waiting for?

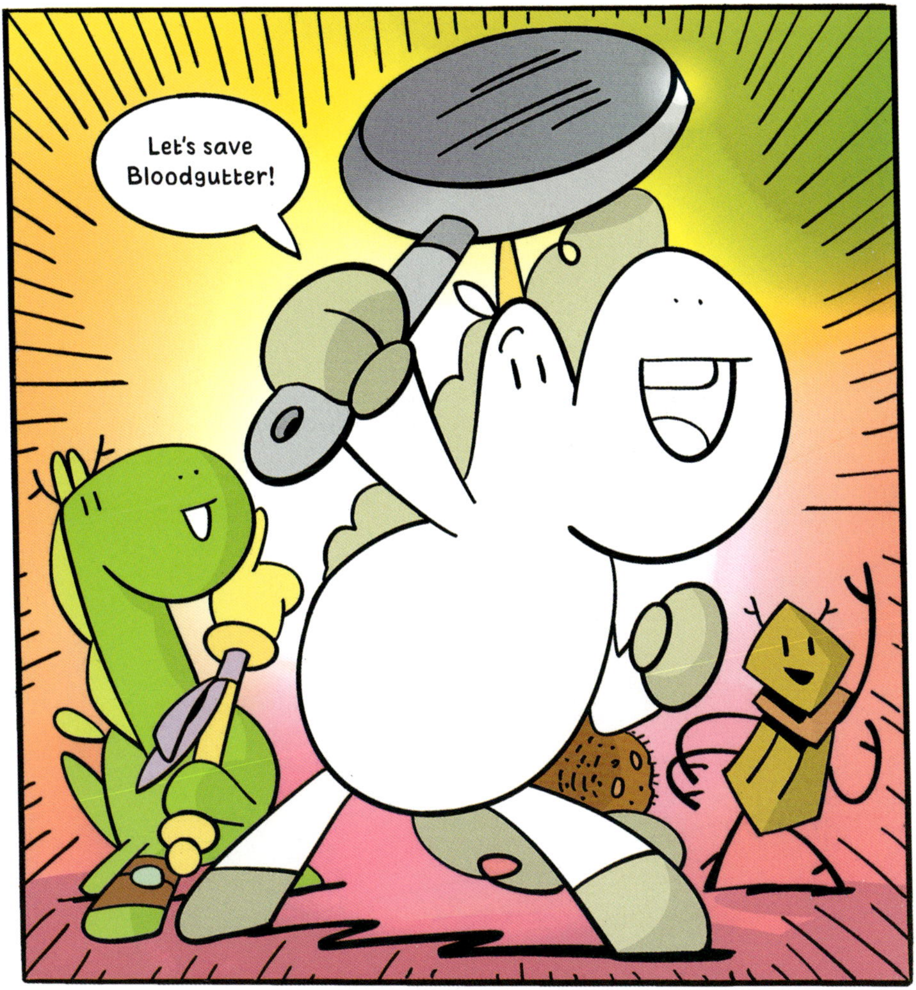
Let's save Bloodgutter!

Clarion Books is an imprint of HarperCollins Publishers.
HarperAlley is an imprint of HarperCollins Publishers.
Punycorn and the Princess of Thieves
Copyright © 2025 by Andi Watson
All rights reserved. Manufactured in Johor, Malaysia. No part of this book may be used or reproduced in any manner whatsoever without written permission except in the case of brief quotations embodied in critical articles and reviews. For information address HarperCollins Children's Books, a division of HarperCollins Publishers, 195 Broadway, New York, NY 10007.
www.harperalley.com

Library of Congress Control Number: 2024940770
ISBN 978-0-35-857200-8

The artist used pens, pencils, paper, Procreate on iPad, and Adobe Photoshop 2023 to create the illustrations for this book.
Design by Celeste Knudsen and Stephanie Hays
25 26 27 28 29 PCA 10 9 8 7 6 5 4 3 2 1
First Edition

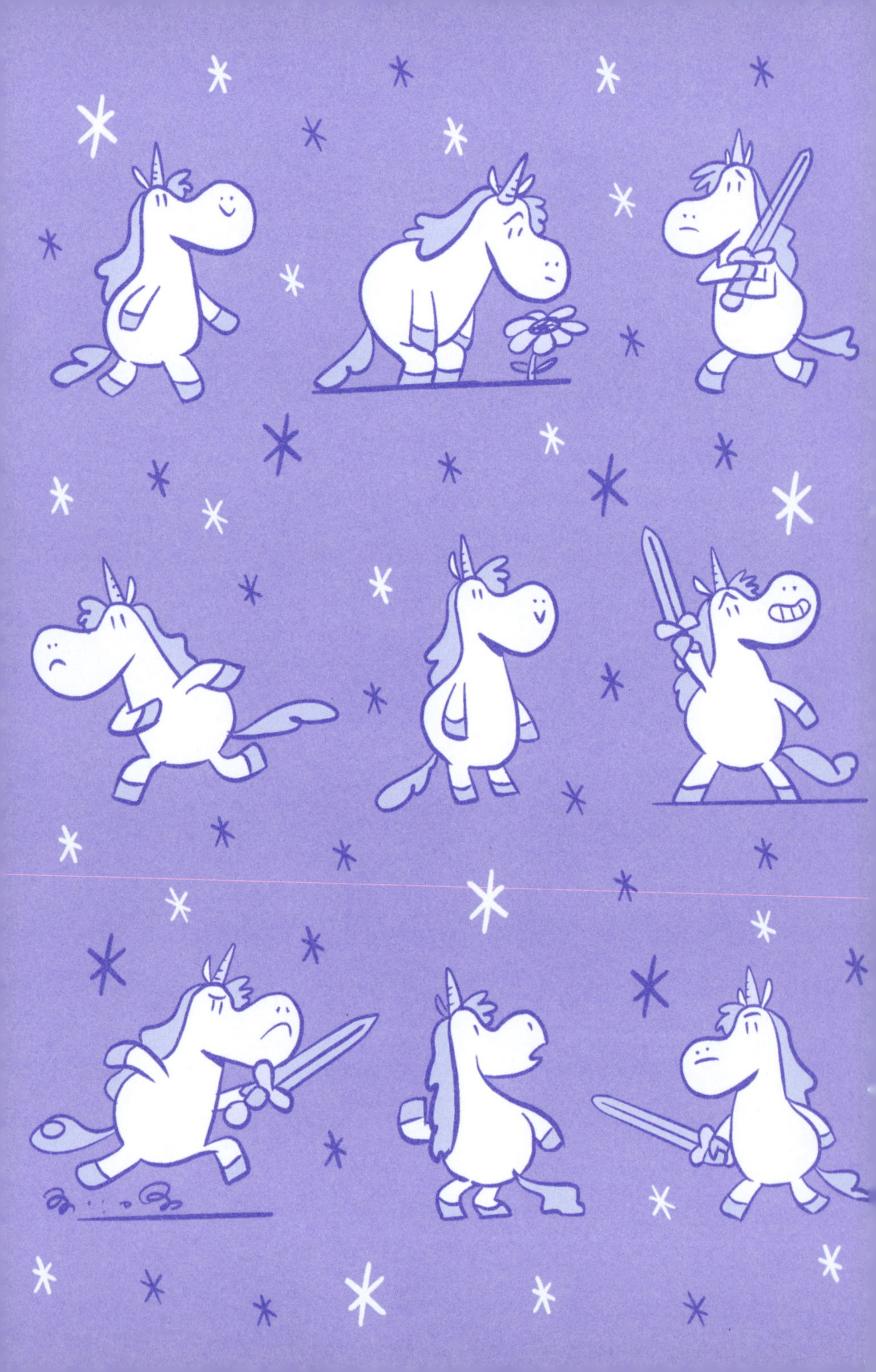